THE JAMES BOYS

RICHARD
LIEBMANN-SMITH

RANDOM HOUSE
NEW YORK

The

JAMES BOYS

A Novel Account of

Four Desperate Brothers

—◆—

Published in the United States by Random House, an imprint of The Random House Publishing Group, a division of Random House, Inc., New York.

RANDOM HOUSE and colophon are registered trademarks of Random House, Inc.

LIBRARY OF CONGRESS CATALOGING-IN-PUBLICATION DATA
Liebmann-Smith, Richard.
The James boys : a novel account of William, Henry, Frank, and Jesse /
Richard Liebmann-Smith.
p.   cm.
ISBN 978-0-345-47078-2
1. James family—Fiction.   2. James, William, 1842–1910—Fiction.   3. James, Henry,
1843–1916—Fiction.   4. James, Jesse, 1847–1882—Fiction.   5. James, Frank,
1844–1915—Fiction.   6. James, Garth Wilkinson, 1845–1883—Fiction.
7. James, Robertson, 1846–1910—Fiction.   I. Title.
PS3562.I443J36 2008
813'.54—dc22   2007038423

Printed in the United States of America on acid-free paper

www.atrandom.com

2 4 6 8 9 7 5 3 1

FIRST EDITION

Book design by Dana Leigh Blanchette

For my brothers in blood and spirit,
and for Joan and Rebecca

Introduction

———•◆•———

During the winter and spring of 1998–99, the meticulously foot-noted pages of *The New York Review of Books* crackled with a heated debate over the life of William James. At issue, along with such weighty matters as the existence of free will and the etiology of clini-cal depression, was whether or not the great Harvard philosopher and psychologist had been a compulsive masturbator. Evidence for this in-cendiary assertion was gingerly marshaled and reviewed by Professor Louis Menand, then of the City University of New York, who pre-sented as Exhibit A this famous passage from James's *The Varieties of Religious Experience,* describing a state of mind that James called "panic fear":

Here [wrote James] is an excellent example, for permission to print which I have to thank the sufferer. The original is in French, and though the subject was evidently in a bad nervous condition at the time of which he writes, his case has otherwise the merit of extreme simplicity. I translate freely.

"Whilst in this state of philosophic pessimism and general depression of spirits about my prospects, I went one evening into a dressing-room in the twilight to procure some article that was there; when suddenly there fell upon me without any warning, just as if it came out of the darkness, a horrible fear of my own existence. Simultaneously there arose in my mind the image of an epileptic patient whom I had seen in the asylum, a black-haired youth with greenish skin, entirely idiotic, who used to sit all day on one of the benches, or rather shelves against the wall, with his knees drawn up against his chin, and the coarse gray undershirt, which was his only garment, drawn over them inclosing his entire figure. He sat there like a sort of sculptured Egyptian cat or Peruvian mummy, moving nothing but his black eyes and looking absolutely non-human. This image and my fear entered into a species of combination with each other. *That shape am I,* I felt, potentially. Nothing that I possess can defend me against that fate, if the hour for it should strike for me as it struck for him. There was such a horror of him, and such a perception of my own merely momentary discrepancy from him, that it was as if something hitherto solid within my breast gave way entirely, and I became a mass of quivering fear."

This harrowing vignette has long attracted the attention of James's biographers because in 1904, two years after its original publication, he revealed to his French translator that the man whose terrifying experience of "panic fear" he had described was none other than himself. There had been no original translation from the French, no gracious permission to print; the psychologist had, he confessed, presented his own case history.

As a result of James's revelation, many students of his life have tried to fit the story of the epileptic patient into a crisis-and-recovery narrative according to which James had suffered, in the early 1870s, what might be described in lay terms as a kind of nervous breakdown. The notion that this crisis may have been precipitated by—or at least have been associated in James's mind with—compulsive masturbation originated, Menand discovered, in an article published in 1968 by the historian Cushing Strout of Cornell. "Strout's idea," wrote Menand, "is that the vision of the epileptic occurred some time between 1866, when James returned from a trip to Brazil and decided he didn't want to be a naturalist, and 1869, when he received his medical degree and decided he didn't want to be a doctor." Strout speculated that James was convinced there was a link between introspection ("speculation and contemplative *Grüblei*") and masturbation, and between masturbation and insanity. The hideous figure of the epileptic patient, Strout concluded, was an objective representation both of William's "self-punishing guilt" and of his dread at being stuck in a medical career—the only professional path that appeared open to him after he abandoned the field of natural history.

Additional support for such an interpretation, Professor Menand went on, was provided by University of Chicago polymath Sandor Gilman. In his book *Disease and Representation,* Gilman suggested that James's description of the epileptic might have been based on a portrait of a mental patient that had appeared in an 1838 treatise on insanity, *Des maladies mentales,* by the pioneering French psychiatrist Jean-Étienne Esquirol. Not only was this work written, as Gilman pointed out, in the language of James's ostensible subject, but the patient depicted in Esquirol's book—who bears a striking resemblance to the asylum inmate described by James—is explicitly identified as an idiot and a masturbator. To support his assertion that James had a fear of descending into madness as a result of his own behavior, Gilman cited an entry from James's diary, dated February 1, 1870, in which he claimed James referred "in a direct manner" to his habitual masturbation: "Hitherto I have tried to fire myself with the moral interest, as an aid in the accomplishing of certain utilitarian ends of attaining certain difficult but salutary habits."

Biography, of course, is hardly an exact science, and Professor Menand, as we shall see, ultimately arrived at a very different—though perhaps even more disturbing—conclusion about the story of the epileptic patient. But do we, or should we, even *care* if William James (to use a more colorful, if less suitably Victorian, expression) was a major jerk-off artist? Or, for that matter, if his brother Henry, widely venerated as one of the greatest novelists in the English language, was as queer as the proverbial three-dollar bill—a proposition with which his biographer Leon Edel played literary footsie for five long volumes? William James himself, we must recall, once warned that the art of being wise is the art of knowing what to overlook.

Yet we cannot overlook such embarrassing or inconvenient possibilities, nor should we; for biographical probing in this instance transcends mere prurient interest in the private activities of private men. The Jameses, after all, present much more than a fascinating case study in psychopathology and twisted family dynamics. As Stanford historian Otis Pease once remarked, virtually the entire story of nineteenth-century America is encompassed in the saga of the James brothers—William and Henry in the East, Frank and Jesse in the West. Or, as the narrator of Peter De Vries's comic novel *Consenting Adults* observed, "If America can be thought of as polarized between two sets of James brothers, Jesse and Frank at one end and you know who at the other, why, we dramatize to ourselves in this one configuration its infinite cultural variety."

Indeed, it would be nearly impossible to overstate the magnitude of the mark the James family has left on the American cultural landscape. The intellectual and literary achievements of "the scientist who wrote psychology like a novelist and the novelist who wrote fiction like a psychologist" (a commonplace even in their own lifetimes) were so influential that the critic Jacques Barzun was moved to designate an entire quarter century of our cultural history as "the reign of William and Henry." Between them, the two older James brothers practically cornered the market of ideas in their age. In addition to the aforementioned *Varieties of Religious Experience* (1902), William's groundbreaking writings include his magisterial *The Principles of Psychology* (1890) and such popular works as *The Will to Believe* (1897) and *Talks to Teachers* (1899). Henry James, of course, gave us a groaning shelf of novels, novellas, short stories, travel writings, and critical essays, highlighted by such enduring masterworks of fiction as *Daisy Miller* (1878), *The Portrait of a Lady* (1881), *The Wings of the Dove* (1902), and *The Golden Bowl* (1904).

The reign of Frank and Jesse, while briefer and based on only a single idea, was no less impressive: Their towering oeuvre includes the seminal daylight bank heist at Liberty, Missouri (1866); their ambitious (if failed) First National Bank job in Northfield, Minnesota (1876); and the storied robbery of the Glendale train (1879). To poet Carl Sandburg, Jesse James is "the only American bandit who is classical, who is to this country what Robin Hood and Dick Turpin are to England, whose exploits are so close to the mythical and apocryphal."

In recent decades, considerable scholarly attention has also been lavished on Alice James, the James brothers' long-neglected sister, in whom such feminist writers as Jean Strouse and Susan Sontag discovered a paradigm of Victorian patriarchal hegemony run amuck. "To be a James and a girl," wrote Strouse, "was a contradiction in terms."

Of course, it might also seem a contradiction in terms to be a James and a ruthless bushwhacker. Born Garth Wilkinson and Robertson James, and overshadowed in childhood by their gifted older siblings, the two younger brothers (not to be confused with the Younger brothers, with whom they were often professionally associated) were to demonstrate a peculiarly American genius for reinventing themselves, gaining national notoriety as the desperate border bandits Frank and Jesse. "While the older brothers came of age slowly under the protective cover of ill health and parental bounty," wrote Cornell psychiatrist Howard M. Feinstein, "the younger pair was forced into premature manhood by battle, so that this minor theme in the lives of William and Henry became the central chapter, the climax of their work lives. Thereafter uncannily they reenacted the plot laid out in their father's early stories. Like so many of the elder Henry's boyhood friends, in spite of 'brilliant promise' and 'romantic charm,' both younger sons 'ended badly.'"

Perhaps it was this familial fear of "ending badly" that overtook William James in his frightening identification with the famous epileptic patient. If so, what, if anything, did masturbation have to do with it? The flap over William James's putative propensity for "self-abuse" reveals not only the extent to which scholars have been fascinated with the minutiae of the Jameses' private lives, but also the degree to which the Jameses were bent on protecting their privacy. Not surprisingly, there is no explicit reference to whacking the wand in any of the writings that William James left. (Those "salutary habits" to which he referred in the diary entry cited by Sandor Gilman were likely nothing more titillating than the routine of getting up early in the morning, according to Professor Menand.) Indeed, the reddest flag on the subject is not anything James left but what he didn't leave. "The biggest impediment to getting a coherent crisis-and-recovery narrative out of the materials of his life between 1867 and 1873," Menand explained, "is that large portions of the record are simply missing." James, he noted, "was never a daily diarist, but the entries in the notebook he used for a diary are fairly regular from April 1868, when it begins, to February 1869. Then twenty-one pages (or as much as forty-two pages of writing) have been cut out, apparently with scissors."

Despite this suspicious excision, Professor Menand not only took issue with the diagnosis of William James as a compulsive masturbator, he went even further, questioning the veracity of the account that James had confessed to be his own case history. The story of the epileptic patient, Menand concluded, was a piece of "biographical flotsam," unmoored to any known event in James's life. "It can be interpreted," he wrote, "as a precipitating crisis, as a psychological breakthrough, as simply one among many crises, most of which are now unrecoverable—or as a partial invention, a little work of semi-fiction."

These proclivities for writing "semi-fiction" and destroying documents—and William was by no means the only, nor even the worst, offender of the lot—bring us to the crux of the dilemma faced by any biographer of the James family: The Jameses were a notoriously slippery bunch who, as Jean Strouse put it, "grew adept at giving eloquently ambiguous voice to the way things were supposed to be: they learned to see and not see, say and not say, reveal and conceal, all at the same time." The father, Henry James, Sr., wrote a version of his life story, *Immortal Life: Illustrated in a Brief Autobiographical Sketch of the Late Stephen Dewhurst,* hiding behind the wholly fictitious character of the title. Henry James, Jr., in his own autobiography, Professor Menand pointed out, "freely changed dates, suppressed facts, and rewrote passages from other people's letters, and then often added injury to insult by destroying the originals." According to Leon Edel, Henry had "a kind of rage of privacy and dealt in mystification to confound those who would treat his life." In 1909, toward the end of that life, the master novelist went so far as to heap forty years of correspondence onto a roaring bonfire in his garden, in accordance with what he referred to as "the law that I have made tolerably absolute these last years as I myself grow older and think more of my latter end: the law of not leaving personal and private documents at the mercy of any accidents, or even of my executors!" Frank and Jesse, it goes without saying, had an abiding professional commitment to covering their tracks. Their recorded lives present a Gordian sheepshank of alibis and aliases in which, according to their biographer William A. Settle, Jr., of the University of Tulsa, "fact and fiction are so entwined that it is difficult—at times, impossible—to untangle them." (Indeed, until the 1995 exhumation and DNA analysis of Jesse's remains, there had even been lingering doubts that the body buried beneath the headstone bearing his name was in fact the outlaw's.)

None of which is to suggest that the Jameses were compulsive liars (except perhaps Frank and Jesse, whose mendacity was the least of their crimes). But they were all famously flexible in their notion of the truth. William, one of the founders of the pragmatic school of philosophy, claimed that "truth *happens* to an idea; it *becomes* true, is *made* true by events." And Henry, who once remarked that "facts themselves are often falsifying," justified altering documents in his autobiography by proclaiming, according to another of his biographers, Lyndall Gordon, that "what he had written was no common memoir; it was a work of imaginative, not literal, truth. The ghosts of the dead had his ear, his spirit had communed with theirs, and the result was a biographic truth that was truer in its suggestiveness, its closeness to the 'unspeakable past,' than figures nailed down by cast-iron facts."

"What makes partial biographical information generally worse than no information at all," Professor Menand complained, "is that speculation fills the gaps and eventually becomes indistinguishable from 'the facts.'" Faced with all these scissored diaries, doctored documents, incinerated correspondence, multiple aliases, and horses with their shoes on backward, a biographer of the Jameses could well be forgiven for speculating that an entire Halloween of skeletons might yet be found lurking in the family closet. (To further fan the flames of such suspicions, even today—nearly a century after Henry's death in 1916—many of the family papers still remain sealed to scholars.)

Certainly the numerous histories of their lives available now leave many crucial questions unanswered: How, for example, was William James (compulsive masturbator or not) able to consider establishing the first laboratory of experimental psychology in America—"raising the money himself," according to his Harvard colleague George Herbert Palmer—on an assistant professor's salary of only twelve hundred dollars a year? And what exactly did William mean when he confessed to his wife long after their 1878 wedding that for two years during their courtship, he had behaved like "a man morally utterly diseased"?

How could the younger brothers, Garth Wilkinson and Robertson, Union officers once so deeply committed to the abolitionist cause that they volunteered for service in the first black regiments of the Civil War, have metamorphosed into those Rebel icons Frank and Jesse? And what drove Henry James to take it on the lam from the United States in the early 1880s and hole up in Europe until after the dawn of a new century?

The account that follows, though by no means a thorough cradle-to-grave biography, may help shed some light on these vexing conundrums. It focuses on only a single year (1876) in the long saga of the Jameses, but that year, as we shall see, was a crucial one indeed, involving perhaps the strongest extrafamilial link among the brothers in their adult lives—a young woman named Elena Hite. Alluring, impetuous, free-thinking, by turns vivacious and sullen, this errant daughter of the minor Hartford railroad baron Asa Hite likely served among the real-life models for some of Henry James's most celebrated fictional heroines, including the scandalous Daisy Miller, the histrionic Verena Tarrant of *The Bostonians,* and the high-spirited Isabel Archer of *The Portrait of a Lady.* Miss Hite was herself hardly a prolific diarist, but neither was she so swift with the scissors and flames as the Jameses. Through the unique prism of her surviving journals and letters, in conjunction with recently unearthed material from the archives of the Pinkerton National Detective Agency, we are privileged to view the James family in a new and revealing—if sometimes painfully embarrassing—light.

That curmudgeonly critic H. L. Mencken once wrote that in choosing to live and work in Europe, Henry James had gone in the wrong direction. "What he needed," contended Mencken, "was intimate contact with the life of his own country. . . . The West would have amused, intrigued and finally conquered him." But Mencken was wrong on at least two counts: Henry James did indeed visit the West, and it neither amused nor intrigued him. It did, however, in a sense conquer him, and here our story begins.

THE JAMES BOYS

Chapter One

———◆———

At four-forty-five on the afternoon of July 7, 1876, the Number 4 Missouri Pacific Express, made up of two sleeping cars, three day coaches, and two baggage cars, pulled out of Kansas City, headed east for St. Louis. Among the passengers aboard that day, along with the usual contingent of rough-clad farmers, itinerant preachers, and high-collared Chicago drummers, was Henry James, who was completing a tour of the western states and territories he had embarked on six weeks earlier at the behest of John Hay, editor of *The New York Tribune.* Such journalistic journeys had become all the rage ever since the great linkage of the nation's eastern and western rail lines in 1869, opening the continent for commerce, settlement, and an exotic new brand of tourism that the railroad companies and newspapers hoped might appeal to wealthy Americans jaded with the fashionable Grand Tour of Europe.

In fact, Henry was not so much completing his western tour as aborting it—cutting short his travels, as he complained to his editor, on account of "excruciating gastric distress." Indeed, the Jamesian digestive apparatus had been in chronic disrepair ever since its exposure a month earlier to the cuisine of St. Louis, a series of "desperate variations upon the inherently unpromising culinary theme of fried catfish." To make matters worse, Henry's back was killing him. In the terminology of today's psychiatry, the Jameses were notorious somaticizers: Their psychological conflicts often manifested in the form of such physical symptoms as painful digestive disturbances, crippling constipation, mysterious visual weaknesses, and blazingly aching backs. (William James, fresh out of the Harvard medical school, diagnosed his brother's spinal symptoms as "dorsal insanity.") In this instance, we might suspect that an underlying reason for Henry's distress—and Henry James was never one to deny any reason its fair weight and then some—was that the young author had come to realize he had neither talent nor taste for newspaper writing. "Try as he might," wrote his biographer Leon Edel, "Henry James could never speak in the journalistic voice. It was as if a man, fluent, suddenly reduced himself to a stutter." In his own mind, James was destined to be a great literary artist, not a newspaper hack, and his true vocation would hardly suffer a whit, he no doubt told himself, if he were never to describe another thundering herd of bison, painted Red Indian, or towering Rocky Mountain. Mark Twain could have the lot. Henry's idea of "roughing it" was any hotel under a two-star rating, and the truth, which must have been painfully apparent to him as he stared out over the western Missouri landscape described by Jesse James's biographer T. J. Stiles as resembling "a rug pushed into a corner: rumpled, wrinkled, rippled with ravines," was that all of that open space—those endless empty miles with scarcely a shanty, much less a café or cathedral to break the sheer *geology* of it all—had literally made him sick.

Fortunately, the interior scenery of the coach was to prove far more to Henry's taste: Across the aisle from the writer sat a young woman who would soon introduce herself as Elena Phoenix and who would come to play a singularly significant role in the lives of the entire James clan. Though he scarcely could have been characterized as a ladies' man in the vulgar, predatory sense, Henry James was nonetheless a connoisseur of what he once described as the "more complicated" sex. Even at this early stage of his literary career, he had long since determined that womanhood, particularly the freshly emerging American strain, was to be a salient subject of his work. ("My Bible is the female mind," declares a diarist in Henry's 1866 tale "A Landscape Painter.") Like Winterbourne, the protagonist of *Daisy Miller*, Henry had a great relish for feminine beauty; he was addicted to observing and analyzing it, and though the features of the specimen presently under his scrutiny were partially obscured by the magazine in which she was engrossed, he could not have helped but discern that the coils of her golden tresses framed a face of remarkable beauty—though it was a beauty, he might have been compelled to note, of the sort more properly designated "handsome" than "pretty." If contemporary photographs of Elena are a suitable guide, Henry's practiced eye doubtless would have registered a slightly too firm set to her mouth, which seemed to war with the sensuous fullness of her lips, and that the angles of her glowing cheeks were perhaps a shade too sharply chiseled for one of the "gentle gender." Nonetheless, the softness of her sex and age—she was then only twenty-two—no doubt lent a sweetness and vulnerability to her patrician countenance that served to take the chill off its sheer sculptural *achèvement.*

On this occasion, the softer facet of her being was accentuated by a fashionable mauve frock, which blossomed with fantastic frills and flounces and from which a daring flash of lemon-yellow petticoat peeped fetchingly at the ankle. Her narrow waist was garnished with a crimson sash, and around her neck, falling low over her rounded bosom, hung a double strand of glowing amber beads. But more striking to Henry James than the young woman's fine features and modish attire would have been a certain larger-than-life aspect of her bearing, an altogether "finished" quality proclaiming the presence of a public personage. She might have seemed to him—in a phrase he would later apply to Isabel Archer in *The Portrait of a Lady*—to have "the general air of being someone in particular." Here, he could have been moved to speculate, was a talented diva bearing the bright torch of the operatic art to the benighted provinces of the West, or perhaps a celebrated comedienne—a radiant Juliet or heartrending Camille honing her art on the coarser sensibilities of the hinterlands before essaying to captivate the more sophisticated audiences of the great metropoli back east.

Yet it was neither her elegant apparel, nor her exquisite facial contours, nor even her "general air," to which his gaze was ultimately drawn, but rather to the reading matter upon which her own attention appeared so fiercely fixed. Henry could not have helped but recognize the familiar typography of *The Atlantic Monthly*—indeed, one of the issues in which his first novel, *Roderick Hudson,* had recently been serialized.

In his later years, after the turn of the century, James would be widely revered as "The Master," with an imposing oeuvre comprising dozens of novels, scores of novellas, and hundreds of short stories. But in that centennial summer of 1876, all of this was far ahead of him and by no means assured as his destiny. He was still in the thrall of what he once called "the hungry futurity of youth," and we can only imagine the maelstrom of emotion generated by the fledgling author's realization that this lovely young woman was in fact perusing his very own words. Her lips moved silently, voluptuously forming the shape of his every syllable—a reading habit he might normally have deemed jejune but which, considering the exquisite syllables in question (to say nothing of the exquisite lips), must have struck him as infinitely charming.

To achieve a better view, he cranked his reclining chair to its forwardmost position so energetically that he may have feared pitching himself headlong into the aisle. Sensing the high voyeuristic voltage being generated across the way, the young woman lifted her eyes to intercept the writer's intense gaze with a cool, quizzical look of her own. (Though proper ladies of the era were conventionally admonished never to encourage "acquaintanceship" with strangers on trains, Elena was hardly one to abide by the rigid strictures of mid-Victorian propriety.)

"I beg your pardon, sir?"

Henry James colored as if caught in some particularly unclean act.

"I gather from your, ah, oscillations," she went on, "that you must be exceedingly interested in my magazine." She held out *The Atlantic,* offering it across the aisle. "Would you care to peruse it at closer range?"

"I . . . I . . . I . . . no . . . I . . . ," Henry stammered, for however gracefully his words may have glided across the smooth plane of the printed page, in the more turbulent atmosphere of the three-dimensional world, they often flapped wildly about, like chimney swallows flushed into a drawing room.

"Well, if you don't care to read it, then I would be most grateful if you would kindly desist from staring at it so." The young woman delivered this remonstrance with a prim nod and a satisfied half-smile, feeling, as she later recorded in her diary, in equal measure pleased and amused by the firmness of tone she was taking with this imposing stranger. James was now thirty-three and, by at least one account, a fine figure of a man: "He had mildly swelled, not to fatness, not to stoutness, but well nigh to the brink of plumpness," wrote William H. Huntington, a colleague at the *Tribune.* "Also hath whiskers, full but close trimmed. By reason of these fulfillments . . . he has much more waxed in good lookingness, and is in his actual presentment (specially *qua* head) a notably finer person than one in the next 10,000 of handsome men."

All these fine fulfillments notwithstanding, at this moment Henry appeared to Elena "for all the world like a schoolboy harshly scolded" as he hurriedly averted his gaze and made an elaborate show of scribbling in the pages of the notebook on his lap.

"Really," the young woman insisted, "I'd be most happy to let you have the magazine. But I simply cannot abide anyone reading over my shoulder. It gives me the willies."

This remark, accompanied by an exaggerated mock shudder that no doubt struck Henry—especially in conjunction with the slang expression—as disarmingly girlish, at last emboldened him to speak.

"I'm terribly sorry," he said, seeming relieved with the smoothness and profundity of his vocal presentation, "I would be loath to knowingly inflict 'the willies' upon anyone. I was merely curious about that story you're reading."

"*Roderick Hudson?*"

"Oh, is that the title?" Henry asked disingenuously. In his preface to the 1907 edition of that early work, he recalled the "quite uplifted sense with which my idea, such as it was, permitted me to at last put quite out to sea. I had but hugged the shore on sundry previous small occasions; bumping about, to acquire skill, in the shallow waters and sandy coves of the 'short story' and master as yet of no vessel constructed to carry a sail." *Roderick Hudson,* then, was his maiden voyage into the deep waters of full-length fiction. In it he had sounded the opening chords of his great themes: the artist and society, European decadence versus American innocence, the labyrinthine divagations of the female mind. It had taken him over a year of intense labor to bring forth his opus, and upon its popular success rode all of Henry's hopes for a career that would permit him to devote his efforts exclusively to fiction.

"Oh, it's dreadful," pronounced the young woman.

Whatever head of steam had built up behind Henry's vocal machinery suddenly fizzled. "D-d-d-dreadful?" he stammered.

"Well, you may judge for yourself. I certainly have no desire to finish it," she said, again offering the magazine across the aisle.

Henry waved aside the proffered journal as though it were yet another portion of detested fried catfish.

"Of course, there are many other perfectly excellent pieces in this number," the young woman chattered on enthusiastically. "Mark Twain has a charming description of old times on the Mississippi, how he became a cub pilot on a steamboat, and Oliver Wendell Holmes has a fascinating essay on crime and automatism in which he argues, if I understand him correctly, that the criminal is not necessarily the same thing as the sinner, since the former is, in some sense, a moral idiot, or morally insane; that just as some men are unable from birth to distinguish between certain colors—red and green, for instance—"

"In what way . . . dreadful?"

The young woman, caught up in her breathless synopsis of the Holmes piece, was momentarily confused. "The story?"

"Yes, the story. This *Roderick Hudson*," Henry insisted. He was now breathing through his nostrils. "In what way is it so . . . dreadful?"

"Why, in almost every way, really." The young woman delivered her harsh evaluation with a tinkling laugh, amused by the boldness of her critique and pleased with the opportunity to display her erudition. "To begin with, it's far too mannered. The characters seem very stiff, the language is often unpleasantly *curly*, and the whole thing is completely void of any recognizable human emotion. It's very . . . chilly, if you know what I mean."

"Chilly," repeated Henry with a glacial smile. It was the very word his brother William had used in his own critique of the novel. Henry was anxious to end this ungratifying exchange, no doubt sorry he had let himself be drawn forth from his cozy cocoon of observation. But his interlocutress, delighted to be liberated from the rigors of her reading, kept her elegant shoulder to the conversational wheel.

"And might you by any chance be a literary gentleman yourself?" she inquired brightly, dropping her gaze toward Henry's open notebook, a handsome black leatherette volume with wine-marbled endpapers.

Henry shifted uncomfortably in his seat and closed the portfolio with a sharp snap. "In a manner of speaking," he answered, then hastily added: "That is, I write the occasional travel piece—herds of bison, Rocky Mountains, Red Indians—that sort of thing. Nothing in the fiction line."

"And might I be familiar with your work, Mr. . . . ?"

"Jones," the writer supplied quickly. "Harry Jones." (Though the surname he blurted was randomly, almost comically, fictional, the Christian name he appended to it was in fact his old family moniker, employed during his youth to distinguish him from his father, Henry Sr., and the numerous other Henrys festooning the James family tree.)

The young woman squinted in a pretty pantomime of cogitation, but clearly, she was drawing a blank. "I'm afraid I've never heard of you, Mr. Jones," she confessed with some embarrassment.

"It would have surprised me immensely if you had," Henry replied dryly.

"But now that we've met, I'd love to read something of yours."

"Oh, you mustn't be too certain of that." At this point Henry was becoming visibly irritated. He must already have been irked with this woman for having made him lie about his name—and such a clumsy, unimaginative lie at that—and he would have had no wish to become any more profoundly enmeshed in this fruitless web of deceit. We can imagine him finding himself conscious of the distinctly ungallant compulsion to discover some hint of imperfection in her apparently flawless appearance, as if some subtle misalignment of feature—some soupçon of coarseness about the mouth or blemish in the smooth complexion—might have established grounds for discounting her painful literary judgment. But the more closely he scrutinized her, the more he would have been obliged to concede that his initial assessment of her beauty had been, if anything, insufficiently generous: She was as bright and soft as an April cloud, and beaming at him with such a fresh, open smile that he no doubt could have throttled her.

"Oh, I'm terribly sorry," she pressed on, extending a hand across the aisle. "Here you've told me your name, and I haven't introduced myself. I'm Elena Phoenix."

Henry took her creamy-kidskin-gloved hand and gave it a perfunctory pump. "Ah, yes," he ventured, "that marvelous mythical bird that perishes in flames and rises from its ashes."

"Indeed," she replied with a practiced enigmatic smile, "that marvelous mythical bird."

"And would it be *Miss* Phoenix, then?" Henry inquired.

At this Elena abruptly withdrew her hand. Her lips pursed and her cheeks colored. "If you mean to inquire whether or not I'm married, Mr. Jones," she replied tartly, "the answer is certainly not. I'm in no hurry for *that* when there are so many other, more rewarding things a woman might achieve."

The vehemence of this short piece of oration seemed to take Henry aback. In searching for the proper term of address, he had no doubt intended merely to provide assurance that any ensuing conversation would be conducted at the highest level of propriety. He could scarcely have expected to provoke a lecture.

"You're making a face, Mr. Jones."

"A face?"

Elena Phoenix scrunched up her fine features to mirror a contorted grimace of disgust.

"I'm dreadfully sorry," said Henry. "One tends to have such imperfect control over one's physiognomy."

"Perhaps," Elena countered, "that may be because one tends to believe that a woman's proper place is in the home." She was building up a considerable head of rhetorical steam. "But let me assure you, Mr. Jones, women are awakening in this land. We have the ability—and the right—to do anything you men do. A woman can go to school or teach school. She can be a doctor, a lawyer, an architect, an artist, a writer. . . ."

Henry James nodded mechanically at the enumeration of each line of work to which the awakening American woman might rightfully aspire. In fact, he felt not so much out of sympathy with feminist politics as weary of them. He had noted on his visit to Boston that winter how the boundless emancipatory energies that had once fueled the abolitionist movement of the 1860s now seemed to have been redirected from Negroes to women. His sister, Alice, when not incapacitated by one of her chronic neurasthenic "episodes," was an active advocate of the cause, especially in the area of female education. She had managed to convince her literary brother of the justice of at least that portion of the feminist agenda. Yet whatever opinions Henry may have held on the subject, at the moment he probably clung to them less tenaciously than to his desire not to be betrayed once again by his facial musculature.

"Or, if such be her inclination," Elena Phoenix concluded with a proud heavenward thrust of her chin, "she can walk the streets and peddle her favors to the highest bidder!"

Henry's eyes widened. He searched Elena's face for a clue as to whether she might be joking, but her countenance evinced nothing beyond its loveliness. If indeed this were a joke on her part, Henry must have felt, it was one entirely too provocative for the circumstances. In Europe a proper young lady would scarcely dare ride a train unescorted, much less engage in such familiar badinage with a perfect stranger. On the other hand, he couldn't have helped but think that if this woman turned out to be—the word would have rushed to his mind with a tingle of excitement and revulsion—a common *whore,* why then might he not discount her poor opinion of *Roderick Hudson* entirely?

"And which of these, ah, worthy professions," asked Henry, "might it be your pleasure to substitute for the sorry satisfactions of the wedded estate?"

The answer to this pointed query was not to be forthcoming—at least not for the moment—since no sooner had it escaped Henry's lips than the coach lurched violently and, with a piercing screech of iron wheels on iron rails, ground shuddering to a halt. There was a loud hiss of steam outside, then a portentous silence.

Somewhere up ahead, the nervous nickering of horses broke the stillness of the hot night air. Peering out the window of the coach to see if any station was apparent, all Henry would have been able to discern would have been the stark rock walls of a construction cut, void of any sign of human habitation or commerce. His fertile imagination might have leaped to wild Indians, herds of bison, or flash floods.

His fellow passengers, however, being far better acquainted with the hazards of the route, were quicker to comprehend the true nature of their plight.

"Train robbers!" shouted one of the Chicago drummers.

———◆———

Contrary to the tenets of American mythology, the art of the train robbery was not invented by the James Gang; that dubious distinction is more properly accorded to the Reno brothers of Seymour, Indiana, who first struck an Adams Express car in 1867. Yet just as it was J. S. Bach who codified and extended the conventions of European music without having created them de novo, so it was the James Gang who perfected the techniques of robbing trains and with whom the classic methodology, even as early as 1876, was already most strongly identified in the popular imagination.

Furthermore, the so-called James Gang was only a loosely organized and ever-shifting cadre of personnel, a larcenous pickup ensemble of which the nucleus was the James brothers themselves—Frank and Jesse—and the Younger brothers—Cole, Jim, and Bob. On July 6, 1876, these core brotherhoods, minus Jim Younger and augmented by Clell Miller, Sam Wells (alias Charlie Pitts), and William Stiles (alias Bill Chadwell), along with a neophyte outlaw named Hobbs Kerry, had assembled near California, Missouri, and ridden west in two groups toward the town of Otterville in what is now Cooper County. The following afternoon, as the Number 4 Express was chugging out of Kansas City, the members of this odious octet had converged a couple of miles east of a forbidding gash in the railroad bed known locally as Rocky Cut, where a bridge was being constructed across the Lamine River. Because of this excavation, trains passing through the cut were obliged to slow to a crawl. A lone watchman was stationed at the construction site, his main job being to cross over and inspect the structure before and after the passage of each train.

As the sun was setting behind the bridge, Bob Younger, Sam Wells, and Clell Miller burst out of the woods and accosted the hapless watchman at gunpoint. "You ain't going to hurt me," he whimpered as they blindfolded him. "What would we want to hurt you for?" replied one of his assailants. "We want that money, that's all we care for."

While the other members of the gang took up positions along the banks of the cut, Bill Stiles and the rookie bandit Hobbs Kerry stayed behind and piled a barricade of railroad ties across the tracks.

It was shortly after ten in the evening when the Number 4 Express finally approached the cut. The blindfolded watchman was shoved across the rails to flag it down with his lantern. According to one witness, "the engine climbed up on the ties, rising fully ten inches off the track and then stopped and of its own weight settled back on the track." Stiles and Kerry quickly scurried to the rear of the train to pile additional ties on the tracks behind the caboose, effectively eliminating the possibility that the engineer might make an escape by throwing the train into reverse.

Owing to the summer heat, the side door of the express car had been left open. Three of the bandits quickly boarded while two others climbed onto the engine, whooping and firing their revolvers into the air.

The commotion was precipitating a mad scramble inside the coaches: The terrified travelers hurried to divest themselves of potential booty, the men sliding greenbacks and gold eagles into their shoes or under their reclining seats, stuffing their pocket watches and jewelry into their baggage on the overhead mesh racks or dropping them into the watercooler, the stove, even the mouths of the brass spittoons. The women—those of whom who had not fainted outright—shrieked or sat paralyzed in their seats. From up the line in the express car came muffled shouts and bangings, then a volley of sharp pistol reports. "The passengers," the baggage master, Peter Conkling, later recalled, "had every reason to believe a massacre was in progress."

Almost immediately, the door of Henry's car swung open to reveal a pair of masked gunmen. Both bandits were armed with big Colt Navy revolvers; the shorter of the pair also cradled a Winchester carbine across his chest.

"Okay, we're comin' in and goin' through you all," announced the taller of the duo, "so be quick, damn you, and hold up your hands!" His strong voice boomed through a mask of diaphanous white muslin, apparently fashioned from a lady's handkerchief or undergarment. Next to the dirty bandanna of blue calico carelessly knotted over the bridge of his partner's nose, this delicate swatch gave the speaker a strangely refined air. In his left hand he toted a two-bushel wheat sack, which he held aloft as he strode into the car.

"Now, I wouldn't advise any of you to hold back on your donations," he warned. "We'll have your money anyway, and if you get smart, we'll have your life as well." The bandit punctuated this harsh caveat by sending a staccato triplet of pistol blasts ringing into the stamped tin ceiling of the coach. (In fact, despite these well-rehearsed theatrics of terror, the gang seldom made off with any significant loot from the riders of the trains they attacked. Such tactics were employed less as a way of increasing the haul from the holdup than of ensuring that the passengers, who of course outnumbered the outlaws, would remain cowed and distracted while the real work of the heist went on up in the express car.)

In the long annals of the James Gang's larcenous exploits, the train robbery at Rocky Cut is best remembered for the unprecedented behavior of one of the passengers, the Reverend J. S. Holmes of Bedford, New York: "To comfort the frightened passengers and crewmen, huddled under the guns of the guards," wrote Jesse James's biographer William A. Settle, Jr., "a minister who had been on board the train prayed loudly that the lives of all might be spared. In the thought that his prayers might go unanswered, he exhorted those about to be killed to repent of their sins while there was yet time. Following the prayer, the passengers mustered enough spirit to sing religious songs, an accompaniment to robbery odd enough to unnerve most bandits."

The outlaw pair, however, appeared not in the least unnerved by this impromptu display of Christian fervor. With the nonchalance of conductors taking tickets, they advanced along the aisle, relieving passengers of pocket watches, cash, rings, and brooches, all of which they crammed unceremoniously into the waiting grain sack.

Elena Phoenix kept her eyes fixed on the lean figure of the leader as he made his way toward her through the acrid stench of gunpowder hanging in the air. Only when he was standing directly over her did she drop her gaze from his angular face. Without a word, the bandit reached down and began to unfasten the clasp of her double chain of amber beads. His touch at the nape of her neck lingered as he gently brushed aside the fine golden wisps of hair above her collar with the muzzle of his pistol. At this criminal caress, Elena lifted her soft sea-green eyes to the hard steel-blue orbs of her assailant.

"Fear," wrote William James in his *Principles of Psychology*, "has bodily expressions of an extremely energetic kind, and stands, beside lust and anger, as one of the three most exciting emotions to which our nature is susceptible." Just which of these exciting emotions Elena was experiencing—or what puissant admixture of all three—is impossible to determine from our historical distance. Henry James, observing from the edge of his seat, saw her lips part and her bosom heave with what at the time he took to be a dry gasp of terror, but what he later surmised might have been the sign of some more succulent response. He was conscious of something like an electrical discharge in the air between Elena Phoenix and the outlaw, a palpable frisson to which he could not help but respond with a sympathetic shiver.

The gunman, as if sensing—and resenting—Henry's vicarious participation in this charged moment, spun quickly on his heel and thrust his revolver directly into the writer's face. "All right, mister! Fork out!" barked the bandit.

Henry James, who had doubtless never imagined himself the victim of any crime more violent than plagiarism, obediently dug out his pocket watch and struggled to unfasten its gold chain from his waistcoat, but the outlaw impatiently ripped it away, along with a ragged swatch of the vest's patterned silk lining.

To Henry's surprise, as he later recounted to his brother William, he found that he was not afraid, at least not in the pulse-pounding, sweat-dripping fashion of the dime novels. Rather, staring up into the barrel of the bandit's cocked six-shooter, he experienced only an overwhelming desire to be in Paris. It was the same "irresistible longing" he had felt often enough in recent weeks, but seldom with the intensity it carried now. He could almost smell the floral perfume of the Luxembourg Gardens wafting across his table and mingling with the aroma of fresh-baked croissants in the Odéon *bistrot* where he had so often taken his *petit déjeuner* on his most recent tour of the continent.

The cold steel of the bandit's revolver against his right temple prodded the writer abruptly back to the less civilized side of the Atlantic. Henry hastily deposited his wallet and gold tiepin into the open sack. Yet the masked desperado still seemed unsatisfied. "I'll take the book, too," he said, motioning with his pistol toward the handsome leatherette portfolio perched on Henry's lap.

Henry always considered his written impressions to be "property," and it would be difficult to overstate the importance of his notebooks to him. "If one is to undertake to tell tales and report with truth on the human scene," he wrote in later life, "it could but be because notes had been from the cradle the ineluctable consequence of one's greatest inward energy . . . to take them was as natural as to look, to think, to feel, to recognize, to remember." However nonchalantly he might have parted with his pocket watch or billfold, Henry James was not about to willingly chuck the accumulated literary capital of his entire western journey into a grimy grain sack. He demurred with a tight shake of his head.

"Seems to me you may have missed the gist of my little sermon back there," the robber hissed. Through clenched teeth, he added, "Now either you hand over that item pronto, or I'm going to blow your damn balls out your asshole."

This graphic threat, underlined by the presentation of the Colt's barrel at the appropriate anatomical altitude to make good upon it, was sufficient to loosen Henry's grip on his precious portfolio—and very nearly on his precious consciousness as well.

"I thank you very kindly, friend," the bandit drawled with a deep bow, holding his prize aloft. Then, to Henry's unfeigned horror, rather than depositing it into the wheat sack and moving on, the outlaw began flipping through the notebook with surprisingly delicate fingers, stopping at the page on which Henry had most recently been scribbling. " 'The softer facet of her being," the outlaw intoned, "is accentuated by a fashionable mauve frock, which blossoms with fantastic frills and flounces and from which a daring flash of lemon-yellow petticoat peeps fetchingly at the ankle. . . .' "

Neither the reader nor anyone within earshot of his leering, lip-smacking recitation had any difficulty identifying the subject of these observations. Elena Phoenix stiffened in her seat, staring straight ahead and coloring strongly at this public enumeration of her charms.

The author of the portrait colored no less strongly. Henry squirmed in his seat and massaged his forehead with his palm. This train robbery, so promising at the outset as a thrilling vignette of Western history on the hoof, now seemed to be turning into a major literary embarrassment. "That isn't meant to be read," he protested. "Those are merely notes."

The bandit ignored the author's complaint. "Sounds to me," he went on, closing the book and addressing himself to the blushing Elena Phoenix, "like you've got yourself a real admirer here."

Elena kept her eyes forward, her chin high. "I don't believe Mr. Jones appreciates my views, and I'm not certain I appreciate his."

"Ah, but I appreciate *your* views just fine," said the bandit, chuckling. "Front, side, and back!" All of this was very much a public performance, another jaunty bit of terrorist theater carefully calculated to burnish the outlaw's growing legend.

Elena, who was not unaccustomed to inspiring such attempts at roguish repartee, merely sighed and muttered, "Well, I'm afraid I've seen quite enough of *you.*"

The outlaw stepped to Elena's side and placed the notebook gently on her lap.

"I just don't believe that's true," he said, raising his hand to his cheek. "Doesn't every Christian woman, deep down, long to gaze upon the very face of evil, to behold the marks of sin and degradation upon the human visage, to confront the naked countenance of hell?"

With a dramatic flourish, he ripped off his sheer muslin mask.

Elena Phoenix, the very portrait of arch composure in her recent conversational contretemps with Henry James, could now, staring up at the handsome features so familiar from every post office rogues' gallery and train depot wall west of the Mississippi, find for vocal expression only a shrill schoolgirl squeal: "Jesse James!"

If the young woman's composure cracked in registering the presence of the notorious bandit, that of Henry James positively crumbled. The author, who was to become one of the masters of the nineteenth-century ghost story, looked as if he had just seen one. "My God!" he blurted. "It's Robbie!"

At this ejaculation, the outlaw turned and faced the writer again, squinting hard to penetrate the glossy brown-black beard that obscured Henry's facial features nearly as effectively as the muslin mask had concealed his own. His mouth worked dumbly, twisting into an expression that on any countenance less formidable than that of the most dreaded desperado in the country might have been taken as the grin of a halfwit. The silly smirk seemed to take on a life of its own, spreading slowly into a smile as wide as all the West.

"Holy shit!" hollered Jesse James. "It's Harry!"

Chapter Two

————◆·———

The young woman who introduced herself to Henry James as Elena Phoenix was born Elena Brownlee Hite on August 28, 1853, in Hartford, Connecticut, the only child of Asa Billings Hite and his wife, Amelia. As a young man, Asa Hite had enjoyed remarkable success in Hartford's burgeoning insurance industry, first as a salesman for the Aetna, then as a manager at Connecticut Mutual Life. He had married well and made the most of it by becoming an early investor in the Hartford & New Haven Railroad, which had opened its books in 1835. By the 1850s, when Elena was born, Asa Hite had already amassed a considerable fortune, most of it in railroad stocks and bonds. Elena grew up in the fashionable Lord's Hill district of that prosperous New England city (a prominent neighbor was Junius Morgan, father of the fabled financier J. P. Morgan). She attended Miss Draper's Seminary and later the Hartford Female Seminary, founded by Catharine Beecher, the older sister of Harriet Beecher Stowe of *Uncle Tom's Cabin* fame.

It might be tempting to credit Elena's subsequent fierce advocacy of female emancipation to this early immersion in feminist ideology, but it is important to note that Catharine Beecher, though considered progressive by many in her day, actually represented the conservative wing of the women's movement. Her educational agenda, rather than being geared toward preparing women to achieve social, political, and economic equality with men, was based on the assertion that managing a home, raising a family, and teaching—the only occupations Miss Beecher deemed appropriate for women—were every bit as important and challenging as running a business or a nation. (In 1871 Beecher signed a petition *against* female suffrage, arguing that women gaining the right to vote would only cause "the humble labors of the family and school to be still more undervalued and shunned.")

Despite its emphasis on "domestic economy," Miss Beecher's curriculum was surprisingly rigorous: Elena studied algebra, chemistry, ancient and modern history, rhetoric, French, Greek, and Latin, along with draftsmanship, written expression, and physical education, which consisted of calisthenics, archery, and "light chest weights"—all designed to improve "the grace and carriage" of the young *seminariennes*.

Academically, Elena proved a superior student, though one of her teachers reported that she could be "headstrong," and another described her as being occasionally "sullen." Her fellow students apparently found her somewhat standoffish—one even called her "haughty"—though from Elena's viewpoint, this was merely a misconstruction of her natural reserve, even shyness, at that awkward age. For whatever reason, she did not make any close friends at Miss Beecher's seminary (or, if she did, those adolescent bonds unraveled abruptly and permanently in the wake of her subsequent transgressions).

At home, even in her teens, Elena was virtually the mistress of the household. Amelia Hite, never a robust woman, had nearly died in giving birth to her daughter, leaving her a semi-invalid and effectively terminating conjugal relations with her husband. (Elena once described her mother, who, in addition to her other infirmities, was most likely addicted to laudanum, as "a living ghost haunting her own house.") Consequently, Elena received considerably more hands-on training in domestic economy than even Miss Beecher would have prescribed for one of such tender years. In an era when young women were often little more than "ornaments in their fathers' parlors, waiting," in the apt phrase of Brown University professor Nancy Hoffman, Elena became something of a surrogate spouse to her father, taking on—along with much of the responsibility for running the household and overseeing her mother's care—many of the social obligations and prerogatives of a Victorian wife. Asa Hite, when not traveling on "railroad business," as he did widely and frequently, was bent on entertaining the upper crust of Hartford society and came to depend upon Elena to help arrange the lavish dinner parties through which he hoped to secure a place among the city's better-established families.

After graduation (with high honors) from Miss Beecher's, Elena began socializing with the provincial yet pretentious young "artistic" crowd in Hartford, centered in the tony Nook Farm enclave of the city, which harbored such literary luminaries as Mark Twain and Harriet Beecher Stowe. Specifically, she took up with one George Goodwin Stanley, an aspiring painter already in his mid-twenties. To the adolescent Elena, who, despite her manifest beauty and bountiful talents, had always felt uncomfortable in the gilded society toward which her father was propelling her, George Stanley must have seemed a dashing figure indeed: Not only did this handsome "older" man boast impeccable social and financial credentials—his father, Aaron Stanley, was an important early backer of Samuel Colt's thriving firearms business—the younger Stanley had even been to Paris, where he had studied with Thomas Couture, a neoclassical painter whose scandalous "orgy" picture *Romans of the Decadence* had been the sensation of the 1847 Salon and who had gone on to instruct Édouard Manet and a number of well-known American artists, including William Morris Hunt, with whom William James later studied at Newport.

Elena's association with young Stanley began innocently and properly enough. Together they studied the Old Masters, participated in gay soirées of charades, musicales, and parlor games of the era, and painted in George's exquisitely appointed north-lit studio, which had been converted from a carriage house on the Stanley estate. She became George's pupil, displaying a talent with brush and oils that he once graciously intimated promised to eclipse even his own.

One of Elena's few surviving canvases from this period treats the classical theme of the Greek goddess of the hunt Artemis (the Roman Diana) surprised while bathing by Acteon, prince of Thebes. Such a subject was of course a highly ambitious undertaking for a fledgling artist, but Elena always took pride in being ahead of herself. (The headmistress at Miss Draper's once reported to her father that upon counting up to ninety-nine, Elena had proudly blurted out "*two* hundred," insisting that she had every right to do so since she had already counted one hundred.) Thanks to her excellent school training in draftsmanship, to George Stanley's attentive tutelage, and to her own native gifts, Elena's work demonstrated a precociously keen sense of composition and expression, particularly in her rendering of the human face and form.

According to the ancient myth, the virgin goddess was so enraged at being spied naked that she transformed her accidental admirer into a stag, which was swiftly and fatally set upon by his own hunting dogs. Conventional treatments of this subject, following Titian's 1559 masterpiece, depict the prince observing the naked goddess surrounded by her nymphs, usually in a bathhouse setting. But Elena's canvas tellingly advances the focus of the great cinquecento master's work by presenting a subsequent moment in the story: In Elena's painting, based on that of Guiseppe Cesari ("Il Cavaliere d'Arpino," 1568–1640), Acteon has already been partially transformed into a stag, his hounds hard at his heels. The bloodied prince's eyes are wide with animal terror, but the fully, proudly naked goddess, to the left and in the foreground, seems to regard the unfortunate voyeur's suffering with true Olympian detachment, her satisfied smile suggesting nothing so much as smug pride with her divine handiwork.

Asa Hite at least initially approved—indeed, encouraged—his daughter's association with young Stanley, pleased by the prospect of the cultural and social advantages she might garner from rubbing elbows (he naïvely assumed it would never be more than elbows) with the scion of such a well-educated, well-heeled, and widely traveled family. He no doubt foresaw a brilliant marriage for his only child.

But Elena had scant desire to rush into what she saw as "the tyranny of wedlock," especially in light of the disheartening model of her parents' own unhappy union. Moreover, during her postbellum adolescence, a new, more assertive—even combative—brand of feminism was rapidly gaining adherents, spearheaded by such militant reformist firebrands as Susan B. Anthony, Elizabeth Cady Stanton, and, most notably, the colorful and charismatic Victoria Woodhull, whom Elena heard speak at the Hartford Opera House in the fall of 1871. In that year—nearly half a century before women ultimately won the right to vote—Woodhull, who had worked at various times in her life as an actress, a prostitute, a clairvoyant, a stockbroker, and a newspaper publisher, had declared herself a candidate for the presidency of the United States, running on a platform that included not only universal suffrage but free love. (Needless to say, "The Woodhull," as she was known, found herself at loggerheads with the likes of Catharine Beecher, who once described the self-nominated candidate as "either insane or the hapless victim of malignant spirits.")

To the impressionable and irrepressible Elena Hite, however, Woodhull's radical creed arrived as a revelation. Freshly liberated from the strictures of Miss Beecher's seminary, she was brimming with a youthful sense of her own artistic and personal possibilities. Above all, she wanted *experience*. She yearned for a Paris of her own, and with characteristic impatience, if she couldn't have the one on the banks of the Seine, she was determined to create one for herself on the banks of the Connecticut.

Her posing with George Stanley became increasingly daring: While his early portraits of Elena depicted her in such quaint and modest guises as that of a mock-shepherdess Marie Antoinette, in time the pair were painting each other, as the delicate Victorian euphemism had it, "from life." (In her Artemis study, Elena used her own likeness for the naked goddess and that of a naked and antlered George Stanley—with facial features somewhere between those of a stag and a socialite—as the model for the young prince.) Such artistic liberties led, perhaps inevitably, to those of a more carnal nature, which, given a wishful "continental" and free-love gloss, somehow evolved into dalliances with others in their circle. (Elena once proclaimed that she was like a man in all things save love, but it appears that in love, especially, her behavior could be masculine in the extreme.) Like Daisy Miller, Elena—upon whom Henry James may have partially based the eponymous heroine of his wildly successful 1878 novella—came to enjoy "a great deal of gentlemen's society." And while in her own mind, she may have been living out a daring bohemian fantasy of free love, the sordid truth, from the perspective of proper Hartford society, was that she was being "passed around" among George Stanley's coterie of overprivileged, overheated young bucks. When one of them, apparently consumed by residual Puritan guilt, confessed these raunchy goings-on to his minister, Elena came to learn that, as Victoria Woodhull's biographer Barbara Goldsmith pointedly noted, "it was one thing to believe in the theory of free love and quite another to practice it." Suddenly, everyone in Hartford, it seemed, was talking *about* her, while no one would talk *to* her.

Finding herself to have become, like Daisy, "a young lady whom a gentleman need no longer be at pains to respect," Elena reacted with alternating bouts of shame and rage—shame not so much for having behaved badly as for having so grossly miscalculated the public consequences of what she had naïvely assumed to be private acts, and rage at knowing that the "crimes" for which she was being shunned were no more heinous than those for which the young men of her acquaintance were summarily exonerated, not to say tacitly applauded.

Most of all, she bridled at the notion that she might be thought of as a victim. Though accepting such a judgment could have provided her with something of a moral "out" from her dire predicament, she refused to allow herself to be seen as the pathetic protagonist of a classic Victorian fallen-woman narrative in which an innocent young girl, usually of lower birth, is led astray by a heartless upper-class rogue. She determined she would rather be treated as an object of scorn than one of pity; indeed, as William James later astutely remarked of her downfall, she seemed "not so much to have fallen as to have leapt."

Her mother, however, proved far less resistant and resilient in the face of the scandal; in fact, it may have killed her. In the wake of the shocking revelations about her daughter's comportment, Amelia Hite took to her bed and never left it, dying—possibly from an overdose of laudanum—within a week.

Elena's father responded to the double blow of his daughter's disgrace and his wife's demise by throwing himself into grim business mode, retreating into his oak-paneled library and occupying himself day and night with railroad investment affairs. He was unwilling or unable to share his anger, disappointment, and grief with his wayward daughter, though all were painfully apparent to her from the distance he put between them. (Besides, sexual misconduct was hardly a subject Asa Hite could have broached with Elena, and not merely out of a sense of Victorian propriety. For years, it was rumored, he had been a regular client at a number of the tonier "sporting houses" of New York City.) Certainly, the easy camaraderie of their surrogate-spouse relationship was gone: There would be no more lavish dinner parties to be arranged chez Hite. Elena and her father rattled around in the big Lord's Hill house in stony silence.

Local gossips, the "Hounds of Hartford," as Elena called them in her diary, chastised her as a heartless and remorseless Jezebel—doubly so for having "driven the final nail into her mother's coffin." Hartford, having demonstrated its intolerance of Elena, soon became intolerable to her.

Fortunately, she was not without means to strike out on her own. At twenty-one, even before her mother's death, she had received a sizable bequest from the estate of her maternal grandfather, Charles Brownlee, a leading Baltimore textile broker. It was a windfall that, under radically different circumstances, might have served as her dowry, but she put it instead toward an extensive cross-country speaking tour. Under the nom de guerre Elena Phoenix, she enlisted as a foot soldier in the "petticoat brigade" of feminist proselytizers then storming the nation's lecture halls in an oratory assault on the citadel of masculine privilege.

Though her message appears to have been little more than basic Bloomer Girl boilerplate advocating female enfranchisement, property rights, and higher education (with particular emphasis on women's sexual prerogatives), Elena's style at the lectern set her dramatically apart from her speechifying sisters on the lyceum circuit. Her seminary training in rhetoric and elocution, coupled with her youth and striking good looks, brought her stunning success throughout New England and even as far west as Kansas City, her last lecture venue before her fateful encounter with Jesse James & Co. A handbill from that occasion reads:

TONIGHT!
THE RISING WOMAN
Miss Elena Phoenix
* Her views on the Emancipation of Women
* Humanity and Political Equality of Women
* The Sleeping Giantess
* Bonds of Matrimony, Shackles of Dress
* The Natural Rights of Females
Miss Phoenix: Author and Lecturer

News of the train robbery at Rocky Cut flashed almost instanta-neously across the telegraph wires of Missouri and the entire nation. The bandits—preliminary reports varied as to whether there were six or a dozen of them—had made off with over fifteen thousand dollars from the Adams and United States Express strongboxes aboard the train, then disappeared like will-o'-the-wisps into the summer night.

When the Number 4 Express finally pulled in to Union Station in St. Louis early the following morning, it was greeted by a clamoring phalanx of reporters, policemen, and detectives. Among the latter were St. Louis chief of police James McDonough and William Pinker-ton of the Pinkerton National Detective Agency, who, as soon as he had gotten word of the latest James-Younger escapade, had hopped the first train down from his home office in Chicago in the hope of picking up the gang's trail while it was still warm.

Not that the seasoned sleuth would have nurtured any serious ex-pectation of gleaning anything useful about the robbery from wit-nesses aboard the train. He was all too familiar with the depressing propensity of the James Gang's victims to develop a convenient and global amnesia for their experiences, either out of raw fear of retalia-tion or from a nostalgic sense of secessionist solidarity with the former Confederate irregulars who made up the gang. Elena Hite, however, being unfamiliar with the mores and bloody history of the region, ap-parently felt little trepidation about submitting to an interview with the detective. She accepted his offer to escort her to her hotel and in-vited him up to her room to be debriefed.

It must have been one of the odder interrogations in Pinkerton's career. Like many a fashionable young lady of her time, Elena, even in high summer (and despite her rhetorical attack on "the shackles of dress"), sported more layers of apparel than a napoleon pastry. Be-neath her frilled mauve frock, she wore three long petticoats: The out-ermost, a "Balmoral," was woolen, with red and green stripes; the inner two were of lace-trimmed muslin, stiffly starched, one white and the other—as noted by the perspicacious Henry James—a soft lemon yellow. These, in turn, covered a pair of tubular cotton drawers, also stiffly starched and secured about her waist with tape strings. The drawers, in a shower of elaborately embroidered ruffles, reached well below her knees, covering a pair of burgundy lisle pantalette stockings that were themselves adorned from calf to ankle with three tiers of white flounces.

After a long hot night toting about this considerable stock of dry goods—she complained to Pinkerton that she felt "rigged up like a schooner in full sail"—Elena was naturally eager to get out of her traveling togs and into a refreshing bath. She proceeded to perform what could only be described as a slow striptease, shedding her garments and laying them one by one atop the flimsy silk-and-bamboo screen that stood between herself and her interlocutor. "So much is made of our so-called feminine modesty," she asserted breezily from behind the lotus-motif screen (reciting verbatim from her own stump speech), "but I'm certain it's all just another ruse by which men, under the guise of elevating us, conspire to render us all the more deeply enslaved."

This line, usually greeted with appreciative applause when delivered from the podium, was met by her present audience with embarrassed silence. Pinkerton's nervous smile did little to conceal the intense discomfort occasioned in him by the increasingly extreme state of dishabille of his star witness. Outside of the racy pages of *The National Police Gazette,* the detective had seldom been exposed at point-blank range to such a thorough catalog of a young lady's inexpressibles. His dark eyes darted over every detail of the suite, registering the magenta velvet drapes, the oak bedstead, the equestrian chromoliths on the walls—everything, in short, but the provocative silhouette of the room's current occupant. Elena, for her part, was not in the least unconscious of the discomfiting effect her immodest behavior was having on the detective, any more than she had been of the shocking impression her remark the night before about walking the streets and peddling her favors to the highest bidder was bound to have made on Henry James. In fact, she quite relished her ability to discombobulate the self-proclaimed dominant sex. ("I must confess," she once wrote, "to deriving an unseemly pleasure from thoroughly confounding the poor creatures at every turn, displaying brashness where they expect reserve and modesty where they anticipate audacity.")

Indeed, Pinkerton was thoroughly flummoxed by Elena. She failed to fit into any of his convenient mental pigeonholes: As an attractive young lady of apparent good breeding, she should not have been gallivanting about the countryside unaccompanied, and certainly not casually disrobing in the presence of strange men. Yet as a women's liberationist, she should have been older, crustier, and far less easy on the eye—more in the mold of that "glorious phalanx of old maids" who "seldom marry and never die" and whom Henry James later skewered in *The Bostonians*.

Pinkerton was experiencing both intense erotic provocation and something very much its opposite, an unpleasant sense of being somehow neutered, like a servant whose sex was irrelevant to the transaction at hand. In fact, he need hardly have flattered himself that Elena was out to seduce him; he was distinctly not her type. Though then only thirty, "The Big Man," as he was known in criminal and law-enforcement circles, had already become, in the description of British journalist Ben Macintyre, "stout and florid," with pudgy cheeks and a huge, drooping, bushy mustache—scarcely a hottie even by Victorian standards—and a prime specimen of those portly "prosperous walruses" that Elena always associated, not in the least romantically, with her father and his stogie-puffing business cronies. Under the circumstances, the detective was anxious to get down to business, as much for whatever information he might elicit from this extraordinary young woman as to keep his mind off the titillating proceedings taking place behind the lotus screen.

By the summer of 1876, hostilities between the James Gang and the Pinkertons had long since achieved the intensity of an all-out war. "I know that the James-Youngers are desperate men," wrote Allan Pinkerton, William's father and the agency's founder, "and that if we meet it must be the death of one or both of us . . . they must repay . . . there is no use talking, they must die."

The crimes for which the Pinkertons were seeking capital redress were not merely the James Gang's depredations upon the railroads and express companies controlled by the agency's wealthy clients. There had been casualties on both sides. In March 1874, a young Pinkerton operative named J. W. Whicher had attempted to infiltrate the gang by passing himself off as a hired hand looking for work on the James farm near Kearney, in Clay County. His body was found bound and gagged, sprawled in a ditch by the side of the road with bullet holes in the temple, neck, and shoulder—some of the shots having been fired at such close range that they left powder burns on his flesh and hair. The twenty-six-year-old Whicher's face, according to some accounts, had been half chewed off by wild hogs. A week later, another Pinkerton operative, Louis J. Lull, a former Chicago police captain, had met a similar fate (sans hogs) in a showdown with John and Jim Younger. On that occasion, Lull, accompanied by fellow Pinkerton agent John Boyle and local deputy sheriff Edwin Daniels, had been accosted by the two Younger brothers on the road near Monegaw Springs in St. Clair County. When a suspicious John Younger trained a double-barreled shotgun on the trio and ordered them to drop their holsters, Boyle spurred his mount and galloped off. He lost his hat to a blast from the shotgun. Daniels lost his life a few moments later, after Lull drew a small Smith & Wesson No. 2 revolver from his boot and shot John Younger through the neck. Jim, the older Younger, retaliated by blasting Daniels into oblivion with his pistol, while the mortally wounded John Younger pursued Lull on horseback, dropping the detective with two shots before falling dead himself. Lull died three days later. Only Jim Younger and the hatless John Boyle, later castigated as a coward by Allan Pinkerton, had survived the encounter.

The following winter, in retaliation, the Pinkertons had mounted a midnight raid on the James farm. On January 26, 1875, a cadre of heavily armed men had surrounded the farmhouse and hurled an incendiary device through a kitchen window. This device may have been, as the Pinkertons' defenders later claimed, an iron-clad ball of "Grecian Fire"—an early precursor of napalm—intended to illuminate the premises or at worst to smoke out its inhabitants. But when it rolled into the open kitchen hearth, it exploded like a bomb. Zerelda Samuel, a woman numerous historians have erroneously described as Frank and Jesse's mother, lost her right arm in the blast, and her eight-year-old son Archie perished when a red-hot chunk of the fireball's cast-iron casing tore into his belly. If Jesse and/or Frank James were at the farm that night—which was never proved—they escaped unscathed. The deadly attack on the Kearney farmhouse had not only failed to bring down the James boys; it had turned into an enormous public relations debacle for the agency. Though the Pinkertons always denied any involvement in the incident, many local citizens who might otherwise have been happy to have seen the region ridded of the robber band came to sympathize with their outlaw neighbors against the invading detectives. Following the raid, a bill was introduced in the Missouri legislature calling for amnesty for the gang, and Jesse James, emboldened by this newfound popular support, lashed out against his pursuers. In a letter published in the *Nashville Republican Banner* in August 1875, the outlaw threatened that Pinkerton "better never dare show his Scottish face again in Western Mo. . . . or he will meet the fate his comrades Capt. Lull and Witcher [*sic*] met."

Since then the frustrated Pinkertons, feeling themselves as much the hunted as the hunters, had redoubled their efforts to bring the gang to justice, desperately clutching at any forensic straw that might blow their way.

Thus, Billy Pinkerton hung heavily on Elena's every word as she described the Rocky Cut robbery and its dramatic culmination in Jesse and Henry's mutual recognition. The long-lost brothers, she told him, had embraced and kissed. Then Jesse and Frank had called Cole and Bob Younger into the coach and presented a thoroughly dazed Henry James to their skeptical associates, proudly introducing their brother as a distinguished man of letters. Elena was able to vouch for the veracity of this characterization on the basis of her reading of *Roderick Hudson* and Henry's travel notebook, though here she withheld a crucial piece of information from Pinkerton—and not for the last time in their relationship: She actually had the notebook in her possession, having slid it off her lap and secreted it in her reticule in the wake of the author's hurried departure from the train. In what Elena described as an entirely "jolly" mood, Frank and Jesse had hustled the bemused novelist off the train with them, remarking on what a fabulous haul they had made that evening.

While recounting these bizarre events, Elena deftly unhooked the three dozen tiny brass clips at the front of her corset, a cumbersome contraption of steel, lace, whalebone, and gutta-percha that reached from her armpits to the fullest part of her hips, shaping her impossibly narrow waist. With an audible sigh, she liberated herself from the girdle's harsh mechanical embrace and stood silhouetted behind the translucent screen draped only in a high-necked, long-sleeved cotton underbody and an embroidered linen cambric chemise.

Pinkerton was not about to be further distracted by the ecdysiastic activity taking place behind the screen. At the mention of an additional James brother—and a literary one at that—the detective's practiced forensic feelers had been set aquiver. While the Younger brothers were clearly every inch the ill-bred backwoods louts they appeared, there had always been something fishy about those James boys: For example, how could one explain Frank James's well-known penchant for reciting flawlessly and at length from Shakespeare and Milton, or his famous facility with the French and German languages? And what of Jesse's courtly demeanor, the high diction and impeccable grammar of his frequent self-serving letters to the local newspapers? If what this woman was telling him was true, Pinkerton surmised, he had every reason to believe it might prove the big break in the case.

He pressed Elena for details, particularly for a precise description of Henry's physical appearance. Unlike his father, Allan, who had been gifted with a born detective's nose for sniffing out crime, Billy Pinkerton lacked an instinct for effortlessly worming his way into the criminal mind. The son had picked up the family trade more or less by rote, depending not so much on feel from his substantial gut as on the nascent science of criminology. Unfortunately, the rigorous Bertillon system of facial measurements, to say nothing of fingerprinting or DNA analysis, had yet to be developed, and the identity of criminals in those benighted times usually had to be ascertained on the basis of such gross physical characteristics as height, scars, and facial features, including the notoriously mutable traits of hair color, weight, beards, and mustaches. To this end, the Pinkerton agency maintained an archive of photographs—the world's earliest and most extensive catalog of mug shots—of which William Pinkerton had carried a selection down from Chicago on the off chance that they might help jog the memory of any recalcitrant witnesses. He now dealt out his little deck of tintypes across Elena's bedspread, a portable rogues' gallery that included pictures of the Younger brothers, Frank and Jesse James, and various other suspected members of the gang, along with a photograph of William Pinkerton's younger brother Robert, which the detective had included partly because any lineup required the presence of a few "ringers" who could not possibly have been involved in the crime in question, and partly for his own fraternal amusement.

When Elena emerged from behind the screen, wearing—much to Pinkerton's relief—a full-length and mercifully opaque cerulean satin dressing gown, she immediately pointed to the images of Frank James and Cole Younger. There were a couple of others she thought she might have recognized, though she couldn't be certain, and on the rest she drew a blank. The likeness of Harry Jones, aka Henry James, was nowhere to be found in the makeshift lineup.

But the picture that most riveted her attention was the one of Jesse James. In this photograph, the infamous outlaw appeared much younger than he had on the occasion of the recent robbery; it dated from his early days as a guerrilla fighter during the Civil War. "Jesse James had a face as smooth and innocent as the face of a school girl," wrote Major John Newman Edwards, describing the outlaw during late adolescence in his secessionist apologia *Noted Guerrillas, or the Warfare of the Border* (1877). "The blue eyes—very clear and penetrating—were never at rest. His form—tall and finely molded—was capable of great endurance. On his lips there was always a smile, and for every comrade a pleasing word or compliment. Looking at his small white hands with their long tapering fingers, it was not then written or recorded that they were to become with a revolver among the quickest and deadliest in the West."

Elena was transfixed by the image. If William Pinkerton was a portly walrus, this photo was of a lithe, lean panther. "Oh, my!" she exclaimed, almost involuntarily. And with that, she excused herself and headed for the bathroom.

Pinkerton called out after his witness, asking what, if anything, she knew about Jesse James.

"All I've heard," came the reply from behind the bathroom door, "is that he steals from the rich and gives to the poor."

At this Pinkerton cut loose a raucous hoot. "He steals, Miss Phoenix, from everyone. And he keeps it all for himself," the detective bellowed over the gurgle of the running faucets. "All that Robin Hood bunkum you've been hearing has been fabricated of whole cloth a yard wide by a bunch of sensationalist newspaper editors and die-hard secessionists who simply refuse to accept the blunt truth of Appomattox. These jokers like to pretend that the James boys are still fighting the Civil War, but even during the war, the regular rebel army wouldn't sully their ranks with the likes of those varmints. They had to fight as guerrillas with Bloody Bill Anderson's brigade—the vilest band of bushwhackers and cutthroats that ever disgraced the Stars and Bars. And I can assure you they haven't changed a whit in the decade since—unless it's for the worse. Sure, they may be cunning and daring and all that, but you'd better just forget all your sweet widow-and-orphan fairy tales and that damned newspaper rot about how the poor James brothers were driven from their farm by those evil railroads built with Northern money and Southern blood."

"They weren't?"

"No, they were not!" boomed the detective. "For your information, the James boys were never driven off that farm—by the railroads or anyone else. As a matter of fact, they're still on it!"

Had she just been informed that the bandit was holed up in the adjoining suite of the hotel, Elena could not have been more astonished. "You mean you actually *know* where he lives?"

"Everyone does. That's the devil of it. The place is outside of Kearney in Clay County."

"Then why don't you just go out there and arrest him?"

Pinkerton gave a bitter snort. "It's not just a farmhouse—it's an armed fortress," he explained. Especially since the botched midnight raid of 1875, "Castle James," as the locals called it, had become virtually impregnable. There were gunports in all the walls and rumors of secret underground escape tunnels. The Jameses had a hundred ways in and a thousand ways out, and with loyal neighbors and others serving as lookouts, they were always warned of approaching strangers.

"Others?" Elena asked in a strange flutey tone.

"Of course."

"Then, on this farm, they don't live . . . alone?"

Pinkerton ignored this pointed question. He was finding his witness highly exasperating. A suspicion was beginning to grow on him that Jesse James might have made off with something more of this young lady's than her amber necklace. She seemed to be in the grip of what the detective would later describe as a "morbid fascination" with the dashing desperado. And if Elena was one of that peculiar breed of women who were fatally fascinated by "bad boys," she hardly could have chosen better (or, more properly, worse): "I consider Jesse James the worst man, without exception, in America," Pinkerton's brother Robert once wrote. "He is utterly devoid of fear, and has no more compunction about cold-blooded murder than he has about eating breakfast."

But why, Elena mused aloud from her bath, would such a man— handsome, clever, courageous—devote himself to a life of crime?

Pinkerton shrugged. "Bad eggs. Rotten apples. What's the difference?"

Yet the difference, to Elena, was everything. "Our entire system of justice depends upon it," she lectured the lawman. "If you would read, for example, the article by the noted physician Oliver Wendell Holmes in *The Atlantic Monthly*, you might appreciate that the criminal suffers from a kind of moral insanity, and that to judge him by our own moral standards may not be at all appropriate to his condition. We cannot, according to Dr. Holmes, apply the common concept of free will to the behavior of these poor wretches, for the sad fact is that, for whatever reason, they simply have no free will."

To the battle-hardened and world-weary detective, all this talk of moral insanity and free will was mere academic twaddle, but to Elena, who had once been treated as something of a moral moron (if not an outright criminal), these questions were of burning personal significance. Like William James—albeit without that brilliant scholar's thorough conversance with the relevant philosophical literature—she was obsessed by the question of free will: Could people (could *she?*) actually *choose* their destinies, or did external factors predetermine their thoughts and behavior? She wondered especially if women were somehow either born or bred to have less free will than men. Were females, like criminals, congenitally excluded from participating fully in the social contract?

"You sound just like Belle Starr," remarked Pinkerton.

"Belle Starr?" Elena thought the name had a lovely ring to it.

"Sure. She's always going around saying that since all the laws are made by men, they needn't be obeyed by women."

"Oh, I *like* that!" Elena laughed. "And where does she lecture?"

"She doesn't *lecture,* Miss Phoenix; she shoots people and steals their money. She's an *outlaw.*"

At this juncture, Elena emerged from her tub and stood framed in the bathroom doorway, clad again in her dressing gown. "I do believe you're making sport of me, sir," she complained with a girlish pout.

"On the contrary," the detective rejoined earnestly, "I happen to be one who believes that our nation's greatest untapped wealth lies not in our land but in the potential achievement of our female citizens, who have too long been tethered to hearth and home."

Elena came into the room and seated herself at the small vanity beside her bed. "Why, that's very nicely put, Mr. Pinkerton," she replied curtly, "but you needn't feel obliged to patronize me." Her celebrated golden tresses, released from their coil and highlighted in the glow of the morning sun streaming through the window, cascaded freely over her shoulders. "I hardly expect men to concur with my views."

"Oh, but I do!" the detective insisted. He was now in the grip of an inspiration. "You may not be aware of it, Miss Phoenix, but my father hired the first female detective in the country."

On a sunny afternoon twenty years earlier, he recounted, a young widow named Kate Warne had appeared at the agency's Chicago offices seeking employment. Assuming the slender brunette was applying for a clerical position, the elder Pinkerton had been dumbfounded when she announced that she was responding to a newspaper ad he had recently placed for new detectives. At that time, the notion of a female detective was virtually unheard of, and Allan Pinkerton had brusquely informed Mrs. Warne that he had never employed a woman in such a capacity. But the aspiring private eye had persisted, arguing that as a woman, she could be "most useful in worming out secrets in many places which would be impossible for a male detective." A woman might be able to induce suspected criminals to brag about their exploits, or develop useful information by befriending wives and girlfriends. After a sleepless night of mulling over the proposition, the elder Pinkerton had offered her a detective job the next day. "She succeeded far beyond my utmost expectations," he later wrote. "Mrs. Warne never let me down!" (In fact, Kate Warne—outside of business hours, he called her "Kitty"—almost certainly became Allan Pinkerton's mistress.)

As he recounted this familiar piece of company lore (leaving out the mistress business, of course), Billy Pinkerton continued to study Elena applying herself to her toilette with the serene confidence of one whose task at the mirror had always consisted of bringing out her beauty, never of having to conceal its opposite.

"She must have been a very admirable woman," Elena allowed warily, uncertain where all this might be leading.

"She was," Pinkerton agreed eagerly. "My brother and I used to call her Aunt Kate when we were little. Whenever she visited us, she always brought a piece of chocolate or caramel candy." The detective began digging through the inner pockets of his waistcoat, and for a moment Elena feared he was about to produce one of the ancient bonbons. Instead, he withdrew a folded and dog-eared envelope, which he handed to Elena.

The letter inside was written on stationery bearing the imprint of Pinkerton's National Detective Agency, with the famous logotype of a single staring eye over the motto WE NEVER SLEEP (an image often cited as the origin of the expression "private eye"). The letterhead listed as general superintendents William A. Pinkerton of the Western Division and Robert A. Pinkerton of the Eastern Division. Allan

Pinkerton, over whose signature the body of the text appeared, was listed as the founder. Elena lowered her hairbrush and read:

Dear Billy,

What in hell is going on down there? All I have is reports of continued marauding, and many of our clients are beginning to express the gravest dissatisfaction with our inability to end this protracted war. I seem to have no soldiers but all officers in my regiments—all are capital men to give orders, few will go forward unless someone goes ahead.

Men like Lull and Whicher are hard to find, I know, but you must replace them in the field. Surely the state of Missouri must have a few tough, honest men in it to do the job. You simply have to try harder to find them. I suppose, too, that you have not yet hired a female detective, but I think that with some effort you will. I give you a description of the class of woman you will require: Say a lady about five feet six or seven inches high, hair dark or light brown. I don't think blond would do. She should be either married or single, but if married her husband must be dead. Face oval, forehead large and massive. Eyes should be large, whether black, blue, or gray, her feet moderately small. An easy talker but careful and one who can keep her own counsel yet be able to carry on a conversation on any subject and be always self-possessed and natural, although assuming a character. I am anxious to have such a female detective, and if you are able to find such a one, I will be highly pleased. We will find plenty of work for her to do bye and bye. I am anxious for you to give this your strict attention and let me know what you are doing.

Elena looked up from her reading to catch Pinkerton's expectant gaze. "I'm afraid my hair is hopelessly blond," she said with a wry smile. "My eyes are green, and my feet are hardly small. Not even moderately."

The possibility that Elena might have colluded with the Pinkertons in their war against the James Gang, either as a hired operative or a paid informer, has gained credence among some historians in light of her feminist agenda ("a woman can do anything a man can do") and the supposition that as the daughter of a railroad magnate, she might have wanted to rid the rails of the gang's wanton brigandage. But it seems more likely that the prospect of serving her father's interests would have been anathema to the rebellious young woman, and that her subsequent "pursuit" of the Jameses was motivated more by her own lively curiosity than by any passion for advancing the cause of womanhood, pleasing her father, or serving the forces of law and order. If Pinkerton ever did make such a proposition, either on this occasion or subsequently, there is no conclusive evidence that Elena ever agreed to work with him. Nothing in the Pinkerton archives suggests such a deal was ever struck, and Elena's diary is uncharacteristically mute on the subject (though she did once later refer to Billy Pinkerton in her journal as "that big old snoop").

What is certain is that after concluding her interview with the detective that morning, and delivering her scheduled lecture in St. Louis that evening, Elena headed back out west on the Hannibal & St. Joseph line the very next day. Whatever arrangement she may or may not have made with Billy Pinkerton, in the weeks to come and throughout the summer, the Eye That Never Sleeps would be keenly focused on "Elena Phoenix."

Chapter Three

———◆———

For William James, the summer of 1876 was to prove a memorable one. The novice professor had just completed his first full year of teaching psychology at Harvard; the depression that had been plaguing him for years was finally beginning to lift; and—perhaps not coincidentally—he had recently made the acquaintance of a young lady named Alice Howe Gibbens, a relationship that was shaping up to be the first real love affair of his life, long overdue. For despite his trim good looks, piercing blue eyes, legendary conversational brilliance, and abundant charm, William James was, at the age of thirty-four, to the best of our historical knowledge (his putative compulsive masturbation notwithstanding), still a virgin. This was not just a manifestation of how notoriously difficult it was to get laid in the nineteenth century. Many of William's contemporaries had long since managed to take the plunge into erotic manhood, even into marriage: His old friend Oliver Wendell Holmes, Jr., whose father's essay on the criminal mind had so impressed Elena Hite, had tied the knot over four years earlier with Fanny Dixwell, a woman William once moonily described as "decidedly A-1" and "about as fine as they make 'em." Granville Stanley Hall, William's first graduate student in psychology, often regaled his professor with tales of his romantic exploits among the local fräuleins during his year of studying in Germany. Hall, who had trained for the ministry at Union Theological Seminary before turning to psychology, extolled his "loss of puritanical inhibitions" on the continent. "I learned how great an enlightener love is and what a spring of mind Eros can be," he later wrote in his *Life and Confessions.* "Not only did these companions facilitate my use of German but, what was vastly more important, they awoke capacities hitherto unusually dormant and repressed and thus made life seem richer and more meaningful."

But for William James—whose German was perfectly serviceable to begin with—the richness and meaning such romantic liaisons might have provided had remained perennially elusive. One of his biographers, Linda Simon of Skidmore College, described him in his twenties as having "no experience in treating women in any way except with condescension." Which is not to suggest that he was a cold fish. On the contrary, according to Simon, William's mother worried that he "was inclined to become carried away with emotion and would fall in love too easily and not wisely." Once he even begged his sister, Alice, to find him "some spirited & romantic creature whom I can fall in love with in a desperate fashion." During his own year of study in Germany, he had swooned over the enchanting *mädchen* at a boarding school across from his pension in Dresden, but he had never advanced beyond gazing wistfully at the objects of his desire through a telescope. Even earlier, on an exploratory voyage up the Amazon with the celebrated naturalist Louis Agassiz, William had experienced the hots for some of the beautiful native Brazilian women he encountered, whose "splendid soft black hair" and "most wildly melodious perfume" caused him to bemoan his inability to communicate "shades of emotion" to them. And for years, before Holmes finally claimed her, William had carried a torch for the pretty and flirtatious "A-1" Fanny Dixwell.

Part of the explanation for his chronic romantic reticence may lie in the fact that intellectually and morally, William James truly believed in the virtue of abstinence. "No one need be told," he wrote in *The Principles of Psychology,* "how dependent all human social elevation is upon the prevalence of chastity. Hardly any factor measures more than this the difference between civilization and barbarism." He even went so far as to posit, in that same tome, the existence of an "anti-sexual instinct," one of personal isolation, that he described as "the actual repulsiveness to us of the idea of intimate contact with most of the persons we meet." He saw this countererotic force as a powerful antagonist to the sexual one, which was usually given pride of place among human drives. "Thus it comes about that this strongest passion of all," he concluded, "so far from being the most 'irresistible,' may, on the contrary, be the hardest one to give rein to, and that individuals in whom the inhibiting influences are potent may pass through life and never find an occasion to have it gratified."

On a more personal level, William was concerned that he may not have been cut out for love and marriage. To begin with, there were his recurring physical and emotional ills—the bad back, the bad eyes, the bad digestion, the periodic "pessimistic crises"—that he feared disqualified him from an intimate relationship. Even when not actively suffering from one (or some unpleasant combination) of these myriad ailments, he sometimes thought of himself as "feeble, egotistical, cowardly, hollow." He was unable to imagine that any desirable woman could ever love the real him. On top of these perceived shortcomings was his shameful sense of lacking a career: While men like Holmes had charted their professional courses early in life and hewed steadfastly to them, James had drifted from art to science to medicine to psychology without ever steering by any visible vocational star. As a practical matter, he doubted his ability to support a wife and family.

So it must have been with considerable skepticism, if not outright alarm, that he greeted his father's announcement one evening in the winter of 1876 when the elder James, upon returning from a meeting of the Radical Club in Boston, proclaimed that he had just met William's future bride.

Playing Cupid was only the latest gambit in a long tournament of wills in which Henry James, Sr., had tried to mold the life of his oldest son to his own quixotic ideals. Practically from the moment William emerged from the cradle, his father had subjected the brilliant boy to a quirky educational agenda that entailed bouncing him from school to school and country to country, his younger siblings thrashing in his wake. When it appeared in William's late teens that he had "prematurely" set his heart on a career in painting, his father adamantly determined that science was the only proper calling for a young man of his manifold gifts. William had gone along with all of this, even to the point of entering medical school, but as he matured, the two found themselves increasingly at odds. They disagreed especially on the subject of religion, with the father tending to see the hand of God in practically everything, and the son in almost nothing. Thus the Radical Club must have struck William as an especially unpromising hunting ground on which to bag him a mate. The group had been founded by Unitarian ministers and progressive-minded laypeople dedicated to purging Christianity of all vestiges of supernatural boogedy-boogedy in favor of emphasizing the spiritual and moral aspects of the faith. The agenda was often touted as "The Second Wave of Transcendentalism," and while the club's airy theological debates were doubtless meat and potatoes to the garrulous and God-obsessed Henry Sr., they would have seemed thin gruel to his rationalistic, agnostic son. William might well have balked at being "fixed up" with a young lady who would willingly subject herself to endless evenings of such sanctimonious palaver.

Yet if he bridled at the old man's matchmaking pretensions, his curiosity must have been piqued, for he dutifully attended the very next meeting of the club, where he was introduced to the paternally anointed Miss Gibbens. Though by no means a great beauty—she was short, "sturdily" built, and frankly plain of feature—the elder Henry's choice was in many ways an apposite one: Alice Gibbens was a teacher at Miss Sanger's School for Girls in Boston and, like William's mother, Mary, radiated an air of being loyal, energetic, and eminently sensible. All of which virtues had been hard won and thoroughly tested: Her father, a physician who never practiced medicine, had struggled with alcoholism and depression throughout his daughter's childhood and had died of a shot from his own revolver when she was only sixteen, leaving Alice and her two younger sisters to care for their delicate and distraught mother (yet another classic Victorian neuras- thenic). Clearly, Alice Gibbens was a woman whose solidity ran more than skin-deep. Despite the somewhat dumpy initial impression she must have made on him, William would have appreciated that the twenty-seven-year-old schoolteacher was not without her share of physical charms: She was blessed with a crown of luxuriant soft brown hair, a "wild rose" complexion, an engaging smile, large dark eyes, and a lovely musical voice. (In fact, she had studied singing in Baden- Baden with Clara Schumann, widow of the great composer Robert Schumann and a world-class musician in her own right.) "As soon as she spoke," wrote James's biographer Gay Wilson Allen, "William felt the weight of his father's prophecy."

In the ensuing weeks and months, and throughout the spring, the weight of that prophecy had grown sweetly heavier on William James. However much they may have disagreed on theological matters—Alice was an active and devout member of the Congregational church—they found that they had numerous tastes and interests in common. They shared a passion for long brisk walks, Browning poems, and European literature. Both had spent considerable time on the continent. (Alice's proficiency in German was equal to William's own, and she easily sur- passed him in Italian.) Better still, the high-minded schoolmarm turned out to have a deliciously irreverent sense of humor. In March she sent William a satirical poem that she had clipped out of *The Boston Sunday Times,* a wicked squib lambasting some of the more pretentious members of the Radical Club—Bronson Alcott, Julia Ward Howe, and Elizabeth Peabody (often cited as the model for the crusty old Miss Birdseye in Henry's *The Bostonians*). Perhaps best of all, Alice Gibbens took a lively and sincere interest in William's work at Harvard.

The graduate course he had been teaching that year was called The Relations Between Physiology and Psychology. Trained as a physician—the only academic degree he ever earned was his Harvard M.D.—William James, like Alice's father, had never formally practiced in what he once termed the "flesh pots" of medicine. Even after he entered medical school, his view of the profession was notably jaundiced. "My first impressions," he wrote at that time, "are that there is much humbug therein, and that, with the exception of surgery, in which something positive is sometimes accomplished, a doctor does more by the moral effect of his presence on the patient and family, than by anything else. He also extracts money from them."

William's interests had always been more deeply rooted in the less financially fertile pastures of psychology and philosophy, and long before receiving his medical degree, he had become caught up in the dream of a scientific psychology. ("It seems to me," he once wrote, "that psychology is like physics before Galileo's time,—not a single *elementary* law yet caught a glimpse of.") During his student year in Germany, between taking spa cures for his depression and scoping out the lovely schoolgirls across the street, he had boned up on the work of such pioneers of the so-called new psychology as Hermann von Helmholtz and Wilhelm Wundt, who believed that the only hope of raising the field to the stature of a natural science lay in a program of rigorous experimentation that would wrest it down out of the lofty realms of metaphysics and ground it in the biological nitty-gritty of the nervous system.

William was largely self-tutored in this emerging discipline. (He once wryly remarked that the first lecture he ever heard on the subject was the first one he himself delivered.) What was more, he felt physically and temperamentally unsuited to the tedious and fussy demands of laboratory work, in which typical experiments of the era involved decapitating frogs and whirling them around on a special apparatus, or amputating their feet and applying acid to the remaining stumps, all the while carrying out and recording meticulous measurements of the poor creatures' nervous responses. Nevertheless, it became his fondest dream to establish a laboratory of experimental psychology at Harvard.

At the time there was not yet even a psychology department at the university—William was doing his teaching in the philosophy department of Harvard College and in the anatomy department of the Lawrence Scientific School—so he had lobbied Harvard's president Charles W. Eliot to approve a curriculum in the field that would incorporate the latest findings about the nervous system (and, not incidentally, guarantee himself a job teaching it). "It is my firm belief," he wrote to Eliot, "that the College cannot possibly have Psychology taught as a living science by any one who has not a first hand acquaintance with the facts of nervous physiology. On the other hand, no mere physiologist can adequately realize the subtlety and difficulty of the psychologic portions of his own subject until he has tried to teach, or at least to study, psychology in its entirety."

President Eliot concurred. As the icing on William's potential wedding cake, the head of the university asked him to return in the fall as an assistant professor with a promised hike in annual salary from twelve hundred to two thousand dollars, "which will be a sweet boon if it occurs," William wrote to Henry. (A couple of thousand dollars was, of course, mere peanuts to what Frank and Jesse were raking in from a basic bank or train job, but William's out-of-pocket expenses were considerably lower than those of his outlaw brothers, in part because he was still living at home with his parents and sister, Alice, on Quincy Street in Cambridge.) For the era, President Eliot's offer represented a fairly decent living wage, with a promise of the financial independence and professional stature so crucial to William's self-esteem. "As the term advances," he wrote to Henry, "I become sensible that I am really better than I was last year in almost every way; which gives me still better prospects for the future."

But William's euphoria with his newfound professional and romantic vistas was severely dampened in mid-July by a letter he received from deepest Missouri. The envelope, which his correspondent had addressed to William's Harvard office so as not to risk alarming the rest of the family, bore the postmark of Kearney, Missouri, and even by Henry's daunting standards of prolixity, the missive it contained was a lengthy one. It began:

> *Dearest Wm.*
>
> *I am afraid that I have neglected writing home longer than has been agreeable to you: but the delay has been inevitable, & when I describe the perfectly infernal circumstances that have stayed my pen, I fancy you will surely forgive my silence.* Que vous en dirai-je? *In brutal summary, our late soldier brothers Rob and Wilkie are neither late nor soldiers: They are very much alive & they are outlaws, having adopted the* prénoms de guerre *"Jesse" and "Frank," while retaining our illustrious surname, wh. they drag through the mud at every criminal outing. Just how this sordid transmogrification occurred they have not as yet deigned fully to confide in me, & I must confess that I am little inclined to press them on the matter. The natural ties of consanguinity notwithstanding, I feel but the feeblest of sympathetic vibrations with them. Excuse the freedom of my speech, which I shall not stint, but better, I daresay, that they had perished honorably in battle—as we had been led to believe—than that they should have survived to arrive at this disgraceful pass. . . .*

The Civil War, of course, is fabled in the annals of American history for having pitted brother against brother—a reference usually to those who fought for the Union versus those who fought for the Confederacy. But the war also sometimes engendered a more subtle yet no less pernicious rift: a deep and lasting enmity between those who sprang to the colors and those who never fought. In the James family, this internecine breach played itself out across a fault line between the older and younger sets of brothers that had already been established long before the outbreak of hostilities between the states. As Alice James's biographer Jean Strouse observed, "Wilky and Bob formed a unit as soon as Bob left the nursery, and they remained paired in all the major activities of their lives. They shared as well a sense that they lacked the special qualities of mind that seemed to distinguish their older brothers." Indeed, early in their teens, years before the younger pair went off to battle, William had already disdainfully written off Rob and Wilky as "destined for commerce," effectively staking out the higher intellectual and artistic ground for himself and Henry. (Alice would always be the odd girl out.) Though much has been made of the supposed rivalry between William and Henry, the two older James brothers—both of whom managed to avoid military service—were exceptionally close. Their interests, if not always identical, were often parallel, overlapping, or complementary, and in a lifelong exchange of letters in which William once saluted Henry as "my in many respects twin bro," they kept each other apprised of much of the minutiae of their intellectual, emotional, physical, social, and professional lives.

In the present specimen of that voluminous correspondence, Henry spared his older brother few details as he went on to recount being unceremoniously hustled off the eastbound Number 4 Express "amidst a melee of wild whooping and deafening pistol reports," then being hauled up onto Jesse's powerful bay mare and taken on a wild night gallop through the brambles and thickets of the Missouri backcountry. For hours Henry clung desperately to his newfound brother's muscular back, his ample posterior smarting from the pounding it was taking against the high cantle of Jesse's saddle, his cheek pressed hard against the outlaw's sopping shirt, which exuded, he reported, a "manly mélange of whiskey, tobacco, leather, and perspiration." From the scene of the crime, the gang headed south, passing through the sleeping township of Florence a couple of hours after midnight, then cutting back into the woods and splashing along the bed of a shallow creek to throw off any trackers who might have picked up their trail.

It was nearly dawn by the time Jesse reined his famously fine mare to a halt on the bank of that moonlit stream. The brothers had exchanged barely a word since the robbery. They now quickly dismounted, and as soon as the gang finished watering their lathered horses in the creek, Frank got down to the business of divvying up the loot, doling out portions according to an arcane system of seniority and function, with the lions' shares going to the more experienced James and Younger brotherhoods. During this tense transaction, Henry hung off to the side, tending to his blazing behind, which he was "sorely tempted to douse in the soothing rush of that babbling brook." Cole Younger, already apprehensive about the inclusion of Hobbs Kerry and the other newcomers to the gang in the Otterville operation, looked askance at the unexpected presence of this novel James brother in their midst. The alliance between the Jameses and Youngers had been forged on the hard anvil of guerrilla warfare over a decade earlier, a bond sealed in shared bloodshed and one that Cole no doubt felt should have been stronger than the ties of mere shared blood.

Cole scrutinized the exquisitely tailored Henry James with undisguised contempt. "What in hell did you say he is, Buck?" he asked, addressing Frank by his old wartime nickname.

"Why, he's a novelist," replied Frank with a knowing smirk. "A *romancier*, if you will. He skewers the foibles of the international set." He gave the writer a broad wink. "Ain't that right, Harry?"

Henry was uncertain what to make of his brother's arch characterization, which, however accurate, could scarcely have been calculated to endear him to the likes of the cutthroat Youngers. Flustered, the author merely nodded, senselessly pointed to his aching ass, and flashed Cole Younger what he hoped would be taken as an ingratiating smile.

Frank grinned and redirected his attention to the task at hand, methodically doling out the greenbacks and negotiable banknotes from the haul into neat piles. Jesse, after making a point of retrieving Elena's amber necklace from the heap of booty, began pacing the bank of the stream, taut and prickly as a strand of barbed wire, his own attention darting nervously from his men to the surrounding landscape, his keen eyes and ears taking in every subtle shift of light and shadow, every random rustling in the cottonwoods, every startled whinny of the horses.

By now the ever-perspicacious Henry James had already come to intuit the dynamics of the gang: While Jesse was clearly the leader in action, Frank appeared to be the brains of the outfit. (If Jesse was a lean panther, as Elena had seen him, Frank was a sly fox.) James William Buel, a Missouri journalist, made a similar observation in his 1880 book *The Border Bandits*. Of Frank James, he wrote: "His cunning and coolness are remarkable, and to compare the two boys in this respect would be like comparing the boldest highwayman with the lowest sneak thief, so great is Frank's superiority. In the matter of education Frank . . . is a student, being a lover of books and familiar with different phases of life." By contrast, the newspaperman described Jesse as being "very limited" in the education department and "revengeful by nature, always sanguine, impetuous, almost heedless. It is due to Frank James' strategy and Jesse's desperate bravery that the latter has not long since been punished for his crimes."

The possibility of being punished for his crimes was very much at the forefront of Jesse's present concerns, informing his every move. At the time of the Rocky Cut robbery, according to the outlaw's biographer T. J. Stiles, "paranoia seeped through his words and actions, along with a continuing obsession with his enemies." Even after the loot had all been properly apportioned and the other members of the gang had mounted up and ridden off in separate directions, Jesse remained vigilant, patrolling the banks of the brook as if expecting a posse to burst forth from the buttonbushes and ninebarks along its edges at any second. The outlaw's slender fingers, Henry observed, were tensely curled, hovering over the grip of his holstered Navy revolver "like the hooded head of a cobra poised to strike." In his letter to William, the writer went on:

> *I must confess to a certain sinking of the heart at finding our brothers in such dire straits—hunted, haunted, with prices on their heads, & the more especially as there appears to have developed something of a bounty on my own* belle tête, *owing to which wholly unwarranted cranial premium my movements have of necessity been severely curtailed—at least until "the heat" is off. Please be assured that I am guilty of no crime, & yet the course of justice in these benighted parts is such that I dare not simply ride into town, proclaim my innocence & trust that a fair trial wd. exonerate me. The more likely outcome were I to embark on such a rash course of action, I am assured, wd. be that I shld. be set upon by an overzealous citizenry to be summarily strung up & left, as the colorful local idiom has it, "for buzzard bait." Rather than risk ornamenting an oak as the guest of honour at such a "necktie party," I have chosen, at the forceful invitation of our felonious brethren, to "hole up" & "lay low" here as their guest for an indefinite period.*

Despite his game attempt at maintaining the characteristic jaunty tone of his correspondence with William (and his apparent grim delight at flexing a new outlaw vocabulary), Henry must have been scared stiff. The "here" to which he referred was the infamous "Castle James," which Pinkerton had described to Elena Hite, although, as the writer went on to portray the place, it was scarcely so imposing an edifice as its grandiloquent sobriquet might have suggested. Indeed, it wasn't much more than a modest single-story clapboard cabin surrounded by split-rail fences and set on 275 acres of rolling farmland.

There was little to distinguish it from countless other rustic homesteads in the region, nor to hint that it might have been the lair of a
gang of notorious desperadoes, other than the fact that the walls were
riddled with a series of peculiar cone-shaped holes set at about eye
level. From the outside, these appeared only as little circles no larger
in circumference than a silver dollar. But inside, they widened out like
inverted funnels. At first glance, Henry confessed, he had taken these
odd borings to be some sort of primitive rural ventilation system, but
Jesse had quickly apprised him of their proper purpose: From within,
a sharpshooter was able to slide the barrel of a rifle through a hole and
swing the stock freely in the wide opening, allowing the marksman to
cover a broad range of the surrounding countryside with scant danger
of being struck by a shot from the perimeter. These were the dreaded
gun ports to which Pinkerton had alluded in his interview with Elena
Hite. Henry had immediately appreciated the workings of the system;
in France he had observed similar installations, designed for crossbows,
along the crenelated parapets of the medieval citadel at Carcassonne.

Convinced that he was implicated as an accomplice in the Rocky
Cut robbery, Henry found himself a de facto prisoner at Castle James,
with his brothers as his wardens. The farm, however, was not the most
horrendous hoosegow he could have imagined. While the surrounding western Missouri countryside lacked the studied old-world charm
of his beloved "wide purple" Roman Campagna, he had to concede
that it was not without a certain unassuming bucolic beauty: The
early-summer fields were burgeoning with corn, hemp, tobacco, and
hay; flocks of bluebirds flitted through the dogwoods and huckleberry
bushes; and the vast open sky provided a wide canvas for the long
lovely sunsets of the season. Moreover, with the influx of hard cash
from the Rocky Cut heist, a splendid store of groceries had arrived at
Castle James—thick Kansas City beefsteaks, savory sides of sugar-
cured bacon, tubs of silky apple butter, tins of aromatic Mojav coffee,
imported English toffee and treacle, and even a few fifths of bonded
Scotch whisky.

And to Henry's surprise—"delight," he insisted, would have been too strong a word under the demoralizing circumstances of his incarceration—his prison turned out to offer a sterling selection of reading matter. Frank James had amassed an extensive private library that included, along with a number of editions of the Bible, the complete works of Shakespeare, a choice collection of Spenser, Milton, Thackeray, Trollope, Balzac, Flaubert (in the original French), and, most remarkably, a well-thumbed copy of his own *Roderick Hudson*. (Had Frank stolen all of these precious volumes? Henry could not help but wonder.) Whatever the source of his literary treasure trove, the senior outlaw's storied scholarship was apparently authentic: Henry recounted to William an incident that occurred shortly after his arrival at the farmhouse, in which he had remarked upon the changes that the passage of the years had wrought upon his brother's appearance. (Gone was the "adipose, genial" Wilky of their school days; the man before him was now craggy and creased, with a "scrawny gamecock" physique that made him look a full decade older than Jesse, though in reality, the outlaw pair were separated by only a couple of years.) Frank had laconically acknowledged that "time is the rider that breaks youth," an expression Henry had assumed to be some cornball cowboy aphorism until Frank had curtly informed him of the quote's proper provenance: "The Temple," by George Herbert, metaphysical poet and orator of Cambridge University.

Faced with such undeniable evidence of his brother's erudition, Henry was unable to contain his curiosity about what this well-read bandit might have thought of his first novel. His coy query on the subject unleashed a critique that began with an all too familiar litany of complaints about the book's coldness, the extraneous "knots, bows and ribbons" of its prose, and the overly rapid pace of its title character's downfall, but which Frank soon managed to hijack into a self-serving disquisition on the aesthetic merits of his own larcenous oeuvre: A well-planned, well-executed holdup, the outlaw argued, was every bit as much a work of art as any literary production. It had structure, drama, and pace; it had a beginning, a middle, and an end. And so much more was inevitably at stake: Unlike the perpetrator of a novel, the armed robber risked far more severe opprobrium than mere carping reviews or lackluster sales; he faced prison or death. Henry found it difficult to discern whether his brother was joking, given the latter's deadpan delivery. (The novelist Ron Hansen depicted Frank as "a stern and very constrained man; he could have been a magistrate, an evangelist, a banker who farmed on weekends; rectitude and resolution influenced his face and comportment; scorn and even malevolence could be read in his green eyes.")

Jesse proved considerably easier to read, but the emotional weather vane of his handsome face could swing unpredictably in the rapidly shifting gusts of his mercurial moods. One evening when the younger bandit was cleaning his big Colt Navy revolver, Henry committed the cardinal faux pas of addressing him as Rob, unaware of the fierce pride his brother took in his famous outlaw moniker. (Jesse believed, not without some justification, that a considerable portion of his national renown derived from its catchy alliterative appeal.) He informed Henry that as a matter of fact, his name was Jesse James, to which the punctilious author replied that, no, properly speaking, Jesse James was his alias.

Jesse begged to differ: He pointed out that, properly speaking, his alias was Thomas Howard. His name, he insisted again, was Jesse James.

"Then perhaps what you mean to say is that Jesse is your nickname," Henry offered.

"Nope," Jesse contradicted his literary brother yet again, an ominous edge creeping into his voice. "My *nickname* is Dingus." More menacingly, he repeated slowly, "What I mean to say is that Jesse James is my *name.*"

Henry, who had spent a year at Harvard Law School during the Civil War, then played what he thought would be his trump: "Ah, but you haven't had it legally changed, have you?"

At this, a dark cloud scrimmed across Jesse's already forbidding countenance. He paused in his gun polishing and shot his brother a murderous glance over the gleaming barrel of the revolver. The writer at last came to comprehend the gravity of his transgression. He cowered and began to stammer, fully cognizant of the possibility that his canny juridical remark might well have been his last. At which point Jesse burst out laughing. "Legally?" he yawped. "*Legally!* I'm an *outlaw,* you asshole. I don't do *shit* legally!"

All of this, as Henry was hardly unaware, might have been the stuff of fiction: The saga of a reunion among long-separated brothers of widely divergent social strata—and such colorful characters, at that—could doubtless have provided enough material for a whole series of novels. But even the prolific Henry James—who, especially in his early tales, was never one to shy away from the lurid conventions of melodrama—was finding his present predicament a bit too raw to consider subjecting to the alchemy of his art. He just wanted it over.

Still, if there was one talent Henry possessed in abundance, in addition to his prodigious literary gift, it was a capacity for sheer endurance. The James brother who would ultimately outlive every one of his siblings knew how to make the best of a bad situation. In an oft-recounted vignette of family lore from their peripatetic childhoods, the James children—Henry was then twelve or thirteen—were once taken on an outing to the home of their French governess Marie Bonningue at Boulogne-sur-Mer. After a luncheon topped off with a memorable dessert of frosted cake, the children were shooed out into the garden to play. William was not in attendance that day and Rob and Wilky soon ran off to explore the surrounding terrain, leaving Alice and Henry alone in the flat sandy garden for the remainder of the long afternoon. As the sun slanted slowly in the sky, Henry sat patiently on a swing, content to muse his musings. "This," the future author observed to his little sister, "might certainly be called pleasure under difficulties!"

Under his present difficulties, Henry managed to keep his wits about him by establishing a routine for himself, passing the long hot days out under the shade of the coffee-bean tree in front of the house, reading his way through Frank's library and scratching away at his detailed dispatch to William. "This was the young Henry in his familiar disguise," as his biographer Leon Edel described him, "trying to bide his time, avoiding all overt action and hoping, by a kind of dogged persistence, to triumph." Henry's letter concluded:

> *Behold me writing this on a rustic table, the rusty nails of which dig into my hand as I drive the pen. I weep for what our brothers might have become, but I do not delude myself about what they are— desperate hardened criminals little resembling the sweet seraphim of the nursery or the sturdy schoolyard striplings their names might evoke in your memory. I am already more than satiated with their society & leur manière d'être, but I am determined not to speak to you except with the voice of stoicism. Patience, I trust, will see any game out. In the meantime, please do not breathe a word of these baleful scribblements to the tender parental ears. The shock & shame of it all, I am certain, wd. simply undo them. I will write anon as events unfold. Until then, my blessings on yourself and all from your fraternal,*
>
> *H.J., jr.*

As events unfolded, however, Henry's plight was soon to become even further complicated by the arrival of an unexpected visitor at the Kearney farm.

On a sunny morning a few days after Henry posted his long letter to William, the reunited James boys were sharing a leisurely late breakfast in the kitchen when a buckboard came bouncing up the dusty drive in front of the house. At the crunch of carriage wheels outside, Jesse sprang up from the table and scrambled into position at one of the gun ports, sliding a seven-shot Spencer carbine into the slot and tensely training the weapon on the approaching intruder. Though he immediately recognized the woman in his rifle's sights as the young beauty from the robbery at Rocky Cut, the outlaw was deeply suspicious of her presence at the farm and especially concerned that she might not be unaccompanied. It would hardly have been above those devious detectives, Jesse must have reckoned, to employ a woman as a decoy to draw him into a fatal ambush. He ordered Henry out the door to greet the interloper.

The writer stumbled into the yard, frantically pulling up his suspenders. He was wearing only an undershirt, his rumpled suit trousers, and a pair of Frank's old cavalry boots—hardly a sartorial ensemble in which he would have liked to imagine himself greeting a refined young lady. "Miss Phoenix?" he inquired, squinting into the bright morning sunlight. Elena had gotten herself up for the occasion in her idea of western women's garb: a cornflower-blue calico print dress with long leg-o'-mutton sleeves, a matching sunbonnet, white pantalettes, and high lace-up prairie boots, none of which served in the slightest to camouflage her congenital air of citified elegance. (She probably looked no more like a real country gal, she later confided to her diary, than Marie Antoinette had ever resembled an authentic shepherdess.)

"Mr. Jones?" she responded with a wry smile, enjoying their private little name joke, to which Henry was still privy to only half. "I believe this belongs to you," she went on, reaching into her reticule and withdrawing the author's notebook.

Jesse kept his carbine trained on Elena's heart as she leaned down from the buckboard and handed Henry his portfolio. Fortunately for her, the man with his finger on the trigger was totally ignorant of his target's recent tête-à-tête with William Pinkerton. If the outlaw had had even the slightest inkling of the hours she'd spent in a hotel room with his archenemy, he might well have dropped her on the spot.

Henry began flipping through the pages of his notebook, becoming momentarily absorbed in the painfully plodding sentences of its hackneyed travel writing. He must have felt that he was reading ancient history, so far removed was his erstwhile journalistic predicament from his present, more life-threatening one.

"I cannot believe you would have come all the way here just for this," he told Elena.

The author's skepticism was well founded. Elena had led William Pinkerton to believe that she would be continuing east on her lecture tour, but if she ever did plan such an itinerary, she had abruptly abandoned it following her dramatic encounter with the James Gang at Rocky Cut. (In truth, even before that fateful meeting, her enchantment with feminist politics had been waning. Victoria Woodhull's premature run for the presidency in 1872 had come to naught, and the movement had been subsequently enervated by the economic depression that had gripped the country the following year, as well as by a profusion of splinter factions and the attendant unproductive bickering.) Though she may not yet have been willing to acknowledge it with her full consciousness, Elena had been wearying of her peripatetic life of "talks and teacups" amid the high-minded company of "brittle old biddies." After years of lecturing about her God-given sexual rights, she was ready to stop talking about them and start exercising them.

She reminded Henry that she had just made a long, dusty journey on his behalf, adding that she would be much obliged if he would kindly ask her in to freshen up. The writer looked questioningly back toward the house, where Jesse, apparently satisfied that his brother was not about to be blown to bits by a Pinkerton firebomb or felled by a fusillade from behind the rail fences, nodded the tip of his rifle barrel affirmatively up and down in the gun port. Henry graciously invited Elena into the house to refresh herself.

She would stay for nearly six weeks.

Chapter Four

———•◆•———

The plundering of the Number 4 Missouri Pacific Express at Rocky ·Cut had economic repercussions well beyond Missouri and the fifteen thousand dollars with which the bandits had absconded. While his operatives out of St. Louis and Kansas City were following the rapidly cooling trail of the perpetrators, William Pinkerton himself was making a command appearance back east to consult with a representative of a consortium of railroad and express company investors who were deeply concerned about the rash of robberies blighting the western lines. The representative in question turned out to be none other than Mr. Asa Hite of Hartford, Connecticut, who, as we have noted, had thrown himself headlong into railroad affairs in the wake of his wife's demise and his daughter's subsequent precipitous departure.

When Pinkerton arrived at Hite's Lord's Hill estate for this tusk-to-tusk tussle of bull walruses, his host invited him into the mansion's exquisitely appointed library and wasted no time in small talk before giving the detective a substantial piece of his mind: Here, he complained, was a gang of two-bit border bandits wreaking havoc with the nation's rail lines. And the losses they were inflicting were hardly confined to the booty they were hauling out of the passenger and express cars. In fact, whatever paltry trinkets and greenbacks were ending up in their grain sacks and saddlebags were by far the least of the problem. More important, their marauding was discouraging business, and not simply the business of moving passengers and freight across the continent. Even further to the point—and here Hite jabbed Pinkerton in the chest with a sausagelike finger—it was the *investment* business that was suffering. The growth of the railroad industry, and hence of the entire national economy, was being held hostage by a small band of pissant desperadoes. It all stank, in Asa Hite's carefully chosen word, of *pusillanimity,* and what especially galled him and his colleagues was that they were pissing away a small fortune on the Pinkertons, who apparently knew who these men were and even where they lived. Why couldn't the damned agency simply eliminate them?

This plaintive query uncannily echoed the one Elena had posed to the detective from behind the bathroom door of her St. Louis hotel room scarcely a fortnight before. It was at this moment that Pinkerton's experienced eye was drawn to a painting on the wall of Asa Hite's library—George Stanley's study of Elena as Marie Antoinette *en guise de bergère.* The likeness was striking, especially to William Pinkerton, who took immense professional pride in his sensitivity to the nuances of human physiognomy and had so very recently been face-to-face with the model. (The detective had no idea that the young woman he had interrogated as "Elena Phoenix" following the Rocky Cut robbery might have been related to his powerful client; nor, for that matter, had Asa Hite the slightest inkling of his daughter's present whereabouts.) But when Pinkerton, in what he hoped might seem a perfectly innocuous bit of what Henry James once dubbed "the mere twaddle of graciousness," inquired about the handsome portrait, he could hardly help noting his interlocutor's patent discomfort. "I per-

ceived," the detective later reported to his father in Chicago, "that Mr.
Hite appeared decidedly ill at ease with the topic. He was clearly dis-
inclined to discuss the painting or its subject, remarking only that it
was an amateur work which he kept 'as a reminder that beauty and
goodness are not necessarily one and the same.'"

Though Hite's remark was ambiguous—it might as easily have referred to the former queen of France ("Let them eat cake") as to the
portrait sitter—Pinkerton deduced from the older man's tone and
bearing that it would be imprudent to pursue the topic "a jot further."
He quickly returned the conversation to the matter at hand, assuring
Asa Hite that fresh, highly promising information had recently
emerged about the James Gang, and that it would be only a matter of
time before the brigands were brought to justice. Hobbs Kerry, the
novice bandit who had helped pile the rail-tie barricade fore and aft of
the train at Rocky Cut, had been captured by the St. Louis police and
jailed in Booneville to await trial. Under intense interrogation, the inexperienced outlaw had squealed like a sow in heat, spewing forth a
full confession of his own part in the crime and providing detailed descriptions of the entire gang, including Henry James, whose role in
the affair the young coal-miner-turned-train-robber was understand-
ably fuzzy about. Kerry had even guided lawmen to the bank of the
stream where the band had divided up the loot and where, according
to Jesse's biographer Ted P. Yeatman, "payroll checks, bank drafts, and
bond coupons, damaged by rain, were found scattered about the site,
along with some stray pieces of gold jewelry," substantiating the veracity of the fledgling felon's account.

After taking his leave of Hite's Lord's Hill mansion with a pledge
to single-mindedly direct the agency's efforts against the James Gang,
Billy Pinkerton repaired to a tavern in downtown Hartford not far
from the railway station. Long investigative experience and a powerful thirst had taught him that such seedy venues could often prove the
source of much useful intelligence, and there, for the price of a couple
of shots of whiskey, he was able to confirm that Mr. Hite did indeed

have a daughter, and one with a racy past at that. The informant, however, a local lush named Dick Perry who was not notably reliable even when sober, was purveying an account of the scandal that had become, with the passage of time and the distortion of drink, considerably more lurid than even the sordid circumstances of Elena's disgrace warranted. In the version of events that Pinkerton elicited from Perry, young George Stanley had been acting as a virtual pimp for Elena, selling his girlfriend's services to his buddies for "horse and cigar money," while her own cut of their ill-gotten gains had gone to bankrolling her subsequent speaking tour.

Thus, in the course of a single day, William Pinkerton came to develop an impression of Elena Hite as both a distinctly higher and lower sort of woman than he had surmised. And while he had yet to reach the point where he would see her as the key to this most frustrating case, he determined that his next step should be to get a line on the present whereabouts of this very interesting young lady.

———✦———

Elena, upon entering Castle James, had discovered that the *ménage* of the place was a bit more complex than she had foreseen; in fact, it was even more so than Henry James had let on in his letter to William. In addition to Frank, Jesse, and Henry, the resident population of the farmhouse included a wizened former slave called Aunt Charlotte, an ancient addle-brained doctor named Reuben Samuel, and, most notably, Samuel's wife, Zerelda, a tough old termagant whom the James Boys, out of a combination of respect, affection, and fear, called "Mamaw."

Mrs. Samuel, who had been none too thrilled about the recent encroachment of Henry James upon her little domain, looked even less kindly upon the unexpected arrival of Elena Hite. Having lost an arm and a son to the Pinkertons in the firebombing of her kitchen two years before, Mamaw detested the railroad dicks with a virulence that was at least the equal of Jesse's. She glared at the suspect intruder with gimlet-eyed hostility—until Frank, sensing the lay of the emotional land, adroitly stepped in and introduced Elena as Henry's wife. This came as something of a surprise to Henry, who had barely digested the image of himself as a fugitive from justice and who now found himself obliged to swallow the identity of a married man—a role he doubtless found even less plausible and considerably more alarming. (He once wrote to William that he believed "almost as much in marriage for most other people as I believe in it little for myself—which is saying a good deal.") Elena, however, was highly amused with the charade Frank had thrust upon her. She threw herself into her part with impressive gusto, immediately calling Henry "darling" and "sweetlingtons" and subjecting the author to a wifely display of affection that served only to compound his consternation and to inflame Jesse's already powerful attraction to her.

Of the force of that attraction there can be no doubt, nor of the fact that it was mutual. Both Jesse and Elena were physically alluring beings, though there was clearly more than mere animal magnetism drawing them together: Both had in their personal histories what a geologically minded psychologist might have recognized as an uncomformity—an abrupt perturbation in the even strata of their development that had set them painfully apart from their peers in late adolescence and subjected them to the scorn of polite society. Jesse had often seen himself portrayed in the press as Satan incarnate, and Elena, having been savaged by the gossiping Hounds of Hartford, had more than a little sympathy for him.

Yet for all their ardor, these two horny devils found themselves at first strangely shy with each other, perhaps lending credence to William's notion of an antisexual instinct or, more likely, merely reflecting mid-Victorian mores and the chilling presence of Mrs. Samuel. (If Mamaw bought in to the taradiddle of Elena being Mrs. Henry James, she doubtless would have seen that improbable union as all the more reason to keep the pretty young thing away from Jesse, who, according to his biographer Marley Brant, "loved as aggressively as he hated.")

At the moment, however, the handsome outlaw had something far more pressing on his mind than a romantic dalliance: Hobbs Kerry's copious confession to the St. Louis police had been receiving prominent front-page play in the newspapers, and Jesse was seething over the turncoat's treachery—as well as perhaps being envious of all the attention the traitor was garnering with his story. As much a pioneer in the dark arts of self-promotion and public relations as of bank and train robbery, Jesse possessed, as Marley Brant observed, "an irrepressible need to be known." It was he, according to T. J. Stiles, "of all the outlaws, who was most obsessed with his public image, who sought to push himself into the news." On one widely publicized occasion, the 1874 holdup of the Iron Mountain Number 7 Express at Gads Hill, Jesse had even gone so far as to prepare in advance a detailed press release for the *St. Louis Dispatch,* which he handed out to his victims to wire to the paper at the conclusion of the robbery.

The myth that Jesse was building for himself was founded on two principal pillars, both designed to inspire popular support for his depredations. The first was his image as the last rebel of the Civil War, as Stiles labeled the outlaw in the subtitle of his biographical study. Even over a decade after Lee's surrender at Appomattox, the Missouri countryside, especially the "Little Dixie" section of the state in which the Samuel farm was located, was rife with former slaveholders and Confederate sympathizers who remained bitter about the war and nostalgic for the lost cause, and who saw themselves as being ground under the boot heel of what one unreconstructed secessionist called "Yankee avarice, Yankee oppression, Yankee intolerance, Yankee hypocrisy." These disgruntled "seceshes" formed the core constituency of Jesse's admirers.

The second mainstay of the outlaw's myth was his claim to be no common criminal but, rather, a populist marauder in the tradition of the great peasant avengers of European folklore—Dick Turpin, Jack

Shepherd, Claude Duval, and that fabled scourge of Sherwood Forest, Robin Hood. In postbellum Missouri, it was not the sheriff of
Nottingham but the banks and railroads that were widely seen to be
holding an oppressive sway over the common man—even over many
of the common men who were not necessarily die-hard Southern
sympathizers. In an oft-cited letter to *The Kansas City Times* in 1872,
Jesse had grandiosely proclaimed: "Some editors call us thieves. We
are not thieves—we are bold robbers . . . I am proud of the name, for
Alexander the Great was a bold robber, and Julius Caesar and
Napoleon Bonaparte. . . . [W]e rob the rich and give to the poor."

It was in this myth-making mode that the outlaw doubtless saw
Hobbs Kerry's newfound notoriety as yet another irresistible opportunity to thrust himself into the limelight and burnish his legend. While
taking a stroll around the farm on the afternoon of her arrival at Castle James, Elena was surprised to come upon the famous robber sitting
at the "rustic table" under the coffee-bean tree, pen in hand.

"Why, I thought Henry was supposed to be the literary James
brother," she remarked lightly.

Jesse was startled. He had been so deep in thought that his celebrated hair-trigger reflexes had for once failed him. (Had Elena been
armed, she easily would have gotten the drop on him.) Regaining his
composure, he told her that what he was writing was not a novel but
a letter to the *The Kansas City Times*—the follow-up to a note he had
sent the newspaper a few days earlier.

He showed her that earlier note:

*Dear Sir: You have published Hobbs Kerry's confession, which makes
it appear that the Jameses and Youngers were the Rocky Cut robbers.
If there was only one side to be told, it would probably be believed by
a good many people that Kerry has told the truth. But this so-called
confession is a well-built pack of lies from beginning to end. I never
heard of Hobbs Kerry, Charlie Pitts and William Chadwell until
Kerry's arrest. I can prove my innocence by eight good, well-known*

*men of Jackson County, and show conclusively that I was not at the
train robbery. . . . Kerry knows that the Jameses and Youngers can't
be taken alive, and that is why he has put it on us. . . . I will write a
long article for the* Times, *and send it to you in a few days, showing
fully how Hobbs Kerry has lied.*

Clearly, Henry was not the only resident purveyor of fiction at
Castle James. The "eight good, well-known men of Jackson County"
who Jesse claimed would prove his innocence were either figments of
his imagination or, at best, former bushwhackers and Confederate vet-
erans he hoped could be counted on to cover for him under questioning by the authorities. And by showing her this letter, Elena realized,
Jesse must have been testing her own trustworthiness; if she—who,
after all, knew perfectly well that he had been at Rocky Cut—had
protested the blatant falsehoods he was trying to foist off on the
Times's readership, she would not only have forfeited any chance of
getting into his britches, she would have been putting herself, as a potential witness against him, squarely in league with his enemies. She
nodded and smiled.

"That's actually quite nicely written," she told him, hoping that
the tone of her voice wasn't betraying too much of a sense of either astonishment or condescension.

Jesse thanked her, even blushing a bit, and not without cause; he
could hardly in good conscience—to the limited extent that he was
burdened with such an encumbrance—have considered himself the
rightful author of the missive. Nor, for that matter, was Frank, who as
the better-lettered of the bandit brothers might have been the one
Elena would have expected to be writing on behalf of the gang. The
older outlaw, however, had always been staunchly against such "carrying on" in the press and had consistently refused to have anything to
do with Jesse's self-aggrandizing epistolary campaigns. So Jesse had
come to rely upon the editorial guidance (if not the out-and-out ghost-
writing) of Major John Newman Edwards, author of *Noted Guerrillas*

and a cofounder of *The Kansas City Times.* It was the major's heavily redacted version of Jesse's most recent missive that Elena had just pronounced so "nicely written."

At the moment, however, the newspaperman and former Confederate officer was no longer available to provide any further such assistance, being, as he put it, "off in the Indian Territory"—the alcoholic Edwards's jocular private euphemism for a drunken binge. Jesse, who had always been more comfortable wielding a six-gun than a pen, had been left alone to wrestle with a severe case of writer's block as he struggled to produce the "long article" he had promised the *Times.* Under the circumstances, he was only too happy to accept Elena's offer of her rhetorical prowess.

She drew a chair up next to him and, side by side, the pair set to work. Elena, with her Hartford Female Seminary training, might have lent a proper stylistic gloss to the text, but she shrewdly advised Jesse to garnish his writing with a folksy touch, even encouraging him to commit a number of blatant misspellings and grammatical no-nos she was certain would have set Miss Catharine Beecher's well-brushed teeth on edge. Their collaboration began:

> *Dear Sir: I have written a great many letters vindicating myself of the false charges that have been brought against me. . . . Detectives have been trying for years to get positive proof against me for some criminal offence, so that they could get a large reward offered for me, dead or alive; and the same of Frank James and the Younger boys, but they have been foiled at every turn, and they are fully convinced that we will never be taken alive, and now they have fell on the deep-laid scheme to get Hobbs Kerry to tell a pack of base lies. But, thank God, I am yet a free man, and have got the power to defend myself against the charge brought against me by Kerry, a notorious liar and poltroon.*

Elena found herself exhilarated by the freewheeling, rough-hewn cadences of their prose, and curiously excited at the notion of labeling

Hobbs Kerry "a notorious liar and poltroon." She had always wanted to call someone a poltroon; it was just the sort of histrionic and romantically archaic epithet her father liked to trot out when venting his spleen. (And neither she nor Jesse seemed to notice that this harsh characterization contradicted the outlaw's earlier assertion that he had never heard of Hobbs Kerry.) After a detailed laying out of Jesse's alibi, the conspirators moved on to leveling a resounding broadside against the Pinkertons while bolstering the outlaw's Robin Hood bona fides:

> *What sense is there in spending so much money in trying to have us arrested? I am sure we have thousands of friends which can't be bought, although the Detectives think they are playing things very fine. Poor fools they are. . . . If the Express Company wants to do a good act they had better give the money they are letting thieving detectives beat them out of to the poor. Now take my advice, express companies, and give your extra money to the suffering poor, and don't let thieving detectives beat you out of it.*

And once embarked on their rant against the Pinkertons, Jesse and Elena really cut loose:

> *The detectives are a brave lot of boys—charge houses, break down doors and make the gray hairs stand up on the heads of unarmed citizens. Why don't President Grant have the soldiers called in and send the detectives out on special trains after the hostile Indians? Arm Pinkerton's force, with hand-granades, and they will kill all the women and children, and as soon as the women and children are killed it will stop the breed and the warriors will die out in a few years.*

Flushed with excitement over their collusion, the authors of this fanciful proposal, their heads now close together over the page, indulged in the first of what would come to be many lingering kisses.

———•———

Back in Cambridge, Henry's letter continued to smolder in William James's consciousness. He kept the incendiary document under lock and key in the top drawer of the desk in his Harvard office, never breathing a word of its contents to his sister, Alice, nor to their parents —especially to their father, who that spring had suffered a mild to moderate stroke. As a physician keenly attuned to the emotional component of the healing process, William would not have wanted to introduce any disturbing information that might have hindered the old man's recuperation, tempted though he must have been every evening at the Quincy Street dinner table to blurt out his appalling news.

He had heard, of course, of the infamous Jesse James for years; it would have been impossible, even as far east as Boston, to pick up a newspaper without being assailed by headlines blaring word of the outlaw's latest dastardly exploits. But until he received Henry's letter, it had never occurred to William James that the notorious desperado with whom he happened to share a surname might have been distant kin, much less his own long-lost brother. The psychologist, who was in the habit of polling his emotions on all occasions, was forced to acknowledge that the shock and revulsion he was experiencing in response to Henry's startling revelations were spiced with a guilty thrill at finding himself in such intimate association with unalloyed evil. William had always been intrigued by the dark side of human nature, which he saw as an inevitable, even desirable, aspect of moral life. "No one knows the worth of innocence," he once wrote, "till he knows it is gone forever, and that money cannot buy it back. Not the saint, but the sinner that repenteth, is he to whom the full length and breadth, and height and depth, of life's meaning is revealed."

There was doubtless something more than abstract philosophizing or psychologizing behind William's fascination with depravity. Since childhood, he had been subjected to his father's lurid cautionary tales of relatives gone bad. The James family tree, according to Henry Sr.'s

accounts, was laden with rotten fruit—a motley crop of drunks, sui-
cides, wastrels, philanderers, thieves, and lunatics who had produced
what Henry Jr. referred to in his autobiography as "a chronicle of early
deaths, arrested careers, broken promises, orphaned children." It was
a sorry saga that no doubt informed the opening pages of the novelist's late work *The Wings of the Dove,* in which his protagonist, Kate
Croy, muses about her own fallen family—including, most tellingly,
her "two lost brothers": "Why," she wonders, "should a set of people
have been put in motion, on such a scale and with such an air of being
equipped for a profitable journey, only to break down without an accident, to stretch themselves in the wayside dust without a reason?"

In his own quest for an explanation behind what he once called his
"in various ways dilapidated family," William James tended to con-
flate notions of evil with those of psychopathology. "Evil is a disease,"
he wrote in *The Varieties of Religious Experience,* "and worry over disease is itself an additional form of disease, which only adds to the original complaint." To the extent that he saw evil as an illness, William,
being a nineteenth-century physician, was inclined to view it as congenital, a kind of biological family curse. As Henry's biographer Lyndall Gordon wrote, "William was convinced that he and his siblings
carried a taint of 'infirm health,' an inborn 'evil' which it would be a
'crime against humanity' to propagate."

Yet even acknowledging that the Jameses had been dealt a bad
hereditary hand, William remained stuck with the immediate question
of what to do. He was always a firm believer in action as a healthy-
minded, masculine virtue, though in his own life, he often had trouble
initiating it. (As Louis Menand pegged him in a chapter heading in his
book *The Metaphysical Club,* William James was invariably "The Man
of Two Minds.") William must have felt that some vigorous response
to Henry's plight was called for, possibly along the lines of jumping on
a train and charging out west to the rescue. But how effective, prag-
matically speaking, could such a scheme have been? The cerebral Harvard don would have recognized that he was in no way equipped to

stand down an armed band of ruthless killers, even (or perhaps especially) if a couple of them happened to be his own brothers. Then, too, upon deeper reflection, he would no doubt have come to appreciate that his arrival on the scene at Castle James might only have exacerbated the threat to his literary brother (not to mention posing a grave one to himself). Still further complicating William's quandary was the fact that he had already committed himself to spending the month of August at Keene Valley in the Adirondack Mountains of upper New York State, a vacation that, for one so delicately constituted, offered the welcome promise of refreshing his "tone of mind and health of body." ("The fact is," he once wrote, "that every man who possibly can should force himself to a holiday of a full month in the year, whether he feels like taking it or not.") The Adirondacks were James's private Arcadia, a region to which, according to James family biographer R. W. B. Lewis, he was becoming addicted. "I love it like a peasant," he declared late in life, "and if Calais was engraved on the heart of Mary Tudor, surely Keene Valley will be engraved on mine when I die."

With a small coterie of friends he called "The Adirondack Doctors," William had recently chipped in to buy a camp in Keene Valley, a modest shack they nicknamed the shanty. The tiny cabin offered spectacular views of the majestic surrounding summits, along with truly primitive living conditions. (William's sister, Alice, once tartly remarked that "the shanty lacks nothing in the way of discomfort.") The group—comprising William James, Henry Bowditch, James J. Putnam, and his brother, Charles—had all been buddies since their student days at the Harvard Medical School, where James Putnam and Henry Bowditch were now distinguished members of the faculty. It was Bowditch who, in 1872, had recommended William for his first teaching post at Harvard, as a replacement instructor for his course in anatomy and physiology. The Adirondack Doctors thus figured prominently in William's ambition to establish his laboratory of experimental psychology at Harvard—a project for which, he doubtless foresaw, the support of his old med-school chums would prove invaluable.

Even more than the comradeship of his influential Harvard hiking companions and the invigorating mountain air, what was most powerfully drawing William James to Keene Valley in the summer of 1876 was the prospect of visiting with Alice Howe Gibbens, who would be staying with a friend nearby. Throughout the spring of that year, the couple had been seeing more and more of each other. As they shared long sunlit walks along the Boston Commons and stimulating evenings at concerts and public lectures, their relationship began inexorably growing from a lighthearted friendship into a serious romance. One evening when he called on Alice at home, William found her alone and noticed, according to his biographer Linda Simon, "a certain enigmatic expression on her face that puzzled and captivated him." Though relatively inexperienced in the rites and rhythms of courtship, William became aware that he was being swept more deeply into the whirlpool of passion than he had ever let himself be. The stakes could hardly have been higher, since what he was yearning for in a woman was not merely an object of affection but, in Simon's phrase, a "source of deliverance." William's desire to spend more time with Alice was thus exerting a potent countervailing tug to his filial and fraternal obligations. His choices that summer: to spend a glorious month in the mountains—hiking, swimming, reading, relaxing with friends, and being near the woman with whom he was beginning to fall in love— or to go out west and possibly be shot dead.

The man of two minds chose the Adirondacks.

———◆———

As a child of the city of Hartford, Elena Hite had seldom, if ever, spent any time on a real working farm. Her experiences of rural life while growing up had been limited to picturesque outings and pretty picnics along the banks of the Housatonic and Connecticut rivers. Yet, to her surprise, she discovered in the days following her arrival at Castle James that she actually thrived in an agricultural environment. She found the clucking, quacking, lowing, and grunting of the livestock unexpectedly soothing, and the pungent scents of the barnyard provided a bracing contrast to the cloying clouds of rose and lavender that had perfumed her lecturing life. By mid-July the corn was standing tall in the fields, with the pole beans that had been planted to climb up around the stalks ready for picking. Elena enjoyed pitching in on the interminable chores of farm life, displaying a knack for many of them and even managing to arrive at a kind of détente with the crusty Mrs. Samuel. As the two women toiled side by side, jarring berry preserves and "working up" tomatoes for the winter, Zerelda came to develop a grudging respect for the quick-learning, hardworking Yankee girl, while Elena, for her part, was impressed that the fiercely energetic and opinionated older woman had managed—without apparent benefit of formal feminist dogma—to be living, rather than merely preaching, the doctrine of female independence.

Still, for Elena, the principal attraction of the farm remained Jesse James. Whenever Frank and Jesse stayed there, they took the precaution of bedding down for the night out in the nearby woods rather than in the house, in order to be able to make a quick getaway or to get the jump on any intruders in the event of a raid. Henry had been included in this alfresco sleeping arrangement, but Elena was given a proper bunk in the family room on the east side of the farmhouse, from which she began regularly slipping away, after the others had drifted off, to join her lover in the hayloft of the barn or out under the stars.

Comparing these charged erotic encounters with the fumbling advances of what she now thought of as the "fresh-faced boys" of Hartford, Elena remarked upon the finely chiseled contours of the outlaw's face, the steely sinews of his arms, and especially the "practiced, knowing" touch of his surprisingly delicate hands. As they explored each other's bodies, she lightly fingered the scarred indentations of two bullet wounds on Jesse's chest near his right nipple and kissed the blunt nub of his left middle finger, of which the first joint was missing. Her curiosity about his past was nearly boundless; but, like Henry, she was reluctant to pry too deeply into what he had been through, for fear of inadvertently setting off his trip-wire temper.

She did, however, tell him her own story—or at least a strategically bowdlerized version of it. Having apparently picked up some of Jesse's self-mythologizing ways, Elena presented her disgrace back in Hartford as a feminist parable she hoped would resonate with the outlaw's aggrieved sense of being misrepresented and misunderstood. In Elena's imaginative rendition of her ruination, George Stanley had begged for her hand in marriage, a step she described herself as having been unwilling to take, on principle. Thus scorned, her rejected suitor had retaliated, she told Jesse, by inventing and spreading dreadful rumors, rendering her continued residence in Hartford untenable and driving her defiantly onto the lecture circuit to decry such weaselly masculine injustices on behalf of all womankind.

On the night following these revelations, Jesse told Elena he had something he wanted her to try on. For a moment she imagined he might produce the string of amber beads he had snatched from her neck during the Rocky Cut robbery, but instead, he presented her with his old guerrilla shirt, a loose-fitting, colorfully embroidered pullover with capacious front pockets designed to carry an ample supply of percussion caps and lead balls. As she playfully modeled the oversize garment for him, Jesse joked that the pockets had to be so large in order to "hold my heavy balls." Rather than being offended by this raunchy humor, Elena delighted in seeing the outlaw so uncharacteristically relaxed. Her sensual ministrations seemed to bring out his light-hearted side. He even kidded about her supposed marriage to Henry and how terribly wrong it was for Jesse to be lying with his brother's "wife"—a sin for which, he mock-solemnly intoned, he would surely burn in hell.

In a certain sense, Elena might as well have *been* Mrs. Henry James. As the languorous weeks of high summer glided by, she found herself spending almost as much time in the company of her putative husband as of her lover, who was frequently absent from the farm, sometimes for days at a time. During Jesse's mysterious disappearances, Elena discovered that Henry, who once described "summer afternoon" as the two most beautiful words in the English language, could almost always be found sitting out under the shade of the coffee-bean tree, either reading or pushing his pen—perhaps composing another letter to William, perhaps working on the "aching fragment" of what would ultimately become *The Portrait of a Lady.* On these occasions Elena often brought out glasses of lemonade and joined the author for long, leisurely chats that at times turned into private literary seminars. Among the works from Frank's library that they discussed was Gustave Flaubert's scandalous *Madame Bovary,* which Elena responded to as a parable of stifled female sexuality and which Henry declared a masterpiece of the novelistic art wherein "the form was as much the essence of the subject as the idea." (What Elena tactfully refrained from mentioning to her companion was that even through the cloudy lens of her admittedly imperfect seminary French, the characters in Flaubert's book seemed infinitely more alive to her than the "dolls with names" that inhabited *Roderick Hudson.*) Despite having to endure Henry's propensity to pontificate ad nauseam on the proper nature of literary fiction, and his bouts of "insufferable pomposity," Elena felt that he had much to teach her. She appreciated that he seemed to take her opinions seriously, and she especially admired—even envied—the young author's profound commitment to his work. ("I am that queer monster the artist," he once wrote to his old friend Henry Adams, "an obstinate finality, an inexhaustible sensibility.") Would that she had ever been able to dedicate herself with such tenacity to her painting!

But the languid tenor of life at Castle James came to an abrupt end one evening in early August when Jesse returned from one of his extended absences in the company of Cole, Bob, and Jim Younger, along with Clell Miller, Samuel Wells, and William Stiles. The outlaw band was gathering for a powwow in the farmhouse kitchen, a war council from which Henry and Elena were pointedly excluded. Elena sensed that something big was up.

For the James-Younger gang, the Rocky Cut robbery had never been intended as a profit center in its own right; rather, the proceeds had been earmarked from the outset to fund a much grander, far more lucrative operation, the details of which the gang now embarked on a series of late-night meetings to hammer out. Among the issues on the table— along with the where, when, and how of their next strike—was what to do about Henry James. Hobbs Kerry's capture and confession had set the Youngers on edge, and they made no attempt to conceal their strong misgivings about Henry and his "wife." (The Youngers apparently had little trouble accepting Elena as Mrs. Henry James—the couple, after all, had been traveling together on the Number 4 Express—but Cole nonetheless joked that maybe they should all share her among themselves as part of the spoils of the robbery, a coarse jest that Jesse must have found less than amusing, though he held his tongue.)

There were few men Jesse James feared outright, but his respect for Cole Younger was considerable: The oldest Younger brother was built like a bull, and even among the brutal fraternity of former guerrilla warriors, he stood out for his unmitigated ferocity. Jesse once told Henry a famous anecdote from Cole's days riding in the border wars. Cole had been given a new Enfield rifle, and to essay the merits of the weapon, he had tied up fifteen prisoners back-to-belly against a tree and blasted a shot into the line. The frontmost three victims fell immediately, but the remaining dozen survived. "Cut the dead men loose," Younger was reputed to have ordered in disgust, "the new Enfield shoots like a popgun!" It had taken, Jesse said, half a dozen more blasts for Cole to complete his macabre product test. What rendered this gruesome vignette doubly disturbing to Henry was that his out-law brother had recounted it to him not as an indictment of Cole Younger but of the Enfield rifle.

Cole's present concern was that Henry knew too damn much. The last thing the gang needed was another blabbermouthed loose cannon rattling about the countryside to be picked up and grilled by the Pinkertons or the St. Louis police. Nor was it lost on the vainglorious Youngers that this rank newcomer was already commanding a "cranial premium" comparable to their own. As Cole saw their dilemma, they could either expel the writer, with the consequent risk of his being captured and interrogated, or draw him more deeply into the new op-eration, in which case his inexperience might pose a dire threat to both himself and the rest of the gang. Frank argued for including Henry in the new plan, less out of any fraternal solidarity than as a way of keeping an eye on him. Cole, whose true preference doubtless ran along the lines of offing the author then and there, grudgingly concurred.

Henry was thus let in on the gang's subsequent deliberations and given a crash course in some of the finer points of horse-and-revolver work. Instead of reading, writing, and engaging in leisurely book chat with Elena, he began passing his cherished summer afternoons blast-ing away with a Colt .45 at rows of empty booze bottles perched along the farm's split-rail fences. Under Frank and Jesse's anxious (and occa-sionally amused) tutelage, the novelist was duly instructed in such useful gunfighter's moves as "fanning" the hammer of his six-shooter and avoiding getting shot through the heart by jumping to the left when confronted by an enemy armed with a revolver, on the grounds that a pistol wielded by a right-handed assailant tends to swing to the assailant's left. Henry was also encouraged to sharpen his equestrian skills. Though he once declared himself "a stranger to the mysteries of horse flesh," like any well-bred nineteenth-century gentleman, Henry James liked to think of himself as at least a competent rider. ("He had never been much of horseman, but he knew how to stay in the saddle," wrote Leon Edel.) The difference between Henry's notion of horsemanship and that of his western brothers was the difference, in the author's literary terms, between being able to crank out a readable letter to a newspaper and producing an elegant full-length novel. Frank and Jesse could ride hell-for-leather for hours or days on end over rugged terrain with little apparent fatigue or discomfort. They apprised Henry of such secrets of the craft as riding switchback across hill faces or dismounting to go straight up or down them; trying to keep to a trot so as not to wear out the animal; using a sheepskin saddle pad to cushion the rough ride and absorb the horse's sweat; choosing a lightweight saddle like the McClellan cavalry model that could be quickly adjusted to fit any horse one might have to appropriate along the way; and always carrying a spare horseshoe, nails, and a hammer for on-trail emergency blacksmithing. One afternoon the brothers even tried, over Henry's strident protestations about his fragile spine and ample girth, to teach the writer the old Comanche Indian trick of "laying low" in the saddle and shooting from beneath his mount's neck—a maneuver Frank swore had saved his life on numerous occasions but which, on this one, nearly cost Henry his.

Falling off a horse turned out to be the least of the traumas that Henry James was to suffer during this period. One bright moonlit night a couple of weeks into his intensive initiation in the outlaw arts, the author awoke to the call of nature and abandoned his bedroll to relieve himself in the bushes behind the barn. He may have been still half asleep from his arduous exertions of the day, but what he observed no doubt brought him brusquely to full Jamesian consciousness.

Much has been written about the voyeuristic strain in the works of Henry James, who, as Leon Edel remarked, "invariably preferred to see rather than be seen." It was a motif for which W. Somerset Maugham chided the author long after his death: "Poor Henry, he's spending eternity wandering round and round a stately park and the fence is just too high for him to peep over and they're having tea just too far away for him to hear what the countess is saying." On this occasion

Henry's voyeurism was not so much literary as literal, and we can only imagine the degree of shock and/or excitement with which he greeted the scene of his supposed wife and his outlaw brother going at it buck naked under the stars. Indeed, it is entirely possible that until that moment Henry James had never in his life witnessed—and most certainly had never participated in—any carnal act more intimate than a familial hug or a chaste social peck. Coming upon the couple in flagrante delicto no doubt made an indelible impression on the sensitive author, and it may well have supplied the *donnée* for the famous scene in *Daisy Miller* in which Winterbourne spies on Daisy's scandalous assignation with her cicerone in the ruins of the Coliseum—the moment when the narrator prudishly judges her to be "a young lady whom a gentleman need no longer be at pains to respect."

Nor, as it happened, was Henry James the only clandestine observer of that stimulating spectacle.

Throughout July 1876, William Pinkerton had been receiving field reports of an attractive young blonde staying at the Samuel farm, rumored in some accounts to be the wife of the notorious belletristic bandit Hank James. The detective, naturally, was quick to divine the true identity of the lady in question and to appreciate the use to which he might put this juicy morsel of intelligence. Being as much a player in the public relations game as Jesse James, Pinkerton had become concerned that in nabbing and debriefing Hobbs Kerry, Chief McDonough and the St. Louis police department had gotten a leg up on the agency in cracking the James Gang case. (While in principle the Pinkertons were supposed to cooperate with official law enforcement, the private detective—especially in light of his recent contretemps with Asa Hite—desperately desired to put himself at the forefront of any triumph over the gang, both for the greater glory of the agency and to convince the railroad and express companies footing the bill that he and his private eyes were earning their keep.) He thus determined that the moment had arrived to head out to Missouri and sniff around a bit for himself.

To reconnoiter the territory, he had assumed the persona of an itinerant Jewish peddler. In the decade following the Civil War, such alien characters had become relatively common denizens of the region, schlepping their bundles of yard goods, needles, threads, notions, tinware, and other household sundries from farm to farm. They were warmly welcomed by the isolated housewives of that era before the advent of national mail-order catalogs. Although the detective's rendition of a Yiddish accent would never have passed muster in the teeming streets of New York or Chicago, it was sufficiently bizarre to be taken for the real thing in Clay County, Missouri. Even heavily disguised, Billy Pinkerton must have been aware that he was assuming an enormous risk in daring to snoop around anywhere in the vicinity of Castle James. The threat that Jesse had issued after the firebombing of the place two years before—warning Pinkerton that if he ever showed his "Scottish face" in these parts, he would meet "the fate of Lull and Whicher"—had technically been directed against Pinkerton's father, Allan; but the son—whom Jesse had always suspected of having personally led that disastrous raid—obviously would have been as splendid a trophy for the gang as the agency's founder.

Arriving at the farm on that sultry summer night, Pinkerton was hoping to pick up a general sense of the lay of the land; he didn't expect to hit pay dirt on his very first foray into enemy territory. But while scouting the outbuildings of the homestead, he spotted Henry James standing in the bushes behind the barn with, as the detective later reported back to Chicago, "his generative member in hand, fully exposed." Following the author's line of sight, the detective took in the torrid tableau of Jesse and Elena rolling in the hay, and his excitement at this scene was at least as much professional as erotic: In one fell swoop, he had not only pinned down the whereabouts of the elusive Jesse James, he had gotten the goods on Henry James and Elena Hite as well.

The lovers, of course, were well out of earshot of both Henry James and William Pinkerton. Had these secret spectators been able to hear as well as see, they would have become even more thoroughly enlightened, for it was on this night, as Jesse and Elena lay in each other's arms gazing up at the celestial fireworks of the annual Perseid meteor shower, that the outlaw spun a full account of his "sordid transmogrification" from a New England child of privilege into a desperate western bandit—much of it the truth, the rest pure self-serving horseshit.

Chapter Five

————◆————

The James boys' odyssey into outlawry, as Jesse recounted to Elena that soft starlit night, effectively began in 1860 at the Sanborn Academy in Concord, Massachusetts, where the younger pair of brothers had been sent in realization of yet another of Henry Sr.'s quixotic educational enthusiasms. The academy, headed by Franklin B. Sanborn, was one of the first coeducational boarding schools in the nation's history. "I can't but felicitate our native land," Henry Sr. gushed to a friend, "that such magnificent experiments go on among us." Nor did it hurt that the school had been commended to Rob and Wilky's father by no less eminent an advocate than Ralph Waldo Emerson, or that its student body boasted the offspring of some of the cream of Yankee intelligentsia—among them Emerson's own son Edward, his daughters, Ellen and Edith, and Nathaniel Hawthorne's son, Julian. Louisa May Alcott's sister Nan was the drawing instructor, and Henry

David Thoreau was often on hand to take the boys and girls on guided nature walks.

Besides being radical in its mixing of the sexes, the Sanborn Academy in those years was also a hotbed of vehement anti-slavery sentiment. Franklin Sanborn had been one of the "Secret Six" coconspirators of the militant abolitionist John Brown, who, the year before the younger James brothers enrolled, had been hanged for attempting to instigate a slave uprising in Virginia by leading a raid on the federal armory at Harpers Ferry. (One of Brown's daughters was a classmate of the James boys.) "In the eyes of Wilky and Bob," wrote their biographer Anna Robeson Burr, "there could have been no greater hero than John Brown, and no doubt they listened with hunger to the accounts of his visit to Concord before their own arrival."

Nonetheless, Rob had never wanted to attend Sanborn, nor indeed any academic institution. Julian Hawthorne described the future outlaw in his high school years as "robust and hilarious, tough, tireless as hickory, great in the playground, not much of a scholar." In fact, at the age of fourteen, Rob had confided to William that what he really wanted to do in life was run a dry-goods store, a vocation for which he may well have been better suited than for book learning, and which, had he pursued it, might well have spared the country considerable mayhem in the decades to come. After only a single year at the academy, Rob refused to return the following fall, insisting on staying at home with the family in Newport, Rhode Island, where William and Henry were studying art with William Morris Hunt. In Newport, "Rough Rob," as William teasingly dubbed his youngest brother, passed much of his time sailing his boat the *Alice,* at one point even threatening to run away to sea. Wilky managed to put in another year at Sanborn before dropping out to enlist in the Union army.

But as Rob and Wilky were itching to get out of school, William and Henry were angling to get in. Neither of the older James brothers saw themselves as fit for military service, on the grounds of ill health. While helping to put out a fire at a Newport stable in 1861, Henry had sustained what the family's biographer R.W.B. Lewis called "the most famous injury in American literary history." This was the trauma to which the novelist cryptically alluded in his autobiography as "a horrid even if an obscure hurt," a coy characterization of his infirmity that subsequently gave rise to much catty conjecture, including Ernest Hemingway's wild speculation that Henry had been emasculated. The truth, however, was almost certainly neither quite so lurid nor so grave. Leon Edel argued convincingly that what the writer had sustained was most likely a garden-variety lower-back injury—"a slipped disc, a sacroiliac or muscular strain"—painful, no doubt, but hardly the catastrophe of castration. Indeed, when Henry Sr. trundled his suffering son up to Boston for a consultation with "a great surgeon, the head of his profession there," the prominent doctor treated his young patient "but to a comparative pooh-pooh," leaving Henry ever thereafter "to reckon with the strange fact of there being nothing to speak of the matter with me."

Hypochondria among the Jameses, as we have seen, was more than a familial affliction; it was something of a competitive sport. Not to be outdone by his brother's inscrutable impairment, William managed to come up with a stunning litany of no less recondite complaints of his own, including eyestrain, headaches, backaches, and "nervousness of temper"—none of which, as Lewis pointedly observed, impeded the young sufferer from "reading assiduously in literature, science, and philosophy, and expressing himself as articulately as ever on many a subject." Nor did William's manifold symptoms deter him from signing on with Louis Agassiz for that arduous and stimulating expedition up the Amazon in the spring of 1865, just as the war was safely winding down.

Yet given the obscurity of their infirmities, William and Henry must have felt a need to avoid the appearance of an unseemly idleness at a time when so many of their contemporaries were risking life and limb in the Union's defense. To this end, the older James brothers apparently saw attending Harvard as a rigorous-seeming alternative to taking up arms. William enrolled in the university's Lawrence Scientific School in the fall of 1861, and Henry entered its law school the following year. In opting for the groves of academe over the fields of battle, the senior pair had the blessing of their father, who, despite his vigorously professed belief in abolition and the Union cause, was initially dead set against any of his sons' joining the army. "No existing government," he wrote, "nor indeed any now possible government, is worth an honest human life and a clean one like theirs. . . . I tell them no young American should put himself in the way of death until he has realized something of the good of life: until he has found some charming conjugal Elizabeth or other to whisper his devotion to, and assume the task if need be, of keeping his memory green."

However, as his younger boys approached enlistment age, Henry Sr. altered his tune. On the day when Rob went off to sign up for duty, with his two older sons safely ensconced on the Cambridge campus, he wrote to a friend: "I cannot but adore the great Providence which is thus lifting our young men out of indolence and vanity, into some free sympathy with His own deathless life."

The youthful bandits-to-be were hardly passive victims of their father's vacillations. Their own adolescent antsyness, idealism, and appetite for adventure—and not of the intellectual sort—obviously played no small role in fueling their fervor to enlist, as, no doubt, did the changing political climate of the nation at large. With the signing of the Emancipation Proclamation in September 1862, President Lincoln hoped to inspire a resurgence of the patriotic passion that had galvanized the Union in the opening months of the war (and perhaps to put off having to resort to a draft); while in the more intimate sphere of the James household, the younger pair of brothers, having lived their entire lives in the long shadows of their older, more gifted siblings, doubtless hoped that by volunteering for military service, they might get to bask in the warm glow of the family limelight for a change.

The first to go was the "adipose, affectionate" Wilky, who joined the Massachusetts 44th Infantry in September 1862, at the age of seventeen. After a few weeks of drilling on the Cambridge Commons, his regiment shipped out for New Bern, North Carolina, where the raw recruit discovered that he possessed a veritable lust for combat. Within a couple of months, he was promoted twice, first to corporal, then swiftly to sergeant. In a letter home written after a skirmish near Kinston, North Carolina, on December 14, Wilky described a hail of bullets whistling over his head "as if all the devils of the Inferno" were milling about him. He concluded, "I don't think Sergeant G.W. has ever known greater glee in all his born days." He also discovered that he had a previously unsuspected appetite for literature and began to acquire the signature erudition of the future killer/scholar Frank James. "The young man who had hitherto shown such an aversion to reading books," wrote Lewis, "could now be observed, on rest periods between marches, reading Victor Hugo's *Les Misérables*. . . ."

Wilky's enlistment was supposed to have entailed only a nine-month commitment to the colors, but in the winter of 1863, Governor John Andrew of Massachusetts launched one of the boldest experiments in American military history: the establishment of an all-black regiment of Union soldiers, the storied Massachusetts 54th Infantry. Frederick Douglass, a former slave and the nation's leading black abolitionist, two of whose sons joined the new regiment, proudly proclaimed that "once the black man gets upon his person the brass letters 'U.S.,' a musket on his shoulder and bullets in his pocket, there is no power on earth which can deny that he has earned the right to citizenship in the United States." The men of the 54th were keenly aware that all eyes would be upon them—and that not a few Americans (in the North as well as the South) were hoping they would fail. There was even a call in Congress to equip the black infantry with pikes instead of firearms. Lieutenant G. W. James—he had been promoted yet again—with his certified combat experience, manifest abolitionist bona fides, and sterling social pedigree, was tapped to serve as an officer in the newly formed unit. In accepting his commission,

Wilky was putting himself in substantial jeopardy, greater even than the significant peril he had faced by joining the army in the first place. Shortly after the establishment of the 54th, the Confederate Congress had issued this daunting proclamation:

> Every white person being a commissioned officer, or acting as such, who, during the present war, shall command negroes or mulattoes in arms against the Confederate States, or who shall arm, train, organize, or prepare negroes or mulattoes for military service against the Confederate States, or who shall voluntarily aid negroes or mulattoes in any military enterprise, attack, or conflict in such service, shall be deemed as inciting servile insurrection, and shall, if captured, be put to death.

In his autobiography, written over half a century after the event, Henry James recounted a memorable visit he made that spring to Camp Meigs, the regiment's training grounds at Readville, outside of Boston. There the author, who had always felt himself constitutionally excluded from such blatantly butch realms of endeavor—he confessed that he couldn't "do things"—was struck by the romance of his little brother's "quick spring out of mere juvenility and into such brightly-bristling ranks," marveling that "this soft companion of my childhood" should have mastered "such mysteries, such engines, such arts." (All of which mysteries, engines, and arts would serve the future Frank James splendidly in his felonious postbellum endeavors.) At Readville, Henry found his brother surrounded by a cadre of "laughing, welcoming, sunburnt young men who seemed mainly to bristle . . . with Boston genealogies." Foremost among these was the regiment's strikingly handsome and patrician commander, Colonel Robert Gould Shaw, eulogized decades later by William James as "the blue-eyed child of fortune." Shaw chose Wilky to be his adjutant.

The Massachusetts 54th Infantry shipped out of Boston for South Carolina on May 28, 1863. Among the throng lining the route of their valedictory march through the city to the harbor that day were Frederick Douglass, John Greenleaf Whittier, and Henry James, Sr. Though he confessed to being "helplessly absent" due to illness on that historic occasion, Henry James, Jr., nonetheless described the stirring scene of the regiment parading through Boston on its way to war, led on horseback by "its fairest of young commanders," the tawny-bearded Colonel Shaw, his upraised sword gleaming in the sun, to "great reverberations of music, of fluttering banners, launched benedictions and every public sound."

Around the time of this inspiring spectacle, Robertson James, at the illegally tender age of only sixteen, signed on with the all-white Massachusetts 45th Regiment, from which he, too, soon transferred to a black outfit, the newly mustered Massachusetts 55th. According to R. W. B. Lewis, the youngest James brother had never found "any moral or psychological sustenance in the slavery issue," but in deference to Elena's Yankee roots and ardent emancipatory proclivities, he played up his adolescent abolitionist sympathies to the hilt, saying that he'd enlisted with "a heart willing to temper every uttermost anguish of the slave in every form" (a phrase she later learned he had pilfered from Wilky's description of Robert Gould Shaw). His actual motives were doubtless less monolithically exalted. Indeed, in light of his father's remark about military service "lifting young men from indolence and vanity," we might surmise that he was more or less booted out of the house. Thus Rob may well have identified psychologically, if not politically, with the persecuted Negro race, having often felt himself to be in some sense the "nigger" of his family, even to the extent of fantasizing that he might not be a James at all. In later life, he wrote:

> I never remember being told anything extraordinary about my babyhood but I often like to contemplate myself as a baby and wonder if I was really as little appreciated as I fully remember feeling at the time. I never see infants now without discerning

in their usually solemn countenance a conviction that they are on guard and in more or less hostile surroundings. However that may be, in my own case, at a very early age the problems of life began to press upon me in such an unnatural way and I developed such an ability for feeling hurt and wounded that I became quite convinced by the time I was twelve years old that I was a foundling.

Though he may have felt that by enlisting he was extricating himself from an increasingly untenable family situation, *"l'ingénieux petit"* Robertson James, as one of his French governesses once called him, could have had only scant suspicion of what he was getting himself into. In woeful contrast to the rousing public displays of patriotism and the spit-and-polish discipline of the training camps, the Civil War was in many respects a proverbial Chinese fire drill. General Helmuth Karl von Moltke, the great Prussian military historian who observed the fratricidal conflict at first hand, declared it to be little more than "two armed mobs chasing each other around the country, from which nothing could be learned."

A tragic instance of this endemic ineptitude—and one that nearly cost Wilky his young life—was the disastrous storming of Fort Wagner in July 1863, a battle described by the younger James brothers' biographer Jane Maher as "one of the worst debacles of the Civil War . . . poorly planned and even more poorly executed." The edifice in question was the principal Confederate installation defending Charleston Harbor and "the strongest single earthwork known in the history of warfare," according to the 54th Regiment's historian, Luis F. Emilio. On the day before the doomed assault, the unit had acquitted itself admirably in an engagement with a squadron of Confederate cavalry that had pinned down the Connecticut 10th Infantry on nearby James Island, an action for which the 54th was widely credited with saving the lives of many of their fellow New Englanders. It was the black regiment's first taste of heavy combat, and Wilky never forgot the sight and stench of mutilated bodies on the beach. On closer inspection, the mutilation turned out to be the work not of enemy soldiers but of ravenous fiddler crabs; yet these horrors were only a grim prelude to what was to follow: After two days without rations or sleep, the men of the 54th were chosen to spearhead the assault on the massive battery itself, a battle in which it became rapidly apparent that the black soldiers were woefully outnumbered and outgunned. Almost half of the regiment's enlisted men and nearly two thirds of its officers were shot down or bayoneted in front of the fortress or within its walls. Colonel Shaw, leading the charge, was felled by a bullet through the heart and unceremoniously interred in a ditch with about fifty of his Negro troops. Wilky took a rifle slug in the side and a cannister ball an inch and a half in diameter in the ankle—grave wounds from which he doubtless would have died had he not been miraculously discovered in a field hospital by the father of his fallen comrade Cabot Russell and delivered, unconscious, back home to Newport for a "long and tedious" recuperation.

———◆———

Even as the 54th was being decimated at Fort Wagner, Rob was shipping out for South Carolina with the 55th. His destination was Charleston Harbor, where his regiment's major mission was to pile up timber and sandbags on the marsh between James and Morris islands to form the foundation for an immense Parrott cannon nicknamed "The Swamp Angel." Constructing the emplacement for this formidable piece of artillery—together with its carriage, it weighed over 24,000 pounds—was grueling, backbreaking labor, made all the more onerous by a scorching Southern sun, swarms of malaria-bearing mosquitos, and sporadic enemy shelling that often sent the soldiers scuttling for the trenches "like so many land-crabs in distress." As Rob later recalled the hellish scene, "the flies of a whole continent had congregated there to harass the emaciated creatures who were dying by scores in the field hospitals." The stinking water in the shallow wells swarmed with rats, and "with the advent of vermin," the men felt they were "reverting to the animal state." Rob contracted a severe case of dysentery, and in addition to his unrelenting physical miseries, he was suffering deep distress over the plight of the wounded Wilky, the brother with whom he would be "paired in all the major activities of their lives."

It wasn't long before the young officer—still just barely seventeen—had become desperately demoralized and homesick. In keeping with the James family's propensity for misplacing or destroying unbecoming documents, all but one of Rob's letters from the front have been lost, but apparently, the impetuous adolescent had begun flirting—much to his father's alarm—with the idea of quitting the army, just as he had cut and run from the Sanborn Academy.

"It is a temptation which your manhood is called upon to resist," Henry Sr. wrote back to his youngest son. "I know perfectly well that if you should yield to the weakness it prompts, you would regret all your days having done so, provided of course your aspiration towards a manly character be genuine." The letter concluded: "Cheer up then my dear boy, and be a man, where you stand . . . this is all you want to evince you an infinitely better manhood. . . . Resist it like a man, and it will flee from you."

Manliness, evidently, was something of an obsession with Henry Sr., and doubtless a bit of a sore point as well, in light of the fact that the figure he himself cut in society was by no means a conventionally masculine one. He had lost his right leg in a childhood accident and was condemned to hobble about on a prosthetic cork limb for the rest of his life. Furthermore, he had never engaged in any recognizable business or profession, much to the embarrassment of his growing sons. (When, as a child, Henry Jr. once asked his father how to describe his occupation to his schoolmates, Henry Sr. had replied, "Say I'm a philosopher, say I'm a seeker of truth, say I'm a lover of my kind, say I'm an author of books if you like; or best of all, just say I'm a student.") But this superannuated scholar had no academic affiliation and earned virtually no money from his writings, living off an inheritance from his father. Even in his own home, it was his wife, Mary, who wore the financial pants, overseeing the household budget and making most of the practical decisions while mothering her husband "as she mothered her offspring." On top of everything else, "this childlike father," in the characterization of Jean Strouse, had suffered, at the age of thirty-three, a kind of nervous breakdown. One evening, while sitting alone at the table after a comfortable dinner, he had been overcome by a "perfectly insane and abject terror," for which he could account only by the imagined presence of "some damned shape squatting invisible to me within the precincts of the room, and raying out from his fetid personality influences fatal to life. The thing had not lasted ten seconds," he later wrote, "before I felt myself a wreck; that is, reduced from a state of firm, vigorous, joyful manhood to one of almost helpless infancy." Following the formulation of the Swedish mystic Emanuel Swedenborg, Henry Sr. came to refer to this frightening collapse as his "vastation"—one of the steps in the regeneration of the soul, according to the Scandinavian seer—thus managing to force a positive spin onto what otherwise might have been more naturally experienced as a *de*vastation. Nevertheless, the episode had left him psychologically shaky, kept spiritually afloat only by the idiosyncratic interpretation of Swedenborgian mysticism to which he clung thereafter. Yet this damaged and pampered trust-fund dilettante, who seldom in his adult life had been obliged to do anything he didn't care to, pressed on in his correspondence with his errant son. In a letter dated August 31, 1864, he wrote to Rob: "I conjure you to be a man and force yourself like a man to do your whole duty," concluding with yet another entreaty to the demoralized adolescent to remain "manfully at your tracks."

All these blustering paternal exhortations served to foment in the nascent bandit a seething rage at his progenitor, next to which his animosity toward the Confederate foe paled to insignificance. Faced with the harsh realities and mortifying cruelties of war, Lieutenant Robertson James came to feel that he'd been had. What he suspected was nothing less than the awful proposition that his dad wanted him dead. As the future outlaw came to interpret it, the old man's message, stripped of all its patriotic posturing and chivalric rhetoric, was simply that his two younger sons were little more than cannon fodder whose heroic demise in battle might glorify the James family name while sparing his more intellectually promising progeny for the chance to achieve higher—and less fatal—forms of greatness. (Jesse's sense of being used for his father's purposes must have resonated powerfully with Elena Hite, who had long suspected her own father of employing her beauty and talents to advance his standing in Hartford society.)

By the end of the summer of 1864, the elder Henry had become so exercised over the young officer's threatened desertion that he implored Wilky, who had recently rejoined his regiment in South Carolina, to pay a visit to his brother and talk him out of his "passing effeminacy." Wilky dutifully embarked on his father's mission, but the G. W. James who returned to the front would have been nearly unrecognizable to the rash young sergeant who had rhapsodized with glee over bullets whizzing about his head. During his long convalescence at Newport, Wilky had come to question the benevolent God of Henry Sr.'s Swedenborgian visions, and had begun to think of himself as "a mite sacrificed on the altar of our father's wartime pieties." In a letter home written shortly after his return to South Carolina, he described his physical appearance—though he might as well have been reporting on his state of mind—as "no longer the stout party on crutches of six months ago, but a meager, sallow, highly moustached cavalier with more mud on his clothes than on his boots."

This soiled cavalier was appalled to discover that his younger brother was in even worse shape than he had been led to believe. On the heels of a bout of sunstroke, the shining-eyed Rob was hollow-cheeked, gaunt, and addle-brained from fever. He was also drinking heavily. But something in his determination to desert fanned the flames of Wilky's own smoldering resentments, among them the brothers' shared grudge against the administration in Washington for first offering the black enlisted men in their regiments lower federal pay than their white counterparts, then not paying them at all—a congressional scam that planted the seeds of rebellion in the future desperadoes. "Bob was disgusted by the government's behavior," wrote Jane Maher, "and for the rest of his life he remained suspicious of and often hostile to most forms of bureaucracy, particularly the federal government." Wilky, too, could never shake the gnawing suspicion that the gallant 54th had been granted the dubious "honor" of leading the doomed assault on Fort Wagner not in recognition of the regiment's valor or effectiveness but simply because its colored troops had been deemed the most readily expendable of the Union forces on hand.

Given these grievances, Wilky's fraternal loyalty came to trump his dedication to the army: He wanted to get his anguished little brother the hell out of there, and rather than convincing Rob to stay the military course, he found himself persuaded to join his brother in abandoning it. One night, as Jesse recounted it to Elena, the disgruntled pair "just upped and lit out."

In thus taking "French leave," the younger James boys were far from unique. The desertion rate for Union troops during the Civil War was scandalously high, among officers as well as enlisted men. Over the course of the conflict, by conservative estimate, more than two hundred thousand federal soldiers bolted from their units. Many of these absconders headed home, but Rob and Wilky—being subject to what Jean Strouse described as "the Jamesian system of moral absolutes," according to which "anyone who was not all good was all bad"—felt that they were effectively severing ties not only with the army but with the James family itself.

Likewise, in heading off to Harvard, William and Henry had managed to extricate themselves from both the clutches of the military and the bosom of the family. The bosom, however, had not been long in coming after them. During the spring of 1864, Henry Sr. once again decided to absquatulate, this time transporting his household from Newport to Ashburton Place in Boston. The new seat of the James clan was a three-story redbrick house, "as substantial as Boston itself," in the description of Leon Edel. It was within the walls of this imposing edifice that the reunited family waited apprehensively all September for word of Rob and Wilky. But the army, as Jane Maher noted, "had no efficient system of notifying families of their sons', fathers' or husbands' injuries or death." Even allowing for the distressingly spotty wartime mall service, after several weeks of ominous epistolary silence from the front, the Jameses could no longer help but suspect that no news was bad news. Haunted by the Confederate decree of death for officers commanding black troops, and by grim visions of the boys' bodies lying in the sand, the family anxiously scoured the newspapers and hung by the mailbox until hope gave way to resignation and, finally, to despair.

"In the mystical creation," Henry Sr. had written to Robert Gould Shaw's parents after their son's death at Fort Wagner, "we are told that 'the evening and the morning were the first day,' and so on. This is because in Divine order all progress is from dark to bright, from evil to good, from low to high, and never contrariwise. And this is the reason why, though I feel for you the tenderest sympathy, I cannot help but rejoicing for him even now with unspeakable joy, that the night is past, and the everlasting morning fairly begun."

It is unlikely that Henry Sr. greeted the apparent demise of his own offspring with such unspeakable joy. Indeed, as Henry Jr. wrote around this time, the James household had become "about as lively as an inner sepulchre."

Back down in South Carolina, having made their fateful break from the army, the renegade James brothers, still very much alive, found themselves in a quandary. Being absent without leave from their units, they dared not head north back into Yankee country; nor could they push any farther south, a direction that would take them even more deeply into enemy territory. Since they were already on the shores of the Atlantic, there was no farther east they could venture without shipping off for Europe. So, setting their sights on California as their ultimate destination, the apostate pair headed west across South Carolina, Tennessee, and Kentucky, traveling mostly on foot and by night, as furtively as any runaway slaves following the drinking gourd to freedom.

But if, by fleeing the battlefields of the Carolinas, Rob and Wilky had hoped to escape the hardships and insanities of war, they had miscalculated catastrophically. While the nation as a whole was in turmoil, the Missouri they reached in late September 1864 was in utter chaos. Even before the outbreak of the Civil War proper, that beleaguered border state had been the scene of some of the most violent and vitriolic bloodletting in American history—the gory "Bleeding Kansas" wars over whether the neighboring western territory should be admitted to the Union as a free or a slave state. (As early as 1856, the James boys' erstwhile abolitionist idol John Brown had been active in Kansas, where on one occasion he and his sons had abducted five Southern settlers and summarily split open their pro-slavery skulls with a cutlass.) Though nominally in the Union camp, Missouri was in fact deeply divided, torn by a war within a war that pitted neighbor against neighbor, waged by marauding partisan bands sowing terror among the populace. Most feared among these were roving gangs of rebel guerrillas operating independently of the regular Confederate army's chain of command, slaughtering and plundering their way around the state, striking random targets, conducting furtive raids, and engaging in savage skirmishes whenever and wherever the opportunity presented itself.

On the afternoon of Tuesday, September 27, 1864, in keeping with their routine of traveling by night and lying low during the day, the fugitive James brothers bedded down in the woods outside of the railroad village of Centralia in Boone County, unaware that only that morning one of the great atrocities of the war had been perpetrated a couple of miles from their clandestine campsite. The Centralia Massacre, as this bloody episode came to be known, had begun a little before noon when a band of about eighty rebel irregulars swept into town bent on mayhem. The guerrillas, many wearing purloined Union army uniforms, had set about terrorizing the populace, looting the tiny town's two stores and helping themselves to whatever goods they pleased, including a barrel of whiskey that they smashed open and guzzled down in short order. After holding up an arriving stagecoach, the gang, drunk on booze and bloodlust, had boarded a North Missouri express train as it pulled into the Centralia station and begun robbing and brutalizing the passengers. Among these were a score of unarmed Union soldiers, many on furlough from service in Sherman's march on Atlanta. The rebels hauled them out of their coach and stripped them of their uniforms. As the distinguished University of Missouri historian William E. Parrish described the grisly scene that followed, "[t]he guerilla chieftain turned to Little Archie Clement, his second in command, with instructions to 'muster out' the enemy. Clement, a perpetual smile on his twisted face, did so with a vengeance, firing point blank at the stunned troops with a pistol in each hand." Before galloping out of town, the drunken bushwhackers torched the train and sent it roaring down the tracks in flames at full throttle with its whistle wailing.

It didn't take long for federal forces in the vicinity to get wind of the atrocity. A battalion of the Missouri 39th Infantry, U.S. Volunteers under the command of Major A.V.E. Johnston, arrived on the scene later that afternoon and quickly fanned out across the surrounding countryside to hunt down the perpetrators. One of Johnston's search parties descended on the James boys' makeshift bivouac and rousted the sleeping brothers from their bedrolls, roughly rummaging through their belongings and discovering the Union uniforms and government-issued sidearms in their rucksacks. The intruders also came upon a volume of Shakespeare's sonnets, with Wilky's name and rank in the Massachusetts 54th proudly inscribed on the flyleaf.

"Pretty far from your colored boys, ain't you, Lieutenant James?" observed the sergeant in charge.

Wilky tried to convince the officer that the book belonged not to him but to his late cousin Garth W. James, who he claimed had been killed at the battle of Fort Wagner. Identifying himself as Frank James—a name chosen, perhaps unconsciously in the heat of the moment, in tribute to his former headmaster Franklin Sanborn—Wilky explained that he carried the pistols and uniforms as mementos of his fallen kinsman, and that he and his brother were on their way to Columbia to enlist in the Union army.

But the sergeant was having none of it. He remarked snidely to his squad that either these boys were deserters from the U.S. Army or else "damned seceshes" trying to pass themselves off as Union soldiers with stolen government property. In either case, he concluded, they were not fit to live and ought to be executed on the spot.

Sensing that the jig was up, the James boys made a wild run for their lives, scrambling through the brush with the bluecoats in hot pursuit, blazing away with muskets and revolvers.

Ironically, it was only the fact that the federal troops were so hard on their heels that saved the brothers' lives. Their desperate dash brought them out of the woods and smack into a guerrilla encampment on a meadow at nearby Young's Creek, where the resident rebels, more than two hundred strong, made short bloody work of their pursuers. The guerrillas, upon spotting the federals, had followed the wartime logic of "the enemy of my enemy must be my friend," assuming that Rob and Wilky were fellow Confederates—a life-sparing misapprehension of which the James boys had scant desire to disabuse their saviors.

As they were about to discover, the brothers had fallen in league with no less formidable a figure than William "Bloody Bill" Anderson, who, in the unequivocal characterization of Jesse's biographer

T. J. Stiles, "was quite simply, the most vicious man in Missouri." A white supremacist who dressed in black, rode a black horse, and flew the black flag of no quarter in battle, Anderson was a notorious murderer, rapist, torturer, scalper, and beheader. It was he who had led the Centralia Massacre and upon whose orders his cutthroat lieutenant Little Archie Clement had served as the eager executioner of the furloughed Union soldiers.

The James boys, barefoot and clad only in the long johns in which they had been sleeping, were brought before Anderson and Clement at their campfire. Little Archie was diminutive indeed: Only eighteen years old, the gray-eyed killer was barely five feet tall and, according to Stiles, "looked more like a jockey than a guerrilla." Bloody Bill, though slim and wiry, was a more imposing presence, with sharp feral features, icy blue-gray eyes, a wild dark beard, and a majestic mane of rippling black locks flowing over his shoulders. When the fearsome guerrilla chieftain asked Rob his name, the nervous teenager meant to answer "Just call me Rob" but instead stuttered, "Jus . . . jus . . . jus. . . ."

Bloody Bill, perhaps taking the flustered youngster for a halfwit, laughed. "Spit it out, boy! Is it *Jesse?*"

"Yes, sir!" Rob replied, and thus the name that would come to be one of the most feared in all the West was coined in an attack of jitters.

The rebel leader explained to the newcomers that he had contrived a classic guerrilla ambush for Major Johnston's battalion: A small decoy contingent led by Dave Pool was about to lure the federal troops down into the meadow, where they would find themselves facing the full force of Anderson's Confederate irregulars. The James boys were naturally expected to "show their stuff" by participating in this lethal scheme. They were outfitted with horses and revolvers and clad in Union uniforms that had been stripped from soldiers massacred that morning at Centralia.

For the newly self-christened Frank and Jesse, the ensuing battle was a baptism by fire. As Frank described the scene to a journalist many years later, "we dismounted to tighten the belts on our horses, and then at the word of command started on our charge. . . . Our line was nearly a quarter of a mile long, theirs was much closer together. We were some six hundred yards away, our speed increasing and our ranks closing up, when they fired their first and only time. They nearly all fired over our heads. . . . Up the hill we went, yelling like wild Indians. . . . Almost in the twinkling of an eye we were on the yankee line. They seemed terrorized. Hypnotized might be a better word. . . . Some . . . were at 'fix bayonets,' some were biting off their cartridges, preparing to reload. Yelling, shooting our pistols, upon them we went."

The Battle of Centralia, as the ambush and its aftermath went down in history, turned out to be a brutal rout in which only a handful of rebels perished while nearly 150 Union soldiers lost their lives. Those who weren't killed outright in the meadow were picked off one by one as they fled back toward town. Many of these unfortunate federals had their throats slashed, their ears and/or noses lopped off, their scalps taken, and their severed heads impaled on local fence posts. At least one of the dead bluecoats had his penis sliced off and shoved into his mouth. Early in the engagement, Jesse James, eager to exhibit his courage and commitment to Bloody Bill and his new comrades-in-arms, bolted to the head of the charge. Riding straight for Major Johnston, he brought down the commander of the Yankee battalion with a single shot from his revolver, then finished him off with a second bullet to his head. "Having killed Major Johnston," wrote T. J. Stiles, "Jesse's fame—and his fate—were sealed."

——◆——

The question of character and fate, as it happens, was a major theme of William James's thought, and it is worth considering at this juncture one of his best-known pronouncements on the subject:

The issue here is of the utmost pregnancy for it decides a man's entire career. When he debates, Shall I commit this crime? Choose that profession? Accept that office, or marry this fortune?—his choice really lies between one of several equally possible future Characters. What he shall become is fixed by the conduct of this moment. Schopenhauer, who enforces his determinism by the argument that with a given fixed character only one reaction is possible under given circumstances, forgets that, in these critical ethical moments, what consciously seems to be in question is the complexion of the character itself. The problem with the man is less what act he shall now choose to do, than what being he shall now resolve to become.

Ignoring for the moment William's striking substitution of "marry this fortune" for the more conventional "marry this woman," the case of Rob and Wilky becoming Jesse and Frank seems to have been less a matter of choosing any particular course in life—some future Character or being—than of simply resolving to go on living. In assuming their new personas, the younger James brothers clearly did not enjoy the luxury, as did William and Henry, of taking their own sweet time to "find themselves." Their own crises of identity played out under the immediate imperative of quite literally saving their own scalps. (The rebel guerrillas were a notoriously paranoid lot, with little compunction about ruthlessly culling from their ranks any members suspected of the slightest doubt or disloyalty.) Fortunately for the James boys, identity in the wartime border country was famously fluid: The Confederate irregulars, as we have noted, wreaked much of their havoc in Union uniform; conversely, Unionist Missouri militiamen often carried out raids on suspected secessionist homesteads posing as rebel bushwhackers. Nor were such identity swaps limited to masquerading as the enemy: During the course of the war, many border combatants actually switched sides, following shifts in the political and military winds or the mandates of private vendettas. (William Clarke

Quantrill, known to history as one of the fiercest of the guerrilla chief-
tains, had been born in Ohio and, like the Jameses, had begun his sanguinary career as an anti-slavery partisan before flipping allegiance to
lead his notorious Black Flag Brigade.)

Thus, contrary to F. Scott Fitzgerald's celebrated assertion that
there are no second acts in American lives, the nation has always fostered a robust tradition of its citizens reinventing themselves, few perhaps so dramatically as the younger James brothers. Though initiated
by sheer fear and a blind will to survive, their attachment to Anderson's band must also be seen as the expression of an adolescent desire to belong. For all their military experience, Frank and Jesse were
nonetheless still impressionable teenagers at heart, hardly immune to
the allure of being part of a group of hard-riding, hard-fighting com-
mandos. Jesse especially, being younger and doubtless more of a born
psychopath than Frank, would have been particularly susceptible to
the blood-knit camaraderie of the guerrilla tribe. In adopting the
homicidal mores and trying to win the esteem of the likes of Clell
Miller and the Younger brothers, the former "foundling" and future
outlaw was forging familial bonds that would endure well beyond the
war years. "He now belonged," wrote T. J. Stiles, "to a group that believed a man must murder for respect."

Following Centralia, the James brothers continued to ride with
Anderson's band, crisscrossing the state and engaging in a series of
raids and skirmishes, during which time Jesse "paid his dues" to the
cutthroat cult in both the violence he wreaked and the wounds he received. (Though here again, the outlaw tried to gussy up the truth by
telling Elena that he had taken a bullet in his lung during a pitched
battle with the federal foe, whereas in fact he'd been shot during the
considerably less heroic escapade of trying to steal a saddle off the
fence of a German farmer. Likewise his missing fingertip, which he attributed for Elena's benefit to the blade of a Yankee bayonet, was more
likely the result of his own clumsiness in loading pistols.)

Within a month of Centralia, Bloody Bill was gunned down in

that Henry Sr. went too far: "He charges society with all the crime committed," complained the sage of Walden Pond, "and praises the criminal for committing it."

How could Frank and Jesse, in their formative years, have failed to absorb their father's subversive message? And there was more: "In the eyes of this novel parent an interesting failure seemed far more worthy of appreciation than any 'too obvious success,'" remarked Jean Strouse, who also observed that Henry Sr. "urged on all five of his children a strenuous individualism that stressed *being extraordinary* no matter what one chose actually to do."

In taking up the outlaw life, Jesse found not merely a way of making a living, but may well have felt he discovered his genius. During the decade following the war, in satisfying their "instincts of infinitude," the James Gang blazed a trail of mayhem across the region, an epic catalog of the crime that began with the looting of the Clay County Savings Bank at Liberty, Missouri—the first daylight bank robbery during peacetime in U.S. history—and continued through the plundering of the Alexander Mitchell & Co. bank at Lexington, Missouri; the Hughes & Wasson bank at Richmond, Missouri; the Nimrod L. Long & Co. bank at Russellville, Kentucky; the Daviess County Savings Association at Gallatin, Missouri; the Ocobock Brothers' bank at Corydon, Iowa; the Bank of Columbia at Columbia, Kentucky; the box office of the Kansas City Exposition, Kansas City, Missouri; the Ste. Genevieve Savings Bank at Ste. Genevieve, Missouri; a Chicago, Rock Island, and Pacific train at Adair, Iowa; a stagecoach at Hot Springs, Arkansas; an Iron Mountain train at Gads Hill, Missouri; an omnibus stagecoach at Lexington, Missouri; a Kansas Pacific train near Muncie, Kansas; the Bank of Huntington at Huntington, West Virginia; and most recently, the Missouri Pacific Express at Otterville, Missouri.

By the summer of 1876, the haul from these depredations had totaled almost two hundred thousand dollars, with nearly a dozen bank tellers, engineers, express car guards, and innocent bystanders left dead or maimed. But in yet another instance of the outlaw tailoring his narrative to Elena's perceived sensibilities, Jesse made an assiduous attempt to downplay the savagery of his escapades. Whenever possible, he framed his violent behavior as "self defense," though it was hardly lost upon the perspicacious young woman that Jesse's broad interpretation of situations in which he deemed it necessary to defend himself with deadly force included such trivial provocations as being looked at "the wrong way." Some folks, the bandit professed, simply "needed" killing: "A man who is a d——d enough fool to refuse to open a safe or a vault when he is covered with a pistol ought to die," he once wrote to *The Kansas City Times,* adding with implacable outlaw logic, "If he gives the alarm, or resists, or refuses to unlock, he gets killed."

The "Rough Rob" of William's jocular appellation had become rough indeed. Now there would be no turning back, no going home— though all he had originally wanted was to go home. The younger James boys had been irrevocably transmuted into Frank and Jesse. *"L'ingénieux petit"* Robertson and the "adipose, affectionate" Garth Wilkinson were every bit as dead to the world as if they lay beneath the cold clay of the Carolinas.

Chapter Six

⸻ •⸱• ⸻

Elena Hite awoke after her night under the stars with Jesse James to discover that her lover and his brothers were gone. Sometime during the wee hours of the morning, the trio had slipped away from the farm in a tarpaulin-covered cart, en route for parts and projects unknown. At breakfast, Zerelda complained from bitter experience that whatever "the boys" were up to would inevitably result in the law descending upon the farm in short order. She insisted that Elena vacate the premises immediately, a decree to which the younger woman readily acceded, concurring with her hostess—especially in light of the outlaw's revelations of the night before—that she indeed knew too much about Jesse James.

"Maybe not so much as you think, missy," Mrs. Samuel responded with a cryptic smirk.

Elena loaded up her buckboard and set out up the road toward St. Joseph, fifty miles to the north. She had not been altogether surprised by Jesse's precipitous departure, which, considering all the late-night scheming that had been going on at the farmhouse, she might well have anticipated—though she would have appreciated the courtesy of a little advance notice. Still, she couldn't help but revel in a certain lightness, of liberation, a sense of having accomplished her mission and demonstrated (at least to herself) that a woman could pursue her own passions with the same intensity and impunity as a man. She took an immodest satisfaction in the fact that she had not only elicited Jesse's erotic attentions but had in some sense gained the outlaw's trust. She had tamed the panther.

These not altogether unpleasant ruminations were soon impinged upon by the appearance on the roadside of a portly peddler who flagged down the buckboard and begged Elena for a ride up to St. Joe.

"Ich dank aych zeyer, frailin," mumbled the itinerant merchant, hoisting his stout frame with discernible effort up onto the seat beside her. Though it was still early in the day, he was already perspiring profusely under the heat of the mid-August sun and the unaccustomed weight of his pack.

Elena, of course, had no difficulty seeing through the detective's flimsy imposture. "Please, spare me the Hebrew, Mr. Pinkerton," she chided.

Her passenger dutifully dropped his masquerade and, cutting straight to the chase, demanded to know what Elena was doing in these parts. She disingenuously replied that she was lecturing, as usual.

"Well, if you're trying to sell female emancipation to Zerelda Samuel," Pinkerton ventured, nodding back down the road toward Castle James, "you're preaching to the pope."

Elena allowed herself a wan smile. The detective took it as confirmation that she had indeed been a recent resident at the Samuels' farm. Pressing his advantage, he began to pump her for information, his most urgent aim being to get her to spill the beans about the James boys' plans. Yet even had she been inclined to cooperate, Elena, having been excluded from the gang's nocturnal deliberations, would have had precious few beans to spill. She knew only that whatever plot they had been cooking up in Zerelda's kitchen was something significant, though she had barely a clue as to the where, what, how, or when. She told the detective that she hadn't the slightest idea what he was talking about.

But her passenger, still throbbingly cognizant of the previous night's intimacy between Jesse James and the comely young woman on the seat beside him, brushed aside her denial. At first he didn't let on that he knew her true identity, or about her recent assignation with the outlaw. But as she remained recalcitrant, he began laying out his trumps.

"Be that as it may, Miss Phoenix—or should I say Miss *Hite*?"

Elena was taken aback. "Hite is my father's name," she warily conceded.

"Indeed, Mr. Asa Hite of Hartford, Connecticut," Pinkerton pressed on. "And I daresay I find it difficult to imagine that fine gentleman being in the least pleased to know of his daughter's amorous relations with a certain criminal party."

"Amorous?"

"It's hardly a secret around these parts, Miss Hite."

"I don't suppose there's much that is," Elena responded noncommittally, though she was quick to appreciate the implications of the detective's line of interrogation—his none too subtle threat that he could easily inform her father she had been fraternizing with the enemy.

Elena tried to tough it out, insisting that if Pinkerton had deigned to take her feminist rhetoric at all seriously, he would have appreciated that she reserved the right to consort with whomever her heart desired.

"So they say in Hartford," rejoined the detective with a knowing smile. "But I don't think Zee James would see it that way."

And thus it was that on a sunny morning in the middle of August 1876, Elena Hite learned that, in the words of the famous ballad, Jesse had a wife. This was an unwelcome piece of intelligence that the detective was only too eager to document by producing from his peddler's kit a yellowed clipping from the *St. Louis Dispatch* dated June 7, 1874—a letter to the newspaper from Jesse James:

> *On the 23rd of April, 1874, I was married to Miss Zee Mimms, of Kansas City, and at the house of a friend there. About fifty of our mutual friends were present on the occasion, and quite a noted Methodist minister performed the ceremonies. We had been engaged for nine years, and through good and evil report, and notwithstanding the lies that had been told upon me and the crimes laid at my door, her devotion to me has never wavered for a moment. You can say that both of us married for love, and that there cannot be any sort of doubt about our marriage being a happy one.*

The above account of the outlaw's wedding, as we now know, was spurious in a number of its details (including the date of the ceremony, which actually took place on the twenty-fourth); but the marriage itself was perfectly authentic, if not quite so blissful as Jesse had proclaimed. And as Pinkerton no doubt had hoped, Elena received this morsel of old news with considerable consternation. Many of the small mysteries of her recent sojourn at Castle James came clicking into place—Jesse's "experienced" touch, his frequent long absences from the farm, and Mrs. Samuel's cryptic remark that very morning: *"Maybe not so much as you think, missy"*—to say nothing of a stinging suspicion about the likely disposition of her prized string of amber beads.

They traveled on for miles in awkward silence, and instead of chauffeuring the detective all the way to St. Joseph, Elena dropped him off at Kearney to catch a train. At the station, Pinkerton tendered her his card and told her she would know where to find him in the event that her memory suddenly improved. Then, playing of necessity bad cop to his own good cop, he pointedly remarked in parting that it would be a shame to see such a well-bred young lady arrested as an accessory to a crime. Elena observed that, to her knowledge, no crime had been committed, but as she was delivering this canny riposte, her words were being drowned out by the hissing and chugging of the arriving locomotive.

She proceeded on to St. Joseph, where, exhausted from the physical and emotional vicissitudes of the day's drive, she took to her hotel bed almost immediately upon finishing her supper. And whatever the subterranean workings of her psyche, the detective's revelation had its intended effect on the young woman: It unleashed her devils. In the early hours of the morning, Elena awoke from a nightmare to the sound of shattering glass and found herself smashing the mirror on the vanity table by her bedside. More than the physical injury (which turned out to be superficial, despite the alarming quantity of blood on her hands, nightgown, and bedclothes), the sheer ferocity of this eruption unnerved her terribly. She was appalled to discover how much anger she must have had roiling within her to drive her to punch a pane of glass. Staring down at her blood-soaked hands and back up at her splintered reflection in the shards of the mirror, she experienced "an abject horror" at her unaccustomed loss of control.

By a certain naïve logic, it might be difficult to understand why Elena Hite would have been so devastated by the unexpected disclosure of Jesse's marital status. Was it jealousy? Could she have been so deeply in love with the outlaw that she found the thought of sharing him with another woman intolerable? Yet certainly she had shared her men with other women before. (In her Hartford days, one of George Stanley's circle of young rakes had been betrothed, and another had been recently married.) It would be difficult to imagine that Elena ever dreamed of actually committing matrimony with the outlaw. Indeed, she had put herself on record with him as being foursquare against the institution. She knew "in her bones," she had told him, that they would never be a couple, and she had repeatedly insisted that despite their lovemaking, he could never "have" her in any proprietary sense. In diary entries written during her sojourn at Castle

James, she described their liaison as a fling, an adventure, perhaps something of a carnal reward for her years of "being good" on the lecture circuit, when so many men—to their ultimate regret, bewilderment, and anger—had taken her brazen free-love rhetoric as an invitation to try to bed her.

Or was it less the existence of a documented Mrs. James that disconcerted Elena than the fact that the outlaw had concealed it from her? Yet this, too, would be a difficult notion to credit: Could she really have imagined Jesse James to have been a straight shooter in any but the most literal sense? After all, the man was a notorious murderer and thief, so why not an adulterer and liar as well? Indeed, Elena knew perfectly well from her own complicity in the bald-faced falsehoods he had foisted off on *The Kansas City Times* that he was not in the least averse to playing fast and loose with the truth.

In writing about men, even in the private pages of her journal, Elena often affected a precociously jaunty and jaded tone, referring to the soi-disant stronger sex as "the little dears" or "those silly beasties," especially in the context of how easy she found it to manipulate them with her feminine charms and graces. But while, by her own admission, she didn't mind occasionally acting the *cocotte*—even taking a perverse pleasure in the sheer audacity of the role—apparently, she could never abide feeling like one.

As a woman of relatively meager years and abundant privileges, Elena was used to enjoying both a protective illusion of invulnerability and a hefty sense of entitlement. Even in the face of the harsh lesson of Hartford, she had continued to live as if she could carry on very much as she pleased without suffering any untoward consequences. But now, in the middle of a bad night, she became cringingly aware of the jeopardy to which she had so recently exposed herself—in putting herself not only at the mercy of a gang of notorious cutthroats, but also in the path of possible arrest, with the attendant prospect of even greater shame and disgrace than she had already known.

After all the comfortable certainties of her doctrinaire feminist vocation and the earthy pleasures of her erotic eclogue at Castle James, she found herself disoriented and deracinated, as if some plush epistemological carpet had been yanked out from under her.

All she knew for sure was that her twenty-third birthday was approaching, and she wanted to go home.

———◆———

With William Stiles (alias Bill Chadwell) at the reins, the cart in which the James brothers stole away from the Samuel farm under cover of darkness made its way north through the night. At daybreak, they ditched the wagon and met up with the rest of the gang near the Iowa border. Other than Jim Younger, who replaced the traitorous Hobbs Kerry—and, of course, the newcomer Henry James—the band was made up of the same personnel who had robbed the Missouri Pacific Express at Rocky Cut: Frank and Jesse James, Cole and Bob Younger, Clell Miller, Sam Wells (alias Charlie Pitts), and Bill Stiles. Together they all rode to Council Bluffs, where, to avoid arousing suspicion, they split up into three smaller groups and boarded separate trains for Minneapolis. Stiles, a Minnesota native, had cut his teeth on horse-and-revolver work up in the North Star State and was looking forward to returning to his old stomping grounds to "shake it up." He tantalized his comrades with visions of easy pickings in that somnolent and prosperous northern region whose credulous citizens, he joked, wouldn't know an outlaw band if they were surrounded by one. He had friends up there who would help them, he promised, and he convinced the gang that they would reap handsome rewards by employing the time-tested guerrilla tactic of striking where least expected.

When the gang reassembled in Minnesota, it was in the raunchy red-light district of St. Paul, where they checked in to the Nicolett House Hotel under assumed names: Frank and Jesse signed in as J. C. Horton and H. L. West of Nashville, Tennessee; Jim Younger was

W. G. Huddleson of Maryland; Cole became J. C. King of Virginia; and Charlie Pitts registered as John Wood (or Ward), also of Virginia. Henry raffishly took the *nom de voyage* of "Rod. Hudson." (Clell Miller and Bob Younger stayed at the nearby Merchant's Hotel.) In St. Paul the outlaws mingled with the local population to glean what they could of Minnesota mores. They played poker at Chinn's & Morgan's gambling house, boozed and dined on oysters at McLeod's Ladies' and Gents' Restaurant and Sample Room, and got their rocks off at Mollie Ellsworth's sporting house—although, as Jesse's biographer Marley Brant recorded, "[o]ne of the more popular girls, Kitty Traverse, later claimed she noticed that one of the men appeared ill and never left his room."

This doubtless would have been the whore-shy and intestinally impaired "Rod. Hudson," for in addition to whatever discomfort Henry James was experiencing by virtue of his novel status as a rough rider, he was also suffering from a flare-up of one of his old psychosomatic nemeses: severe constipation. The author had been periodically plagued with this affliction for much of his adult life, most grievously when traveling. On a tour of Italy in the autumn of 1869, he had endured an especially debilitating bout of what he referred to at the time as "my old enemy no. 2—by which I mean my unhappy bowels." (Old enemy no. 1, we must assume, was his unhappy back.) In a letter to William, which by the estimation of Leon Edel, "in the history of literature may well be the most elaborate account of the ailment extant," Henry had bemoaned "this hideous repletion of my belly" in excruciating detail. William, on the authority of his newly minted M.D., had responded at equally exhaustive length, providing his ailing brother with an annotated roster of the most eminent bowel boffins in Europe and prescribing various therapies, including croton oil, senna, Epsom salts, and enemas of soapsuds and oil ("as large and hot as you can bear"). Most drastically, William proposed a regimen of electricity in the form of "a strong *galvanic* current from the spine to the abdominal muscles, or if the rectum be paralysed one pole put inside the rectum." Shortly thereafter, without having resorted to this shocking treatment, Henry had reported from Rome that he was "immensely relieved of those woes concerning which I sent you from Florence such copious bulletins."

Now, as the gang ventured out across the Minnesota countryside in search of promising pickings, Henry spent much of his time holed up in the bathrooms and outhouses of the hotels and farmhouses where they stayed. The writer's costiveness served only to exacerbate Cole Younger's already pronounced disdain for the interloper. More than once Younger suggested to Frank and Jesse that they dump their ailing brother—or, better yet, "just put the son of a bitch out of his misery." But the outlaw James brothers insisted on hewing to their own agenda, perhaps by way of extracting interest on what they perceived as a decade-old family debt, or perhaps because Henry's continued presence, however ineffectual and inconvenient, provided the Jameses at least numerical parity with the Youngers, against whom they found themselves locked in a perennial tug-of-war for domination of the gang.

Over the next couple of weeks, the outlaws reconnoitered the region in groups of three or four, often posing as cattle dealers, civil engineers, or land speculators while they sized up various possibilities for plunder. During this period they provisioned themselves for their forthcoming exploit—whatever it would turn out to be—with an imposing arsenal of new Colts and carbines, a wardrobe of long white cattlemen's linen dusters under which to conceal them, and a small herd of splendid, speedy thoroughbreds on which to make their getaway. "[A] connoisseur in horseflesh," wrote Jesse's biographer Frank Triplett, "might view with delighted eyes the long barrel, thin limbs and velvet coats of these horses; some of which were fit to make a race almost for the price of a king's ransom."

Thus impressively armed and mounted, the gang ultimately set its larcenous sights on the town of Northfield, about fifty miles south of Minneapolis, which Frank and Jesse, posing as land buyers, went down to reconnoiter. The municipality, with a population of about two thousand, had been founded in 1855 on the banks of the Cannon River, across which a dam had been constructed to power the Ames Mill's production of prizewinning flour ground from the grain grown in the fertile fields of the surrounding region. Though relatively small, Northfield already boasted two institutions of higher learning: Carleton College (founded in 1866) and St. Olaf College (founded in 1874). More to the point, Jesse and Frank discovered that the town was policed by only a single elderly lawman, that it had no gun shops—just a couple of hardware stores carrying a limited selection of firearms—and that its major financial institution, the First National Bank of Northfield, would be flush with funds generated by the recent harvest.

For the former Confederate guerrillas who made up the majority of the gang, Bill Stiles provided an additional incentive to target the Northfield bank: He informed his companions that one of the town's leading citizens was Adelbert Ames, whose family owned the eponymous mill that drove the local economy. While a brigadier general in the Union army, Ames had commanded the division that brought down Fort Fisher in Wilmington, North Carolina, the last Confederate seaport to fall. After the war, he had served as governor of Mississippi, where he was known as "Grant's bayonet governor" and where he had acquired a reputation among die-hard secessionists as a carpetbagger who had plundered the state during Reconstruction. Ames had been impeached when the Democrats came to power, but he had been exonerated of all charges and had eventually retreated to Northfield, where his family, Stiles reported, not only owned the profitable flour mill but also held a substantial interest in the bank. (Adelbert's brother John was on the board of directors, and his father, Jesse, was a vice president.) To further sweeten the deal, Stiles revealed that Adelbert Ames's father-in-law was none other than Benjamin F. Butler, who, according to Jesse's biographer T. J. Stiles (no relation, he claims, to the bandit), had been universally regarded as one of the worst generals in the Union army. As the federal overseer of New Orleans during the war, Butler had earned the nickname "Beast" for his harsh and corrupt administration of that vanquished city. (He was also known as "Silver Spoons," reflecting the popular calumny that, given half a chance, he would swipe his own grandmother's flatware.) General Butler, it was widely rumored, had made a killing in kickbacks from a cotton-smuggling operation and had deposited a juicy chunk of his ill-gotten fortune in his son-in-law's Northfield bank. "Butler's treatment of the Southerners during the war," Cole Younger later wrote, "was not such as to commend him to our regard, and we felt little compunction, under the circumstances, about raiding him or his."

On Wednesday, September 6, the gang arrived in the vicinity of Northfield, traveling in two groups. Frank, Jesse, Charlie Pitts, and Bob Younger took lodgings at the farm of C. C. Stetson on the Faribault Road five miles outside of town. The others, including Henry, upon whom Cole Younger insisted on keeping a watchful eye, stayed at the Cushman Hotel in nearby Millersburgh, where, according to Marley Brant, "it was later reported that one of the men claimed he was ill and stayed in his room during dinner."

It was on that evening that the outlaws plotted out the next day's escapade, and if Henry had previously been skeptical of Frank's boastful conceit of armed robbery being a form of art, he came to appreciate the degree of care and cunning that went into the realization of such a work. It was not simply a matter of riding up to the nearest bank and storming in with six-guns blazing, any more than writing a novel involved sitting down one day with pen and paper and starting to scribble from the top of page one. In both endeavors there had to be inspiration, outlines, rough drafts, false starts, an openness to improvisation, and a thorough conversance with the conventions of the genre. Given all that could go wrong, success in either enterprise could never be guaranteed. What Henry later wrote of the novelist's métier, he might now have conceded, could well apply to those who aspired to pull off a bank holdup: "We work in the dark—we do what we can—we give what we have. Our doubt is our passion, and our passion is our task. The rest is the madness of art."

———◆———

Up in the Adirondacks, life in the shanty that summer had been proving—at least at the outset—every bit as rustic and convivial as William James could have desired. The climate of the mountain retreat, both meteorological and social, proved ideal for "tramping and camping," and he delighted in the company of his medical buddies. James Putnam and Henry Bowditch were among the select group of William's oldest and closest friends—it also included Oliver Wendell Holmes, Jr.—with whom he relished gossiping "on generalities"; though, given the professional proclivities of the Adirondack Doctors, the generalities toward which their chat tended to gravitate were those centering on psychology and neurology.

Despite the fact that they were all more or less contemporaries, the other Adirondack Doctors struck William as far more comfortably settled in their professional and personal lives than he could ever imagine himself being: Henry Bowditch had married a couple of years earlier, and both he and James Putnam were already firmly established in their medical and academic careers. Bowditch, whom William always admired as "honest" and "worthy," had pursued three years of postgraduate study with the renowned physiologist Karl Ludwig in Leipzig and had returned to the Harvard Medical School to become its first full-time faculty member, charged by President Eliot with revamping the curriculum to emphasize hard science. (Bowditch subsequently became dean of the school and the first president of the American Physiological Society.)

James Putnam, after earning his Harvard M.D., had gone on to

Europe for further training, working with Karl von Rokitansky and Theodor Meynert in Vienna, and with the eminent neurologist John Hughlings Jackson in London. The focus of Putnam's studies was clinical neurology and psychiatry. (He was especially intrigued by the enigma of neurasthenia, which the celebrated French neurologist Jean-Martin Charcot once called "the American disease.") Upon returning to Boston, Putnam, too, had taken up teaching at the Harvard Medical School while serving as "Head of Electrics" at Massachusetts General Hospital, where he pioneered the use of electrotherapy—mild galvanic stimulation—as a cutting-edge modality in the treatment of nervous disorders. By 1876, having established the hospital's first outpatient clinic for the mentally ill, he had taken the title "Physician to Out-Patients with Diseases of the Nervous System." Later, he was to become a founding member and president of the American Neurological Society and an early proponent of Freud's theories in the United States. William, with only a single year of college teaching under his belt, had been doing experimental work back in Boston with both of these rising stars of American medicine. Bowditch ran a laboratory on North Grove Street near the Massachusetts General Hospital, to which James was a frequent visitor and in which he vastly enjoyed "paddling around." With Putnam, he had been carrying out neurological experiments in a makeshift home lab, sometimes using animals—they had published a paper on "Cortical Stimulation in the Dog"—and sometimes themselves as subjects. William looked to his more experienced colleagues for suggestions and support for his plan to launch a laboratory of experimental psychology at Harvard, and by the end of the summer, he was confident that they would stand solidly behind him in his campaign to get his pet project approved, funded, and equipped. That aspect of his estival agenda, at least, appeared to be a done deal.

It was in the romantic realm that things were proving dicier, for if Jesse James was possessed of an irrepressible need to be known, William lived under the sway of a no less powerful longing to be recognized, though not necessarily in the sense of becoming a household name. The recognition that William craved was the less public—though perhaps rarer—distinction of being fully acknowledged and embraced by another human soul. "James yearned for someone to perceive and love the authentic, the dark, self that lay somewhere in the deep recesses of his being," wrote his biographer Linda Simon. In a passage about the human need for God in his essay "The Meaning of Truth," William spelled out the essence of this special thirst for "recognition":

> The flaw was evident when, as a case analogous to that of a godless universe, I thought of what I called an "automatic sweetheart," meaning a soulless body which should be absolutely indistinguishable from a spiritually animated maiden, laughing, talking, blushing, nursing us, and performing all feminine offices as tactfully and sweetly as if a soul were in her. Would any one regard her as a full equivalent? Certainly not, and why? Because, framed as we are, our egoism craves above all things inward sympathy and recognition, love and admiration. The outward treatment is valued mainly as an expression . . . of the accompanying consciousness believed in. Pragmatically, then, belief in the automatic sweetheart would not *work*. . . .

In Alice Gibbens, William was discovering that summer a real flesh-and-blood sweetheart with whom he was experiencing, much to his astonishment, the wholly unaccustomed sense of being precisely where—physically, spiritually, and socially—he would most want to be. He delighted in his easy intercourse with Alice as they passed blissful afternoons picnicking on the gentle wooded banks of the east branch of the Au Sable, hopscotching over the boulders of lovely little Johns Brook, and hiking the high trails of Mount Marcy, Haystack, and the daunting Gothics. "As a walker," Putnam once recalled, James "was among the foremost. He had the peculiarity, in climbing, of raising himself largely with the foot that was lowermost, instead of planting the other and drawing himself up by it, as is so common. This is a slight thing, but it was an element counting for elasticity and grace." Alice matched William stride for graceful stride.

In the evenings they often joined their friends around a crackling campfire to sing such old Stephen Foster favorites as "Jeanie with the Light Brown Hair" and "Beautiful Dreamer," to which Alice lent her charming soprano in haunting high harmonies that echoed through the pure mountain air. With the flickering light of the piney blaze illuminating their faces, they lay side by side under the huge starlit dome of the Adirondack sky to gaze up at the same Perseid meteor shower that had provided the heavenly sparks for Jesse and Elena's lovemaking out in Missouri.

As their summer idyll was drawing to a close, William made a daring declaration: "To state abruptly the whole matter," he told Alice, "I am in love, *und zwar* [forgive me] with Yourself."

Such a bold pronouncement—one that he had never made to any woman—was for William James nothing less than a giant step down the path toward the fulfillment of his father's matrimonial prophecy. But in the nervous Newtonian mechanics of William's mind, all thinking tended to produce equal and opposite rethinking. Having laid his amatory cards so audaciously upon the table, the psychologist found himself besieged by a nattering swarm of characteristic second thoughts. "To a certain extent," he wrote to Alice at summer's end, "I will suppose you feel a sympathy with me, but I can furnish you with undreamed arguments against accepting any offer I might make." Among these counterarguments would have been his fragile health, his questionable ability to support a family, his dark moods, his sexual inexperience, and, of course, the dread "family taint." Though he desperately desired to be both known and loved, William feared that the more any woman truly *knew* him, the less she might truly *love* him— a line of squirrel-cage thinking that inevitably brought him around to the even more demoralizing conclusion that the very fact that he so often obsessed over his unlovableness was, in itself, grounds for her not to love him.

Increasingly, a corrosive anxiety came to eat away at William's simple alpine pleasures, and not just on the romantic front; he also fretted that any day he might pick up a newspaper to read that his brothers—including his "in-many-respects twin" Henry—had been arrested or worse. Despite his deep yearning for an open soul-to-soul relationship with Alice Gibbens, he was reluctant to share these preoccupations with his potential bride, entailing, as such confidences inevitably would have, the unsavory revelation that some of her prospective in-laws were outlaws.

———◆———

On the morning of September 7, the two bandit parties met up outside of the tiny village of Dundas and headed for Northfield as a unit. They must have made an impressive spectacle, cantering toward the town on their magnificent mounts, their white linen dusters flapping snappily in the morning breeze. Despite a bad night at the mercy of his blocked bowels and the fact that he was virtually a hostage, for the first time in his life, Henry was experiencing, however reluctantly and unexpectedly, the masculine thrill of riding into battle with comrades-in-arms—a delayed taste of what it might have been like to have been the solider (and the man) he had never become. "Henry James's early stories," wrote psychiatrist Howard M. Feinstein, "can be read as the creation of a young artist who had become painfully aware of himself as a female consciousness masquerading in the body of a man." (This was what Leon Edel referred to as the author's "literary transvestism," a stance that informed not only James's writings but his entire existence.) As a boy, Henry had once begged to tag along with William and his chums on some bit of childish mischief, only to have his older brother dismissively remark, "*I* play with boys who curse and swear."

The author had never forgotten the sting of that schoolyard snub; but henceforth, in the unlikely event that the appropriate occasion should ever present itself, he would now be able to retort: "Well, *I* play with boys who rob and kill!"

On this occasion the robbing and killing began at about one P.M. when, as planned, Jesse, Frank, and Bob Younger crossed the iron bridge into the center of town, hitched their horses in front of the bank, and strolled across the street to Jeft's restaurant. After a hearty repast of ham and eggs, the trio moseyed back across Division Street to Lee & Hitchcock's dry-goods store, located in a large building known as the Scriver Block, which also housed the bank. The outlaws bided their time sitting on some packing crates piled in front of the shop. At two P.M. sharp, they rose from the wooden boxes and sauntered nonchalantly around the corner into the bank. Taking this as their signal to deploy, Cole Younger and Clell Miller left their post at the near end of the bridge and rode slowly into town.

On his way up Division Street, Cole observed that there were far too many people out and about for his taste, including, to his surprise, Adelbert Ames, whom the outlaw recognized strolling with his father and brother. "Look, it's the governor himself," Cole remarked to Miller as they trotted by.

Ames overheard this comment and eyed the pair warily. "Those men are Southerners," he alerted his companions. "Nobody up here calls me governor."

Arriving at the front of the bank, Clell Miller noticed that his colleagues inside had left the door ajar—the first of the afternoon's many missteps. While Cole dismounted and made a show of casually fiddling with the girth of his saddle, Miller got off his horse and strolled over to the door to ease it shut. At that moment J. S. Allen, a local hardware dealer who had become suspicious of the tough-looking strangers on their fine-looking horses, walked up to the door and tried to enter the building. Miller grabbed the merchant by the arm to block his way, but Allen had already gotten a glimpse through the window and had immediately discerned what was going on inside. He tore free of Miller's grasp and took off down Division Street, shouting, "Get your guns, boys! They're robbing the bank!"

Clell fired a warning shot over the fleeing hardwareman's head. Across the street, a young medical student named Henry Wheeler, who was lounging outside his father's pharmacy, saw what was taking place at the entrance to the bank. He, too, began yelling, "Robbery! Robbery!" Then he ducked into the drugstore to get a gun.

Inside the bank, Frank, Jesse, and Bob Younger had good reason to believe, at least at the outset, that everything would go according to plan. There were no customers in the establishment and only three employees on duty: the teller Alonzo Bunker, the clerk Frank Wilcox, and the bookkeeper Joseph L. Heywood. The door of the vault behind the counter was wide open, and a massive iron safe sat clearly visible against its back wall. The outlaws approached the counter, drew their guns, and ordered the employees to drop to their knees with their hands in the air. "We're going to rob this bank," barked Jesse. "Don't any of you holler. We've got forty men outside."

The robbers scrambled over the counter and demanded to know which of the workers was the cashier. Each of them replied in the negative, including Heywood, who, strictly speaking, was telling the truth in that the regular cashier, George M. Phillips, was in Philadelphia visiting the Centennial Exposition and had designated the bookkeeper to act in his stead during his absence. Jesse, however, observing that Heywood was the oldest, best dressed, and most well spoken of the group, leveled his pistol at the bookkeeper's head. "You *are* the cashier," he insisted. "Now open the safe, you goddamned son of a bitch!"

But Joseph L. Heywood was not one to be easily intimidated. The thirty-nine-year-old bookkeeper was a veteran of the Illinois 127th Infantry and the treasurer of Carleton College, of which he was also a trustee. Just a week earlier, he had told the president of the college that in the event of a bank robbery, he would under no circumstances hand over the institution's assets. Indeed, even the most rabidly partisan of Jesse's biographers have felt compelled to acknowledge the bookkeeper's extraordinary calm and courage in the face of the gang's coercions. Looking straight into the muzzle of Jesse's revolver, Heywood quietly informed the outlaw that he was unable to comply.

When Frank James stepped forward to get a closer look at the safe, the bookkeeper made a lunge for the bandit and tried to shove him into the vault, catching Frank's arm with the heavy slamming door and almost crushing it. Frank cried out in pain as Bob Younger sprang at Heywood, sending him sprawling to the floor with a brutal blow to the skull from the butt of his pistol. Younger then ordered Alonzo Bunker to lie down next to the dazed bookkeeper while Jesse drew a bowie knife from his billowing linen duster and pressed the long gleaming blade against the prostrate Heywood's windpipe. "Let's cut his damned throat," he proposed (probably with more of an aim to terrorize than to murder). Yet even as the blade of Jesse's "Arkansas toothpick" etched a thin line of blood across Heywood's Adam's apple, the doughty bookkeeper remained obdurate. He gaspingly explained that the safe had recently been set on a chronometer and could be opened only at certain prespecified times. (This, too, was technically the truth, although what Heywood neglected to mention was that the safe, containing at least fifteen thousand dollars in cash, was in fact already unlocked—a crucial piece of information that the increasingly distracted robbers were never to discover.)

Jesse, growing impatient, yanked the bookkeeper to his feet and frog-marched him into the vault. Meanwhile, Alonzo Bunker struggled to his knees and tried to retrieve a small Smith & Wesson .32-caliber handgun from its hiding place on a shelf beneath the counter. But Bob Younger, who suspected that there was a teller's cash drawer somewhere, quickly snatched the weapon away and forced Bunker back down to the floor, pressing the tip of his pistol to the teller's temple and demanding, "Show me where the money is, you son of a bitch, or I'll kill you!"

Inside the vault, Jesse threw Heywood down in front of the safe and fired a shot into the floorboards within inches of his head. With Bob Younger and Frank James momentarily distracted by the report of Jesse's revolver, Alzono Bunker took the opportunity to scramble once again to his feet and make a dash for the rear door of the building. Bob gave chase and fired at the fleeing teller, wounding him in the shoulder. But Bunker managed to stagger out into the alleyway behind the bank, hollering, "They're robbing the bank! Help!"

Out in front of the building, things were going even less propitiously for the men on guard than for the robbers inside. To clear the street of carriages and pedestrians, Cole Younger and Clell Miller had sprung to their horses and were galloping back and forth, discharging their pistols and shouting, "Get in! Get in!"

Seeing the commotion from their post at the bridge, Jim Younger, Charlie Pitts, Bill Stiles, and Henry James spurred their horses and came thundering down Division Street into the fray, whooping, hollering, and firing their revolvers into the air; Cole Younger had given the gang strict orders to shoot only to frighten, not to kill—a directive that, at least in Henry's case, proved entirely superfluous. The author was packing a pair of big Colt .44s, but it was all he could manage simply to control his high-strung mount: He kept both hands clutched tightly on the reins and never unholstered his pistols. Nonetheless, the other members of the gang, especially Jim Younger, kept a close watch on the writer, concerned that he might do something rash to endanger them all, or that he might try to abscond from their custody.

Under the onslaught of this second contingent of horsemen, most of the citizens on the street scattered like leaves before a storm; but, as the outlaws were about to discover, they were not to be afforded the respectful latitude to which they had become accustomed when operating on their home turf. Out of either raw courage or sheer foolhardiness, the staunch citizens of Northfield were choosing to express a far less indulgent attitude toward armed robbery than their battle-cowed counterparts back down in Missouri. Henry Wheeler, the medical student, had procured an old Civil War–era carbine with which he ran into the Dampier Hotel across the street from the bank. With a handful of cartridges supplied by the hotel clerk, he raced up the stairs to one of the top-story rooms overlooking Division Street, from which he began firing down on the outlaws. Meanwhile, J. S. Allen, the hardware dealer who had provoked Clell Miller's initial warning shot, hurried into his store and began passing out guns and ammunition to the townspeople. Anselm R. Manning, the proprietor of Northfield's other hardware store, grabbed a breech loading rifle from his stock and hurried out into the street. Another citizen, Elias Stacy, picked up a double-barreled shotgun and a pocketful of shells. All over the town, the enraged Northfielders armed themselves with whatever weapons they had handy and took up positions on rooftops, in stairwells, on porches, and at windowsills to begin blasting away at the bandits.

With shots ringing out all around him, Cole Younger continued firing into the air and bellowing orders to clear the street. One hapless pedestrian, a Swedish immigrant named Nicolaus Gustavson, stumbled into the bandit's path and stared blankly up at the furious horseman. "Get off the damn street!" Younger yelled again. But Gustavson, who had only recently arrived in Minnesota, spoke no English, and was most likely drunk to boot, simply stood there as, to Henry's horror, Cole lowered his revolver and fired a shot into the befuddled Swede's head. (So much, Henry must have thought, for not shooting to kill.) As the mortally wounded Gustavson staggered toward the gutter, Cole caught Henry's appalled regard and glared back at the author as if to say, "What the fuck are *you* looking at?" Henry quickly averted his gaze and did his utmost to emit a bone-chilling rebel yell. But instead of a full-throated whoop, all he managed to squeeze out was "a frightened little pig-whistle."

Meanwhile, Clell Miller dismounted once again and ran over to the bank to warn the men inside. "Hurry up!" he shouted through the doorway. "They've given the alarm!" As he climbed back on his horse,

Miller was rocked in the saddle by a spray of birdshot from Elias Stacy's fowling piece. The cloud of lead pellets riddled the outlaw's face, blinding his left eye and pocking his flesh into a gory moonscape. Still, he kept his seat and continued firing off his pistols.

Amid the chaos of swirling dust, acrid gun smoke, shouting, shooting, shattered windows, and splintered hitching posts, Henry James was making the potentially fatal blunder of lapsing into his characteristic posture of observation. Among the vivid impressions he registered was that of Anselm Manning, armed with the breech-loading Remington rifle he had taken from his hardware store, peering from around the corner of the dry-goods shop and plugging Bob Younger's tethered thoroughbred squarely between the eyes. As the exquisite animal let out a startled whinny and crumpled to the ground, Manning reloaded and fired at Cole Younger, clipping the outlaw in the left shoulder as he galloped by.

The gang on the street was caught in the lethal cross fire between Henry Wheeler at his hotel window and Anselm Manning around the corner from the bank. Manning had been joined by Adelbert Ames, who had gotten word of the robbery in progress at his office at the mill and come running toward the action at the Scriver Block. Reverting to his old military mien, the former general began commanding the hardware dealer as one of his troops, directing his fire toward the most promising objectives. Bill Stiles, at well over six feet tall, presented a prominent target even from a block away. With Ames's calming and coaching, the nervous Manning took careful aim and squeezed off a shot that went straight through the big bandit's heart. Stiles tumbled off his horse, dropping dead only a few feet from Henry James.

So engrossed was Henry in the unutterable carnage unfolding all around him that he forgot he himself was a target—at least until a shot from Wheeler's perch at the Dampier Hotel blew off his high-crowned "Boss of the Plains" Stetson hat. (Had Henry not been hunched down in his saddle owing to his constipated condition, the slug doubtless would have pierced his skull.) The author, abruptly awake to his peril, made a game attempt to execute the old Comanche maneuver of lying low in his saddle, hoping that his horse's neck and shoulders might shield him from the barrage. But as he leaned farther forward, the placket of his linen duster caught on his saddle horn, leaving him dangling against his horse's flank like a floppy rag doll.

Wheeler, assuming that Henry was out of commission, shifted his attention to the other bandits. One of his subsequent shots hit Jim Younger in the left shoulder. Another struck the half-blinded Clell Miller just below the collarbone, sending the outlaw toppling to the dust, spurting bright red blood from what the doctor in training surmised was his subclavian artery. Cole Younger dismounted and ran over to aid his fallen comrade but, realizing that Miller was already moribund, stripped him of his gunbelt and ammunition, even as Wheeler's next bullet caught him in the left vastus lateralis. Younger hobbled back to the door of the bank, frantically yelling, "They're killing our men! Get out here!"

Inside, the robbers were reaching their wits' end. With the appearance of his wounded brother at the door, Bob Younger concluded that the moment had arrived to abandon the premises. He hurried out of the bank, closely followed by Jesse James, who paused only long enough to snatch the meager wad of cash on the counter. The last to leave was Frank James. Frustrated that all of his careful planning was coming to naught, and still furious with Heywood for having slammed his arm with the vault door, the outlaw aimed his pistol at the bookkeeper and fired. Heywood lurched toward his desk and crumpled into his chair. Then, with Frank Wilcox looking on in helpless horror, the robber vaulted the railing, pressed his revolver hard against the bookkeeper's right temple, and fired again. Heywood slumped across his desk, his blood and brains soaking into the blotter as Frank turned and coolly strolled out of the bank to rejoin what was left of the gang.

Bob Younger had burst from the building to discover his horse lying dead in the dust along with Clell Miller and Bill Stiles, whose riderless mounts were prancing loose. As the robber tried to grab one of the fallen men's horses, Anselm Manning began taking potshots at him, driving Younger to scurry for cover under a wooden staircase. The outlaw and the hardwareman fell into a pitched gun duel, exchanging fire until a bullet from Henry Wheeler's carbine across the street smashed Younger's right elbow. The former guerrilla deftly executed a "border shift," flipping his gun to his left hand and continuing to fire at Manning, though he was badly injured.

Frank and Jesse had made it safely out of the bank and up onto their horses. Immediately appreciating the futility of the situation, they signaled to the others that it was time to skedaddle. "It's no use, boys! Let's go!" called Frank, even as a bullet ripped into his right leg.

It was at this moment that a stinging blast of birdshot from Elias Stacy's shotgun caught Henry's high-spirited horse in the rump. The startled animal was instantly transformed into a savage bronco— rearing up, wheeling, and bolting down the street with the author, still entangled on the saddle horn, clinging for dear life as Frank and Jesse lit out after him.

Seeing the Jameses beating their ragged retreat, Bob Younger stumbled out from under the staircase, his shattered right arm dangling limp at his side, just as another shot struck him in the left leg. "Don't leave me, boys!" he cried. "I've been shot!"

Despite Wheeler's slug lodged in his thigh, Cole Younger had managed to remount after calling the men out of the bank. Now, as Charlie Pitts covered him with a pair of pistols, Cole galloped through a hail of gunfire toward his wounded brother and, with a superhuman effort, grabbed hold of Bob's cartridge belt and hauled him up on the back of his saddle. Bob clung to his brother's waist with his good left arm as a volley of shots tore off Cole's saddle horn and sliced through his reins. With one hand clutching his horse's mane and the other still wielding his pistol, Cole took off after the Jameses.

The exquisitely plotted robbery had devolved into a rout. Desperately hugging the neck of his spooked horse, Henry "led" the remains of the gang back across the Cannon River bridge through a final flurry of bullets whistling past his ears—a couple of them possibly fired by Cole Younger. Frank and Jesse were hot on Henry's tail, followed by Jim Younger and Charlie Pitts, with Cole and Bob, riding double, bringing up the rear. Pitts, who had managed to remain unscathed throughout the robbery, now caught a bullet in his left arm. Jim was struck in the right leg. Cole was hit in the left hip, the right side, and the right arm. Those citizens who had been unable to procure firearms hurled stones and pitchforks at the fleeing bandits.

On the far side of the bridge, Jesse and Frank finally caught up with their brother, galloping alongside his runaway mount to rein in the frightened animal and its even more frightened rider.

It was at this juncture that Henry James discovered, not entirely to his relief, that the cursed constipation which had been vexing him for weeks was now suddenly and utterly behind him.

Chapter Seven

On the afternoon of September 7, 1876, over a thousand miles from
the chaos and carnage taking place out in Minnesota, Elena Hite arrived in Cambridge to meet with William James. It was a glorious late-
summer day in the academic suburb. Students were moving in for the
new semester, shouting their hallos across the Harvard Yard or lounging in laughing groups under the shade of the slender elms that lined
its crisscrossing paths. Elena, togged up to the nines for the occasion in
a cloud of Valenciennes lace, swanned her way along a gauntlet of admiring glances and breezed into William's office in Lawrence Hall.

She had girded herself for an immaculate clinical setting bristling
with an armamentarium of gleaming medical instruments. But the
doctor's lair turned out to be distinctly unclinical and almost comically
unprepossessing. The tiny chamber was barely more than a cubbyhole,
strewn willy-nilly with books, academic journals, sketch pads, framed
collections of Amazonian lepidoptera, a metronome, horopter charts,

and a couple of pieces of tarnished brass scientific apparatus. Other than the disconcerting presence of a large apothecary jar full of decapitated frogs bobbing in formaldehyde, the overall ambiance of the room was casually inviting, as was the man himself. William greeted Elena in his shirtsleeves and offered her a chair he had apparently just appropriated on her behalf from a nearby lecture hall.

At barely five feet eight, the oldest James brother was not nearly so tall as Elena had imagined, yet he carried himself with a limber grace and a bounce to his step. What struck her most pleasantly about the doctor was his voice, which James Putnam once described as having "a resonance and charm which those who had once heard it, especially in conversation, never could forget."

Elena took her seat and arranged the frilly flounces of her skirt about her ankles. She had a secret "test" for the men she encountered, staring into their eyes with a decidedly unladylike directness to gauge their moral—and perhaps erotic—mettle. (She was particularly drawn to those who unflinchingly met and returned her probing gaze.) On this basis she now completed her comparative taxonomy of the James men, of whom she was beginning to fancy herself something of a connoisseur: "While Jesse's steel blue eyes seem to look *through* you," she wrote in her diary, "Frank's look *around* you, and Henry's darker orbs peer *into* you." William, she recorded approvingly, "looks *at* you."

When the young doctor gently inquired what had brought her there, Elena sighed and let her elegant shoulders slump a bit, hardly knowing where to begin.

Back home in Hartford after her collapse out in Missouri, she had failed to regain her equilibrium. Whatever comfort she might have imagined deriving from being under her father's roof again and amid the familiar furnishings of her childhood had been short-lived at best. She slept poorly, ate either too much or scarcely at all, and found herself cross, restless, and too distracted even to read. All around her, the city rattled with ghosts. Most of her former schoolmates were either married or marrying, and she found herself still shunned. The stigma of her youthful offenses, which had mercifully receded in her memory to little more than a talking point for her gender politics, had come back to nettle her with the full, fresh force of its original sting. Not a day or night went by when she managed to avoid ruminating over her deplorable youth. On Lord's Hill, the once-fiery feminist orator regressed back into sulky adolescence. Asa Hite neither knew—nor cared to know—the particulars of his daughter's lecturing life or the crisis that had brought her back to Hartford. She and her father, Elena complained in her journal, merely had "that much else *not* to talk about."

What most haunted Asa Hite, after enduring years of travail in catering to his neurasthenic wife, was the dispiriting specter of history repeating itself with a deranged daughter. He was determined to procure for Elena the very best medical care money could buy, for which he had naturally turned to Dr. James J. Putnam of Boston, who had once treated Amelia Hite at Massachusetts General Hospital during his stint as head of electrics at that illustrious institution.

While in his neurological research Putnam was still very much in thrall to the nineteenth-century agenda of what Jacques Barzun called "bodifying the mind," as a clinician he was beginning to suspect that the mind had a mind of its own. " 'The man' is, above all else, the mind of the man," he would later write, "and not only the mind as an organ of conscious thought but the mind as an organ of bodily nutrition, and the mind as a vast theatre for the interplay of contending forces that do not always recognize the personal consciousness as their ruler. This is the man that the doctor should learn about and treat." Having determined that there was nothing organically the matter with Elena, Putnam had struck upon the notion—which he would ultimately come sorely to regret—of referring her for a consultation with William James, who, he once wrote, "was one of the first among professional psychologists to recognize the full bearing of the contributions which medical observation—that is, the psychology of the unusual or the slightly twisted mind—has made to the more classical psychological attitudes and insights." James, he trusted, would be able to provide a unique and useful perspective on the patient's condition. And Elena, Putnam hoped, might prove to be not the sole therapeutic beneficiary of his referral: Being painfully aware of William's distressed state at the end of the summer—he once spoke of James having "a real tendency to occasional depression"—Putnam believed he would be helping take his friend's mind off his love troubles by passing along this attractive, lively (if somewhat disturbed) young woman for a second opinion.

The eminent neurologist knew nothing of Elena's recent imbroglio with his colleague's brothers, although the patient was of course keenly cognizant of William's familial provenance. One might suppose that she would have balked at the prospect of any further entanglement with the family of the man who had so recently broken her heart; but Elena's heart, as we have seen, was no uncomplicated organ. If nothing else, she had a dangerously high threshold for stimulation, and after a couple of weeks of moping about her father's Lord's Hill mansion, she was beginning to suffer, along with her other woes, an intolerable itch of sheer boredom. To Asa Hite's uncomprehending yet profound relief, his despondent daughter seemed to perk up at the notion that she would be consulting with the brilliant Dr. James.

In the event, however, Elena was finding herself more than a little apprehensive. Face-to-face with the senior James brother, she became uncomfortably aware of the power he wielded over her as a physician: Might he declare her a madwoman? Make her undress? Pack her away to an insane asylum? Hypnotize her? (She had heard they were doing a great deal of that in Paris.)

We will most probably never know precisely what transpired between William James and Elena Hite that afternoon. The young doctor took no notes; or, if he did, they have long since gone the way of the mysterious twenty-one pages snipped from his 1869 diary. And there are passages in Elena's journal jottings describing their session together in which she is uncharacteristically circumspect. Certainly the encounter could hardly have been a clinical interview in any sense that a modern-day psychiatrist would recognize. To begin with, William was not a trained psychiatrist, even by the relatively primitive standards of the nineteenth century. What was more, he was William James and doubtless would have been constitutionally averse to a rigid clinical protocol, just as he was loath to lecture from notes, stick to a course curriculum, or perform the meticulous measurements and rigorous routines of a laboratory experiment.

Nonetheless, he was a sensitive and discerning listener. "By a kind of admirable divination," wrote the Swiss psychologist Theodore Flournoy, "he fathomed without disturbing them, minds that were very different from his own. Thus he was in touch with the moods and phases of the inner life of others, which to most of us are inaccessible, imprisoned as we are by the fixed barriers of our own egoism." And, of course, the doctor was no stranger personally to "nervous breakdowns": There had been his own ghastly crisis of seven years earlier, which he later presented as the case study of the epileptic patient in his *Varieties of Religious Experience,* as well as his father's famous "vastation," which had become a staple of James family lore. Perhaps even more germane to his present patient were the periodic "attacks" suffered by his sister, Alice, who, from late adolescence, had undergone a series of debilitating nervous episodes that, according to her biographer Jean Strouse, had been variously diagnosed as "neurasthenia, hysteria, rheumatic gout, suppressed gout, cardiac complication, spinal neurosis, nervous hyperesthesia, and spiritual crisis." Symptomatically, Alice's breakdowns took the form of fainting spells, mysterious physical pains, nervous prostrations, overwhelming anxieties, terrors, and suicidal thoughts, for which she had been subjected to the full, futile panoply of Victorian therapeutic maneuvers. As Leon Edel wrote in his introduction to her published diary, "All the remedies of the time were attempted: massage, visits to specialists in Manhattan for ice and electric therapy, special 'blistering' baths, sad sojourns to the 'Adams Nervine Asylum' near Boston—but they proved ineffective."

Fortunately, Elena Hite's case did not appear so grave or intractable as to call for Manhattan, baths, or galvanizing electric currents. Yet when William asked her to describe her symptoms, she became defensive: There was nothing "wrong" with her, she insisted, but only with this weary world, wherein it was so hard for one soul to know another under all the necessary and unnecessary guises that kept them apart. Her "big crime," she complained, was merely that of seeking "the full expression of love."

William, it hardly need be said, had accused her of no crime. The answer he had doubtless expected to his perfunctory clinical query was a familiar litany of complaints along the lines of headaches, fatigue, insomnia, and eyestrain. He must have been taken aback, then, not only by the vehemence of Elena's response but by the unforeseen direction in which it wrenched the course of their consultation; in bringing up the torments of love, the patient had cut directly to the essence of William's agonizing over his relationship with Alice Gibbens, thus threatening to undermine all of James Putnam's noble intentions in making his referral. Elena, who often relished discombobulating her interlocutors, was not altogether displeased with the effect her reply seemed to have on William James. If she sensed, as she undoubtedly did, that he was upset by her outburst, such a perception served only to spur her on. In response to William's chary request for elaboration, she proceeded not only to provide him with a skeletal (if spicy) account of her dalliances with George Stanley & Co., but also to divulge that she recently had been "deceived" by a married man. Even without dropping the bombshell that the scoundrel in question was the doctor's own undeceased brother, she managed to visibly disconcert him with her revelation: He rose from his desk and stepped over to the sole window in the office, where he stood for a moment, pensively inhaling deep drafts of bracing Harvard air.

Though hardly unappreciative of what he once referred to as "the animal potency of sex," William James was never to accord that sub-

ject the uniquely determinative stature to which Freud would elevate
it. (Of the nearly fourteen hundred pages in his *Principles of Psychology*, James devoted a scant two and a half to the subject of love, with
the bulk of that discussion being a description of the "anti-sexual"
instinct.) And while never a knee-jerk Victorian bluenose, he was
nonetheless something of a traditionalist in his views on chastity and
the sanctity of matrimony: "That the direction of the sexual instinct
towards one individual tends to inhibit its application to other individuals," he wrote, "is a law, upon which, though it suffers many exceptions, the whole *régime* of monogamy is based."

Elena Hite, apparently, was one of those vexing exceptions. In fact,
William had gleaned from James Putnam that Mr. Hite had expressed
concern about his daughter's "penchant for indiscretion"; yet the doctor was unprepared for either the extent of Elena's transgressions or
her unblushing candor. Indeed, Elena was surprised at how comfortable she was—under both the assured confidentiality of the doctor/
patient relationship and the encouragement of William's intense and
sympathetic attention—dumping the details of her sexual peccadil-
loes and predilections on him. ("I'm afraid I may have scandalized the
poor man dreadfully," she later reported somewhat disingenuously in
her journal, "with these allusions to my—ahem—'past.'")

Returning to his desk, William scrutinized the exquisite creature
before him as she insouciantly brushed a few errant strands of golden
hair from her eyes. Like Henry on the Missouri Pacific Express two
months earlier, he was taken by the sculptural perfection of Elena's
beauty—with an appreciation that, unlike his literary brother's cool
aesthetic assessment, was heated through an unequivocally heterosexual sensibility. Even in her present distressed state, the young woman
radiated a freshness and openness that seemed disturbingly at odds
with the corrupt history she had just recounted.

"Do you believe I suffer from a hopelessly unregenerate nature, Dr.
James?" she coyly inquired.

"Do *you*?" William asked.

Elena considered, then replied that while she sometimes regretted her behavior, she could never be sorry for it—a distinction that must have struck William as being without a difference, until the patient explained that she believed much of her suffering derived from the attitudes and behavior of others toward her, rather than from any internal sense of her own guilt or "ruin." She would forever refuse, she asserted, to apologize for the way she was. "Or do you propose that one ought to spend one's life slavishly courting the good report of others?" This was as much a challenge as a question, and it was perhaps then that William formulated his impression of Elena—which he later confided to his brother—as being less a woman who had fallen than one who had willfully leaped.

"So you like to feel that you're the captain of your own canoe?" he remarked.

She answered that she did indeed, but perhaps in response to William's unexpectedly colloquial tone, she relented from her hardline stance and added that she had recently read of a class of persons who were morally blind—who seemed to have been born without free will. She trusted that she was not among them, but sometimes, she admitted, she did feel helpless to moderate her appetites and affections. She wondered, in such states of mind, how much of her behavior was the expression of her own choices or to what degree it might be driven by forces or passions beyond her conscious control—a feeling for which she had scant tolerance. (What she did *not* mention to William was that for all the colorful social and political bunting with which she liked to drape it, sex itself had often proved something of a disappointment to her.) "I wonder why," she continued, "since they sometimes seem to cause me such unhappiness, I nevertheless feel compelled to persist on my evil courses." Elena delivered this last locution with a peculiar half-smile that was, at the very least, ironic and, if William was not mistaken, may have bordered on coquettish. In any event, it had the effect of inflaming the young doctor, whose erotic juices, freshly primed during his summer idyll with Alice Gibbens, now threatened to flow freely—and perhaps to overflow.

He seized upon the opportunity to steer the conversation away from the rocky shoals of sex and out toward the deeper but, for him, far more comfortably navigable waters of philosophy. "Throughout the first two decades of his professional life," wrote his biographer Gay Wilson Allen, "the philosophical subject which interested James most continued to be free will *versus* determinism." For William, this classic conundrum was of more than technical interest: He had always felt the prospect of living in a wholly determined, clockwork universe to be viscerally depressing, so he was looking not just for an intellectual solution but for an emotional way out. Taking the flagrantly unpsychiatric tack of revealing something of his own troubled history, he confided to his patient that during the late 1860s and early 1870s, he had experienced a prolonged and distressing bout of doubt, debility, and depression so severe that it had brought him nearly to the brink of suicide. (If his condition at that time had been to any degree precipitated or exacerbated by his conflicts over masturbation, William demurred from mentioning this possibility to Elena.) During that disconsolate period, in which he later described himself to Henry as having been "melancholy as a whippoorwill," William had despaired of ever being able to influence the course of his own life; and though he despised his tendency toward morbid introspection and sterile intellectualization, he had expended much of his depleted store of energy on obsessive rumination over the philosophical dilemma. Before he could exert his free will, he believed, he first needed to convince himself that such an entity existed.

It had been the French philosopher Charles-Bernard Renouvier, he told Elena, who had helped to usher him out from beneath the dark shadow of materialistic predestinarianism and into the sweet sunlight of self-determination. In April 1870, shortly after the period of the excised diary pages, he recorded: "I think that yesterday was a crisis in my life. I finished the first part of Renouvier's second 'Essais' and see no reason why his definition of Free Will—'the sustaining of a thought *because I choose to* when I might have other thoughts'—need be the definition of an illusion." It had been at that juncture, William recounted, that he had exultantly declared: "My first act of free will shall be to believe in free will."

To William's undisguised delight, his patient appeared to hang on every word of his psycho-philosophical apologue with an attentiveness he could not have dreamed of eliciting from his blasé undergraduates. Elena's shining green eyes remained raptly fixed upon his expressive face, and as she later confessed in her journal, it was all she could do to suppress a girlish urge to applaud the doctor's oration, enthralled as she was not only by his resonant baritone and keen reasoning but by his arrant passion. (She no doubt also would have been tempted to applaud Leon Edel's astute observation of a century later that "William was all idea and intellect warmed by feeling; Henry was all feeling—intellectualized.")

Having happily ascertained that Elena could read French, William rose again from his desk and retrieved his precious volume of Renouvier's essays from its place of honor on the bookshelf, ardently pressing it upon his patient, who clutched the unlikely prescription to her bosom with such a bright and grateful smile that he may well have found himself wrestling with an impulse to unload his entire library on her. That evening she made the following breathless entry in her diary: "Finally met Dr. William James today. What a *real* person he is! He is in nearly all respects head and shoulders above his brothers, having the largest heart as well as the largest head, and is thoroughly interesting to me."

———•———

Back out in Minnesota, from the far side of the Cannon River bridge, the surviving members of the James-Younger Gang galloped hell-for-leather out of Northfield until they reached Dundas, the village where they had met up that morning. There they stopped briefly to rest and water their steaming horses, bandage their wounds with shreds of clothing, and take stock of their situation, which was clearly dire. Bill Stiles, who was to have served as their guide out along the back roads and byways of the Minnesota countryside, lay dead on Division Street with a bullet through his heart. Clell Miller, his face riddled with birdshot and his subclavian artery severed, had also been killed. (The bodies of the two slain outlaws were unceremoniously dragged off the dusty thoroughfare and hauled into the local photographer's shop, where they were stripped to the waist and propped up on a wooden bench, still oozing blood from their mortal wounds, to be photographed and gawked at by the townspeople.) The majority of the gang members who made it out of town alive had also been shot: Frank James, his arm still smarting from the bank vault door, had taken a bullet in the right thigh. Cole Younger carried at least five slugs in various parts of his anatomy, and Jim Younger held three. Charlie Pitts had a single bullet wound in his left arm. In the worst shape of all was Bob Younger, who was hemorrhaging profusely from his shattered right elbow and leg wound. Of the entire band, only Jesse and Henry James had managed to get through the melee unharmed (although Henry was obliged to endure the discomfort and embarrassment of riding wreathed in a clinging nimbus of his own stink). The whole wild affair had lasted under a quarter hour and had grossed the gang a grand total of—accounts vary— between $26.01 and $26.70.

And their nightmare was only just beginning. In the days and weeks to come, as news of the robbery and killings brattled across the telegraph lines of the state and the nation, the gang would become the quarry of what Jesse's biographer William Settle called "the most widespread manhunt in Minnesota heretofore." More than a thousand men were on their trail at various times, in posses composed of irate citizens, bounty hunters, curiosity seekers, fame-chasers, and professional lawmen, some from as far away as Cincinnati and including policemen and detectives from Minneapolis and St. Paul.

The gang's first encounter with such a group took place late that afternoon in the town of Shieldsville. While watering their horses at a trough outside of Haggerty's saloon, the bandits noticed a pile of rifles and shotguns stacked at the door of the establishment. When the owners of the firearms, a squad of men from nearby Faribault, exited the bar, they found themselves staring straight into the robbers' drawn revolvers. Jesse ordered the posse members not to touch their guns on pain of death, then quickly led the gang out of town before any further bloodshed could be added to the already appreciable charges against them. But the posse, fueled by the Dutch courage of Haggerty's brew, soon collected their weapons and lit out after the fugitives, catching up with them about four miles out of town. After a sobering exchange of gunfire, the Faribault contingent apparently thought better of pressing their pursuit and allowed the desperadoes to slip away into the descending darkness.

The outlaw band took cover for the night in part of a dense forest known locally as "The Big Woods." Wounded, famished, and demoralized, they had nothing to eat and dared not even light a campfire for fear of alerting any additional pursuers to their whereabouts. With banks of ominous clouds gathering in the night sky, they bedded down beneath the pines to the hoots of owls and the distant howls of timber wolves. Henry, still reeking mightily, was made to sleep well away from the rest of the gang—to the extent that he was able to sleep at all. Though his body was wracked with fatigue, the strain of the day's events was beginning to take an even heavier toll on his psyche: It was distressing enough to have lost control of his horse and his bowels; now he may well have feared losing his mind, if not his life. While back in Missouri, his status as a wanted man had seemed merely theoretical—and perhaps even a trifle romantic—that day it had sunk in that there were real men with real guns and real bullets on his trail. Assuming they didn't kill him outright, he realized, no posse would ever credit his outlandish tale of being held hostage by his own brothers. To steady his nerves, the writer tried to force himself to focus on a mental review of the works of Anthony Trollope, a novelist he had once admired as being "charged with something of the big Balzac authority." He hoped to lull himself to sleep with a soothing reverie of that author's quaint and cozy Barsetshire world of venial vicars and dotty dowagers, but— William's felicitous philosophical epiphany notwithstanding—Henry found himself unable to steer his thoughts down the desired path. Instead, he ended up seething with resentment at the Englishman's smug, self-satisfied approach to literature and, by extension, to all of life: Obviously, the genteel Mr. Trollope had never been obliged to re- tire for the evening on the hard, cold ground plastered in his own shit, with a bloodthirsty posse breathing up his ass. Henry wept himself into a fitful slumber.

And then came the rains. Beginning early the following morning and continuing unabated for the next two weeks, a series of torrential downpours swelled streams, washed out bridges, flooded fields, and turned the rural dirt roads into rivers of mud. The deluge proved something of a mixed blessing for the outlaw band: Though it ham- pered their escape, it also washed away their tracks and hindered their pursuers, even to the extent of discouraging many posse members from persevering in their hunt for the bandits. It achieved little, how- ever, toward improving Henry's odor or his state of mind. The pelting rain soaked through his clothing down to his skin, inducing a painful, purulent rash on his legs and rear end and dampening his spirit with a pervasive hopelessness.

Without Bill Stiles or any maps of the region to guide them, and with the sun and stars obscured by furious rain clouds, the fugitives were effectively lost. The best they could do was keep pressing toward what they hoped was the southwest, in the general direction of far-off Missouri. But being unfamiliar with the lay of the land, they were often obliged to seek the guidance of local residents, even of some of the very men who were on their trail—a dangerous exigency that led them on occasion to masquerade as their own pursuers. By the following afternoon, the Cannon River had become unfordable, and the gang was forced to take a detour along the Cordova Road, where they came across a group of workers who had taken shelter from the rain in a makeshift hut. Most of the laborers were German, and Frank addressed them in their native tongue, explaining that he and his companions were part of a posse on the trail of the Northfield robbers and asking where they might safely traverse the swollen stream. When the workers got a whiff of Henry and eyed him inquisitively, Frank came up with a stirring tale of his brother having taken shelter from the robbers in an outhouse and being driven to lower himself into its putrid pit to hide from his assailants. This provided the German roustabouts a hearty laugh, and they cheerfully pointed the way to a nearby bridge.

That night, after two nearly fatal run-ins with posses and a desperate escape across Tetonka Lake, the outlaws set up camp in the woods near the town of Janesville. Jesse and Henry, being the only two gang members with no suspicious wounds to conceal, approached yet another posse camping nearby. The brothers managed to cadge a small supply of victuals for themselves and the others. In response to the inevitable skeptical inquiries about Henry's odor, Jesse told them that his comrade was a halfwit suffering the ill effects of having recently gobbled down a bad batch of peaches.

Whatever fascination the rough-and-ready macho life may have held for Henry James at the outset of his criminal adventure was fading fast, especially during the difficult days that followed, as the gang fell to bickering among themselves about who was responsible for their plight. There were certainly more than enough recriminations to go around: Jesse was berated for his decision to enter the bank when the streets of Northfield were so crowded with pedestrians; Cole Younger was chastised for his cold-blooded gunning down of the drunken Swede; and Frank was admonished for blowing out the brains of the hapless bookkeeper. But much to Henry's dismay, the brunt of the

blame seemed to fall upon him. The author's edgy presence at the robbery, Cole griped, had "thrown us off our game." What was more, the
alpha Younger asserted, Henry's reluctance to whip out his pistols and
join in the shooting had created "a bad impression," emboldening the
townspeople by making the gang appear "a passel of pussies."

Henry's brothers demurred from springing to his defense, which
may have had less to do with any lapse in fraternal solidarity than with
their desperate desire to move on. Jesse, especially, was becoming frustrated with their plodding pace. By September 14—a full week to the
day after the botched robbery—the gang had gotten only as far as the
outskirts of the town of Mankato, a distance of barely fifty miles from
the scene of the crime. And Bob Younger appeared to be on his last
legs: His shattered elbow had become badly infected, leaving him so
weak and dizzy from his high fever and loss of blood that he could
barely hold himself upright in the saddle. He rode clutching the saddle horn with his left hand, while another of the gang led his horse
along by the reins. Jesse made no secret of wanting to abandon the
gravely wounded man to his fate—he argued for "saving six by sacri-
ficing one"—but Cole and Jim Younger were appalled at the notion of
deserting their failing brother.

Frank proposed what he hoped might be a more palatable alternative: He suggested that a group of the less badly wounded men split
off from the others, thereby buying some time for the more severely
injured outlaws to slow down and recuperate while the faster-moving
party divided and diverted their pursuers. In terms of personnel, this
scheme meant that the James brothers and Charlie Pitts would strike
out from the Youngers. It is likely that at this juncture, Frank and
Jesse wanted to leave Henry behind as well, but the Youngers would
have had nothing to do with such a proposition, in part because the
writer had already shown himself to be less than useless under fire,
and in part because, as Cole Younger indelicately put it, he "stunk like
shit." (After a week in the saddle, none of the crew smelled like roses,
but Henry's fecal fragrance had by then risen to a high ripeness that

his comrades found truly rebarbative. As William James pointed out in his discussion of the "native repugnancy" of "excrementitious and putrid things" in his *Principles of Psychology:* "That *we dislike in others things which we tolerate in ourselves* is a law of our aesthetic nature about which there can be no doubt.") Frank and Jesse reluctantly assented to taking their malodorous brother along with them, if only to seal the deal; at which point Charlie Pitts, though but slightly injured himself, opted to throw in his lot with the more badly wounded yet less odiferous Youngers.

There has long been an assumption on the part of some historians that the two outlaw groups must have parted ways on less than amicable terms, but such a supposition is belied by Cole Younger's subsequent testimony that the Jameses took off "with the knowledge and consent of the others." More tellingly, before splitting up, the Youngers turned over a number of their personal belongings to Frank and Jesse for safekeeping, along with the bulk of what remained of the fat Rocky Cut bankroll—a sum that must have been considerable. Minnesota historian John Koblas cited a news story from the *Faribault Democrat* in which the fleeing James brothers were later reported to have stopped at a farmhouse to purchase a loaf of bread, a hat, and two grain sacks. "One of the men," wrote Koblas, "took out a wad of bills, which according to the farmer, was as long as his arm. It consisted mostly of $100 and $50 bills, and they paid him a dollar and a half."

————◆————

The morning after their first meeting, Elena Hite arrived back at William's Harvard office for a follow-up visit, still aglow with the warmth of the doctor's free-will pep talk of the previous afternoon. Indeed, that therapeutic encounter seemed to have bolstered both of their spirits. In place of his informal shirtsleeves of the day before, William was sporting a natty box-pleated belted tweed jacket, striped trousers, a sky-blue Italian silk foulard, and an impeccably polished pair of dark tan oxfords. He had always been something of a dandy—his letters to Henry in Europe were frequently larded with requests for special-order apparel and accessories to be shipped from the continent—and Elena had apparently brought out the Beau Brummel in him. ("We so appropriate our clothes and identify ourselves with them," he once wrote, "that there are few of us who, if asked to choose between having a beautiful body clad in raiment perpetually shabby and un-clean, and having an ugly and blemished form always spotlessly attired, would not hesitate a moment before making a decisive reply.")

Elena handed William back his volume of Renouvier's *Essais,* which she had dutifully perused overnight; although, as she sheep-ishly confessed, between the difficult French and the arcane philo-sophical jargon, much of it had left her head spinning. Fortunately, the professor reassured her, he had no intention of administering a quiz, gallantly adding that even he had struggled with the book in his initial readings.

The doctor and his patient fell back into a comfortable colloquy, the stream of their conversation meandering even farther afield from typi-cal consulting-room material than it had the day before, as whatever pretense of a clinical cast they may have tried to maintain dissipated into a fizzy orgy of general chat. William, whom Henry's biographer Lyndall Gordon called "the most captivating of the Jameses," must have been at his most scintillating. (As his sister, Alice, once wrote of him, "he is simply himself, a creature who speaks in another language as Henry says from the rest of mankind and who would lend life and charm to a treadmill.") Elena, having long been frozen out of Asa Hite's confidence, reveled in the opportunity to partake in the kind of precocious and sassy badinage with an older male authority figure that she had always yearned to share with her father. William, for his part, was falling easily into the avuncular role of mentor, a stance that was always charged for him, according to his biographer Linda Simon, with "a decidedly romantic, if not erotic, aura."

They discovered, among other common interests, a shared love of painting and a mutual connection to that discipline in the person of the French artist Thomas Couture, who had instructed both Elena's degenerate guru George Stanley and William's former teacher William Morris Hunt. While studying with Hunt in Newport during the early 1860s, William told Elena, he had briefly entertained an adolescent flirtation with making a career in painting, an ambition that had devolved into yet another contest of wills between himself and Henry Sr.; despite his effusive admiration for Art in the abstract, William's father, in Linda Simon's phrase, was "repulsed by the idea that his son would engage in an occupation so spiritually and intellectually vacuous." (Another of William's biographers, Howard M. Feinstein, diagnosed his abandonment of his dream to stain canvases for a living as nothing less than a form of "self-murder.") At least on this occasion, William maintained that he had never really regretted his decision to pursue science over art, and that he had even found his trained painterly eye a distinct asset in his subsequent endeavors, especially his study of anatomy, in which it had sharpened his ability to discern and delineate the underlying structural secrets of the human form.

"Oh and what, pray tell, do you discern in mine?" Elena laughingly asked. By her own admission, she had a "boundless appetite" for knowing how she appeared to others, whether in her public speaking, in her romantic relationships, or even, in this case, as the subject of a clinical evaluation. (During her own adolescent fling with brush and canvas, she had once executed a challenging dual study of her lovely face and its reflection in a limpid lotus pool—actually, George Stanley's watering trough—that she had pointedly titled *Narcissa*.)

Rising to Elena's teasing challenge, William picked up a drawing pad and began to sketch out a likeness of his patient. This artistic exercise not only gave him license to shamelessly ogle her alluring contours, it also facilitated their conversational give-and-take, allowing him to elicit an informal psychiatric history of his model.

As she posed for William's pen, Elena rambled back over the bleak landscape of her isolated childhood—her mother's long illness; her father's relentless pushing of her into society; and her often testy relationships with her schoolmates, to whom she felt intellectually superior yet socially inferior. William, who was as much fascinated with the female mind as Henry—although without enjoying his literary brother's seemingly effortless ability to vibrate sympathetically to its mysterious wavelengths—was especially intrigued by Elena's paradoxical mélange of both very high and very low self-regard and her penchant for whipsawing from one to the other with alarming alacrity. He wondered if this might have anything to do with her unconventional behavior.

Perhaps taking her cue from William's confession of his clash with Henry Sr. over the aborted painting career, Elena mused that her behavior—or, more properly, as she knew he meant, her *mis*behavior—might have been a way of "getting back at my father." William cannily remarked that, as things had turned out, it seemed rather to have gotten her back *to* her father. (This was the sort of observation that was to become commonplace among Freudian analysts in the next century, though in 1876 Freud himself was still a mere medical student, dissecting the reproductive organs of eels, with psychoanalysis barely a glint in his ambitious eye.)

The doctor and his patient might have carried on in this affable vein indefinitely, but when Elena reached across William's desk to accept his sketch for closer inspection, her eye happened to fall upon a copy of that morning's edition of *The Boston Daily Globe,* which lay atop the cluttered surface. At the bottom of the newspaper's front page was a small headline reporting that a daring daylight bank robbery and murder had been perpetrated the day before out in Northfield, Minnesota.

Elena blanched.

William, who had picked up the paper on his way to the office and tossed it onto his desktop without having scanned its contents, was oblivious to the headline, which, in any event, contained no mention of the Jameses or the Youngers by name. But he couldn't help observing the plunge to pallor of Elena's normally rosy complexion, nor the fact that her gaze was directed elsewhere than toward his painstaking draftsmanship.

Elena was in a quandary. She was confident that William could have had no notion of her connection to the western Jameses, but she couldn't be certain whether he was aware of his own. If, as she believed, he had been in correspondence with Henry, he might well have known of the existence of his outlaw brothers in Missouri; yet he would have had little reason to link them to the cursory newspaper headline, which specified only that the crimes had been perpetrated in distant Minnesota. Elena, on the other hand, had ample reason to suspect that the gang had been planning to strike far from their usual hunting grounds and thus intuited the true import of the news item before her. To extricate herself from this awkward impasse, she hastily fabricated a cover story, claiming that she had recently lectured in Northfield and was simply flabbergasted to imagine that charming little college town being the scene of such heinous acts.

At this point William and Elena brought their heads together over the newspaper and perused the story more closely. The body of the text was short on particulars, having been pieced together hastily from sketchy telegraphed reports the previous evening, but buried near the end of the item were indeed speculations from local lawmen that the crime may have been the work of the notorious James Gang of Missouri.

Now it was William's turn to blanch.

———◆———

No longer encumbered by the more severely wounded Youngers, the three James brothers, riding freshly stolen horses, at last began to make better time across the sodden North Star terrain, heading due west toward the Dakota Territory. But with posses closing in on them from all points of the compass, ad pickets posted at practically every bridge and crossroads they reached, the Jameses found that after over twenty-four hours of hard riding, they had driven their new horses into the ground. Hoping to throw off their trackers, they dismounted and shooed the worn-out animals in three different directions to serve as decoys.

Now they were on foot and moving slowly over the soggy landscape. Frank cut a makeshift walking stick from a fallen tree branch, but his progress was still ponderous and painful, the old foot wound from the cannister ball he had taken at Fort Wagner adding to the burden of his more recent injuries. Further impeding their pace, Henry's back had begun to act up, obliging him to halt repeatedly to fight off crippling dorsal spasms. The brothers appeared to be approaching the endgame of their flight.

On the evening of September 15, the exhausted trio hobbled up to the door of an isolated farmhouse west of Lake Crystal. Frank, again flexing his polyglot aptitude, explained to the old German immigrant couple who greeted them that he and his colleagues were part of a posse on the trail of the notorious Northfield bandits. They had gotten separated from their fellows, he went on, when the brigands they were chasing had shot their horses out from under them. He then flashed a fistful of greenbacks and offered to pay handsomely for a solid meal and a night's lodging. Even before he could launch into whatever fanciful explanation he had concocted to account for his comrade's stench, the old couple graciously welcomed them in—on the condition that Henry leave his fetid garments outside by the hog pen.

After over a week of sloughing through the mire of the Minnesota plains on horseback and on foot, the Jameses found the humble clapboard shanty a veritable palace of luxury. While the old hausfrau prepared a hearty repast of pigs' knuckles, sauerkraut, and corn biscuits, the brothers took turns bathing in her commodious washtub. Not only did this afford Henry the blessed opportunity to rid himself of his detested odor, it also proved a soothing boon to his aching back. To top off his ablutions and alter his appearance for the first time since the days of the Civil War—and for the last time he would ever do so again until his hair began to gray at the turn of the new century—he shaved off his luxuriant beard.

Just as he was emerging from the tub, he heard the distant nickering of horses and the muffled clamor of male voices outside the cabin.

In the kitchen, the famished Frank and Jesse were about to take their places at the table. Announcing in German that he feared the dreaded robber gang might be approaching, Frank got up and hustled the old couple out the back door and into the woodshed behind the shack "for their own safety." Meanwhile, Jesse dashed into the bedroom and ordered Henry to slip into a faded gingham housedress belonging to the old woman, while he himself threw on a pair of her husband's patched denim overalls. To complete his disguise, Henry knotted a kerchief around his balding pate as the men outside began knocking insistently on the door.

Concerned that they might still be recognizable, the brothers scrambled into the kitchen and hastily applied a layer of sooty grease from the stove as blackface. Henry's entire experience of the colored race had been limited to accepting hors d'oeuvres from the occasional servant and listening to the orations of Frederick Douglass, but Jesse told him not to worry. Citing his deeper familiarity with the Negro dialect and mannerisms from his stint with the Massachusetts 55th, the former Union officer insisted on doing all the talking.

"I'se a'comin', I'se a'comin'!" he muttered, shuffling toward the door. The pounding of gloved knuckles was now accompanied by the ominous ostinato of a heavy boot or rifle butt. Jesse opened it to reveal four men wearing glistening rubber rain slickers and carrying lanterns and carbines.

"Yassuh, massuh?" he greeted the leader, a deputy sheriff named Seward Bovell from the town of New Ulm, to the west. (Fortunately for the Jameses, the posse included no local residents, who might have been familiar with the proper inhabitants of the shanty.)

"Evening," said Bovell. "We're looking for some men. Have you seen any strangers in the vicinity?"

"Ah ain' neva bin to no city," Jesse replied.

"The *vicinity*. The *area*. Have you seen any strange men around these parts?"

"Oh, yassuh! Ah do believe dey wuz some dat come by a wile b'fo', but dey be long gone now."

The deputy peered over Jesse's shoulder into the kitchen, which was lit only by a flickering oil lamp. The table, he could see, had been set for more than a couple. "What's your name, boy?" Bovell inquired.

"Dey calls me Juicy, suh," Jesse replied with a wide ingratiating smile. "An' dis heah be my woman . . . Saliva."

Henry looked askance at his brother.

"Pleased to meet you," said the deputy. "Expecting company, are you, Juicy?"

"Oh, yassuh, we is," Jesse extemporized. "De chilluns a-gwyne be comin' by fo' suppah dis ebenin'. Ain' dat so, Sal?" He took Henry's hand and gazed into his brother's eyes in a touching pantomime of parental pride, which apparently failed to mollify the lawman.

"Hmmmm. Mind if we just take a little look around?"

Without waiting for a response, Bovell and his men barged in and began inspecting the shack, flinging open closets and peering under beds and behind doors while Jesse and Henry, who had secreted their revolvers in the vegetable bin, stood helplessly by. At last, seemingly satisfied that there were no signs of their quarry, the intruders snatched a few biscuits off the kitchen table and headed for the door. "Now, if you see those fellows coming back around here, you'd best be real careful," cautioned the deputy. "They robbed the bank at North-field last week and shot two men dead."

"Lawsy me!" ejaculated Henry in a cracking falsetto, his eyes widening in a grotesque burlesque of fear.

Jesse shot his brother an irritated glance. "Well, I sho' hopes you be ketchin' dem ebil mens!" he called out after the posse as they withdrew back into the night.

As soon as the interlopers were safely out of hearing, Henry and Jesse pointed at each other's outlandish appearance and burst into hysterical laughter. It was not simply a release of the tension that set them off, nor even the minstrel-show silliness of their getups. At some level the brothers must have recognized that the "literary transvestite" and the "nigger of the James family" had managed to effect a transformation into avatars of their shadow selves.

Without even bothering to sample what was left on the kitchen table, the exhausted Henry staggered into the bedroom to collapse into a profound and dreamless sleep.

When he awoke the next morning, he discovered that Frank and Jesse were nowhere on the premises. He looked around the shack, calling out their names, at first tentatively, then with increasing volume and urgency. Nothing. No one. They were gone—their clothing, their guns, every trace of them. Still, it was not until he came upon a generous wad of high-denomination banknotes thoughtfully tucked into one of his boots that it fully dawned on Henry that his brothers had actually deserted him. He secreted the bills down the bosom of his gingham dress and stepped outside the shack. The old German couple's only horse, an ancient half-blind draft animal, was also gone, apparently expropriated by the outlaw pair. They must have skedaddled riding double on the old plug, he surmised.

For the first time in months, Henry James was totally alone. He stood by the front door with the rain gently pitter-pattering on the leaves around him, breathing in the fresh, cool air of freedom.

Shortly, he became aware that his solitude was not quite so absolute as he had supposed. Hearing muffled sniffling from behind the cabin, he went around back to the woodshed, where he discovered the old immigrants, whom Frank had taken the precaution of binding and gagging for the night. They were tied back to back, wide-eyed with fear, and seeing Henry approach in his gingham getup and greasy blackface only compounded their manifest distress.

Henry stepped forward to release them but then thought better of the idea, realizing that by doing so he might be sorely jeopardizing his chances of escape: If he freed the couple before departing, there would be little to stop them from siccing the law on him the moment he was out of sight. Leaving his hosts tied up was, to be sure, unspeakably discourteous, especially in light of their generous hospitality of the previous evening, but Henry's standards of politesse had deteriorated precipitously over the past few weeks, and at least, as he may have consoled himself, he wasn't about to *shoot* them, as the boorish Cole Younger might well have done.

———◆———

During the week following his consultations with Elena Hite, William James became morbidly preoccupied with the manhunt for what *The Boston Daily Globe* called "the Minnesota Brigands." He believed he had managed to get through his final session with Elena without tipping his hand regarding his relationship to the robbers. (On that score, he and his patient had arrived at a Mexican standoff, neither revealing to the other the extent of their connections to the western Jameses, both only lamenting that whatever had transpired out in Northfield seemed a sorry commentary on the state of morality and public order in these United States.) As further details emerged about the holdup and its aftermath, it became increasingly apparent that the infamous Frank and Jesse James were indeed among the fugitive suspects, although there was no mention of Henry. In fact, it remained unclear how many outlaws had taken part in the crime, with some eyewitnesses confidently claiming to have counted eight, while others were equally certain there had been nine. William, always the man of two minds, found himself torn between an up-standing desire to see justice righteously rendered and a furtive frater-nal loyalty that kept him rooting for the perpetrators to make a clean getaway.

Despite being on tenterhooks over the fate of his brothers, the doc-tor dutifully reported back to Asa Hite on his daughter's condition, noting in his best clinical deadpan that Elena appeared to be "a very interesting young lady of abundant charm and high intelligence," who was clearly distraught but not, in his considered medical opin-ion, seriously ill. (She seemed to be suffering, William informally di-agnosed, "more from a broken heart than a broken nervous system.") Under the circumstances, the only treatment he could recommend—which he offered somewhat apologetically—was that conventional Victorian therapy for youthful malaise, a European Grand Tour. ("Europe," wrote Jean Strouse, "had always served as the ultimate James family panacea.") But Mr. Hite, not surprisingly, was worried that his daughter, left unchaperoned on that wicked and worldly con-tinent, might revert to what he indelicately termed her "wild ways." He therefore sought to arrange—also following the conventional wis-dom of the age—that she be accompanied on her therapeutic sojourn by a more mature female companion, for which position Dr. James shamelessly proposed his sister, Alice.

In prescribing Alice James as a duenna for Elena, William may not have been acting solely in the interest of his patient. As we have noted, he had ample reason to be concerned about his sister—a woman who once wrote, "I was born bad, and I have never recovered." After a long summer of helping to nurse her ailing father through the recuperation from his stroke, Alice was beginning to show the signs of strain that often heralded one of her nervous attacks. Especially troubling to William was the apparent negative effect upon his sister of his bur-geoning romance with—and potential marriage to—his "other" Alice, Miss Gibbens. Within the James family, William and his sister had al-ways enjoyed a unique relationship: As Alice was growing up, her oldest brother had developed a teasing, flirtatious mode of dealing with her, lavishing facetiously fulsome praise on her feminine charms and graces, addressing her by such provocative epithets as "Chérie Charmante de Bal," "Charmante Jeune Fille," "Sweetlet" and even "You lovely babe." This playfully seductive tone had both pleased and confused the maturing girl, but with the arrival of the redoubtable Alice Gibbens upon the scene, their special bond was threatening to unravel. As Jean Strouse observed: "Whatever agitation William's flirtatious attentions caused his sister, they also flattered and excited her—and they were the only consistent, overt, amorous attentions she ever received from a man. . . . She returned his mocking banter, and undoubtedly, in a suppressed way, his sexual curiosity. His engagement to a paragon of health and virtue was a profound betrayal."

Indeed, William's "engagement," though not yet formalized, threatened to deal a double blow to his high-strung sister: Not only did it represent the definitive dashing of whatever hopes Alice may have entertained that he would always be there for her, it also increased the likelihood that she would be left alone to care for their aging parents, setting in stone her incipient status as a spinster. "While friend after friend became engaged and married," wrote Linda Simon, "Alice . . . was convinced that she would never marry, that she was not the pretty, winsome, flirtatious young woman her brother had invented, but one among the 'depressed & gloomy females' doomed to become old maids."

By way of compensation for his "betrayal," William no doubt hoped that an all-expenses-paid trip abroad might have as much of a salutary effect upon his sister as upon Asa Hite's distressed daughter. Fortunately, in spite of her manifold afflictions, Alice James presented socially as a thoroughly sober—indeed, somewhat dour—lady of impeccable breeding. Seven years Elena's senior, painfully plain of feature and impeccably proper (not to say rigid) of demeanor, she must have struck Asa Hite as the ideal governess for the unruly engine of his errant daughter's impulsivity.

Elena, for her part, was exhilarated by the prospect of going abroad—of being able to experience, at long last, "a Paris of her own." That she would be accompanied to the storied city by yet another member of the endlessly intriguing James clan rendered her anticipation all the more delectable. And while Alice James, long familiar with the treasures and pleasures of old Europe, took her assignment in stride, William frequently found himself unprofessionally obsessed with imagining how it all would register in Elena's unseasoned yet uniquely acute perceptions. By now, in addition to their mutual interest in painting, the grand conundrum of free will, and an abiding curiosity concerning current events out in Minnesota, the doctor and his patient had something else in common: They were both entranced with Elena Hite.

Chapter Eight

—— ◆ ——

Henry James set sail for Europe from New York Harbor aboard the Cunarder *Bothnia* on October 1, 1876. It was a rough autumn crossing; the capricious currents of the North Atlantic played relentless havoc upon the always delicate Jamesian digestive apparatus. Though the luxury liner, built only two years earlier, boasted the world's first shipboard library, the fugitive author was barely able to read, let alone write, and spent most of the voyage sequestered in his cabin. But his gastric discomforts on this long final leg of his flight from Minnesota were mitigated by the heady exhilaration of escape as the powerful steamer put thousands of watery miles between himself and the law.

From the little shack near Lake Crystal, he had made his way to St. Peter, where, having scrubbed the kitchen grease off his face and swapped his kerchief and gingham frock for more conventionally masculine attire, he had boarded a train for Minneapolis, from whence he had traveled on to Chicago and ultimately to New York. Throughout his journey east, like William in Cambridge, he had kept anxiously scouring the papers for news of the Minnesota manhunt. Thankfully, he had come upon no accounts of any old German couple being found dead in their woodshed in the vicinity of Lake Crystal. But according to widely published reports, on September 21, a posse from Madelia, under the command of Sheriff James Glispin of Watonwan County, had cornered the Younger brothers and Charlie Pitts in a desolate swamp called Hanska Slough. During the ensuing gun battle, Pitts had been killed and the Youngers—badly shot up—had been forced to surrender. They were currently being held awaiting trial in the jail at Faribault, where, to Henry's immense relief, despite whatever animosity or disdain they may have felt toward him, Cole and his brothers were apparently keeping faith with the outlaw code of silence by refusing to divulge the identities of their accomplices in the Northfield robbery. ("Be true to your friends if the Heavens fall," Cole Younger was reported to have scrawled in a note to Sheriff Glispin.)

Frank and Jesse remained at large. Henry perused numerous—and often wildly conflicting—accounts of his brothers being spotted, either on horseback or on foot, all across Minnesota and even into Iowa. One dispatch, from the *Sioux City Daily Journal,* noted: "The greatest excitement prevails, and armed squads are moving to and fro continually. The hundreds of men engaged in the chase appear to have no head or organized leaders, and consequently the chances of catching the fleeing ruffians are growing fainter and fainter each succeeding day." Nonetheless, Henry had become convinced that he ought not to count on his brothers continuing to elude their pursuers, nor on the incarcerated Youngers to keep holding their tongues. His best chance for survival, he reckoned—in keeping with his lifelong propensity for expatriating himself—would be to skip the country as soon as possible. Immediately upon reaching Manhattan, he dispensed part of the money Frank and Jesse had left in his boot on a first-class ticket aboard the *Bothnia.*

Upon arriving in Paris, he nestled gratefully into the welcoming bosom of the old city, taking up lodgings on the fashionable *rive droite* in a furnished fourth-floor apartment at 29, rue de Luxembourg (the present-day rue Cambon). He described his new digs in a letter to his father—his first correspondence with the old man since early summer—as "a snug little *troisième,* with the eastern sun, two bedrooms, a parlor, an antechamber and a kitchen. Furniture clean and pretty, house irreproachable, and a gem of a *portier,* who waits on me." The porter cost Henry six dollars a month; his rent was about sixty-five dollars; his woodpile was five dollars; and his linens were under two—all of which he was able to afford quite comfortably out of what remained of his "take" from the Rocky Cut swag. Safely ensconced amid the ornate clocks, graceful candelabras, and gleaming copper casseroles of his "eminently congenial" new abode, Henry doubtless would have liked nothing better than to have put the traumata of his recent western sojourn behind him; but being "one upon whom nothing is lost"—his famous prescription as the primary qualification for a novelist—he clearly had trouble shaking off his harrowing memories of the previous three months. By way of distraction, exorcism, and reclamation of his proper *métier,* he immersed himself in a frenzy of literary composition.

The novel into which he threw himself at this time, *The American,* has often been criticized for its overabundance of melodramatic elements, including the protagonist's shocking discovery that the mother of his lover had murdered her husband. William Dean Howells, Henry's editor at *The Atlantic Monthly,* in which the work was serialized, begged the author to tone down these Gothic flourishes, but he refused. For ample reason, family secrets—including murder—must have been very much on his mind that autumn.

Also on his mind was the plight of an American struggling to pierce the hermetic bubble of Parisian society. Fresh from his escapades on the frontier, he saw the cultural chasm between the old and new worlds—always a major Jamesian theme—as yawning far wider than he had ever imagined. It should hardly be surprising that he made Christopher

Newman, the protagonist of his work in progress, not merely an American but a hardy westerner to boot, undoubtedly modeled on the physically robust specimens in whose company he had so reluctantly spent the summer. ("Exertion and action," he wrote in describing his title character, "were as natural to him as respiration; a more completely healthy mortal had never trod the elastic soil of the West.")

Unlike his fictional Newman, Henry James was no stranger to the City of Light. Throughout his life, from early childhood, he had been a frequent visitor to the luminous capital. His French, both spoken and written, was impeccable. He had, according to Leon Edel, "a thorough knowledge of the riches of the language and consciously cultivated gallicisms in his English, even as he liberally sowed his earlier prose and even the late with French words." Yet it was one thing to be fluent in the language and conversant with the literature; it would be quite another to crack the rarified coterie of those who actually produced it.

Henry's entrée into the citadel of Parisian literary society was to be a fellow foreigner, the great Russian author Ivan Sergeyevich Turgenev, whose books Henry had read in French and German translations and whom he deemed quite possibly "the first novelist of the day." Two years earlier, on a previous European junket, Henry had written a laudatory essay on Turgenev's fiction for *The North American Review,* praising the Russian's work for its "commingled realism and idealism" and admiring how, in Turgenev's hands, "abstract possibilities immediately become, to his vision, concrete situations." By way of realizing his own abstract possibility of one day meeting his admired subject in the flesh, Henry had mailed a copy of his belletristic mash note to Turgenev in Baden-Baden, following up a few weeks later with a visit in person to the posh spa town—only to discover by the time he arrived that the cosmopolitan author had already decamped for Carlsbad to recover from an attack of gout. Turgenev did, however, answer Henry by post, noting that his review was "inspired by a fine sense of what is just and true," adding that "there is manliness in it and psychological sagacity and a clear literary taste." The Russian gave Henry his Paris address in the rue de Douai and concluded, "It would please me very much indeed to make your acquaintance as well as that of your compatriots."

Now, having settled into his cozy Right Bank flat, Henry wasted little time in redeeming his two-year-old rain check with the Russian literary giant. Number 50, rue de Douai, perched along one of the steep winding streets of Montmartre, was a three-story *maison particulière* set back from the sidewalk behind a low stone wall. There Turgenev cohabited in a long-standing ménage à trois with the French-Spanish operatic prima donna Pauline Garcia-Viardot and her considerably older husband, the French writer Louis Viardot—a scandalous domestic arrangement dating back to their 1843 meeting in St. Petersburg, when the acclaimed soprano was only twenty-one. When Henry arrived chez Turgenev promptly at eleven on the appointed morning, Ivan Sergeyevich greeted his transatlantic visitor warmly and ushered him up into the small sitting room on the second floor. For a novelist's lair, the room struck Henry as surprisingly spare and neat, with only a few books and not a scrap of paper or a writing implement in sight, as if "the traces of work had been carefully removed." Other than "several choice pictures of the modern French school, especially a very fine specimen of prime canvas of Théodore Rousseau," the entire chamber—from the walls to the furniture to the portière—was decorated in various shades of green. The centerpiece of the room was an "immeasurable" divan—also in green—that appeared to have been specially constructed to accommodate Turgenev's enormous frame; the Russian writer proved to be not only a literary giant but a literal one as well. As Henry later described his host:

> It would have been impossible to imagine a better representation of a Nimrod of the North. He was exceedingly tall, and broad and robust in proportion. His head was one of the finest, and though the line of his features was irregular there was a

great deal of beauty in his face. It was eminently of the Russian type—almost everything in it was wide. His expression had a singular sweetness, with a touch of Slav languor, and his eye, the kindest of eyes, was deep and melancholy. His hair, abundant and straight, was as white as silver; and his beard, which he wore trimmed rather short, was of the colour of his hair. In all his tall person . . . there was an air of neglected strength, as if it had been part of his modesty never to remind himself that he was strong.

The Russian proved as powerful conversationally as he appeared physically. Over the course of the next two hours, Henry found his host to be "the richest, the most delightful, of talkers" as the Stendhal of the Steppes shared with his guest some of the secrets of his method of composition, in which, to Henry's immense approval, character— character expressed, character exposed—always came before story. It was his habit, Turgenev revealed, to begin each new work by compiling a detailed dossier on the personages he wished to present, much as a detective might put together a description of the physique, psychology, habits, and social background of his prime criminal suspects. (Here Henry, who, so far as he knew, still had a price on his head, began flushing uncontrollably—a notably peculiar response to a bit of literary chitchat, which the baffled Russian courteously disregarded.) James found Turgenev "a delightful, mild, masculine figure." According to Leon Edel: "Henry had come prepared to like him for his novels. Instead he found a human being he could love."

But the ambitious American was out for even bigger game: He confided to his newfound friend his desire to make the acquaintance of the most eminent fellow practitioners of their art in France, most especially the illustrious Gustave Flaubert, of whom he knew Turgenev to be an intimate. To Henry's unutterable delight, his host offered to take him to the upcoming *réunion* of Flaubert's celebrated *cénacle*, his weekly gathering of the brightest literary lights on the Parisian scene.

Among the world's great novelists the author of *Madame Bovary* occupied a unique niche in James's literary pantheon. Henry's unabashed veneration of Flaubert was born of an indelible incident from his European youth: While staying in Paris with his family in 1856, he had happened upon a copy of the *Revue de Paris* on a table in his father's study. Flipping through the pages of that distinctive yellow-bound periodical, the adolescent author-to-be was drawn to the title *Madame Bovary: Moeurs de Province,* which struck him as "mysteriously arresting, inscrutably charged." For the rest of his life, he would be able to evoke with striking clarity the image of his juvenile self standing before the fire, his back against "the low beplushed and begarnished French chimney-piece" as he greedily devoured the excerpt, knowing nothing of what had preceded it nor of what was to follow, but thoroughly entranced by the vibrant world Flaubert had conjured up on the pages before him. For Henry, as his biographer Robert LeClair described it, the experience had proved "little short of historic," establishing as it did the literary benchmark against which the fledgling writer would measure his own productions for decades to come. Describing Flaubert's masterpiece years later, he would enthuse that "the accumulation of detail is so immense, the vividness of portraiture of people, of things, of places, of times and hours, is so poignant and convincing, that one is dragged into the very current and tissue of the story; the reader seems to have lived in it all, more than in any novel I can recall."

In Flaubert, Henry had discovered "the novelist's novelist." He was particularly admiring of the exacting attention paid by the Frenchman—who, rumor had it, had once spent three full days polishing a single sentence—to producing "perfect phrases, perfectly interrelated, and as closely woven together as a suit of chain-mail." Flaubert, as he later wrote, was "the model for us all."

It was thus with considerable awe and no small measure of trepidation that Henry set out with Turgenev the following weekend to participate in one of Flaubert's famous "Sunday afternoons." Scrambling after the huge Russian up five long flights of stairs to Flaubert's Parisian roost at the end of the rue du Faubourg Saint-Honoré, Henry doubtless would gladly have endured all the dangers, discomforts, and indignities of the previous months a thousand times over if such were the price of being brought to this giddy pinnacle.

Gustave Flaubert himself came to the door and embraced Turgenev as if greeting a long-lost brother. The great French author was wearing "a long colloquial dressing gown" with matching trousers, an outfit that served only to accentuate his "massive physical development." He was largely bald, with his sparse allotment of hair falling in a shaggy mane over the back of his collar. His eyes were pale and "salient," his complexion ruddy and splotchy, his long leonine mustaches swept back along the sides of his prominent jowls. His most striking physical trait was his sheer size: Contemporary observers invariably likened the impression he created to that of a bear or an ox; but to Henry James, the big Frenchman resembled rather a "weather-beaten old military man," calling to his mind nothing so much as an aged Gallic incarnation of Cole Younger.

Flaubert welcomed his guests into a narrow, high-ceilinged salon that Henry found "bare and provisional" in its furnishings, with the striking exception of a great gilded statue of the Buddha gazing down beatifically over the proceedings from its perch of honor on the mantelpiece. For all his girth and forbidding fierceness of mien, Henry's host turned out to be surprisingly gentle and soft-spoken, even timid, as he introduced his transatlantic visitor to the others on hand that afternoon. Among these notables were Edmond de Goncourt, Alphonse Daudet, Émile Zola, and Guy de Maupassant—a veritable who's who of contemporary French realism. And in refreshing contrast to the discourse of Henry's erstwhile colleagues—which had been largely confined to "guns, whores, and horses"—the talk in Flaubert's salon gave the young novelist the intoxicating sense of experiencing genuine con versation for the first time in his life. "What was discussed in that little smoke-clouded room," he later recorded, "was chiefly questions of taste, questions of art and form; and the speakers, for the most part, were in aesthetic matters, radicals of the deepest dye," by which he meant that they shared "the conviction that art and morality are two perfectly different things, and that the former has no more to do with the latter than it has with astronomy or embryology." The only duty of a novel, in the credo of Flaubert's coterie, "was to be well written; that merit included every other of which it was capable."

The afternoon went by in a heady haze of thick smoke and brilliant talk. Though Henry spoke less than the others—in deference to their seniority in the clique and their daunting virtuosity with the French tongue—he felt that he acquitted himself admirably, an impression that was confirmed at the end of the day when his host effusively invited him to return the following Sunday. Later, in his journal, Henry described Flaubert as having "a powerful, serious, melancholy, manly, deeply corrupted, yet not corrupting nature." As Leon Edel wrote, "He liked the man; he was not at all what his books had led him to suspect; and there were moments when he was to wonder whether he wasn't fonder of Flaubert than of Turgenev."

Henry could not help but dwell on the similarities he saw between himself and his literary hero: Both were votaries at the altar of *le mot juste.* ("We believe," Henry wrote, "there is a certain particular phrase, better than any other, for everything in the world, and the thoroughly accomplished writer ends by finding it.") On a more personal level, neither author had ever married, both had briefly attended law school in youth, and both were subject to frequent bouts of ill health—in Flaubert's case, periodic attacks of epilepsy, among other ailments. But there the similarities abruptly ended; for while the American was a fastidious virgin who prided himself on propriety, refinement, and the keeping of a high moral tone in both his life and work, the Frenchman was a notorious *débauché* who wallowed in gluttony, absinthe, alcohol, tobacco, and fornication. On their way home, Turgenev confided to his new American friend his conviction that the trouble with Flaubert was that he had never known a decent woman, or even one that was a little interesting, having passed his life exclusively *"avec des courtisanes et des riens-du-tout"*—an endless, fruitless series of infatuations and dalliances with prostitutes and actresses—Rachel Félix, Marie Dorval, Apollonie Sabatier, Alice Pasca, Béatrix Person, and Sarah Bernhardt, among countless others.

This juicy tidbit of Parisian literary gossip was, for Henry, the cherry on the pudding. Only a month earlier, he had been dodging bullets, coated in his own diarrhea; now here he was, dishing on the author of *Madame Bovary* with the first novelist of the day. Back in his cozy apartment that evening, he stretched out blissfully on the plush chaise longue in his parlor with a glass of port to let the splendid impressions of the afternoon wash over him and percolate in his consciousness. At last the sweet potentialities of his new life in the French capital promised to eclipse the sordid memories of Missouri and Minnesota as he picked up the thread of his artistic destiny among his true peers. He felt that he had taken a seat in the council of the gods. *"Je suis lancé en plein Olympe,"* he wrote a few days later to his old boyhood friend Thomas Sergeant Perry.

But Henry James, who once called Europe "the great American sedative," was about to find the old continent anything but tranquilizing: His euphoric musings were abruptly intruded upon by the appearance at the parlor door of his stalwart *portier,* who discreetly knocked, entered the chamber, and handed his employer a note announcing the recent arrival in Paris of his sister, Alice, and her traveling companion, a young lady by the name of Miss Elena Hite.

———◆———

That very evening, on the other side of the Atlantic, William James was delivering a public lecture at Harvard's Museum of Comparative

Zoology His talk was entitled "Foundations for a Scientific Psychology," the topic closest to his professional heart that autumn and one that was intimately bound up with his hopes to establish a laboratory of experimental psychology at the university.

"We now believe that the uniform correlation of brain-states and mind-states is a law of nature," Professor James informed his audience, explaining that the emergence of psychology from the ethereal realms of metaphysics and into the empirical rigors of the laboratory was largely the result of its recent alliance with the science of physiology, a field in which new discoveries about the functionings of the central nervous system were promising to shed fascinating fresh light on the ancient mysteries of perception, emotion, cognition, memory, attention, and will.

Among William's listeners on this occasion was President Charles W. Eliot of Harvard; Louis Agassiz's son, Alexander, who was running the museum that his late naturalist father, Louis, had founded; and of course, William's faithful new cheerleader and amanuensis Alice Gibbens, who had labored with him for weeks in preparing his address and with whom he had rehearsed it ad nauseam all that afternoon. Front and center in the crowd sat Asa Hite of Hartford, whom William had expressly invited with the unconcealed agenda of hitting up "the old porker" (as he often ungraciously referred to his potential benefactor behind that gentleman's ample posterior) for a generous donation to help fund his planned laboratory. Following his consultations with Elena in September, William had struck up a lively correspondence with the Connecticut railroad tycoon, cementing the bond that had been established when Alice James signed on as Hite's daughter's traveling companion. Mr. Hite prided himself on keeping abreast of all modern developments in science and technology—an informational appetite that was not, however, wholly in evidence at the present moment: Having dined and imbibed with his customary extravagance just before attending the lecture, the tycoon appeared to be nodding off in his seat, his odobenidan snores punctuating the professor's carefully crafted speech like intermittent blasts of a rogue foghorn.

As William launched into a devastating critique of the dominant paradigms of the so-called elementistic psychologies of the day, a less than academically minded observer of the scene might have found his attention diverted to the belated arrival of a pair of strangers at the rear of the lecture hall. The two men, sporting elegant pinchback suits and jaunty bowler hats, were clearly too old and too stylishly attired to be students. The shorter of the pair walked with a pronounced limp, supporting his stride with a silver-headed ebony cane. His sandy-haired companion cautiously scanned the auditorium with his steel-blue eyes before taking a seat in the very last row of the amphitheater, ensuring that no one would be sitting behind him. William, warming to his subject, fortunately took no notice of these well-appointed interlopers, whose unlikely presence at the Museum of Comparative Zoology might otherwise have violently derailed the train of his disquisition.

The long flight of the James brothers from Northfield has gone down in the annals of American crime as one of the grand escape sagas of all time. As an editorialist for the *Sedalia Bazoo* in Missouri admiringly recorded: "They ran the gauntlet of Minnesota and Dakota for a distance of 490 miles, and the wildest exploits in the romance of Dick Turpin will not compare with this bold ride for life."

Free of the Youngers and Henry James, at the earliest opportunity Frank and Jesse had abandoned the decrepit draft mare they had appropriated from the old German couple for a pair of sleeker mounts. Proceeding west at a swifter clip, they had thrown themselves into desperate survival mode: For days and nights, running on sheer guts and cussedness, the aching, exhausted, and starving former soldiers and bushwhackers had ridden as hard and fast as their horses could endure. More than once they had confronted their pursuers face-to-face, and it was during one such encounter that Jesse, who had thus far miraculously managed to avoid injury, had taken a blast from a shotgun in his right knee. Still the brothers pressed on.

The last confirmed sighting of the outlaws was reported on September 25 by a country doctor named Sidney Mosher whom Frank and Jesse had briefly kidnapped on the outskirts of Sioux City, Iowa. Before releasing the terrified physician, the bandits had forced him at gunpoint to dress their wounds and exchange his clothes and horse for Frank's. "They let the doctor go, then rode south into the darkness," recorded T. J. Stiles. "Their trail was never found again. Ruthless, relentless, and utterly iron-willed, they had outrun, outfought, and outsmarted perhaps a thousand pursuers, crossing hundreds of miles of hostile territory. And they had survived." Indeed, there could have been no more vivid demonstration of William's famous observation that "great emergencies and crises show us how much greater our vital resources are than we had supposed."

Yet their ordeal was far from over. Despite the silence of the incarcerated Youngers, it had required no great feat of detective work for Chief James McDonough of the St. Louis Police Department to conclude that their accomplices at Northfield had almost certainly included the Jameses, with whom he knew Cole and his brothers to have been in criminal cahoots for over a decade. And just as Zerelda had predicted to Elena Hite when "the boys" set off on their adventure, McDonough's men had wasted little time in staking out the Samuel farm. (William Pinkerton had correctly surmised that his elusive quarry would never be so foolhardy as to show their faces anywhere around their old Missouri haunts. The Big Man, as we shall learn, had taken a very different tack in his obsessive pursuit of the James brothers.) Meanwhile, just as they had elected to strike in remote Minnesota, the wily ex-guerrillas had once again plotted to go where they were least expected by determining—perhaps under the sway of memories and sentiments stirred up by Henry's recent presence among them—to return to the genteel New England ground of their childhood.

At the conclusion of William's lecture, a small throng of well-wishers gathered around the podium to congratulate the speaker. Only after this knot of admirers had significantly thinned out did Frank and Jesse leave their seats at the rear of the auditorium and venture toward their brother, who was in conversation with only Alice Gibbens and Asa Hite. At closer range, having had the benefit of Henry's descriptions, William had little difficulty divining the identities of the approaching gentlemen. They embraced him awkwardly, calling him Willie and obliging him to introduce them to Miss Gibbens and Mr. Hite.

"Ah, yes, I'd like you to meet—" William looked quizzically toward Frank.

"Dr. Will Franklin," Frank piped up boldly, extending his hand to Asa Hite and bowing gracefully to Alice Gibbens. "And this is my colleague Professor Robert Jessup. We're old pals of Willie's from our student days in Europe, *n'est-ce pas, cher* Guillaume?"

"Yes, of course, Europe," William echoed, somewhat bemused. "Good old Europe."

Mr. Hite was delighted to make the acquaintance of William's distinguished colleagues. "And where are you fellows teaching now?" he inquired.

William, not to be bested by Frank's brazen fabrications, took the liberty of responding for his brothers: "I believe it's Carleton College, is it not?" he answered sardonically. "And you, Professor Jessup—if I'm not mistaken—are at St. Olaf?"

"That's right," Jesse replied. "Full professor—head of the department, as a matter of fact."

"Ah, excellent school!" bellowed Asa Hite, who had doubtless never heard of the institution but who went on to express his surprise and admiration that one so young should have already reached such academic heights—and who would have been even more surprised, if considerably less admiring, to have learned that this professorial prodigy was in fact the "pissant desperado" who was not only ruining

his railroad business but had also recently been enjoying carnal relations with his lovely daughter.

———◆———

Elena Hite and Alice James embarked for the continent aboard the
Cunard liner *Algeria* only a fortnight after Henry's departure. Their
crossing was considerably calmer than the author's; indeed, Elena discovered that the bracing ocean air worked wonders on both her complexion and her disposition. If she harbored any misgivings about
having been summarily booted off the stage of her life in the States to
be "swept beneath the tattered old rug of Europe" (as she teasingly described her plight in her first letter to William), she was determined to
make the most of it. She and her traveling companion were fêted
nightly at the captain's table and enjoyed lively games of backgam-
mon and whist with their shipmates. The men aboard the *Algeria,*
predictably, were all over the fetching young female emancipationist,
though Alice James, never having mastered the flirtatious arts beyond
the bounds of her family circle, left most of them cold.

Despite her militant solidarity with women in the aggregate, Elena,
as she had made painfully clear to William James, had seldom, from
her school days on, enjoyed close relations with individual members of
her own sex. She had little reason to suppose that her duenna would
prove an exception to this trend, especially given that the sole female
James sibling was notoriously "tightly wound." Years later, in her famous diary, Alice would lament her lifelong predicament:

> Conceive of never being without the sense that if you let your-
> self go for a moment your mechanism will fall into pie and that
> at some given moment you must abandon it all, let the dykes
> break and the flood sweep in, acknowledging yourself abjectly
> impotent before the immutable laws. When all one's moral and

natural stock in trade is a temperament forbidding the abandonment of an inch or the relaxation of a muscle 'tis a never-
ending fight.

Having feared that she might find herself in the clutches of a
stodgy old stick-in-the-mud, Elena was pleasantly surprised to discover that Alice, like her novelist brother, was a canny—and catty—
judge of character. The two traveling ladies ended up passing many a
delicious hour dissecting the quirks and qualities of their fellow voy-
agers, especially the men, at whose expense Alice relished displaying
her mordant wit. Of one particularly abhorrent specimen—an aggressively charming Italian count who introduced himself as Salvatore
Terilli—she remarked that he appeared to have "about as much civilization as a gorilla," and warned Elena that "to associate with and
have to take seriously a creature with the moral substance of a monkey becomes degrading after a while, no matter how one may have
been seduced by his 'shines' at the first going off."

Both women professed to holding jaundiced views of marriage, although her duenna's disdain for the institution, Elena apprehended,
seemed to smack less of any profound political or personal conviction
than of plain old sour grapes. In fact, Alice had recently written to her
friend Annie Ashburner that she feared facing "the mortification of
descending to the grave a spinster, not from choice of the sweet lot,
but from dire necessity." To that same correspondent she had subsequently confided: "If I could get any sort of man to be impassioned
about me I should not let him escape." But as Jean Strouse observed,
Alice "appears never to have entered seriously into a relationship with
a man, or even to have surmised what that might mean." In fact, she
"found most men, aside from her brothers, 'queer' and rather frightening."

To history, it is the James brothers who are regarded as "queer"
(Henry) and "rather frightening" (Frank and Jesse). But to Elena Hite,
they—especially William—were a favorite topic of shipboard conversa-

tion. For the woman who had grown up as a lonely only child, all of the lively, convoluted, loving, and competitive give-and-take among the Jameses—the whole thick, eccentric, but nourishing stew of their family life—was a dish of which she could never get her fill, and Alice obligingly served up an endless banquet of anecdote and insight to satisfy her charge's prodigious appetite. Over the course of the long voyage, she treated Elena to a smorgasbord of colorful and candid recollections of Europe, Newport, Cambridge, and the Civil War, offering, among other choice morsels, the observation that Henry—whom she had learned, just before sailing, was back in Paris—was "a native of the James family and knew no other country," along with plentiful reminiscences of the two younger brothers, both tragically lost in battle so long ago.

Arriving in the French capital, the two Yankee ladies settled in at the Hôtel Lorraine near the Quai Voltaire, a favorite Parisian haunt of the Cambridge intelligentsia, where they were joined for dinner the following evening by Henry James. The trio took a corner banquette at the establishment's *table d'hôte,* where the writer, having picked up Jesse's cautious habit, sat with his back to the walls.

Needless to say, the encounter proved an awkward one. Alice James had no idea that her companion had enjoyed any prior acquaintance with Henry—that she had even, for a number of weeks, masqueraded as his wife—much less that Elena had spent any time with Frank and Jesse, of whose continued earthly existence the youngest James sibling remained entirely ignorant. Henry, having known Elena only by her lecturing soubriquet, had no reason to suspect that the Miss Hite whom his sister was accompanying to Paris would turn out to be his own erstwhile Mrs. James.

"Upon spying me," Elena recorded in her journal, "H. positively *recoiled* in his seat. He was flustered & stammering deliciously. I feared he might succumb to apoplexy on the spot, but he miraculously regained his composure and carried off the charade with admirable aplomb, politely enquiring where I was from, how I had enjoyed my first trans-Atlantic voyage, &c. But as soon as A. excused herself briefly between courses, he leaned across the table and grabbed me by the wrist with surprising force, ferociously demanding *sotto voce* what on earth I thought I was doing there. When and why had I stopped being 'Miss Phoenix'? And how the devil had I fallen in league with his beloved little sister?"

Elena explained to Henry that her acquaintance with William— and, *pari passu*, with Alice—had been the machination of her father and Dr. James Putnam of the Massachusetts General Hospital. "I certainly had not the slightest inkling," she insisted, "that Dr. William James of Harvard would turn out to be one of . . . *you.*"

"And what inklings do you suppose Alice might have of . . . *us?*" asked Henry.

Elena quickly reassured him that, to the best of her knowledge, neither his sister nor William knew anything of her prior "associations" out in Missouri. Then she turned the tables on her interlocutor by accusing him of having known all along that Jesse had a wife. This Henry vehemently denied, pointing out that in any event, being married was surely the least of his younger brother's transgressions. He then admonished—virtually threatened—Elena not to divulge a word of any of this to his sister. "You cannot imagine," he cautioned, "how frightfully it would upset her to learn that her trusted traveling companion had recently been consorting with the infamous outlaw Jesse James, nor—even more disturbing—that said brigand just happens to be her own not-so-late brother."

"Indeed," replied Elena. "But might it not upset her at least as much to learn that her darling brother Henry—known in the family circle, as she informs me, by the sweet pet name 'Angel'—had recently knocked over a bank in Minnesota?"

Henry's visage took on the same cringing, scolded-schoolboy cast that it had worn when Elena had first caught him staring across at her on the Missouri Pacific Express. But he quickly recovered. "And what proof do you have of that?" he snapped.

"Oh, please," Elena bluffed, "we both know what we both know."

"Aha! I thought not," retorted Henry. But he conceded that it would be best for all concerned if they agreed to keep each other's secrets.

Returning to the table, Alice discovered her brother and her traveling companion in a conspiratorial tableau of raised wineglasses.

"To a pleasant sojourn!" Henry improvised, bringing his goblet to Elena's with a celebratory clink.

"And to a *quiet* one!" Elena added with a nearly imperceptible wink.

Alice, jumping into the jolly spirit of the occasion, raised her own glass and toasted: "To friends and family!"

———◆———

Alice James was hardly so obtuse as her dining partners may have supposed or hoped. No less perspicacious than her more publicly accomplished brothers, she had already sensed that something was "up" with Elena Hite. Although still ignorant of her traveling companion's clandestine ties to the James family, Alice was astute enough—having had copious experience of her own in the psychiatric arena—to appreciate that the younger woman's interest in William went well beyond a patient's typical curiosity about her doctor. She had especially remarked on Elena's keen desire to hear all about Alice Gibbens—a red flag that led her to suspect that Elena the Huntress had set her cap, as the expression had it, for her beloved brother. Nor, as the days and weeks of their Paris sojourn together went by, could she help but observe that the patient and her physician were corresponding with a far greater frequency than any demands for medical updates could have warranted. Elena was sending William a letter almost daily, sometimes even twice a day, and he was responding nearly as prolifically. His patient was transparently thrilled to receive these missives, poring over them for nuggets of wit and wisdom that she often insisted on reading aloud to Alice. (The mere appearance of her name in William's "beautiful and flowing" script on the face of an envelope, Elena confessed in her journal, was enough to transport her with "delicious gleams" of anticipation.)

It would probably be an egregious overinterpretation to suggest that Alice James, even if unconsciously, had it in mind to toss the monkey wrench of Elena Hite into the whirring gears of the "other" Alice's matrimonial juggernaut; but in her own correspondence with her brother, she seems to have gone out of her way to depict Elena in the most tantalizing possible light, describing her charge as "lovely," "brilliant," "delightful," "such excellent company," "like a living sunbeam," and even "celestial." Whatever his sister's intentions, William James received these glowing reports with a pleasure wholly disproportionate to any professional pride he might have taken in Elena's psychiatric progress, which, by her own account in a letter to the doctor, was nearly miraculous:

> *Dear Dr. James,*
>
> *What a benign medicine this journey is proving! You will doubtless be gratified to learn that my health & moral outlook have improved boundlessly since you last saw me; indeed, I suspect that you would scarcely recognize the glum, tormented creature of your consultation chamber. Paris is my tonic, owing in no small measure to the attentive ministrations of your superlative sister, without whom I'm sure I would simply wander about this marvelous city like a lost Hottentott. (Alice's French, as you know, is excellent—better* than *excellent—whereas I am obliged to muddle through jabbering a dreadful chow-chow of all sorts of languages.)*
>
> *My life here is so full of interest and my time so thoroughly filled that I'm practically bursting to tell you absolutely everything. The other evening, following an afternoon at the dazzling Musée du Louvre, we dined nearby at Le Grand Véfour, a favorite restaurant—or so we were told—of the emperor Napoleon (the first*

one, that is) and his empress Josephine. (I ate a thrush!*) We have also explored the gilded splendor of the recently renovated opera house, the verdant and aromatic treasures of Le Jardin des Plantes, as well as the lofty, sky-pricking spires of the Notre Dame cathedral. Wherever we go we are treated to the splendid spectacle of parading soldiers, all hugely colorful, especially the mounted* cuirassiers *in their shining plumed helmets and snug white* culottes de peau. *(Alice & I attempted to imagine how* you *might appear decked out in such picturesque military attire & we happily concurred that you would make a most dashing dragoon.) Such wonders, of course, may seem merely so much* vieux chapeau *to the cosmopolitan likes of yourself— but to this wide-eyed daughter of Hartford it is all so much like having tumbled into the pages of a fantastical picture-book. . . .*

And if Paris was Elena's tonic, her letters to William from that glittering city were rapidly becoming his own; for with the descent upon Cambridge of the chill gloom of November—along with his outlaw brothers—the doctor's spirits had taken a decided turn for the worse.

To keep them away from Henry Sr. and their mother, and to substantiate the pretense that they were "visiting scholars," William installed Frank and Jesse in Miss Upham's boardinghouse on Kirkland Street, where he himself had been a resident during the early 1860s, before the rest of the family moved from Newport to Boston. The establishment catered to graduate students and bachelor dons, and in Frank's case, at least, the role of academic proved a credible cover, as the older outlaw was more than content to spend his days auditing lectures and prowling through the stacks of the Harvard libraries. Jesse's adjustment to his newly assumed scholarly identity was a bit rockier: William had winced to hear a report from the boardinghouse that his youngest brother, in the heat of a philosophical debate, had countered an aggressive challenge to his logic by declaring, "I refute it *thus!*" and drawing a cocked Derringer from the watch pocket of his waistcoat.

The old family taint was also casting its shadow over William's romance with Alice Gibbens. Indeed, of this troubled period in their courtship, R. W. B. Lewis wrote, "William seemed oddly bent on undermining his case." To whatever doubts and hesitations already bedeviled him—and they were legion—William added the unspoken complication of Elena Hite. His patient had become, in the phrase of Linda Simon, "a luminous figment of his imagination," and as her shapely figure pirouetted incessantly across his mind, she came to exemplify everything that the Boston schoolmistress was not—a dazzling bird of paradise to Miss Gibbens's drab and fussy brood hen. But was Elena, he must have wondered, a symptom or a solution? There was no denying that she was beautiful, bright, and sexually fascinating; nor could it have been lost on the man who once wrote "marry this fortune" that, in addition to her other charms, she was— or would become upon her father's death—an immensely wealthy woman. While Alice Gibbens may have been the choice of Henry Sr., Elena appeared to be gaining the approval of Henry Jr. and his sister, with whom she seemed to be getting along famously. Her letter from Paris continued:

> *Our dear Henry has graciously sacrificed eons of his scribbling time to play cicerone to this pair of idle Yankee ladies. He has introduced us to many of his American friends here, including the delightful Bootts (father Francis & daughter Elizabeth), Mr. Edward Lee Childes, Miss Henrietta Reubell, &c., and even to a smattering of his French* confrères, *among them the estimable M. Gustave Flaubert, with whose masterful* Madame Bovary *you are no doubt familiar.*
>
> *Just yesterday, through the generous offices of sweet Lizzie Boott, we all paid a visit to the* atelier *of the celebrated painter Thomas Couture, erstwhile instructor to George Stanley, of whom you & I spoke in Cambridge, if you will recall. I fear I pestered your poor brother mercilessly to arrange this little pilgrimage, for which I have*

since offered him my most abject apologies. Despite the stellar opinion in which this artist is apparently held in certain quarters, I must confess that I found M. Couture hardly so formidable an entity—either in his art or his person—as I had been led to expect. Even his much-ballyhooed canvas The Romans of the Decadence *struck me as, au* fond, *a tawdry thing. The work seemed an egregious example of the very worst sort of bombastic academic painting—highly impasted, exquisitely rendered in every detail yet totally false in overall effect.* Ugh!

If my appraisal of M. Couture strikes you as unduly sharp, I hasten to confess it may be less in response to his work than to his deportment; for here I must record a shocking fact: As he was showing me about his gallery that horrid little man, to my huge disgust, had the cheek to press his attentions upon me in a most coarse and odious manner, which behavior upset me utterly. (No doubt in light of the candid revelations I made to you last month you may hold me—et bien pour cause, mon cher docteur—*to be the very worst kind of fast; but pray permit me to assure you that I did in no wise seek or encourage that man's obscene attentions. Without vanity, I confess that I am not unconscious of the effect that my visual aspect can have on certain members of your sex—even having shamelessly exploited it upon occasion to further my wicked purposes—but even a poor* ruined *wench like myself must nonetheless reserve the right to select the agent of her degradation, don't you agree?)*

In any event, it was certainly an unsavory excursion for the lot of us—yet happily, I have chosen *not to dwell on such unpleasantnesses, as your esteemed M. Renouvier would no doubt heartily applaud. Indeed, I have been feeling so well lately that I scarcely know what to make of it. I don't remember ever in my life being in such good spirits. And you, sir, have been so very kind and friendly to me—you don't know how much happiness your letters are giving me. I frequently return in thought to our encounters before that eerie*

audience of decapitated amphibians in your office, & I shall live in
eternal gratitude for the comfort & guidance you provided me on
those memorable occasions.

A toute à l'heure, cher docteur ("toodle-oo" in the English!)
Miss Elena Hite

William could hardly have helped but be beguiled by the frisky and flirtatious tone of Elena's correspondence; but notwithstanding her avowed desire to tell him "absolutely everything," there were at least a couple of salient items that she seemingly thought better of mentioning. The first was that on her visit to Couture's studio, she had brought along the sketch that William had rendered of her in his office back in Cambridge, believing that the famous art teacher would be delighted to see the work of a student of his own former protégé, William Morris Hunt. Couture, however, after taking a perfunctory glance at the drawing, had summarily dismissed it as a decent likeness, but artistically "minable." (On the subject of Thomas Couture, Henry's assessment was at least as harsh as Elena's. In his own letter to William describing the episode, he wrote: "I paid with them a long visit to Couture, who is an amusing but a vulgar little fat & dirty old man—en somme (to me) peu sympathique." And without going into prurient detail about the artist's offensive behavior toward Elena, he added: "I hope it will at least have the effect of keeping her from returning to her detestable Couture.")

More significantly, Elena neglected to inform William of a circumstance that may well have been the effective engine of her manifest ebullience: namely, that she had embarked on a liaison with the "estimable" M. Gustave Flaubert—a Frenchman whose attentions she apparently looked upon with immeasurably less "huge disgust" than she did those of the "detestable" Thomas Couture.

Chapter Nine

———◆———

"If I were a woman," Gustave Flaubert once remarked, "I wouldn't want myself for a lover. A fling, yes; but an intimate relationship, no." Yet the very quality in the Frenchman that Ivan Turgenev found so woefully reprehensible—his seeming inability to sustain a relationship with a woman that went beyond the carnal—was immensely (if perversely) appealing to Elena Hite in her present state of mind. Unlike Henry James's Christopher Newman, this American in Paris was looking for not so much a spouse as an experience.

In 1876 the great French author was fifty-five years old, over twice Elena's age. That year he had lost two of the most significant women in his life—the novelist George Sand and the poet Louise Colet, with whom he had carried on a tumultuous affair thirty years earlier. "My heart," he wrote, "is becoming a necropolis." His own health—always fragile despite his robust appearance—was deteriorating precipitously, and age, he complained, had softened him to the consistency of "an overripe Edomite pear." In four years he would be dead. Nonetheless, not long before Flaubert came into Elena's life, the poet François Coppée had written of him: "He carried his head loftily. His whole bearing was that of the romantics. . . . One could still make out fine features in his florid, swollen face . . . and a truly Merovingian mess of hair hung in graying, tousled locks from his half-denuded pate. This old Gustave Flaubert was no longer handsome, but he was still superb."

In her previous relationships with men, Elena had been accustomed to reining in her intellect, her sexuality, or both; but she felt there was no way she could be either too smart or too raunchy for this brilliant and vastly experienced *littérateur.* Reading *Madame Bovary* that summer out at Castle James, she had been deeply impressed by the author's empathy with the feminine psyche. Here, she sensed, was a man who truly appreciated not only a woman's romantic yearnings and the stifling potential of a bourgeois marriage, but also the power of sheer female horniness. ("Madame Bovary, *c'est moi,*" he was reputed to have proclaimed.) And if Elena was attracted by Flaubert's sensibility on the page, she found herself equally drawn to him in the abundant flesh. Though by rights he should have fallen into that category of oversize "prosperous walruses" to whom she liked to think of herself as erotically immune, she gushed in her diary that he was "a great bear of a man in whom a woman might easily lose herself. Everything about him is so BIG—his body, his voice, his mind, his talent, his appetites. . . ." She found herself surprisingly aroused by the old *roué*'s "deliciously lascivious" ways, and just as she had measured Jesse's "experienced" touch against the crude gropings of the "fresh-faced boys" of Hartford, she gave Flaubert's masterful manipulations pride of place over the outlaw's relatively coarse "sawing" motions. Apparently, the sophisticated Frenchman initiated Elena into the art of what the Victorians quaintly designated *gamahucherie.* ("I am like a cigar," he once said, "you have to suck on me to get me going.") In her journal she wrote of "blooming & blossoming" under Flaubert's erotic tutelage, calling him, in a cross-lingual *jeu de mots,* her "Flower-

Bear," and expatiating upon the "exquisite private sensations" his attentions induced in her. ("Every Grand Tour requires a religious epiphany," she exclaimed, "and now I've had mine!")

Happily, the blooming was mutual: Flaubert was surprised and delighted by the rejuvenating effect of this radiant paradigm of new-world womanhood. As he wrote to his niece Caroline Hamard, "I think I've been seriously and secretly ill without realizing ever since the death of our poor dear mother. If I'm wrong about that, why have all the clouds lifted for me recently? It's like a mist clearing. And I feel physically restored."

Contrary to William James's assertion that "the direction of the sexual instinct towards one individual tends to inhibit its application to other individuals," Elena discovered that the sensual awakening she was experiencing with her "Flower-Bear" was intensifying rather than diminishing her infatuation with her *"cher docteur."* Just as her own insinuation into William's erotic consciousness had been lubricated by his nascent romance with Alice Gibbens, so Elena's sentimental education with Flaubert seemed to be opening her up to a whole new appreciation of the possibilities of the male sex—especially of William James, who clearly offered more amatory potential for the long term than the aging Frenchman. In her letters back to Cambridge, she was properly reticent about the salacious details of her liaison with Flaubert, yet she came to feel compelled to at least allude to his presence in her Parisian life, if only to cover her flank in case Alice James was reporting back to her brother on the company she was keeping. Elena furnished William with a number of innocent vignettes concerning her acquaintance with the famous novelist, among them an account of a delightful late-morning *déjeuner* they had shared at a café on the avenue de l'Opéra, a repast that lasted well into the afternoon and throughout which her companion expounded colorfully and eloquently on everything from the barbarism of the ancient Carthaginians to the miraculous restorative powers of the sea salt of Guérande. Upon quitting the café, Elena reported, "we disported ourselves upon the *trottoirs* in a decidedly disreputable manner," ending the day with a long, leisurely promenade along the banks of the Seine, highlighted by "a beautiful rose crimson glow over the water" and "a flock of beggar children with whining voices who sallied out upon us on the *quai*," and to whom Flaubert, with touching generosity, dispensed a pocketful of copper sous. "At present," she concluded, "I am in serene enjoyment of a good conscience and blistered feet," coyly appending: "I don't know why I have tried your patience by writing so about a person you have never seen; unless it's to show you that I haven't irrevocably given up the world, the flesh and the devil, but am conscious of a faint charm about them still when taken in small doses."

Flaubert being Flaubert, the doses of "the world, the flesh and the devil" to which he treated his American paramour were anything but small. When not reveling in the delights of lovemaking *à la française* with her, the celebrated auteur squired Elena all around Paris, where he seemed to know everything and everyone. (He had even been an intimate of Napoléon III's wife, the empress Eugénie, and of his cousin Princess Mathilde.) Especially thrilling to the girl from Hartford were their forays into the louche demimonde of the French capital—the colorful shadow society of artists, actors, poets, courtesans, and randy aristocrats that had flourished during the decadent days of the Second Empire and which persisted in faded form in the more austere atmosphere of the Third Republic. (Among the storied demimondaines to whom Flaubert introduced Elena was the aging courtesan Apollonie Sabatier, known as "La Présidente," who, on one memorable visit to her salon on the avenue d'Eylau in Passy, extravagantly praised the younger woman's classic "champagne-goblet" breasts.) For their sorties into the more respectable cultural establishments of the city—the Opéra Garnier, the Comédie Française, the art galleries and cathedrals—the lovers were often canny and considerate enough to invite Henry and Alice James. It was on one such outing, which found this oddly assorted quartet in the Salon Carré of the Louvre—coincidentally, the setting of the opening chapter of *The American*—that Elena discreetly directed Henry's attention to the presence of a portly gentleman seated on the great circular divan in the center of the hall. The stout stranger sported a too floppy beret and a laughably bogus goatee and was making a great show of being deeply engrossed in the morning edition of *Le Figaro*. But he was wearing heavy American shoes—a dead giveaway to the perspicacious eye of Elena Hite, to whom the detective appeared no more convincing in his impersonation of a Frenchman in the ancient Parisian palace than he had as a Jewish peddler along the dusty roads of western Missouri. She gently nudged Henry, alerting her companion to the presence of William Pinkerton. To her unconcealed amusement, Henry blanched. The detective, he gasped, was *tailing* him!

"Oh, don't be such a worrywart," Elena whispered. "He can't possibly have a clue as to what you look like. He's tailing *me*."

But Elena was wrong, at least on the first count: Having clandestinely observed Henry James on the moonlit night of her tryst with Jesse, Pinkerton had an all too vivid mental image of the author, even down to aspects of his anatomy that would not normally have been visible on a run-of-the-mill mug shot. On the second count, however, she was absolutely correct: It was indeed Elena and not Henry James whom the detective was following.

As the trail had gone cold on the James brothers after the Northfield robbery, Billy Pinkerton had once again been summoned to Hartford to provide Asa Hite with an update on the state of affairs out west. The news he had been obliged to report was hardly encouraging: Despite the arrest of the Younger brothers and the killing of Charlie Pitts at Hanska Slough, the law was still no closer to bringing the Jameses themselves to justice. At one point during the pursuit of the bandits, Chief James McDonough of the St. Louis Police Department—Pinkerton's archrival in the race to capture the fugitive outlaws—was convinced that he had located the wounded Frank James in Independence, Missouri, but as the private eye recounted to Hite with an unprofessionally delectable tingle of schadenfreude, the police chief had been embarrassed to discover that the suspect in custody was only a cattle trader from Louisiana named John Goodin or Goodwin who had shot himself in the knee while hunting squirrels four months earlier. The lamentable bottom line was that the James boys appeared to have eluded apprehension once again.

Pinkerton had braced himself for a tongue-lashing from his host, but to his astonishment and relief, the detective found the previously irascible railroad magnate in excellent spirits. Over cigars and a congenial snifter or two of brandy in his library after dinner, Mr. Hite confided to his guest that the reason he was feeling so chipper was that his daughter, whom he had feared might have inherited her mother's tendency to neurasthenic instability, was recuperating capitally in Europe from an episode of nervous prostration she had suffered out west that summer. (Here Pinkerton winced, knowing full well what the precipitating factor in Elena's breakdown had been, but his host mercifully took the detective's tortured facial gyrations as an expression of sympathy rather than guilt.) In his expansive mood, Mr. Hite went on to regale his interlocutor with an enthusiastic account of his daughter's remarkable recovery under the care of one Dr. William James of Harvard, the doctor's splendid sister, Alice, and even his brother Henry, a noted literary gent who had recently taken up residence in Paris.

For Pinkerton the lights flashed on: There was more to this James Gang, he queasily surmised, than had previously met "the eye that never sleeps." And his consternation turned to outright alarm as Asa Hite ebulliently went on to describe Dr. James's plans to establish a laboratory of experimental psychology up at Harvard. It occurred to the detective that this brilliant professor might well be the "evil genius" behind a complex criminal conspiracy that appeared to have not only an East Coast component but perhaps an international one as well. Pinkerton knew from his considerable sleuthing experience that in the face of such an unlikely assortment of characters and circumstances, no hypothesis—however bizarre—could prudently be ruled out. Was it possible, he speculated, that the ambitious psychologist was bent on developing some kind of nefarious mind-control scheme with which to enslave an unsuspecting populace? Perhaps William James had gotten his brothers under the sway of his powerful intellect, employing Frank, Jesse, and Henry as tools to bring in the loot to fund his grander plan, whatever that might prove to be. And could the mad doctor have already begun "experimenting" on Elena Hite, somehow mesmerically transforming the hapless feminist into an unwitting puppet of his wicked will? (Had Pinkerton fancied himself Sherlock Holmes—the accounts of whose adventures were not published until a decade later—he would have just discovered his Professor Moriarty.)

"These Jameses," he later remarked in his report back to the home office in Chicago, "are a boundlessly depraved family, in which this impressionable young woman has become piteously ensnared. Having recently been coerced into presenting herself as the wife of Henry James, while concurrently—according to an unimpeachable source— fornicating with Jesse James, she has now fallen into the clutches of the senior member of this felonious fraternity, William James, a brainy but doubtless deeply deranged psychologist who appears to have somehow gained control of her mind."

The detective refrained from sharing these baleful suspicions with his cheery host. But he did make a point of worming out of Mr. Hite the whereabouts of Elena in Paris; now, in addition to hunting down the James brothers, he felt duty-bound to rescue the daughter of the agency's star client, lending special urgency to the venerable French maxim *cherchez la femme.*

———◆———

Despite his fascination with the grand mysteries of the human psyche, William James was finding himself uncharacteristically incurious about the history and pathology of Frank and Jesse. Over the course of that autumn, the outlaws provided their oldest brother with a cursory (and predictably self-serving) account of their lives from the time of the Civil

War to the present, but it was all—quite literally—too close to home for William to maintain his customary intellectual objectivity. Much as he may have felt he *should* have been intrigued and concerned, all he really wanted was for them to go away.

Had he been paying closer attention, he would have observed that the bond between the two outlaws was beginning to fray. As Henry noted in his autobiography, his younger brothers were "so constitutionally different," not only from the rest of the Jameses but from each other, and that fall their dissimilar talents and temperaments, which had complemented each other with such deadly synergy over the course of their criminal careers, were driving them in drastically divergent directions. While following newspaper reports of the imprisonment and trial of the Younger brothers, Frank was coming to the conclusion that the time had arrived for him to sever ties with his felonious past. The wounds he had received during the Northfield robbery and its aftermath had left him in chronic pain and incapacitated to the extent that he found it difficult to imagine ever again negotiating the rigors of outlaw life. At a deeper level, he was haunted with having killed the bookkeeper Joseph Heywood, who had appeared to be a serious, well-spoken, scholarly fellow about his own age. There but for the grace of God, Frank couldn't help but feel, went he. And try as he might to convince himself that he had acted in self-defense or out of some vestigial loyalty to his former Confederate comrades, he knew in his heart that what he had committed out in Minnesota was nothing less than cold-blooded, first-degree murder. He was hungering for some form of redemption, and as he wrote to Henry in Paris: "I am tired of this life of taut nerves, of night-riding and day-riding, of constant listening for footfalls, creaking twigs and rustling leaves and creaking doors; tired of seeing Judas in the face of every friend I know—and God knows I have none to spare—tired of the hoofs and horns with which popular belief has equipped me. I want to see if there is not a way out of it. . . ."

His way out, Frank came to hope, might be in the guise of the ac-

ademic "Will Franklin." What had begun as a semi-facetious pose was
showing promise of turning into something more. One of the regulars
at Miss Upham's table was Francis Child, the Boylston professor of
rhetoric and oratory at Harvard, who had been taking his breakfast at
the boardinghouse for over a decade. Professor Child, affectionately
known as "Stubby" to students and colleagues alike, was a distinguished Chaucerian scholar most noted for his magisterial study *English and Scottish Popular Ballads.* He was a gregarious fellow, once
described by William James as "a great joker" and by Henry as a "delightful man, rounded character, passionate patriot, admirable talker,
above all thorough humanist and humorist." The jovial rotund professor and the wiry phlegmatic outlaw hit it off immediately. Frank,
with his fine musical ear and deep love of language, was drawn to the
haunting archaic poetry of Child's ancient troubadour tales of hard-
hearted maidens, ruthless pirates, rapacious highwaymen, bloody bat-
tles, and gory murders—all sweetly sanitized in melody and verse.
Eighteen seventy-six was to be the professor's last year of teaching at
Harvard, and his magnum opus, which would remain incomplete
even upon his death twenty years later, was still very much a work in
progress. "Will Franklin" eagerly offered to assist his learned breakfast
companion with the tedious tasks of cataloging and documenting the
sources of the ballads. Seeing that Professor Child himself had never
earned a doctoral degree, Frank was encouraged to imagine that despite his own unlettered condition, he might have a chance of making
a new life for himself in the university and thus reclaim his birthright
as an eastern James.

"All had changed, changed utterly—and Frank was glad of it,"
wrote T. J. Stiles of the outlaw brothers' situation after Northfield. "For
Jesse, on the other hand," he added portentously, "a terrible boredom
was born." In Cambridge the younger outlaw remained unrepentant
and unfulfilled. Barely wounded, he was still itching for action. He
didn't cotton in the least to the Harvard ambiance, which for him
served only to stir up all the old childhood feelings of anger and resent-

ment, the sense of being underappreciated. Out west he had been accustomed to being known and feared, even if not universally admired; but in the academic suburb, it grated on the bogus "Professor Jessup" that he could never reveal what he had come to feel was his true identity. Unlike Frank, he had neither the talent, the interest, nor the desire to try to make a go of it in university life. (Notwithstanding all of President Eliot's radical curriculum reforms, Jesse understood that Harvard was hardly about to introduce courses in his specialties of bushwhacking and bank robbing.) And without his wife, Zee, or the stern "Mamaw" Samuel around to temper his excesses, he soon reverted to the unruly behavior that had set him on the path to desertion and outlawry during the war. He took to drinking and gambling, which, though they may have counted as only minor vices next to robbing and killing, were sufficiently disorderly to irritate Frank and alienate William. On more than one morning that fall, the psychologist arrived at his little Lawrence Hall office to discover the detritus of an all-night poker game that his wayward brother had been hosting for a crew of dissolute undergraduates—a stinking clutter of empty booze bottles, ashes, and cigar butts, some of them floating in the apothecary jar along with the decapitated frogs.

It was not simply that William was vexed with Frank and Jesse, nor even that he was disturbed about feeling so unfraternally toward them as he did. More distressing was the way his outlaw brothers made him feel about himself. The presence on his home turf of these physically and morally damaged kinsmen was a constant and dispiriting reminder of the ancient "family taint" at a time when he was just beginning to entertain the hope of transcending it. For the first time in his life, William was allowing himself a modicum of optimism about his professional future, as his plans for a laboratory of experimental psychology were rapidly developing a far greater reality and momentum than he had ever dared dream. Asa Hite, delighted with the apparent progress of Elena's continental "cure" (and unaware of her doctor's more than clinical interest in his daughter), had offered to pony up the cash to get the project rolling and had even entered into talks with President Eliot about just how such a facility might be integrated into the educational and physical architecture of the university.

Under the circumstances, William's moods seesawed from an agitated despondency to an almost manic expansiveness. In prose that R. W. B. Lewis called "Whitmanian" and Linda Simon described as "some of the most clotted writing he ever produced," the psychologist wrote to Alice Gibbens about his burgeoning ambitions: "The only single use for which my life was given me," he grandiloquently proclaimed, "[is] *acting* for the deepest, widest most general good I can see and feel." He rejoiced in the notion that he was "giving the moral universe a shove ahead; that I am baffling the powers of night; that I belong to the morning and the flowing tides of health and strength and good. . . ." Still, the flowing tides on which William liked to fancy himself being buoyed were fighting a strong countervailing undertow. Besides the demoralizing presence of Frank and Jesse in Cambridge and the new academic responsibilities entailed by his promotion to assistant professor, William was being dragged down by concerns about his elderly parents, whose needs were weighing especially heavily upon him now that his dutiful sister was abroad—and, of course, by his crippling ambivalence over Alice Gibbens and his insidious preoccupation with Elena Hite. When William confided his growing obsession with his patient to James Putnam, the neurologist had tersely cautioned his old friend that the tantalizing object of his fantasies was "not a keeper."

All this turmoil was taking its toll on William's delicate constitution, especially on his back, which Linda Simon called "the barometer of his emotional state." In desperate pursuit of relief from his mounting burden of physical pain and emotional unrest, he began indulging in "experiments" with chloral hydrate, hashish, opium, mescal, nitrous oxide, and what Simon described as "other substances to expand his view." One evening during this tense and tumultuous period, in which he later described himself as having been "a man

morally utterly diseased," William showed up at the Harvard laboratory of his old friend Charles Loring Jackson, a pioneering organic
chemist. Jackson, who had recently returned from a two-year research
stint in Europe, described to the psychologist an amusing incident
that had taken place in Berlin, where he had been studying the prop-
erties of amyl nitrite. In the course of these investigations, an Englishman working in the laboratory had begun singing and laughing as if
he were drunk, and by the end of the session, Jackson found himself
in a similar state of intoxication. As the chemist later recounted:

> James was immensely interested and asked to try some of it. At
> first he very properly held the bottle at a distance, and waved the
> vapor toward himself; but when to his continual questions, "Is
> my face flushing?" we answered "No," he at last put it against his
> nose and took a good sniff. Then he felt blindly for the table, put
> the bottle on it and said, "O! how queer I feel!" took up two
> battery-jars full of alcohol (two quarts if I remember) and started
> across the Yard.

The man of two minds was in danger of going out of both.

———◆———

At about this time Henry James wrote to William from Paris: "My life
runs on in an even current, very rapidly, but brings forth nothing very
important." This was an entirely disingenuous piece of posturing on
the part of the fugitive author. He, too, was experiencing abundant
agitation, generated no less by the ominous appearance of William
Pinkerton in the French capital than by the scandalous behavior of
Elena Hite. Henry was both appalled and fascinated by his errant
countrywoman's cavalier disregard for the rigid social mores of the
continent. Shortly after finishing *The American,* he would begin writing *Daisy Miller: A Study,* the work that was to bring him his first taste

of international acclaim. And for this celebrated tale of an ill-fated young American woman behaving badly in Europe, Henry drew heavily upon his observations of Elena, who struck him as the very archetype of the "Americana."

Initially, he had been delighted with Flaubert's interest in his brother's alluring patient, not only for providing grist for his literary mill, but also because introducing her into the great novelist's life had lent Henry considerable cachet in the eyes of the famous Frenchman and his circle. Flaubert, who had previously been polite and *accueillant* in his dealings with Henry, had become positively chummy. One unforgettable afternoon he even treated the American writer to a private recitation of Théophile Gautier's haunting poem "Pastel," which he read to Henry—and to Henry alone!—"in his own full tone."

Yet as Flaubert's flirtation with Elena flowered into a full-fledged *affaire de coeur,* Henry—though he may have been loath to acknowledge it—found himself experiencing an unseemly jealousy of his pretty compatriot for monopolizing so much of the older author's attention and admiration, which he must have felt should rightfully have been directed toward himself and his novelistic efforts. What was more, he was becoming concerned that Elena's increasingly public involvement with his literary idol might be reflecting badly on his sister's reputation among the close-knit and gossipy expatriate American colony of Paris and, by extension, upon his own. Having reaped the benefits of encouraging Elena's improper behavior as his "in" with Flaubert, Henry wasn't in a position to castigate Alice James for failing to keep a tighter rein on her charge; yet without wanting to alarm William—nor to reveal anything of his own past association with the woman in question—the author felt obliged to give fair warning of the potential "complications," especially in light of the windfall the psychologist was about to receive from Elena's father. "This young lady," Henry wrote, "appears to be afflicted with a congenital want of perception of certain rudimentary differences between the possible, for decent people, and the impossible."

It all came to a head on a gray Saturday at the end of November when Henry, Alice, Elena, and Flaubert boarded a train for an excursion out to Versailles, where they hired a brougham at the railway station for a tour of the famous château. Elena, having once posed for George Stanley as Marie Antoinette, had expressed a special desire to view the opulent palace where the famous queen had reigned and which had recently been designated as the seat of the French Parliament. But late November, Henry cautioned, was hardly the optimal time of year for such an outing, especially since the celebrated gardens would be lying fallow and the thousand exotic trees of the Orangerie arboretum would be leafless and forlorn. All of the author's previous visits to that regal monument to aesthetic and financial excess had taken place in summertime, when, as he once wrote, "the fountains were playing, the avenues green, and the long polished floors of the gilded halls dotted with Paris holiday-takers or American tourists—looking like flies on horizontal mirrors."

By the time the little group arrived at the château, a chilly rain was falling and the sprawling grounds were nearly deserted. Flaubert and Elena took off in the carriage to view the Petit Trianon and the Queen's Hamlet, that charmingly artificial Norman village that Marie Antoinette had constructed in which to play out her shepherdess fantasies. This left Henry and Alice to explore the stately sculpture gardens and the great shallow basins of the dormant fountains. For what seemed an eternity, the James siblings wandered among the forest of statues, taking in over and over again what Henry described as the "sallow nudities" of "the old Hebes and Floras and Neptunes." It was a distant echo of that sunny day over twenty years earlier when the pair had been stranded all afternoon in their governess's garden at Boulogne-sur-Mer—the unhappy occasion when Henry had made his famous remark about "pleasure under difficulties." Only now, stuck out in the freezing drizzle, they were finding the difficulties more onerous and the pleasures less consoling. When at first they spotted the brougham in the distance, bouncing through the frigid mist, it seemed to Henry that Flaubert and Elena must have felt it was too cold and damp to be strolling around, preferring to survey the vast demesne from the relative comfort of their rented conveyance. But when the vigorously rocking carriage passed a second time, and then a third—and when Henry observed that the curtains were drawn over the windows—the shocking truth dawned upon him: The randy couple within was reenacting the scandalous scene from *Madame Bovary* in which Emma and her young lover Léon, after a tour of the Rouen Cathedral, spent the afternoon fornicating in a carriage as it jounced frantically up and down the thoroughfares of the city.

On the way back to the Versailles railway station, Henry could smell the musky tang of sex in the stuffy confines of the coach. Elena snuggled contentedly against the offending Frenchman, who was blissfully dozing in his seat. Once, when she caught Henry scrutinizing her with his penetrating gaze, Elena muttered dreamily, "I wonder how I shall appear in your novels, Mr. James." But Henry was hardly thinking literary thoughts at that moment. The idea that Elena would dare to carry on as she had, virtually under his sister's nose, was the final straw: He determined that it was time to get his brother's patient and her chaperone out of Paris.

Back in the city, at the entrance to the Hôtel Lorraine, Henry caught Elena by the elbow and pulled her sharply aside. "You have behaved abominably," he scolded her. "You must leave immediately."

Elena yanked herself free of the author's grasp and responded with a derisory elevation of her eyebrows. "Oh, and this from the man who stooped to spying on me in my most intimate moments with his own brother?"

Henry, who had never suspected that Elena had been aware of his presence on that torrid occasion, was taken aback momentarily. Nonetheless, he must have felt that whatever opprobrious acts one might perform in the dark of night out behind a barn in Missouri, one should *never* commit in broad daylight at the Palais de Versailles, the very seat of the French government.

"I was not *spying* on anyone," he snapped. "I was merely heeding, as the common expression has it, the call of nature."

Elena shot him a scornful smirk. "Well, it must have been a very *long* call indeed, *n'est-ce pas?*" she retorted.

It occurred to her that she had more on her former "husband" than a bit of nocturnal voyeurism. There was, after all, still a price on his head back in the States, and she could have, if she wished, turned him in as a suspect for his role in the Northfield robbery. Yet Henry had plenty on her as well: Her affairs with Gustave Flaubert and Jesse James were more than enough to scuttle her prospects with William and perhaps even to get her disinherited. "I fear I am a good deal of a baby—in the sense of not wanting the reproaches of my friends or relatives on this or any other subject," she wrote defensively in her diary that night.

But in her heart she knew her Grand Tour was over.

———◆———

The next morning William Pinkerton decided that the moment had arrived for him to make his move. From the fetid confines of a conveniently situated *pissoir,* he had surreptitiously observed the heated exchange between Henry James and Elena Hite the previous evening outside the Hôtel Lorraine and had concluded that he might be able to take advantage of whatever rift had developed between the two to approach his client's daughter and get to the bottom of what the Jameses were up to. Having spent all that day tailing his quarry around Versailles, and having drawn the same sordid conclusion that Henry had about what Elena was doing in the carriage with Flaubert, the detective felt himself securely in position, should the need arise, to inform Asa Hite that his daughter's vaunted "cure" had fallen far short of what the railroad baron had been led to believe. Though her mood may have improved markedly in Paris, Elena was still up to her old "wild ways," and Mr. Hite's esteemed Dr. William James was at the very least a quack and quite possibly a master criminal.

Before having to resort to so drastic a measure as presenting Elena's father with such disturbing intelligence, Pinkerton elected to pursue the potentially more productive tack of confronting Elena with these hard home truths. Armed with his arsenal of incriminating information, he would take one last crack at trying to recruit her as an ally in his cause. Did they not, after all, have a common enemy in the perfidious Jesse James? And would she not appreciate being disencumbered of the meddlesome Henry? If only she would cooperate with him, he would tell her, he could spare her father the disillusionment and ire of learning about her swelling dossier of misdeeds, while simultaneously liberating her from the clutches of the nefarious James brothers. In Asa Hite's eyes, then—and perhaps even in Elena's own—the detective would appear a hero rather than a snitch. And although he never mentioned it in his dispatches back to the home office, Pinkerton may well have been nurturing the fantasy he had developed when Elena had "stripped for him" in her St. Louis hotel room in July—the dream of making her into his own incarnation of his father's detective/mistress, Kate Warne. Perhaps he even entertained the hope of gaining the hand of the young beauty—and a handsome dowry—as a reward from her grateful father. If, after all, she could tumble for an ancient plumper like Flaubert, could she not be at least equally attracted to his own much younger and firmer bulk?

But when Pinkerton showed up at the hotel on Sunday morning to present Elena with his ultimatum, he was curtly informed that *les mesdemoiselles américaines* had already checked out, leaving no forwarding address. This was an unexpected setback that the detective found troubling in the extreme. It suggested, among other distressing possibilities, that Henry James might have gotten wind of Pinkerton's presence in Paris.

"A man of great bonhomie and charm," wrote the British journalist Ben Macintyre, "Pinkerton could also be utterly ruthless, as many criminals had discovered at the expense of their liberty and, in some instances, their lives." In the course of his assiduous Parisian reconnaissance, the detective had followed Henry out to Flaubert's apartment and thus had a fair idea of where he might find the outlaw author on a Sunday afternoon. Determined not to let a James brother slip through his fingers again, he holstered a heavy pair of Colt revolvers and hightailed it out to the rue du Faubourg Saint-Honoré.

In this instance Pinkerton's conjecture proved to be right on the money. At that very moment Henry James was on his way to Flaubert's Parisian pied-à-terre with the firm intention of informing the *cénacle* that he would no longer be attending their gatherings. His experience at Versailles had brought him smack up against what R. W. B. Lewis called "the inveterate carnality" of the literary community of Paris, which, as Lewis wrote, always made the prim American author "somewhat squeamish." Henry had come to sour utterly on Flaubert, a disenchantment that was to be reflected in his snarky assessment of his former idol's later works in a review he wrote that winter for *The Galaxy.* Lumping Flaubert among the "minor" French novelists—along with such now all but forgotten writers as Charles de Bernard, Octave Feuillet, and Victor Cherbuliez—Henry cited his fallen hero as "an extraordinary example of a writer outliving his genius" and characterized all of the novels after *Madame Bovary* as "unmistakenly stillborn," deriding their "fatal charmlessness." Henry was particularly scathing in his assessment of *L'Éducation sentimentale,* of which he wrote, "the book is in a single word a *dead* one," and the experience of reading it "like masticating ashes and sawdust," adding, "There is no more charm in this laborious monument to a treacherous ideal than there is perfume in a gravel-heap."

By the time Henry arrived chez Flaubert, the regular coterie—Zola, Daudet, Turgenev, de Maupassant, and Edmond de Goncourt—was comfortably ensconced in the salon, thickening the air with their copious tobacco smoke and *chatoyante* conversation. Henry greeted the group with a nervous bow and took a place by the mantelpiece under the gilded statuette of the Buddha. In his most eloquent French, he launched into his valedictory philippic, informing the assembled authors that he could regretfully no longer, in good conscience, attend any of their future meetings, for reasons of which their not entirely esteemed host was perfectly well aware and upon which, as a gentleman, he felt no need to elaborate before the present company.

Henry had a great deal more to say—"The longer I live in France," he had written to William the night before, "the better I like the French personally, but the more convinced I am of their bottomless superficiality"—but at this point his impassioned diatribe was interrupted by a heavy knock at the door.

When Flaubert, who always gave his servant Sundays off, went to answer the door, Billy Pinkerton, whose considerable avoirdupois was every ounce the equal of the sizable Frenchman's, roughly shouldered his way past the great novelist and barged into the center of the fumous salon. Still huffing audibly from the steep stairs, the detective brandished his Colt revolvers and blasted a volley of warning shots into the cciling, plunging the startled assemblage into an unaccustomed state of total silence.

"Henry James!" Pinkerton barked, turning toward the chimneypiece and leveling his smoking pistols at the frightened novelist. "Put your hands in the air and get down on the floor! You're under arrest!"

The Pinkertons, of course, had no legal jurisdiction in France. (Indeed, being private detectives, they were technically without jurisdiction back in the United States as well; but on their home turf, they were accustomed to working hand in glove with local law-enforcement agencies whose confidence and cooperation they gained and maintained not only by relieving them of much of their tedious investigative burden but also by magnanimously stepping aside at the moment of arrest and allowing the glory—and, not incidentally, any applicable reward money—to accrue to those beleaguered public servants.) In Paris, however, Billy Pinkerton was on his own, yet he was confident that his six-shooters and handcuffs would supply more than sufficient authority to make up for whatever the niceties of international law failed to provide him.

Henry hastily complied with the detective's harsh command, dropping to his knees and reaching hard for the bullet-pocked ceiling. What Pinkerton had failed to foresee, however, was the presence in the salon of Ivan Sergeyevich Turgenev, the colossal Nimrod of the North. Unintimidated by the interloper's gleaming guns, the Russian giant sprang to his American confrere's defense, pouncing on the detective from behind with the full weight of his gargantuan frame and sending him sprawling, mustache to the marquetry. As the stunned lawman's revolvers clattered harmlessly across the floor, he tried gamely to struggle to his feet, but he was no match for the massive Muscovite and the furious horde of French realists who, emboldened by the courageous example of the author of *Fathers and Sons,* descended upon the lawman en masse and proceeded, in the common idiom, to beat the living crap out of him. Flaubert, who had studied the military arts as a lieutenant in the National Guard during the Prussian invasion six years earlier, leaped into the fray and held the startled private eye in an eye-bulging headlock while Alphonse Daudet kneed him sharply in the balls and Émile Zola, with his powerful oarsman's arms, pummeled him repeatedly in the belly. Even the fastidious Edmond de Goncourt deigned to risk creasing his shiny patent-leather pumps by getting in a few crisp kicks to the intruder's prominent derrière.

During the dustup, Henry James managed to retrieve Pinkerton's pistols from the floor and make his getaway. The badly shaken author scrambled out the door of Flaubert's apartment, down the five flights of stairs, out of the Faubourg Saint-Honoré, out of Paris, out of France, and out of Europe—all the way back to quiet Quincy Street.

It was all, as Edmond de Goncourt summed up the scene in his famous journal, *"tellement Wild-West."*

Chapter Ten

———◆———

Charles William Eliot served as president of Harvard from 1869 to 1909. During his unprecedented four-decade tenure at the helm of the nation's flagship university, Eliot oversaw the most profound academic makeover in that institution's history: He tightened admission standards, increased enrollment, revamped and expanded the curriculum, introduced a system of electives, abolished compulsory religious worship, beefed up the graduate schools, and brought rigorous biological science to the medical school. In the judgment of Louis Menand, President Eliot was nothing less than "the most important figure in the history of American higher education."

Yet for all the brilliance of his educational and administrative accomplishments, C. W. Eliot was far from scintillating in person. Trained in mathematics and chemistry, he had a methodical stoichiometric mind and a spirit severely steeped in Yankee Unitarianism.

"Eliot was the non-pareil schoolmaster to his age,—an age that worshiped the schoolmaster and clung to him," wrote the political reformer John Jay Chapman, who attended Harvard in the early 1880s. He added that the university's president "regarded cultivation somewhat as Michael Angelo [*sic*] regarded the painting of the Venetian school,—as a thing fit for women. Life was greater than culture. No ideals except ideals of conduct had reality for him." According to another Harvard alumnus of the era, the theologian George Angier Gordon, "something in his look and bearing said plainly, 'I am observing you, you must prove your worth.'"

Even more daunting than Eliot's "look and bearing" was his face: Born with a large nevus—a swollen, angry red welt that covered nearly his entire right cheek—he never allowed himself to be photographed except in left profile. "What all his intimates called his coldness," wrote the literary biographer Edward Wagenknecht, "had been developed, at least in part, by his lifelong knowledge that a stranger's first impulse at the sight of his face was to shudder, and his frequent failure to greet people was due at least in part to vision so defective that he could not recognize a friend fifteen feet away."

Given their many differences in talents and temperament, it is hardly surprising that the long relationship between Charles Eliot and William James was not without its occasional strains. Eliot's initial impression of William, formed when the latter was his student at the Lawrence Scientific School during the early 1860s, was that "James was a very interesting and agreeable pupil, but was not wholly devoted to the study of Chemistry." (He also disapprovingly noted that William's attendance at his organic chemistry laboratory had been "irregular.") William, for his part, had been less than delighted when his former professor was appointed president of Harvard in 1869. As he wrote to Henry Bowditch on that occasion, "His great personal defects—tactlessness—meddlesomeness—and disposition to cherish petty grudges seem pretty universally acknowledged; but his ideas seem good and his economic powers first rate,—so in the absence of any other possible candidate, he went in. It seems queer that such a place should go begging for candidates. . . ."

As president, Eliot endured even greater frustrations with James than he had as his chemistry teacher. In the spring of 1873, he offered William a position teaching anatomy, which the latter initially declined, preferring, as he wrote to his brother Henry, "to fight it out on the line of mental science." But when it became apparent that no offer was forthcoming in that field, William decided to accept the anatomy spot after all. Then he changed his mind yet again, thus engaging Eliot as his unwilling partner in a typical Jamesian waltz of vacillation that the stolid administrator could only have found exasperating in the extreme.

But whatever grievances the president and the psychologist may have held against each other, all were forgiven (if not forgotten) in the fall of 1876, upon William's delivery of the well-heeled Asa Hite to Eliot's growing roster of the school's benefactors—a list that would come to include such prodigiously fat cats as J. P. Morgan and John D. Rockefeller, and which would ultimately make Harvard the wealthiest private university in the world. With his "first-rate economic powers," Eliot well understood the fund-raising function to be among the primary duties of a university president; or, as Frank James snidely put it, he knew perfectly well "which side his buttocks were buttered on."

Eliot also knew how to butter up his benefactors, few of whom were in the least reticent about having their generosity publicly acknowledged and applauded. It was thus that on the evening of Friday, December 15, 1876, the university's leader played host to a lavish soirée in celebration of the funding of the school's new Asa B. Hite Laboratory of Experimental Psychology. The gala event took place at the president's residence, an imposing redbrick edifice with a massive slate mansard roof, situated near the Harvard Yard at No. 17 Quincy Street, directly across from the James family's more modest abode at No. 20. Eliot pulled out all the stops in orchestrating this posh affair in honor of the laboratory's eponymous donor, decking out his parlor and drawing room in the spirit of the season with potted poinsettias, sprigs of holly, ivy, and fragrant sprays of pine. All that afternoon a small army of servants in crimson livery, many of them scholarship students, bustled about lading the buffet tables with a sumptuous spread of goodies—ginger cookies, spice cakes, mincemeat pies, candied fruits and nuts—and strategically situating decanters of port wine and sherry all about the room, the centerpiece of which was a capacious cut-crystal punch bowl filled with a deceptively potent concoction of Jamaican rum, cognac, Madeira, lime juice, guava jelly, green tea, and simple syrup.

The Harvard campus glittered that evening with a blanket of snow that had been falling throughout the day. By the time the guests began to arrive—many by horse-drawn sleigh—the president's mansion was illuminated with the welcoming glow of dozens of gas lamps. The event brought together *le tout* Harvard: a number of department heads, including Francis Child of the English department and George Herbert Palmer of the philosophy department; Alexander Agassiz and his stepmother, Elizabeth (who was to become the cofounder and first president of Radcliffe College); Henry Bowditch and James Putnam of the medical faculty; and Oliver Wendell Holmes, Jr., of the law school, among other Cambridge luminaries—all of whom were scrupulously observed by William Pinkerton, who had arrived earlier in the day accompanied by a pair of armed and uniformed agency guards whose job it was to watch over a polished mahogany chest full of gold bullion that was to be ceremoniously presented by Asa Hite to an appropriately grateful President Eliot as the climax of the evening's festivities. (Mr. Hite's generous gift to the university was likely less an expression of any reasoned belief in the future of scientific psychology than of simple gratitude to William James for having delivered his daughter back to him from Europe a new woman—self-assured yet without the old strident political edge, eminently comfortable with herself and bursting with life.)

As the guests filed in to the parlor to the mellifluous strains of a string quartet and a grand piano provided by faculty members of the nearby New England Conservatory of Music, Pinkerton, still smarting from the drubbing he had received at the hands (and feet) of Ivan Turgenev and his rabid gang of French novelists a couple of weeks earlier, stuck close by his security men and the chest of bullion. The detective did not feel it was his place to be mingling with such distinguished company. After all, he was on duty, and not merely as the guardian of Asa Hite's gleaming largesse. Having let Henry James slip through his fingers at Flaubert's *cénacle,* he was eager to size up the devious Dr. William James at close range, though he had not mentioned anything to Asa Hite of his dire suspicions concerning the psychologist, nor of Elena's misbehavior with Henry's pal Flaubert—either of which admissions would have entailed having to confess that he had once again failed to nab a James brother. In fact, Pinkerton had seen no need even to mention to his client that he had recently been in France.

At about six P.M. the James family—William, Henry, Alice, and their parents—arrived from across the way in a group, led by William in an elegant black swallowtail coat, white waistcoat, and stock tie. (Frank and Jesse, in the guises of Professors Franklin and Jessup, would show up separately a bit later, Frank in the company of his jolly mentor Francis Child and Jesse all by his cantankerous lonesome.) Always leery of large, formal occasions, William had been especially apprehensive about the evening, knowing that he might well be encountering Elena Hite for the first time since her precipitous return from the continent the week before, an anxiety against which he had fortified his spirits with a swift whiff of amyl nitrite before sallying out across Quincy Street. Under the influence of those potent chemical vapors, his face was flushed to a rosy glow, and the usual bounce to his step was pronounced to such a degree that he appeared to Pinkerton almost to be dancing a jig.

The detective's attention was so thoroughly riveted on the preternaturally buoyant professor that he failed to register the concurrent arrival of Henry James, who brought up the rear of the family contingent and who, upon entering the parlor, as was his wont, paused briefly to make a survey of the assembled guests. Alarmed to spot William Pinkerton among them, the author promptly detached himself from his clan and slunk off along the side of the room, keeping his back to the dreaded detective at all times and as much of the company as possible interposed between himself and his nemesis. In originally fleeing Minnesota for Europe, he had hoped to evade the consequences of his involvement with his outlaw brothers; but, as we have seen, the notion that being abroad might somehow have put him out of reach of the long arm of the law had turned out to be cruelly illusory. His brutal confrontation with Pinkerton chez Flaubert had so unnerved him that, rather than devising any ingenious scheme for continuing to avoid arrest, the panicked "native of the James family" had blindly responded to the primal pull of home—a move that had drawn him once again into perilous proximity to the trigger-happy private eye. To make matters worse, as Henry gazed back across the room toward the entryway, he cringed to witness the arrival of his erstwhile "wife," Elena Hite, whom he had effectively booted out of Paris, an act for which he was certain she would unlikely be inclined to look upon him fondly.

The Hites, father and daughter, were making a grand entrance, Asa Hite sporting a double-breasted Prince Albert frock coat and gold-handled ebony walking stick, and Elena appearing exquisitely framed by the archway of the parlor in a princess-line sheath, dramatically fashioned by Charles Frederick Worth from a bolt of verdigris satin that brought out the striking hue of her eyes. The garment—only a small sample of the spoils of her recent couturial sack of Paris—was cut daringly low at the bodice, the audacious effect softened, if at all, by a modest tulle tucker. Standing before William James in the gentle glow of the gas lamps, she appeared even more radiant than he remembered her. He had often wondered during the months of her absence abroad whether he might not have come to overrate her allure, yet if anything, her beauty had burgeoned on the continent. Her

Grand Tour, mysteriously curtailed though it had been—William's sister had never satisfactorily explained the motivation for their abrupt return to the States—had manifestly fulfilled its intended sanative objective.

The arrival of his former patient rapidly cleared William's head of any lingering effects of the short-acting amyl, replacing it with a "high" of a different, though no less puissant, quality. In the months since their consultations in William's Lawrence Hall office, Elena had come to fill a place in his heart that Alice Gibbens, the mate anointed by his father, seemingly never could. Years later, in his *Varieties of Religious Experience,* he would expound upon the distinction between what he called "once-born" and "twice-born" souls: The former were those healthy-minded individuals who seemed to sail through life secure in their sense of its meaning and richness, "developing straight and natural, with no element of morbid compunction or crisis." The latter, by contrast, were "sick-minded," having peered into the dark abyss of despair and disillusionment and become intimately acquainted with the reality of evil in the universe. William, not surprisingly, tended to side with the sick-minded over "mere sky-blue healthy-minded moralists," whose view of life, he argued, was "inadequate as a philosophical doctrine, because the evil facts which it refuses positively to account for are a genuine portion of reality; and they may after all be the best key to life's significance, and possibly the only openers of our eyes to the deepest levels of truth."

In the staunch Miss Gibbens, William perceived the classic embodiment of the once-born soul, which he feared might never be able to empathize with the frailties and flights of his own. Just as Jesse James had vibrated sympathetically to the "unconformities" that he and "Miss Phoenix" had experienced in the course of their disrupted teen years, so William had come to consider his patient something of a soul mate by virtue of the breakdowns they had both suffered in their twenties. Less philosophically, he had been finding that he simply missed her—or, at the very least, his lively correspondence with her, around which he had come to shape his days while she was abroad.

As their eyes met across the parlor, Elena approached William with a twinge of trepidation. After all, she could not have been certain that Alice and Henry James had refrained from tattling to their older brother about her liaison with Gustave Flaubert. But neither of William's siblings had seen fit to let that fraught cat out of the bag, if only because to have done so would have been to acknowledge an egregious lapse of oversight on their own parts. Thus, nothing in William's expression or demeanor gave Elena the slightest suggestion of anything other than an unmitigated delight at beholding her.

"Bonsoir, cher docteur," she said, smiling, daintily offering him her kid-gloved hand.

William took it and brought it to his lips with a courtly bow. *"Enchanté, comme toujours, chère mademoiselle."*

The doctor and his former patient leaned toward each other, barely suppressing—or so it seemed to Pinkerton from his vantage point at the back of the room—a mutual inclination to fall into an embrace. But this unclinical urge, if it existed, was quickly squelched by Asa Hite, who stepped forward and clapped William heartily on the back. "Some shindig, eh, Bill?" he boomed, employing the monstrosity of nominal overfamiliarity with which he had taken the liberty of addressing his correspondent during their months of exchanging letters. William shuddered inwardly to hear it, but, having failed to nip the thing in the epistolary bud, he felt helplessly obliged to abide it spoken aloud.

"I'll say, Asa!" he gamely returned.

Billy Pinkerton, who had left his post by the bullion chest to prowl his way through the crowd for a closer inspection of the suspect professor, caught the attention of Mr. Hite, who called the detective over to introduce him to his daughter and his favorite psychologist.

Elena and Pinkerton eyed each other warily, each fearing that the other might let slip some telltale intimation of their contentious prior acquaintance. But upon being informed that the young lady had recently returned from Paris, the detective made a mighty show of averring that he had never had the pleasure of visiting the storied French capital.

"Oh, you really *must* go sometime, Mr. Pinkerton," Elena teased him gaily. "It's such an *intriguing* city."

"Yes, that's what I hear."

Mr. Hite then introduced William James, whom he presented to the detective as "the man of the hour."

"To say nothing of being the *most* brilliant doctor!" Elena gushed.

"So your father has told me."

"And did he tell you about Dr. James's brother Henry? I had the pleasure of meeting him in Paris. He's *such* a talented writer!" she prattled on, enjoying watching Pinkerton squirm. "They're a *most* extraordinary family, really."

"Exceptional, yes, so I gather," the detective deadpanned. He shook William's hand, noting the evil doctor's grip to be unexpectedly firm for so slight and cerebral an individual.

"Seems to me you fellows are pretty much in the same game," Mr. Hite ventured by way of establishing common conversational ground between the detective and the psychologist.

"Is that so?" replied William. "And what game might that be, Asa?"

"You know," Hite answered, tapping a stubby finger to his temple with a conspiratorial wink. "The human mind and all that."

Fixing William with a penetrating regard, Pinkerton remarked that his own investigations were focused exclusively on the *criminal* mind.

"Ah, fascinating. And what have you learned?" asked William.

"Not nearly so much as I'd like, Professor, " the detective replied, cagily appending, "Although I *have* observed that criminal proclivities often tend to run in families."

William, having no reason to imagine that his interlocutor was cognizant of his relationship to the western Jameses, nor that he himself was an object of the detective's darkest suspicions, breezily conceded that certain degenerate tendencies did indeed appear to be hereditary—like others, such as artistic talent and scientific genius—but at present the data were far from sufficient to disentangle the social from the biological threads of influence.

"And are those the sorts of experiments you're proposing to conduct in this new laboratory of yours?" asked Pinkerton.

William gave a modest chuckle. "I'm afraid we're a long way from being able to address such complex questions at the moment," he explained. "What we'll primarily be looking into are simple nervous responses in the so-called lower animals."

"Well, some of the criminal animals I've been studying get pretty low," Pinkerton commented wryly. "And sometimes mighty nervous, too."

William responded to the detective's gibe with such a natural-sounding chortle that Pinkerton was forced to conclude that if the psychologist was also a master criminal, he was certainly one smooth customer.

"Now, I'm sure you boys could jabber on about this all evening," Mr. Hite broke in, laying a fleshy hand on William's shoulder, "but what say we go pay our respects to the high muck-a-muck?"

William begged his leave of the detective, assuring him what a pleasure it had been to make his acquaintance, then dutifully escorted the guest of honor and his daughter off toward the center of the parlor, where President Eliot and his wife were surrounded by a gaggle of guests, among them Mrs. Agassiz and her stepson, Alexander. As they crossed the room, the psychologist took the precaution of warning Elena about Eliot's disfigurement, yet she was nonetheless startled by her initial view of the president's furious red splotch, which, as she whispered to William, would thenceforth be forever conflated in her mind with the notion of "Harvard crimson."

Upon greeting the Hites, Eliot referred to William James as "this proud son of Harvard" and pronounced the occasion "a splendid moment for the university, and for the advancement of human knowledge."

"And shall Harvard someday also boast of its proud *daughters?*" Elena asked brightly.

Mrs. Agassiz, studying the forward younger woman with an attitude that was at once appalled, amused, and admiring, gave a mock-conspiratorial nod to Mrs. Eliot. "Oh, we've been hounding our poor President Eliot about that for *years,* Miss Hite," she said, sighing theatrically.

"All in good time, ladies. All in good time," Eliot responded with a hint of pique and an apologetic glance toward Asa Hite. "But this evening, let us not forget, we are gathered to celebrate a more immediately imminent milestone in our university's history."

"You bet!" concurred Mr. Hite, and as he and President Eliot launched into a volley of mutual congratulations, William offered Elena his arm and guided her off around the parlor to meet some of the other guests. The first they encountered was Alice Gibbens, to whom William introduced Elena as "the daughter of our generous benefactor, Mr. Asa Hite," presenting Miss Gibbens as "my dear friend," a designation that Alice greeted with a microscopic moue, apparently finding it insufficiently intimate to impress the special nature of their relationship upon the beautiful young woman draped on her near-fiancé's arm, a woman whom she undoubtedly recognized, if only subconsciously, as a contender for his affections.

William must have found the contrast between the two women striking—and not merely according to the measure of how often each had been "born." Alice Gibbens was decked out for the occasion in an ensemble comprising a somber brownish hoopskirt and a high-collared, ruffled beige silk blouse topped off by a broad grosgrain choker—a dowdy getup that did little either to obscure her stoutness or to evidence an even marginally keen sense of style. Indeed, William could hardly have conjured up a more vivid realization of his formulation of the drab brood hen and the dazzling bird of paradise than Alice and Elena standing face-to-face.

"Ah yes, Dr. James has spoken of you as the young lady who was recently traveling with his sister," Miss Gibbens intoned with an overly brilliant smile. "I do hope that you're feeling better now."

"Oh, infinitely so, thank you," Elena replied, scrutinizing her rival with an equally insincere exercise of her own facial musculature and insinuating her hand even more deeply into the crook of William's elbow. "Dr. James knew just what I needed."

"I daresay he must have," Alice answered icily. "But of course one can never be *too* careful, can one?" she added. "I understand that it's imperative for those in your condition to avoid becoming overly stimulated."

"I shall certainly try my best," Elena assured her with a brittle smile.

William was casting anxiously about the room for anyone or anything that might distract the two women from their increasingly sticky encounter. Succor, such as it would prove, arrived in the form of Jesse James, who, wielding a glass of punch in each hand with the same aplomb with which he had once toted a pair of six-shooters, came weaving his way toward them.

William seized upon his brother's appearance as an opportunity to defuse the ladies' potentially incendiary confrontation, ingenuously presenting Jesse as "my distinguished colleague Professor Robert Jessup."

The outlaw was momentarily flummoxed, never having seen Elena so splendidly dolled up, and still laboring under the misapprehension that the young woman with whom he had shared such delightful intimacies the previous summer was named Elena Phoenix. "Pleased to make your acquaintance, Miss . . . *Hite?*" he responded quizzically, addressing his remark as much to her half-exposed bosom as to her face.

Elena executed a crisp curtsy and a tight smile. "Likewise, I'm sure, Professor. And where, pray tell, might be the lovely *Mrs.* Jessup this evening?"

This, to William, must have seemed a strange and overly familiar query to be putting to a gentleman to whom one had just been introduced. (Perhaps he speculated that his patient wasn't quite so far out of the psychiatric woods as he had been encouraged to believe.) He looked askance at Elena, who responded with an inscrutable smirk.

"I'm afraid that my wife is presently indisposed," Jesse replied coolly. Then, directing a nod over at Henry James, who was skulking about the sideboard stuffing his face with a slice of mince pie, the outlaw mischievously said, "As I was just informing your *husband.*"

Elena was astonished to discover Henry among the company. Knowing nothing of the violent episode in the rue du Faubourg Saint-Honoré, she had assumed that after cleansing Paris of her embarrassing presence, he would have been content to have remained there forever, keeping Flaubert and the entire city to himself. Henry sensed the knot of curious guests gazing over at him and, not wanting to draw any further attention to himself, gave them an anemic bow and turned back to the buffet table, with Elena glowering sourly after him.

"I wasn't aware that Miss Hite *had* a husband," Alice Gibbens interjected tartly. "Or have I been misinformed, dear?"

"Not at all," Elena replied. "I fear that it's Professor Jessup who is misinformed. Perhaps he's confusing me with some other Elena of his acquaintance. After all, having a spouse is hardly something one simply forgets, now, is it? Why, that would be virtually criminal."

It was apparent to William James that his quondam patient was amusing herself immensely with these arch remarks, although he was utterly perplexed by what they all meant. He had been prepared, naturally, to negotiate the necessary deceptions surrounding the identities of Frank and Jesse that evening; but in the face of all these odd looks and veiled references, he could only have been experiencing a disquieting sense of having become enmeshed in a far denser web of dissimulation than he had bargained for. Mercifully, the thickening tension was broken by President Eliot, who tinkled a wineglass to obtain the attention of the company. After offering a few perfunctory words of greeting, this unlikely master of the revels announced: "We have a sterling program of entertainment this evening, commencing with Professors Francis Child and Will Franklin, who will grace us with a selection of the old ballads that Professor Child has been so assiduously collecting."

To a polite pitter-patter of applause, Professors Child and Franklin took their places in front of the grand piano and announced their opening number. Of the 305 ballads and their variants in Francis Child's collection, an impressive thirty-eight of them were devoted to the exploits of Robin Hood and his merry men, vastly more than to any other subject. The specimen with which Will Franklin and Francis Child chose to kick off their serenade to the assembled academics was the one known as Child Ballad no. 136, "Robin Hood's Delight." "Stubby" Child's quavering tenor and Will Franklin's light baritone blended in pleasant close harmonies as they sang:

> There is some will talk of lord and knights,
>> Doun a doun a doun a doun
>> And some of yeoman good,
> But I will tell you of Will Scarlock,
>> Little John and Robin Hood.
>> Doun a doun a doun a doun
>
> They were outlaws, as 'tis well known,
>> And men of a noble blood;
> And many a time was their valour shown
>> In the forrest of merry Sheerwood. . . .

Billy Pinkerton, happily tapping his toes to the ancient air, failed to recognize the younger vocalist as the notorious Frank James. The only visual record he had of the bandit was the Civil War–era tintype he had laid out on the hotel bed in St. Louis for Elena to peruse, an image to which the wiry troubadour by the piano no longer bore much of a resemblance. Thus the irony of the infamous Missouri outlaw musically apotheosizing a fellow fabled miscreant was entirely lost upon the detective, as it was upon practically everyone else in the room, with the notable exceptions of Jesse and Henry James. Had Pinkerton been paying closer attention, he would have observed Professor Jessup sidling over to his furtive brother to share the joke. At first Jesse was all wry smiles, but his demeanor abruptly darkened when Henry surreptitiously pointed out the presence of the detective in the back of the room. At the sight of his archenemy, the outlaw's steel-blue eyes narrowed to reptilian slits, his jaw tightened, and he scowled into his tumbler of punch, which he aggressively downed in a single swig. William James and Elena Hite—the only other individuals in the room who might have appreciated the sardonic aptness of Frank's song selection—were far too deeply engrossed in each other to take much notice of the background music to their increasingly immoderate flirtation. With their arms still intertwined, they drifted moonily off to the fringes of the parlor, exchanging reminiscences of their earlier psychiatric encounters and the prolific international correspondence those consultations had spawned.

Back at the piano, Will Franklin and Professor Child now moved on to a rendition of the "A" variant of Child Ballad no. 74, "Fair Margaret and Sweet William," a tragic tale of star-crossed lovers:

> As it fell out on a long summer's day,
> Two lovers they sat on a hill;
> They sat together that long summer's day,
> And could not talk their fill.

> "I see no harm by you, Margaret,
> Nor you see none by me;

Before tomorrow eight a clock
A rich wedding shall you see."

Fair Margaret sat in her bower-window,
A-combing of her hair,
And there she spy'd Sweet William and his bride,
As they were riding near.

Down she layd her ivory comb,
And up she bound her hair;
She went her way forth of her bower,
But never more did come there.

When day was gone, and night was come,
And all men fast asleep,
Then came the spirit of Fair Margaret,
And stood at William's feet.

"God give you joy, you two true lovers,
In bride-bed fast asleep;
Loe I am going to my green grass grave,
And am in my winding-sheet. . . ."

Despite its archaic diction and convoluted syntax, the hoary medieval folk song still had the power to move even a gathering of sophisticated nineteenth-century academics. The familiar rose-and-briar ending of the tune was greeted by a poignant hush, followed by an enthusiastic round of applause; but as he and Francis Child left the piano, Frank was immediately accosted by a highly agitated Professor Jessup, who urgently pulled him aside to alert him to the presence of William Pinkerton at the back of the parlor. Frank, still basking in the approbation of the audience (which he later reported having found "so much sweeter than being blasted away at by an angry lynch mob"), was initially slow to apprehend the full implication of his brother's admonition, until Jesse reminded him that the trial of the Youngers out in Minnesota had recently concluded with Cole, Bob, and Jim pleading guilty to all charges and receiving life sentences in the state penitentiary at Stillwater rather than the trips to the gallows that most observers believed should have been their due. Who was to say, Jesse asked, what sort of secret deal their former comrades may have cut with the authorities in order to spare their own precious hides, perhaps even having gone so far as to finger Frank as the triggerman in Joseph Heywood's murder? And while the crowd was turning its attention to President Eliot's introduction of the next performer on the program— Miss Alice Gibbens—Jesse, who, even as Professor Jessup, never ventured out without packing at least two pistols on his person and a bowie knife strapped to his calf, stealthily handed off one of his guns to his brother before returning to his station by the punch bowl. Though Frank was in no frame of mind to be dragged back into the vicissitudes of his outlaw past, the prospect of being collared by Pinkerton and hauled in to face charges of killing the Northfield bookkeeper must have served as a powerful incentive for him to accept Jesse's weapon and all that went with it. He reluctantly pocketed the pistol.

Miss Gibbens's contribution to the evening's entertainment was a selection of lieder composed by her former vocal coach, opening with Frau Schumann's elegant setting of the poet Friedrich Rückert's "Liebst du um Schönheit" ("If You Love for Beauty"), her Opus 12 no. 4.

> Liebst du um Schönheit,
> o nicht mich liebe!
> Liebe die Sonne,
> sie trägt ein gold'nes Haar!

> Liebst du um Jugend,
> o nicht mich liebe!

Liebe den Frühling,
der jung ist jedes Jahr!

Liebst du um Schätze,
o nicht mich liebe!
Liebe die Meerfrau,
sie hat viel Perlen klar.

Licbst du um Liebe,
o ja, mich liebe!
Liebe mich immer,
dich lieb' ich immerdar.

As she warbled this paean to true love, Miss Gibbens kept anxiously scanning the audience to catch a glimpse of her intended's admiring visage, only to gradually twig to the distressing realization that William and his pretty patient were no longer in the parlor. Peering out toward the hallway, she was appalled to spy the shameless couple beginning to make their way up the staircase toward the private chambers of the president's residence.

After rushing through her next number—Clara Schumann's haunting setting of Heinrich Heine's "Lorelei"—at a breakneck tempo that would have thoroughly nauseated the composer, the flustered singer abandoned her place by the piano and bustled across the room to consult with William's parents and sister over the scandalous disappearance of the man of the hour and his benefactor's captivating daughter. Miss James, never a great admirer of her brother's "other" Alice, merely smirked and shrugged, while Henry Sr., who had become increasingly hard of hearing with age, impatiently shushed the distraught diva, the better to follow the next announcement from the podium. "We are honored this evening," President Eliot was proclaiming, "to have with us not only Dr. William James, the distinguished founding director of our new Hite Laboratory of Experimental Psychology here at Harvard, but also his no less accomplished brother, the author Henry James, Jr., upon whom I would like to take the liberty of imposing at this time to favor us with a reading from one of his marvelous tales."

Henry's cover was thus effectively blown. Earlier in the week he had graciously consented to participating in the evening's entertainment, but that was before he had been aware that William Pinkerton and his men would be in the audience. Desperately attempting to maintain a low profile, the author kept his head down, hemming and hawing. His work, he stammered, was not actually meant for oral presentation; furthermore, he was a sorry reader, and in addition, he had no manuscript at hand from which to recite. President Eliot, in what was probably one of his nearest approximations to the deportment of a party animal, smiled broadly and waved a copy of *The Atlantic Monthly,* jovially cajoling the recalcitrant scribe to take the floor.

To Henry's anguish, the crowd, led by a paternally beaming Henry Sr., began vociferously encouraging him to come forward. The beleaguered novelist, feeling he had no option but to oblige, shambled up to the podium. There President Eliot handed him the journal containing the first installment of *The American,* from which he commenced to read in a nearly inaudible voice—as if somehow not to be heard might magically keep him from being seen as well:

On a brilliant day in May, in the year 1868, a gentleman was reclining at his ease on the great circular divan which at that period occupied the centre of the Salon Carré, in the Museum of the Louvre. This commodious ottoman has since been removed, to the extreme regret of all weak-kneed lovers of the fine arts; but the gentleman in question had taken serene possession of its softest spot, and, with his head thrown back and his legs outstretched, was staring at Murillo's beautiful moon-borne Madonna in profound enjoyment of his posture. . . .

William Pinkerton, of course, had no trouble recognizing the fugitive writer. The moment Henry started to read, the detective alerted his uniformed guards to the presence of a major felon in the room; yet with his every lawmanly instinct screaming for him to storm the lectern and make an arrest, he grudgingly refrained from taking such drastic action, realizing that to do so would be to risk spoiling his star client's moment of glory, and recalling what had recently transpired chez Flaubert—a bitter memory that rendered him fearful of being similarly set upon and ignominiously dispatched by, perhaps, an outraged Harvard English department.

Pinkerton was not the only one in the parlor struggling to suppress an itch for action: Positioned at either side of the room and edging their way inconspicuously toward the back, Frank and Jesse James were keeping close eyes on the detective and his men, poised to spring to the defense of their literary brother in the event that any of the lawmen made the slightest false move.

Henry, having observed Pinkerton in animated consultation with his security detail, terminated his reading only a few sentences into the story. Without so much as a word of explanation or apology to President Eliot, the frightened author handed his host the copy of *The Atlantic* and ducked swiftly into the butler's pantry, from which he scurried out the servants' entrance and back across chilly Quincy Street to the refuge of No. 20.

President Eliot, with his notoriously limited tolerance for the unforeseen, stood momentarily bemused. There being no further performances scheduled for the evening, he had little alternative but to move directly to the main event. Frantically cuing the resident pianist to sound a dramatic fanfare, Eliot called upon Asa Hite and William James to come forward for the presentation of Mr. Hite's handsome donation to the university. Pinkerton signaled his men to lug the heavy mahogany bullion box to the front of the room, where the security detail, flanking the chest, ceremoniously lifted its lid to reveal the gleaming array of gold bars within. The sight elicited a startled gasp from the guests, which Asa Hite took as evidence of their awe at the magnitude of his munificence; whereas most of them, more likely, were appalled by such a blatant and vulgar display of wealth. It was a spectacle, they no doubt felt, that might have played quite prettily down in New York and perhaps even in provincial Hartford, but which up in proper Boston could only be taken as an egregious exhibition of reprehensible taste.

Oblivious to the true significance of the crowd's reaction, Mr. Hite proudly took his place to one side of the mahogany chest. As President Eliot went into his introductory remarks, it became rapidly apparent that William James, who was to have bookended the bullion on the other side, was no longer in the parlor. Eliot became visibly perturbed by the professor's absence, which he doubtless perceived as yet another example of his former student's congenital fecklessness. His testy inquiry as to whether anyone knew the whereabouts of Professor James evoked a confused low murmur that rippled through the room, until Alice Gibbens came forward and whispered into Eliot's ear her suspicion that the missing celebrant had ascended to the upper chambers of the residence. It being entirely unfitting for anyone but the master of the manse to venture into that sacrosanct private domain, it fell upon President Eliot himself to go looking for the "proud son of Harvard." Excusing himself momentarily, he asked if any of the previous performers would be so kind as to furnish an encore during his absence, but none volunteered. (Frank James, having precious little desire to share the podium with William Pinkerton, naturally demurred, and the overwrought Miss Gibbens apologized that she no longer felt herself to be "in voice.") This left Hite, Pinkerton, and his security guards standing silently staring out at the guests while the conservatory pianist nobly essayed to fill the embarrassing void by tinkling out a Schubert sonata. His musical efforts, however, did little to ameliorate the general sense of unease in the parlor.

Into this yawning breach in the evening's amusements strode—or, more accurately, staggered—Jesse James. Reckless and impulsive under the best of circumstances, the outlaw, besides being thoroughly soused and seething with animosity toward Billy Pinkerton, was also doubtless jealous of all the attention being lavished on his older brothers—not to mention on the fabled scourge of Sherwood Forest, whose legendary exploits, he believed, paled in comparison to his own. Taking his place by the piano, Professor Jessup launched into a tipsy recitation of a poem that he introduced as a work of his own composition in the grand tradition of Francis Child's troubadour ballads:

> You may sing about your Robin Hood
> And other famous names,
> But the greatest outlaws of them all
> Are Frank and Jesse James.
> These bold marauders of the plains,
> The bravest in all history
> Strike fear into the banks and trains
> With deeds becloaked in mystery.

Never having seen Jesse in the light—or with his pants on—William Pinkerton took a while to appreciate the extraordinary import of what he was observing. But whatever initial uncertainty he may have harbored as to the true identity of the poet, what he heard next was more than sufficient to remove any lingering shadow of a doubt: Jesse's rhyme turned out to be a lurid fantasy of the James brothers wreaking revenge upon the Pinkertons, a dreadful piece of doggerel in which Frank, Jesse, and a trio of unnamed accomplices staged a bloody ambush on their sworn enemies:

> The Pinkerton detective clan
> (Those craven railroad dicks)
> Tracked the James Gang everywhere
> And thought they knew their tricks.

But when they rode the Iron Horse
On express cars and their engines
The James boys laid in wait for them
And vowed to take their vengeance.

It went on to describe in brutal detail the demise of Allan, William, and Robert Pinkerton at the hands of the James brothers et al.:

Then from out of the woods
With a fierce rebel yell
These bold desperadoes
Sent those cowards to hell.
Made them swallow hot lead
And then dine on the dust
As they ended up dead
Like all railroad dicks must.

No one in the audience knew what to make of this outlandish performance, although most were either too polite or too flabbergasted to give voice to their consternation. Billy Pinkerton was chafing to collar the felonious versifier. He looked over to Mr. Hite with a furrowed brow, clenched teeth, and an angry shake of his head, all of which his employer took as an indication that something had to be done immediately to put a stop to the travesty. The foolhardy railroad magnate thus took it upon himself to step forward and grab the offending poetaster by the arm, unaware that this was the selfsame Jesse James who had an "Arkansas toothpick" strapped to his calf and who, according to T. J. Stiles, may once have employed such a utensil to slice the penis off one of his victims and stuff it into his mouth (the "his" in this instance presumably referring to the victim's mouth and not to the outlaw's own).

"Professor Jessup!" bellowed Hite. "This is entirely unfitting! You must desist immediately!"

Jesse shook free of the older man's grasp and shoved his portly assailant aside, sending him slamming headlong back against the bullion box with a resounding crash that knocked him unconscious. As
Pinkerton and his men advanced to restrain the outlaw, he drew a revolver from beneath his waistcoat and brandished the weapon shakily
at his attackers, commanding the detective and his henchmen to drop
their holsters and spread-eagle themselves across the top of the piano.
As the pianist hastily deserted his bench, the horrified guests, already
disturbed by the fact that the poet was so obviously in his cups and
"making little sense," flew into an absolute panic. Even Oliver Wendell Holmes, Jr., who had seen abundant action during the Civil
War—in which he had been thrice wounded—was shaken by the
flash of a firearm in the Harvard president's parlor. In response to the
commotion, the drunken gunman wheeled and waved his pistol at
the crowd, sending them screaming and crying toward the rear of the
room amid a clatter of overturning tables and shattering glassware.

Meanwhile, upstairs in President Eliot's master bedroom, Elena
Hite was treating William James to a delectable demonstration of her
recently acquired proficiency in the gamahuchic arts. This was undoubtedly a novel sensation for the chaste psychologist, who, even in
his wildest masturbatory fantasies, might never have imagined himself
the object of such exotic ministrations. Yet as his biographer Robert D.
Richardson pointed out: "James possessed what has been called 'a great
experiencing nature'; he was astonishingly, even alarmingly, open to
new experiences. . . . This risk-taking, this avidity for the widest possible range of conscious experience, predisposed him to embrace things
that many of us might find unsettling." (It is also not unlikely that the
psychologist's exhilaration was being enhanced by the effects of another vial of amyl nitrite he had uncorked to get himself "up" for the
illicit interlude.) Amazed and thrilled by Elena's brazen flouting of all
conceivable correctitude, William breathlessly asked her how she could
dare to perform such a louche act with so many proper people so close

at hand. Elena reminded him of what she had once told him about the folly of living for the good report of others: Having scandalized all of Hartford and most of Paris, she professed that mere Harvard was hardly of concern to her.

"Paris?" he asked. "How did you manage to scandalize most of Paris?"

William must have felt himself on the verge of penetrating the mystery of Elena's premature return from the continent, but before she could respond to his charged query, the bedroom door flew open to reveal Charles W. Eliot looming at the threshold.

Despite his wretched eyesight and the darkness of the chamber, the president of Harvard had no difficulty discerning what was transpiring on his Chippendale four-poster. His face turned such a bright scarlet that the shocking hue of his nevus was momentarily eclipsed. "James!" he shouted. "What the devil are you up to?"

To this, the famously articulate professor had no response other than to hastily yank up his trousers and beat a slapdash retreat out past the startled chief executive and down the stairs, where he was greeted by a scene of near-total chaos.

With his revolver directed toward the cowering crowd, much as he would have held a bunch of overly curious onlookers at bay during a Missouri bank holdup, Jesse James was making a point of finishing up his provocative rhyme:

> Then off at a gallop
> These knights of the road
> Did ride hell-for-leather
> Until the cock crowed.
> They rode in like thunder,
> They vanished like mist,
> Back to their hideout
> Where they ate, drank, and pissed.

This could have been one of the gravest missteps of the outlaw's career, and not merely from a literary viewpoint. While Jesse was standing down the terrified guests, and defiantly declaiming the final stanza of his impromptu opus, Billy Pinkerton managed to slip silently away from his position splayed across the lid of the grand piano, and began stealthily moving to retrieve his cast-off holster from the floor. In another second he would have gotten the drop on the drunken Jesse James, had not the scholarly Will Franklin—much to the astonishment of his mentor Francis Child, standing right beside him—whipped out the revolver that Jesse had handed him earlier and squeezed off a shot at Pinkerton's pudgy fingers. The crowd shrieked but, wary of Jesse's gun trained on them, resisted the impulse to bolt en masse. As the detective rapidly withdrew his hand, Frank raced forward and jabbed the barrel of his smoking pistol into the bulging belly of the startled sleuth.

Hearing the report of Frank's revolver and observing Asa Hite lying prostrate beside the bullion box, William jumped to the conclusion that his brother had just killed the goose that laid the golden eggs. He shifted instantly into medical mode and rushed to his benefactor's side, berating his brother, "My God, man, you've shot Mr. Hite!"

When Frank turned to reassure William that he was responsible for no such homicidal act, Billy Pinkerton seized the opportunity to swat the outlaw/scholar's pistol boldly aside and tromp down with the full force of his abundant poundage on Frank's bad foot—the one that had been shattered by a cannister ball during the war—causing him to let out an anguished howl and drop his weapon. As Jesse spun around to see what all the screaming was about, Pinkerton's guards sprang from the piano top and pounced on the besotted poet from behind, forcefully disarming him. In an instant the tables had turned, giving Pinkerton and his men the upper hand.

Mr. Hite struggled to his feet just in time to greet C. W. Eliot descending the staircase with a perceptibly disheveled Elena Hite in tow. Already badly discombobulated by what had been going on in his bedroom, the Harvard president was even further appalled to witness the bizarre and violent turn of events in his parlor, which he could only have seen as better befitting the most unruly frontier saloon than America's premier institution of higher learning. With unconcealed disgust, he remanded Elena to the custody of her father, giving the still-woozy tycoon a curt account of the compromising position in which he had discovered his daughter upstairs. This lewd news brought Mr. Hite to full consciousness as abruptly as a stiff whiff of smelling salts. He glared at Elena, then shot a nasty glance over toward William James, who, at Pinkerton's command, had just been slammed across the piano top and, with his legs indecorously spread, was being vigorously frisked by one of the uniformed agency guards. Under vastly different circumstances, the Connecticut railroad baron might have been pleased to have entertained a proper suit from the young doctor for his daughter's hand, but having gotten an inkling from President Eliot of what William and his erstwhile patient had been up to in the master bedroom, he found his esteem for the brilliant psychologist plummeting precipitously. He was certain that in short order everyone in the parlor would become aware of Elena's misbehavior with the man of the hour, which they would undoubtedly view as a woeful reflection upon his own parental laxity. He was thus seized by a pressing desire to get himself and his errant daughter off the premises and back down to Hartford posthaste. "Come on, Pinkerton!" he shouted. "Pack up the damned gold, and let's get the hell out of here!"

The detective paid little heed, relishing as he was the spectacular prospect of rounding up virtually all of the elusive James brothers in a single swoop. He and his men had their guns trained on William, Frank, and Jesse, and Henry, he reckoned, could hardly have gotten far. Beating James McDonough of the St. Louis Police Department to the punch, Pinkerton gloated to his security guards, would be a stunning coup that was bound to reverberate across the nation's wires to the everlasting glory of the agency.

Unfortunately, William Pinkerton, unlike his rival Chief McDon-

ough, was not a bona fide officer of the law. Having hit the James jack-
pot, the private eye was about to discover that there was little he could
do to cash in his chips. Asa Hite, still under the impression that Professors Jessup and Franklin were no more than a couple of rowdy academics instead of the most wanted outlaws in the nation, was becoming
adamant, with the savage petulance that only a thwarted millionaire
could display. "Pinkerton!" he hollered. "I said get your sorry ass out of
here!"

"You don't understand, sir!" the detective pleaded. "These are the
James boys!"

"I don't care if they're the goddamned Bloomer Girls!" Hite called
back. "We're going home!" With a death grip on Elena's wrist, he began
dragging her out of Eliot's parlor over her vehement protestations. Reduced to a state of infantile rage, she was kicking frantically at her father's shins and screaming, "But *Daddy*! I don't *want* to go home!"

Asa Hite, who had never verbally acknowledged his dissolute daughter's transgressions, now addressed her in the harshest possible terms:
"Shut up, you little *harlot*!" he barked. "You're not going home. You're
going to the *asylum*!" With that, he brought a beefy hand across Elena's
beautiful face with a solid smack that reverberated through the stricken
parlor almost as shockingly as the report from Frank's revolver a few
moments earlier.

As a bright crimson weal rose on Elena's cheek, mirroring President
Eliot's own, an infuriated William James lunged forward to intervene,
only to be violently jerked back by the agency goons.

"Now move it, Pinkerton!" bellowed Mr. Hite.

Recognizing that the man was in no frame of mind to be crossed,
the detective grudgingly acceded to his powerful client and ordered
his guards to holster their weapons, pack up the gold, and start hauling it away. With his own gun trained on his captives as he backed out
of the parlor, Pinkerton admonished the Jameses: "You bastards got
real lucky this time, but don't think you've seen the last of me!"

To which Frank, his injured foot still throbbing fiercely from the weight of the detective's boot, retorted grimly: "Nor you of us, you son of a bitch!"

But Pinkerton was already beyond hearing range. As soon as the detective was out the door, Frank and Jesse retrieved their guns from the parlor floor and skedaddled after William along Henry's route through the butler's pantry, leaving President Eliot to survey the wreckage of his elegant soirée. Shaking his head and doubtless making a mental note to more carefully vet the visiting scholars' program at Harvard, he was oblivious to the traumatized company scurrying past him in a hasty exodus, few even bothering to extend to their host so much as the courtesy of expressing their gratitude for a stimulating evening.

———◆———

On the other side of Quincy Street, William, Frank, and Jesse regrouped in the parental abode. There they discovered Henry cringing in the attic, from whence they coaxed the severely spooked author downstairs for an urgent fraternal tête-à-tête-à-tête-à-tête. This marked the first time that all four James brothers had been together under the family roof since the halcyon days of their antebellum sojourn in Newport, a reunion that might have been the occasion for a round of jolly reminiscences had not Pinkerton's warning still been ringing menacingly in their ears. As Frank cautioned his brothers, the moment the detective delivered the Hites safely home, he would undoubtedly turn straight around and mount a manhunt that would make the aftermath of the Northfield robbery look like a playground game of hide-and-seek.

Whatever peaceable fantasies Frank had fostered of trading his outlaw life for the merry tutelage of Francis Child had evaporated with Jesse's conjecture that the jailed Younger brothers may have ratted him out. Moreover, the Pinkertons' midnight firebombing of Castle James two years earlier still burned fresh in his memory, and the more recent affront of the detective having stomped on his bad foot had stirred in him a blind fury, just as Joseph Heywood's slamming his hand in the vault door of the Northfield bank had unleashed his homicidal rage. Something had to be done to stop the Big Man, Frank insisted—and sooner rather than later.

William, recalling Asa Hite's previous visits to Harvard, surmised that the detective's immediate destination was most likely the Dewey Square station in Boston, where his client's private railway car would be waiting to be coupled to a scheduled train to take them back down to Hartford.

At the mention of a railway car, Jesse, whose mastery of the art of train robbery far surpassed his command of poetic composition, perked up. Still dreaming of a "big score" to make up for the paltry take of the Northfield fiasco, he enthused, "Damn, that's a shitload of gold there!"

The shitload, William tersely reminded his bandit brother, was rightfully the property of Harvard University, earmarked for the construction of his new laboratory.

"Fat chance now, Casanova," Frank observed drily.

The psychologist had yet to fathom the full implications of the evening's events, being, as he was, preoccupied with the fate of Elena Hite. With "the asylum," William knew, Asa Hite had been threatening to commit his daughter to the Hartford Retreat for the Insane, Connecticut's oldest mental institution (today known by the gentler appellation the Hartford Institute of Living). The Retreat was far from the worst of snake pits—indeed, its establishment in 1824 had been predicated on the humane principle of providing "moral" treatment that stressed dignity and respect for the mentally ill. But as historian Lawrence B. Goodheart of the University of Connecticut at Hartford has noted, in the years following the Civil War, "less was heard about 'the law of kindness' and moral treatment of patients and more about moral unfitness and the benefits of eugenics." Having been intimately acquainted with similar institutions in his medical school days, William had no illusions about conditions in such establishments. He would have feared that confinement in the Retreat might destroy Elena—at the very least branding her a madwoman for life and perhaps even driving that spirited young woman truly insane: a stiff penalty indeed for a single aborted blow job.

Over a lifetime of wrestling with the problem of good and evil, William always desired to come down on the side of the former, yet there was in his character a persistent fascination with the latter, which he often argued was an inevitable—and even desirable—aspect of genuine reality. "I personally gave up the Absolute," he once wrote. "I fully believe in taking moral holidays." As his biographer Robert D. Richardson observed, William "could be reckless, even cruel," and "[a] part of James doubtless enjoyed the fray." This abiding appetite for transgression was apparent when, years later, after lecturing to an adoring audience of schoolteachers at Chautauqua, he wrote that he would have been "glad to get into something less blameless but more admiration-worthy. The flash of a pistol, a dagger, or a devilish eye, anything to break the unlovely level of 10,000 good people—a crime, a murder, rape, elopement, anything would do."

What would do on this snowy night was not yet entirely clear, though when it came to Billy Pinkerton, "the man of two minds" was of one with Frank's and Jesse's.

Of the gathered Jameses, Henry alone was reluctant to tangle again with the flagitious lawman. He was still shaken from his encounter with the private eye in Paris and naturally inclined never to run *toward* trouble. Not having been present for the gunplay at President Eliot's soirée, he failed to grasp the extent to which the gloves were off in the war between the Pinkertons and the Jameses. Discretion, he contended, might well be the better part of valor.

Frank laid out the counterargument plainly for his literary brother: "Do you understand what 'dead or alive' means, Harry?" he asked. "Do you want to *hang*?"

At that, Henry scrambled up the stairs to the bedroom he had been occupying since his return from France. While he was there rummaging through his steamer trunk to recover the pair of Colt revolvers he had salvaged from Flaubert's floor, downstairs the front door swung abruptly open. Frank and Jesse reflexively whipped out their own six-shooters and dropped to their knees behind a pair of bookcases in the living room, ready to do battle. The assumptive aggressors, however, turned out to be the benignant elder Jameses and their daughter, Alice.

"Now what in heaven's name was all *that* about?" Mrs. James demanded of William, with a nod back over her shoulder. Then, registering the presence of the gunmen kneeling behind the bookshelves, she pointed to Frank and Jesse. "And who in the world *are* these gentlemen?"

The gentlemen in question emerged from their makeshift battle stations, politely pocketed their pistols, and greeted the proper residents of the house with a couple of crisp bows, introducing themselves as Professors Franklin and Jessup.

Uncharitably dismissed by Henry's biographer Lyndall Gordon as "small-minded" and "that ordinary woman," who "had not a thought in her head beyond maternal nursing," Mary James could in fact be a shrewd observer of the human scene. She scrutinized the gunmen skeptically. "But then what could that dreadful policeman have meant when he said that you were the James boys?" she asked.

This salient query elicited utter silence on the part of the brothers, each of whom looked anxiously to the others to account for Pinkerton's proclamation. They were spared having to come up with an answer by the fortuitous appearance of Henry James, who descended the staircase with a loaded revolver in each hand.

"Angel!" Mrs. James exclaimed. "My Lord, what's gotten into you?"

Henry responded with a bashful tilt of his big balding head and a smile that was at once self-satisfied and diabolic—an expression often colorfully described in the vernacular as a "shit-eating grin."

At that moment—perhaps prompted by the sight of all four brothers together, or perhaps by Pinkerton's remark about the younger pair being Jameses—Mary James's much denigrated maternal instincts came springing to the fore: With a mother's uncanny sense of consanguinity, she recognized the gun-toting interlopers in her living room as the issue of her very own loins. Clutching her bosom and nearly swooning, she cried, "Rob! Wilky!"

"Oh my God!" exclaimed Alice James. "Of course!"

Henry Sr. failed to share in the familial epiphany. "What? What?" he asked.

"These men, darling," Mary breathlessly explained, "are our boys Wilky and Rob."

The elder Henry's eyes, already owlishly magnified by the lenses of his pince-nez, appeared to grow even larger as he inspected the outlaw pair. "Bobbins? Wilkums? But those angelic spirits have consummated their union with the Almighty."

"They haven't consummated anything, dear," Mary assured her husband. "They're right here."

Henry Sr. stepped forward and awkwardly embraced his long-lost sons, possibly less to express paternal affection than to convince himself that they weren't apparitions. "Do you fellows believe in God?" he asked.

But Jesse was in no mood for either a windy theology tutorial or a touching family reunion. "Come on!" he ordered his brothers. "Let's get the hell out of here!"

As they all followed the younger outlaw out to the stable to hitch a team of two up to the family sleigh, William paused in the mudroom to inhale yet another hit of amyl nitrite before charging out into the frosty night.

"Don't forget your galoshes, boys!" Mary James called out after her rapidly departing brood.

———◆———

Careening over the frozen streets of Cambridge at a dangerous gallop, the Jameses' sleigh flew past the plodding horsecars on Massachusetts Avenue, its iron runners striking up bright plumes of sparks as they scraped over patches of exposed cobblestone. Jesse cracked the whip mercilessly over the team. He was now cold sober—or at least less intoxicated with the fading effects of President Eliot's punch than with the prospect of once again robbing a train.

As William had predicted, they discovered Hite's coach berthed on an otherwise deserted siding in the Dewey Square rail yard. Such luxurious cars, known as "private varnish" in the railroading jargon of the era, were the perquisites of investors like Asa Hite, who had become an officer of the newly formed New York, New Haven & Hartford Railroad when the Hartford & New Haven merged with the New York & New Haven in 1872, more than doubling the company's total track mileage and augmenting his personal fortune proportionately. He had spared no expense in the construction and furnishing of his "mansion on rails," as the noted railroad historian Lucius Beebe called such ostentatious conveyances. Mr. Hite's custom-made Pullman Palace boasted a kitchen with a large range and icebox, a dining room with an extension table and sideboard, a spacious lounge and smoking area, an observation parlor with a library and desk, and four commodious staterooms. The interior of the coach was richly appointed with all the characteristic accoutrements of Gilded Age conspicuous consumption: ornate inlaid woodwork of olive wood, hand-rubbed satinwood, Circassian walnut, and curly maple; looped and fringed damask drapes; and delicate silk portieres. Illumination was provided throughout the coach by Pintsch gas lamps mounted in etched and frosted glass sconces set on finely wrought and polished brass fixtures.

Asa Hite had initially dubbed his lavish land yacht *The Charter Oak,* in honor of the most famous tree in Hartford history, but so pleased had he been with his daughter's demeanor upon her return from Europe that he had joyfully rechristened it *Elena*—a decision he must now have regretted, even as the gilded lettering of her name was barely dry on the coach's external cladding.

Approaching the opulent carriage on foot, the James brothers had a clear view of its occupants through its lighted windows. In the smoking section of the central lounge area, the men—Hite, Pinkerton, and his pair of security guards—were already ensconced in handsomely upholstered plush armchairs, contentedly puffing cigars, sipping brandy, and partaking of a congenial game of cards. Elena Hite, still in her party finery, sat writing by gaslight at the mahogany rolltop desk in the library section of the observation parlor, her solitary figure softened by the gently falling snow and framed by the embrasure of the parlor's plate-glass window like a Sargent portrait.

As they stole quietly across the icy rail yard toward the coach, Henry tapped William on the shoulder and offered his brother one of the Colt revolvers, commenting with an unmistakable soupçon of condescension, "I trust you know how to handle a six-gun."

William did not. No sooner had he received the weapon from Henry's hand than, in a kind of pistolic premature ejaculation, the thing went off with a loud report that rang through the deserted rail yard like the roar of a cannon.

If the Jameses had any plan of attack at all, it became moot. Alerted to the presence of armed men outside, the two Pinkerton security guards leaped up from their card game, drew their pistols, and took positions on the front observation platform, from which they began firing at the intruders. With no place to take cover in the open rail yard, the Jameses had no choice but to storm the coach. Jesse took the lead, conspicuously thrilled to have his brothers falling in behind him and to hear the yard echo with the bloodcurdling whoop of his rebel yell. Guns blazing, the brothers rushed the car from the back, scrambling over the filigreed brass railings on the rear observation platform and gaining entrance to the coach through the kitchen and dining room.

The ensuing gun battle was a melee. With the Jameses firing through the coach from the rear and the Pinkertons shooting from the front, many of the elegant gas lamps along the car's walls were soon blasted out. The pungent aroma of volatile Pintsch gas mingled with the acrid, metallic stench of gunpowder, as the silk portieres and damask drapes started going up in smoke. In the fuliginous atmosphere of the coach, it became nearly impossible for the combatants to discern who was shooting at whom, or even where the shots were coming from. Shadowy figures popped up, firing virtually at random, their pistols flashing in the dark. At each report, Henry, harking back to the lessons of Castle James, kept jumping vigorously to his left.

Hearing the bells of an approaching horse-drawn fire engine, the Jameses realized that a police wagon might not be far behind. They decided that in this instance, discretion might indeed be the better part of valor. Taking a page from Henry's book, they all scrambled out of the coach. Of the James brothers, Henry, reliving the horror of the stable fire in which he had sustained his "obscure hurt," was the first to escape, followed by William, Jesse, and finally Frank, hobbling on his bad foot. With flames beginning to engulf the car, everyone else fled the conflagration—Billy Pinkerton, his security guards, and Asa Hite, even the porter and the cook, who had been cowering under the dining room table.

Only Elena Hite failed to emerge from her namesake coach. She had been shot dead in the cross fire.

Epilogue

In his famous 1884 essay "The Art of Fiction," Henry James wrote that "the 'ending' of a novel is, for many persons, like that of a good dinner, a course of desserts and ices, and the artist in fiction is regarded as a sort of meddlesome doctor who forbids agreeable aftertastes." Defending his own artistic notion of what a novel should be, Henry attacked his imagined critics:

> They would argue, of course, that a novel ought to be "good," but they would interpret this term in a fashion of their own, which indeed would vary considerably from one critic to another. One would say that being good means representing virtuous and aspiring characters, placed in prominent positions; another would say that it depends on a "happy ending," on a distribution at the last of prizes, pensions, husbands, wives, babies, millions, appended paragraphs, and cheerful remarks. An-

other still would say that it means being full of incident and movement, so that we shall wish to jump ahead, to see who was the mysterious stranger, and if the stolen will was ever found, and shall not be distracted from this pleasure by any tiresome analysis or "description." But they would all agree that the "artistic" idea would spoil some of their fun. One would hold it accountable for all the description, another would see it revealed in the absence of sympathy. Its hostility to a happy ending would be evident, and it might even in some cases render any ending at all impossible.

The historical biographer, unlike the novelist, has little to dole out at the end of his or her endeavors but death. Not only Elena Hite but everyone else portrayed in these pages has long since passed on and faded from living memory; and, as William James remarked in his eulogy for Ralph Waldo Emerson, "The phantom of an attitude, the echo of a certain mode of thought, a few pages of print, some invention, or some victory we gained in a brief critical hour, are all that can survive the best of us."

What survives Elena Hite, beyond a few paintings, letters, and snippets of her diary, are the reverberations of her encounters with the James brothers. We know her almost entirely through the impressions that she left on their longer, more storied lives. Despite the efforts of the James family and most of their biographers to expunge any hint of her presence in those lives, William, Henry, Frank, and Jesse, each in his own way, was profoundly affected by this uniquely fascinating young woman, and by her violent and untimely death, the details of which remain a mystery to this day.

It seems unlikely that anyone intentionally shot Elena. A case might be made against Jesse, Frank, or even Henry, on the grounds that they may have had it in for her as a potential witness. Even farther-fetched would be the speculation that William could have chosen to euthanize his former patient in order to spare her what he may have seen as a fate worse than death, i.e., rotting away in an insane asylum. More probable is that Elena was gunned down accidentally, in which case the perpetrator could have been practically anyone in Mr. Hite's coach that night. Given the darkness, smoke, and commotion, the possibility cannot be ruled out that no one present ever knew who fired the fatal shot, including perhaps even the gunman himself.

In the absence of any hard evidence, some scholars have thrown up their hands, among them a prominent feminist historian who recently declared that Elena had been done in by "Victorian patriarchal hegemony run amuck—a virtual victim of the 19th century." But centuries don't kill people, guns kill people, and without the insights of modern ballistic forensic technology, it remains impossible to determine whose weapon brought Elena down—an enigma that would be immeasurably compounded by the fact that the pistols William and Henry James were toting that December night in 1876 were those that Henry had snatched up off of Gustave Flaubert's floor, and which would have been identical to the standard-issue agency revolvers wielded by Billy Pinkerton and his security men.

We do not know, and pending any startling new information that may come to light, we likely never will. Such is the sort of ambiguity—forensic rather than "artistic," in this instance—that Henry James cited as ruining the pleasures of his straw-man critics who would demand that all the mysteries of a story be neatly wrapped up and beribboned for presentation to the reader at its conclusion. What we do know is that there was clearly a cover-up of the real cause of Elena's death. No formal inquiry into the incident was ever undertaken, and the official presumption was that she perished as another hapless victim of the notoriously combustive Pintsch gas with which the railway cars of the era were illuminated. The culprit behind this sweeping under the legal rug of the shooting was almost certainly Asa Hite: Weary of scandal and perhaps secretly relieved that Elena would never become yet another crazy burden on him, her father could have been contented to let the whole gruesome business slide. William Pinkerton would doubtless have been more than willing to collude with his client in hushing up the true nature of the affair, not only out of his well-documented deference to Mr. Hite, but also to avoid any further unfavorable publicity concerning his agency's slipshod pursuit of the James Gang.

The Dewey Square debacle proved something of a watershed in the Pinkertons' quest to bring the James brothers to justice. Once again, "the eye that never sleeps" had been caught napping, and in light of the botched raid on Castle James and the fiasco in Gustave Flaubert's Paris apartment, Billy Pinkerton must have felt that he could ill afford yet another major public embarrassment. Having scant desire to provoke his father's wrath, he never reported the sordid occurrence back to the home office in Chicago, and no record of it can be found in the agency archives. But after Dewey Square, it appears that the detective had no further stomach for the pursuit of the James Gang, turning his attention to other, more tractable cases. His glaring failure to nab the most infamous outlaws in the country may have informed his subsequent reluctance to publish a memoir of his otherwise brilliant career. "I have always been opposed to crime reminiscences," he claimed toward the end of his life, "and the reminiscences of the Pinkerton Agency will never be written." According to historian Richard Wilmer Rowan, "He never retracted, refusing many publishing offers for his autobiography, and went to his grave like a gold mine defying its prospectors."

Yet even if Pinkerton had chosen to go after the Jameses, he would not have found it easy. He had no hard evidence against William for any actual crime, and the three others lit out early the next morning, with Henry hopping the first steamer he could book for England and the younger pair heading south to Tennessee, where they took up residence under the aliases Ben J. Woodson and John Davis Howard to begin making peaceful livings at farming, raising horses, and doing odd jobs. (Jesse's paranoid fears notwithstanding, the Younger brothers never did squeal on the Jameses, serving out their sentences at the Stillwater Penitentiary in honorable silence.) Yet Jesse's congenital antsyness came to the fore: After a couple of years of clean living, he felt compelled to put together a new criminal crew and to take up once again the only métier he and Frank had known in their adult lives.

This reconstituted James Gang was but a pallid simulacrum of the band that had terrorized Missouri in the decade immediately following the Civil War. The former guerrillas who made up the core of that original unit had all been interred or imprisoned, and the younger, greener men who took their places—Charley and Robert Ford, Clarence and Wood Hite (no relation to Elena), Dick Liddil, Ed Miller, Bill Ryan, and Tucker Bassham—were a far cry from the likes of those battle-hardened bushwhackers. None of the new gang members had fought in the war, and in terms of criminal credentials, the most heinous offense to which any of them could lay claim prior to hooking up with the Jameses was stealing a horse. What was more, the romantic Civil War mythos in which the first-string James Gang had cloaked their crimes had, by the late 1870s, begun to wear thin, even in those Confederaphilic enclaves of western Missouri that so often provided refuge and apology for the outlaws in the heyday of their postbellum marauding. Reconstruction had crumbled, and as T. J. Stiles noted, "Jesse and his comrades had symbolized secessionist resentments, but when the dust settled after the election of 1876, there was nothing left to resent." Most ominously, some of the new boys lacked the fierce loyalty of their predecessors. Faced with the temptation of a promised bounty of ten thousand dollars for their legendary leader, they had little compunction about selling him out.

Of the assassination of Jesse James by Robert Ford in St. Joseph, Missouri, on the morning of April 3, 1882, little need be recounted here. That sanguinary episode has become an integral aspect of American folklore, immortalized—as Jesse doubtless would have been delighted to hear—in the popular ballad attributed to the otherwise unsung contemporary minstrel Billy Gashade:

Now the people held their breath when they heard of Jesse's death,
And they wondered how he ever came to fall
Robert Ford, it was a fact, shot Jesse in the back
While Jesse hung a picture on the wall

In a letter to William from London written after the shooting, Henry remarked that Jesse had died a "natural death." This took William aback. He wondered if perhaps the English newspapers hadn't mangled the story, to which Henry, in his subsequent missive, ruefully responded that what he had meant was that for a vicious outlaw, being shot in the back by a member of one's own gang *was* a natural death.

Frank James fared considerably better than his younger brother. After Jesse's murder, he lay low for a few months, then arranged through the good offices of Major John Edwards to turn himself in to Governor Crittenden of Missouri in what some historians believe was a secret deal to assure a pardon in the event that he was convicted of any crime. He surrendered to the governor in early October 1882 and was tried almost a year later for the murder of a passenger named Frank McMillan during a train robbery at Winston, Missouri, in 1881, and in Alabama for an 1881 stagecoach holdup at Muscle Shoals. Acquitted in both cases—and never tried for his role in the Northfield robbery or any of his other earlier crimes—Frank spent the next thirty years as a minor celebrity, eking out a meager living as a race starter at county fairs, a horse wrangler, a shoe salesman, and a doorman at a St. Louis burlesque house. After the turn of the century, he took a crack at acting, appearing in bit parts with traveling stock companies in such tacky melodramas as *The Fatal Scar* and *Across the Desert*. When Cole Younger was granted a conditional pardon in 1903, Frank joined forces with his old comrade-in-arms to tour with *The Great Cole Younger and Frank James Historical Wild West Show.* Under the terms of his pardon, Cole was forbidden to perform, but Frank was able put his thespian (and outlaw) experience to good use, portraying a stagecoach passenger in the thrilling holdup finale of the spectacle.

Following the death of Zerelda "Mamaw" Samuel in 1911, the former brigand moved back to Castle James, where he spent his final years tilling the land and palavering with Kodak-toting tourists and curiosity seekers. He never attempted to reestablish contact with his older brothers, though he did read Henry's novels, enjoying *The Bostonians* and *The Portrait of a Lady* but abhorring the author's late "third style," which he found "unreadable," perceiving in it, as he once complained to Cole Younger's sister Henrietta, "the damnedest farrago of constipation and diarrhea." After *The Wings of the Dove*, he lost interest and returned to his beloved Shakespeare and Milton.

Frank died on February 18, 1915. In his last published interview, the year before, when asked about his criminal past by a reporter from *Collier's Weekly*, he replied, "I neither affirm nor deny. . . . If I admitted that these stories were true, people would say, 'There's the greatest scoundrel unhung,' and if I denied 'em they'd say: 'There's the greatest liar on earth,' so I just say nothing." He did, however—perhaps in a belated tip of his Stetson to Elena Hite—make a point of telling his interviewer that he believed women ought to have the right to vote. "Look at what we owe to the woman," he argued. "A man gets 75 per cent of what goodness is in him from his mother, and he owes at least 40 per cent of all he makes to his wife." In what may have been a sly dig at his brother William, he added, "Yes, some men owe more than that. Some of 'em owe 100 per cent to their wives."

———✦———

In the wake of December 15, 1876, William James manfully steeled himself to brave the consequences of his manifold misdeeds. But those weighty shoes never dropped. Indeed, the psychologist may have been the greatest beneficiary of Asa Hite's Dewey Square cover-up. President Eliot remained mercifully ignorant of William's pistol-packing role at the rail yard, which he would certainly have seen as grounds for dismissal from the university, if not for a lengthy prison term. As for William's sexual shenanigans at the soirée, interceding with the head of Harvard on his behalf was Dr. James Putnam, who must have felt appreciable guilt over having gotten his old friend embroiled with Elena Hite in the first place. The distinguished neurologist attempted to convince President Eliot that the young lady whom he had personally examined prior to referring her to Dr. James was a certifiable madwoman. What his colleague had been attempting that night in the presidential bedroom, Putnam claimed, was not so much a selfish exercise in unbridled lust—as it might have appeared to a layman—but rather a desperate, admittedly unconventional, yet perhaps heroic new form of psychotherapy. Henry Bowditch concurred, and together he and Putnam stood behind their fellow Adirondack Doctor, even to the point of intimating that they would abandon their Harvard posts in protest should William get the sack.

Whether or not he found Putnam's case even remotely credible, faced with the potential defection of the two brightest stars of his medical faculty, Eliot warily welcomed William back into the Harvard fold. Despite the president's alleged propensity for holding grudges, he went so far as to scrape together sufficient funding to launch a much attenuated version of the proposed laboratory of experimental psychology.

Alice Gibbens proved a tougher nut to crack. If William's courtship of the soprano schoolmarm had been something of a seesaw affair even prior to his appalling escapades at President Eliot's soirée, it subsequently became more like a roller-coaster ride. For months after that distressing event, Alice refused to have anything to do with her former near-fiancé. (This was the period during which William later described himself as "a man morally utterly diseased.") When summer came, she bolted Boston with her sister Margaret for an extended holiday in Quebec, where she received copious letters of abject contrition and squirmy self-abasement from William in Keene Valley. "Little by little," he wrote to her on August 24, "time will perhaps give me something to think about but my own unspeakable impotence and culpability, and the outrages which they have wrought upon your thrice divine being."

Ultimately, Miss Gibbens relented, though probably owing less to the persuasive power of her suitor than to her own fear of impending spinsterhood and her recognition that whatever threat Elena Hite may have posed to their relationship had been effectively terminated with the younger woman's demise. But she didn't make it easy for her lapsed lover: Reminded once by her sister that she had made William wait two years to seal the deal, Alice acerbically remarked, "Don't you think a woman has a right to take her time?"

The on-again, off-again couple was finally married on July 10, 1878, much to the delight and relief of their friends and families—with the notable exception of Alice James. For William's brickly sister, the wedding of her beloved brother precipitated a severe crack-up from which, by her own account, she never fully recovered, referring to it years later in her diary as "that summer of '78 when I went down to the deep sea, its dark waters closed over me, and I knew neither hope nor peace." Alice never landed a husband of her own (and at heart probably never wanted one), but she did settle in to a "Boston marriage" with her longtime friend and caretaker Katharine Loring, whom Henry once described as "the most perfect companion she could have found, if she had picked over the whole human family." The allegiant pair of Yankee ladies moved to England, where Alice died of a breast tumor in 1892 at the age of forty-three, attended at her deathbed by her devoted brother Henry, whose secrets she took to her grave.

William's long, conventionally heterosexual marriage with Alice Gibbens has often been credited with sparing him from his worst self. "William suffered from nearly clinical depression during the 1860s and early 1870s, and his self-doubts about his sanity and his capacity for living seem possibly connected to his masturbation guilt," wrote Yale comparative literature professor Peter Brooks. "He would find a solution in marriage, after a long and tortured courtship: a marriage from which he often sought escape but which he simultaneously figured as his salvation." Under the stabilizing influence of matrimony, William's professional life flourished, lending credence to Frank's remark about some men owing 100 percent of their livelihoods to their wives. The man who had once feared that he might have no career at all turned out to have several, almost all of them illustrious. As a psychologist, philosopher, Harvard professor, and popular author, he reigned for decades as one of America's leading public intellectuals; but in spite of establishing the nation's first psychology laboratory, he never made much of a mark as an experimentalist. This lapse reflected more than sour grapes over Asa Hite's withdrawal of his lavish support for the laboratory, or even William's long-standing distaste for the rigors of bench science. Rather, he appears to have become disenchanted with the entire agenda of the new psychology, which he suspected would never be able to account for the slippery mysteries of consciousness. "Many persons nowadays," he once complained, "seem to think that any conclusion must be very scientific if the arguments in favor of it are all derived from the twitching of frogs' legs—especially if the frogs are decapitated—and that, on the other hand, any doctrine chiefly vouched for by the feelings of human beings—with heads on their shoulders—must be benighted and superstitious."

But William doubtless yearned for something more than a scientific psychology that would account for the feelings of human beings. Just as Elena had, in life, opened him to the exhilaration of eroticism, in death she drew him to the eerie embrace of spiritualism. His interest in the afterlife is often attributed to the tragic death in 1885 of his infant second son, Herman, though in fact it predated this traumatic filial loss, or even to the passing of his parents in 1882, when he was already a member of the newly founded British Society for Psychical Research. Though he never made it explicit, it is likely that his fascination with the occult was triggered by the death of Elena Hite, and that it was always she with whom he so desperately longed to communicate across the great divide. If Alice Gibbens believed that her late rival's demise would mark the end of her husband's obsession with his beguiling former patient, she was sorely mistaken: William was haunted—or at least yearned to be—by Elena, pursuing her specter in the séances of a comely young medium by the name of Leonora Piper, whose apparent ability to make contact with souls on the "other side" seemed to defy any rational or scientific explanation. As he wrote in *The Will to Believe:*

> If you wish to upset the law that all crows are black, you must not seek to show that no crows are; it is enough if you prove one simple crow to be white. My own white crow is Mrs. Piper. In the trances of this medium, I cannot resist the conviction that knowledge appears which she has never gained by the ordinary waking use of her eyes and ears and wits. . . . As a matter of fact, the trances I speak of have broken down for my own mind the limits of the admitted order of nature. Science, so far as science denies such exceptional occurrences, lies prostrate in the dust for me; and the most urgent intellectual need which I feel at present is that science be built up again in a form in which such things may have a place.

Unfortunately, there is no evidence, either scientific or anecdotal, that William ever made contact with the shade of Elena Hite, but much of her spirit did find its way into the works of his brother Henry, who seems to have done a far better job of conjuring it up than the celebrated Mrs. Piper. While William continued to carry a torch for his departed patient, it was Henry who became the keeper of the flame. "I wonder how I shall appear in your novels, Mr. James," Elena had mused at Versailles. The answer is that she lives on in the "bad lecture blood" of Verena Tarrant in *The Bostonians;* in the beauty, intelligence, and independence of Isabel Archer in *The Portrait of a Lady;* in the wealth and iron resolve of Milly Theale in *The Wings of the Dove;* and, of course, in the fatal indiscretions of Daisy Miller.

It is a commonplace among Jamesian scholars to cite Henry's cousin

Mary "Minnie" Temple as the model for the author's audacious young "Americanas"; but Minnie, who died of consumption in 1870 at the age of twenty-five, though a precociously free thinker on the subjects of gender and religion, was never particularly transgressive on the sexual front. Elena became, for Henry James, the embodiment of the erotic, especially of the demolitionary power of sexuality. "In Henry's novels," wrote Jean Strouse, "sex, though unnamed, often occupies a central place in the characters' preoccupations and actions. It becomes more explicit in his later work (*The Wings of the Dove, The Golden Bowl, The Ambassadors*), but early and late it is nearly always associated with destruction, cruelty, corruption."

Despite Henry's lip service to his "utter disgust" with the "unspeakable horror" of Elena's behavior, he must have secretly admired her sexual hubris. As a closeted and celibate homosexual, in later life he apparently came to feel that for all his smashing literary and social successes, he had never really *lived*, i.e., loved, i.e., laid—a theme that found its haunting expression in his 1903 tale, *The Beast in the Jungle*. (To the journalist Morton Fullerton, Henry once wrote of his "essential loneliness," which he described as "deeper than my 'genius,' deeper than my 'discipline,' deeper than my pride, deeper, above all, than the deep countermining of art.") Tragically truncated though it had been, Elena's life had been filled with more romantic and erotic adventure than Henry's much longer one, and he undoubtedly recalled with awe and pangs of envy the temerity of his erstwhile "wife" in coming to Castle James for the express purpose of seducing Jesse; her shameless liaison with Flaubert; and her reckless tryst with William.

After Elena's death, Henry took it on the lam to London, where, on the heels of the international sensation of his Elena-inspired *Daisy Miller*, he became the toast of the town. (He reported dining out 140 times during the winter of 1878–79.) He stayed in the English capital for over five years before furtively returning to Boston twice in 1882, the year when both his parents died. The elder Jameses went to their graves believing that after President Eliot's ill-fated party, their two youngest sons had vanished back down south or out west, still living under the shameful cloud of having deserted during the Civil War. Neither William nor Henry ever had the heart to tell their parents the rest of the brutal truth. It had been enough of a shock for the poor old dears to learn that Rob and Wilky were still alive; to have found out that their boys had become the most notorious American outlaws of the nineteenth century would only have hastened their passing.

That year was a dangerous one for Henry to be setting foot in the United States. With the assassination of Jesse, the heat was on for the James Gang. At the time of their father's death, Frank was in jail in Independence, Missouri, awaiting trial, and Henry must have been terrified at what details might emerge during his brother's interrogation or in sworn testimony before a jury. While most accounts of the raid on the Northfield bank described the perpetrators as a gang of eight men, there were persistent rumors, based on eyewitness accounts, of an additional bandit. The identity of this supernumerary gang member had never been established, and it was Henry's lifelong fear that he would one day be fingered as the mysterious ninth man. After his father's funeral, he wasted no time in beating it back to England, where he would remain once again in self-imposed exile, this time for nearly a quarter of a century.

———•———

When he finally dared hazard another voyage back to his homeland, in 1904—the year after Cole Younger's pardon—Henry James found America a new country in a new century. At the request of his publisher, Charles Scribner, he embarked on a transcontinental train journey that must have promised the belated consummation of the aborted journalistic junket he had undertaken nearly three decades earlier. The trip, which he documented in a collection of essays published under the title *The American Scene,* took him all the way out to California, where he visited his nephew in San Francisco. "When Uncle Henry came to us, he found the west rather crude," Ned James later recalled. "He was bored by the west, by the 'slobber of noises,' which we call our language, by the stream of vacant stupid faces on the streets and everywhere the 'big ogre of business.'" The ascendancy of what Henry once scornfully referred to as "the rank money-passion" led him to fear that the emerging history of the country would inexorably be written by Asa Hite and his spiritual descendants—to the extent that a horde of rapacious entrepreneurs might be called spiritual. (Compared to the depredations of such profit-addled plunderers, those of the old James Gang must have struck the author as well-nigh quaint.) The explosive new American mania for commerce even threatened to encroach upon the ivy-covered walls of William's venerated Harvard, where Henry observed that many of the young men in the Yard already wore a "business man" face. The philosopher George Santayana, who had been one of William's outstanding students, accused President Eliot of turning education into preparation for "service in the world of business," and William himself, with only the barest trace of irony, once wrote to Eliot warning of colleges becoming "training schools of crime." (Asa Hite was to have revenge of sorts on all four James brothers: He died in 1907, leaving a substantial chunk of his fortune toward the founding of the Harvard Business School, which opened its doors in 1908.)

Having passed the milestone age of sixty, Henry was looking back, acutely aware that the bulk of his life and work was behind him. He convinced Scribner to publish a monumental compilation of what he designated as "all of the author's fiction that he desires perpetuated," to be known as the New York Edition, which he cryptically insisted should comprise precisely twenty-three volumes. As Leon Edel observed, "[t]he figure seems indeed to have a certain magical quality for James; when he needs a date, a youthful age, a general number, he often fixes on 23." Twenty-three was the age at which Elena Hite died, and even if Henry was certain he had not fired the shot that killed her—as at Northfield, he never discharged his pistol—he may yet have suffered the guilt of knowing that by continually jumping to his left on that wild night, he might have taken himself out of the path of the bullet that found her. He must have feared that, like some hoary ghost in one of his many tales of the "supernatural and 'gruesome,'" the sordid specters of his "marriage" to Elena and his attendant outlaw escapades could spring forth at any moment and threaten to "bite him in the ass," as they soon did.

Following the death of William James from heart failure in 1910, his widow, Alice, imposed upon Henry to write up a few memories of his late brother, a project that, in the prolix author's hands, soon ballooned into a full-blown autobiography. By 1914 the work had burgeoned to three volumes—the first entitled *A Small Boy and Others,* the second *Notes of a Son and Brother,* and the third *The Middle Years*—before Henry abandoned it, ostensibly owing to the outbreak of the Great War. More likely he was unwilling or unable to come to grips with what he would have been obliged to reveal had he continued. Faced with the classic Jamesian dilemma of "saying and not saying," the autobiographer seems to have chosen dawdling and, ultimately, death. He succumbed to what he once called "the dusky pall of fatality" on February 28, 1916, the last of his generation to depart. The account of his life was left unfinished, but in what he did complete of it, the writer whose fiction is replete with "unreliable narrators" was to prove himself among the least reliable of all. "To the young," he once told Edmund Gosse, "the early dead, the baffled, the defeated, I don't think we can be tender enough"; yet not only was he ruthless in his expunging of Elena from the James family history—the text ends abruptly in the mid-1870s, just before she made her appearance in the lives of the Jameses—but, more significantly, he had practically nothing to say about the history of his younger brothers after the Civil War, with the exception of this coy but telling reference in the second volume:

> The story, the general one, of the great surge of action on which
> they were so early carried, was to take still other turns during
> the years I now speak of, some of these not of the happiest; but

with the same relation to it on my own part too depressingly prolonged—that of seeing, sharing, envying, applauding, pitying, all from too far-off, and with the queer sense that, whether or no they would prove to have had the time of their lives, it seemed that the only time I should have had would stand or fall by theirs.

Along with Asa Hite's concealment of the true cause of his daughter's death, Henry's bowdlerized memoirs were to become the fountainhead of a long cascade of cover-ups. In addition to fictionalizing and judiciously editing his autobiography, the author also attempted to cover his tracks by destroying thousands of letters, some of them undoubtedly containing references to Elena Hite and the criminal careers of his younger brothers. (According to William's biographer Gerald E. Myers, "William's letters to Henry from August 1876 to October 1882 are lost, with the exception of a single letter of 2 August, 1880.") These missing documents most likely perished in the roaring bonfire that Henry set at his home in Rye, Sussex—his famous "epistolary immolation," which uncannily echoed the fate that Elena had suffered at Dewey Square.

Elena Hite's tragic entanglement with the James brothers began and ended with an assault on a train, that emblematic mode of nineteenth-century conveyance. Her gaslit life was cruelly extinguished before the era of the electric light, the telephone, the automobile, the motion picture, or female suffrage. In effect, like Jesse, she suffered a "double death," having first been shot and then rubbed out of the history of the James family so thoroughly that for most biographers, it is as if she never lived. The present author would therefore, in Henry James's phrase, be "ashamed, as of a cold impiety," not to let her have the last word in these pages, which she provides by way of the singed leaves of what was to be the final entry in her diary, reclaimed from the smoldering interior of her father's private rail coach:

Oh, tonight has been quite the most unpleasant I ever spent. Father is absolutely livid with me. He has threatened to shunt me off to the Retreat, though I do not, I will not believe it. Never before has he raised his voice or his hand to me, having borne in stolid silence whatever "disgrace" I may have heaped upon his cherished good name. Can I now appear so irredeemably wicked in his eyes as to deserve this most ungentle treatment? Fortunately he has always been more fuse than bomb, so I may yet foster the hope that by Sunday his ire will have fizzled. As I write this, he is engaged in a lively game of whist with that atrocious Mr. Pinkerton & his cronies & already his mood appears to have lightened. (From the bellows of triumph I hear emanating from the smoking parlor I gather that he is winning, a state of affairs which never fails to buoy his spirits.)

[SCORCHED SEGMENT]

It was all a horrid muddle, the details of which are so thoroughly seared into my brain that I feel no need to recount them here, as they will certainly abide with me forever. But the fault, I would insist, was not entirely my own. Jesse & Frank James, I gather, were responsible for the introduction of firearms into the evening's festivities, which comportment could only have been inestimably more disruptive of them than whatever my genial disporting with Dr. James upstairs may have contributed to the general havoc.

[MISSING PAGE?]

I am so very weary of being the object of the world's opprobrium, yet my every natural action seems to provoke the most unsparing obloquy, even on the part of those whom I know for a certainty to be no less deserving of it than myself. It distresses me beyond measure to find myself plunged afresh into the Slough of Despond. Per-

haps I am more than usually subject to extremes of happiness and of depression, yet I suppose everyone must have moments, even in the most varied and distracting life, when the old questioning spirit, the demon of the Why, Whence, Wither?, stalks in like the skeleton at the feast and takes a seat beside her. At times like these I fear that my vaunted free will may not be nearly so free as dear Dr. James would have me believe. (Nor his own, for that matter! Perhaps it is all just a fragment [sic] of his imagination.)

I had been longing so very especially to see him again, but of course one would be utterly stupid to lay one's hopes for happiness on this earth in the lap of another human being, even of one who happens to be a medical doctor. Dr. James—dare I say it? Yes, I dare say it!—has the most lovely penis. (Someday, I trust, such a frank reference to the sexual organs will no more cause the blush to mount to one's face than a reference to any other part of the body!) Not that I maintain any fantasy of marrying the man. Too much is claimed for that shabby old institution & Liberty, I daresay, is a better husband than Love. Still, I shudder to imagine the poor fellow getting hitched with that smug singing sow, Miss Givins [sic].

[WATER-DAMAGED PAGE]

I go on, I know, as if I were crazy, and it's a wonder I'm not, but sometimes I feel inclined to think that there is not a good man living; for if I follow my heart with them it seems unfailingly to be to my detriment. (If I were to follow my mind *I should surely have nothing at all to do with the impossible creatures!) I welcome the day when all of this [scorched] will be behind me. I know it is unfashionable, perhaps even unthinkable, for a young lady to prefer the life of a spinster to that of a wife & mother, but I cannot help but imagine the serene pleasures of a life alone, perhaps in a humble cabin in the country with my dogs and my paintings. Or perhaps I might further my education. (I did, before all h*ll broke* loose, have a most enlightening audience with President Eliot. The poor man is stiff as an umbrella and pitifully disfigured, but he— or, rather, his wife & the formidable Mrs. Agassiz—left me with the signal impression that I will yet live to see the day when Harvard deigns to accommodate women in its educational scheme. Won't that *be a wonder!)*

[SMUDGED AND TORN]

In spite of everything I cannot say that I regret having made the acquaintance of the James brothers. It thrills me to know that I hold so many of their secrets, though they, of course, in turn, hold so many of my own. They are such a company of characters & such a picture of differences, & withal so fused & united & interlocked, that I find them all infinitely fascinating & [illegible].

RICHARD LIEBMANN-SMITH was educated at Stanford, Columbia, the Yale School of Drama, and the University of Paris. A former editor of *The Sciences* magazine and at Basic Books, he is co-creator of *The Tick,* the animated television series, and has written for such publications as *The New Yorker, The New York Times Magazine, The New York Times Book Review, Smithsonian Magazine, Playboy, Harper's,* and *The National Lampoon.* He is the father of a daughter, Rebecca, and lives in New York with his wife, Joan, a medical writer. He is one of four brothers.

ABOUT THE TYPE

This book was set in Garamond, a typeface originally designed by the Parisian typecutter Claude Garamond (1480–1561). This version of Garamond was modeled on a 1592 specimen sheet from the Egenolff-Berner foundry, which was produced from types assumed to have been brought to Frankfurt by the punchcutter Jacques Sabon.

Claude Garamond's distinguished romans and italics first appeared in *Opera Ciceronis* in 1543–44. The Garamond types are clear, open, and elegant.